THE
ELECTION

A Willie Mitchell Banks novel

MICHAEL HENRY

Michael Henry

Other books by this author:
Three Bad Years
At Random
The Ride Along (with William Henry)
D.O.G.s: *The Secret History* (with William Henry)
Atmosphere of Violence (with William Henry)

Dedicated to:

To my three sons, Joseph, Stephen, and William; each of whom, in his own way, has made me a very proud father.

Acknowledgements:

Many thanks to reliable and patient readers Pat Austin, David Fite, Kaye Bryant, Martha V. Whitwell, Gayle Henry, and Bill Byrne; to the creative, indefatigable, and indestructible Christine Maynard for her help and encouragement; to Mike Hourin, reader, marketer, and one-man-welcome-wagon extraordinaire; to Jim Wilson for wise counsel; to son William for invaluable creative input.

Yaloquena County District Attorney runs for re-election against Eleanor Bernstein, whose vicious smear campaign against Willie Mitchell is being orchestrated by the Reverend Bobby Sanders, longtime nemesis of the D.A.

At a political rally on the Fourth of July, seven-year-old Danny Thurman goes missing. In spite of a county-wide search, the boy's body is never found. A month after the boy's disappearance, Ross Bullard, son of prominent banker Jules Bullard, shoots himself and leaves a note incriminating himself in the disappearance of Danny. Bullard survives his suicide attempt. Willie Mitchell explains to Danny's parents that the missing body makes winning the murder prosecution of Bullard almost impossible. The parents say they understand, but insist that Willie Mitchell go forward with the prosecution of Bullard for Danny's murder.

Famed defense attorney J.D. Silver fights for Bullard and tries to get the case dismissed, arguing that without a body, there's no proof of murder. Willie Mitchell presses the case forward to a trial before a local jury, even though it's unlikely he can win a jury verdict that will hold up on appeal, and equally unlikely the D.A. can win his own re-election.

For more on the author and D.A. Willie Mitchell Banks and his son Jake Banks, visit www.henryandhenrybooks.com

CHAPTER ONE

The Mayor waved and started my way, parting the crowd like water. I knew what Everett wanted me to do, but there was no way I was getting into the dunking booth. I was determined on that Fourth of July to hang on to what dignity I had left. Looking back, I realize now I had little to lose. After twenty-four years as a prosecutor and local politician, I'm here to tell you there is nothing dignified about either.

"You're not talking me into that dunking booth," I told him as soon as he was close enough to hear.

The big-hearted Mayor of Sunshine, slap dab in the heart of the Mississippi Delta, was a big man. Six-three and two-forty, solid-gray temples framed his coal black matte-finished forehead. He put his hand on my shoulder and gave me his "trust me on this, Willie Mitchell" look. Everett had given me that look many times in the past, and I usually succumbed. Not today.

Everett and I locked thumbs and did the handshake choreography we'd done since the eighties. I'm not sure it was ever cool, but it had always been fun. The Mayor grinned and wrapped his arm around my shoulders, pulling me into his penumbra of Aqua Velva and Right Guard.

"Eleanor did it earlier today, Willie Mitchell, and she was a big hit. You know how straight-laced she is. Nobody thought she'd get in there but she did and she came up out of that water tank laughing like nobody's business. You can do this."

The image of Eleanor Bernstein in the dunking booth confirmed my suspicion that she really wanted my job and was willing to do whatever it took to win. Eleanor spent most of her working days in the Yaloquena courtroom or in her Indigent Defender office on the first floor. She and I had tried scores of cases against each other, and pleaded out hundreds more. The dunking booth was way out of her comfort zone. Eleanor was always a lady, well-dressed and understated in her business suits. She buttoned her blouses all the way up revealing no hint of her mahogany chest. She was smart, well-prepared, and soft-spoken except on occasion when she got irritated with me in trial or plea negotiations. She could be plenty tough when the situation called for it.

Even though I had spent a lot of time trying and disposing of criminal cases with Eleanor, all I knew about her personal life was she wasn't married. She was smart to guard her privacy. Like every courthouse in rural Mississippi, ours was a beehive of gossip spread by small town functionaries with patronage appointments and too much time on their hands.

Everett ticked off the reasons why I need to be dunked. I really did appreciate his efforts to get me re-elected, but the dunking booth was beyond the pale. It wouldn't have been twenty-four years ago when I ran the first time. In those days I was on a mission, knocking on every door, dead set on getting every vote in the City of Sunshine and Yaloquena County. I had the fever. I would have gladly camped out in the dunking booth if that was what it took to win. I don't know why I was so obsessed, so single-minded. Winning that race was all that mattered to me then.

After six terms as the elected District Attorney for Yaloquena County, I was burned out. To a crisp.

No matter how hard I worked at prosecuting, it made little difference in the behavior of the citizens of Yaloquena County. When their blood was up, and their blood alcohol, too, they were going to do as they pleased, consequences be damned. So much for the deterrent effect of diligent and forceful prosecution. In the so-called war on drugs, I had been in the front lines, fighting crack in my first three terms, crystal meth in the last three. I can tell you this for a fact: my aggressive prosecution of the cases made no difference whatsoever. There was still tons of the stuff out there, being used and sold by young people who felt they had no future and by middle-aged dead-enders who had no past.

I don't attribute my burnout to the trial work. I never feel more alive than when I'm in front of a jury. I love it. I want to persuade those twelve people with every word, every reaction, every gesture. I want to win, and not just for the sake of winning. I want to win because when I take a case to trial, I believe with every fiber of my being that the guy sitting next to his defense lawyer is guilty of murder or rape or armed robbery. I believe it because I have vetted the evidence, talked to the cops and the witnesses, and concluded that not only is the defendant guilty beyond a reasonable doubt, he's guilty beyond any doubt.

If I have the slightest misgiving about the evidence, I don't take the case to trial. I just don't. If I'm not dead certain of guilt, I work something out, sometimes making the victim's family mad. I dismiss the charge or take a plea to a lesser offense. At times I give my *imprimatur* to a greatly reduced sentence. I work in the trenches against violent offenders. I rarely deal with white collar criminals. None of my defendants in Yaloquena County merely happened to be in the wrong place at the wrong time. They are people who have gotten away with all kinds of things in the past; they just weren't caught, to wit: Darrell Ross Bullard.

What had me down was the daily grind of making hard decisions that upended people's lives. In my county, the burden is all on my shoulders. I decide who is formally charged with crimes. I decide if there is sufficient evidence to bring a serious case to the Grand Jury to obtain an indictment. And Grand Jurors hear only what I choose to put before them. What little they think they know of the law is usually wrong or distorted, causing them to be more dangerous than helpful.

After their first session or two, Grand Jurors just want my presentation or Walton's to be as brief as possible. They want to get back to work and to their families. The Grand Jury room is an intimate setting, and sometimes I'm ashamed to present the sordid, violent facts of my world to decent people. It's the stuff that I deal with every day but after a while, the Grand Jurors don't want to hear anything else about it. *Just tell us what you want us to do, Mr. D.A.* While I've never heard a juror utter those exact words, I've gotten the message.

Sometimes I get stressed out in cases where I decide there's not enough evidence to bring charges. I make it a point not to blame the law enforcement officers *even if it is entirely their fault.* There have been countless times an investigation was irretrievably damaged at the outset by incompetent deputies or lack of resources. They don't mean to be inept, just like they don't mean to be ignorant and uneducated. They're often the product of a childhood where there were no books in the home and a school system that failed to teach them how to write a grammatically correct sentence. Some of the arrest reports are hilarious. Tragic, too. Truth is, I don't know how Sheriff Jones gets enough able-bodied applicants to become deputies. They're paid nothing and take constant abuse. I guess it's the same way the Catholic Church used to get eighteen-year-olds to enter the seminary: "Now, boys, join our club. You'll always be poor, have no say about where you'll work, and you'll never get to enjoy the most beautiful thing God created—a naked woman." *Oh, yeah. Sign me up for that, padre.*

When the family of a victim hears me say the person who killed or maimed their loved one will not be charged with a crime, they get angry. No matter how many times I explain that either the law or the facts are not there, they pretend they don't hear me. Grief and rage overcome reason. I've been accused of just about everything by the aggrieved families: collusion, bribery, political cowardice, incompetence, and stupidity.

I remember one angry father walking out of my office saying quietly to his crying wife, "Come on, baby, the D.A. done been bought off."

I knew that grieving father needed someone to blame, but after twenty-four years of taking it on my shoulders, absorbing the vitriol with as much stoicism as I could muster, I was sick of it. Let someone else do it for a change.

But here I am, the world's worst politician, running for re-election.

I could say that Everett and Sheriff Lee Jones talked me into it by appealing to my sense of duty, not to mention my ego and pride. When they said Yaloquena County needed me and Eleanor Bernstein could not do what I do, I knew they were right. After twenty-four years, I hated to turn it over to someone who would not do the job as well. Self-centered reasoning, I admit. The truth is, I'm not sure why I agreed to run again.

Susan didn't want me to. She went through all the reasons why I shouldn't: we didn't need the money; we could travel more; we'd spend more time together; our stress level would subside; we could spend time in D.C. with Scott and his girl friend; we would have more time to try to catch up with Jake. I reminded her that no matter how much time we had, we'd never be able to find out where David Dunne was sending Jake and what he was doing.

Susan also made a lot of sense talking about the political repercussions of sending so many people to the penitentiary over twenty-four years. Each one of the convicts I sent to various state facilities, including Parchman Farm, the vast Mississippi state penitentiary in the middle of the Delta, had family who voted in Yaloquena County, and many of them would never vote for me again. It didn't matter that their son, brother, sister, or cousin was guilty as sin of the offense charged. What they remembered was this: District Attorney Willie Mitchell Banks sent their loved one away. I had already heard from demagogues on the campaign trail supporting Eleanor Bernstein that most all the people I convicted and sent to prison were black.

In Yaloquena County, seventy-five per cent of the citizens are black.

I knew Susan was right. There was nothing I could do about the mountain of animosity accumulated against me over twenty-four years. So what did I do? I ran anyway.

As the Mayor drew closer that evening, my restless brain segued to the larger bone I've always picked with myself: what I've done in my life and what I've left undone. I'm sure my dysthymic moaning about opportunities lost was part of what drove Susan away. It was a miserable three years without her. There was too much alcohol, too many wasted days and nights feeling sorry for myself, not to mention the poor judgment I showed letting Mary Margaret Anderson play me like a fiddle. Thank God Susan came back. Thank God.

I continued listening to Everett talk about the dunking booth and election details. I had to force myself to pretend I was interested while wishing I hadn't submitted the one hundred plus signatures of registered voters along with the notice of candidacy to qualify. I was defying the principle I learned in my first election: enthusiasm was contagious. Voters sensed it and liked it. They didn't like ambivalence, not to mention lethargy. And that's just what I was giving Everett and everyone else at this Fourth of July barbecue and political rally. I was mailing it in, half-assing the campaign.

This event was the first time Eleanor and I were scheduled to speak at the same forum. Everett was trying to get me pumped up. I wanted desperately to be somewhere else.

"Let me go shake a few hands," I said to the Mayor. "Winston's about to call us up there to speak. I'll get back with you afterwards."

He nodded and merged back into the crowd, glad-handing and hugging, laughing and teasing, his big laugh shaking his entire body. Mayor Everett Johnson was sixty-five-years-old. He had two inches and seventy pounds on me. He was seven years older, too. Not only was Everett a good friend and close political ally, he was the best vote-getter in Sunshine—an avuncular and natural leader, veteran of many local controversies. He wanted everyone to get along.

I walked toward Clerk of Circuit Court Winston Moore standing near the speakers' platform. Winston was running unopposed for his second term. He was in his element, emcee for the biennial Fourth of July barbecue and fireworks gala in the new downtown park constructed with "stimulus" money from Washington procured for Sunshine by Congresswoman Rose Jackson.

I didn't care for the way the Clerk carried out his official duties, but I always admired Winston's style. He was resplendent in a white Guayabera and loose-fitting cream-colored Tommy Bahama linen slacks and *écru* patent leather loafers. I was thankful Winston kept his chief deputy clerk, transplanted Cajun Eddie Bordelon, on the job after Winston was elected. Eddie kept the Clerk's office and the courtroom running smoothly, seeing to all the details of the Circuit Clerk's operations. Winston didn't know much about the technical workings of his office, but the man was born to emcee.

"Looking sharp, Mr. Clerk," I said and shook Winston's hand.

"Too hot for a coat and tie," Winston said. "Cubans and Mexicans—they know how to dress for this kind of heat."

"Now that it's getting dark maybe it'll cool down."

"Not fast enough," the Clerk said, pulling a bright white handkerchief from his pocket and mopping his dark brown brow. "We're going by the alphabet, so you'll speak before Eleanor."

"Fine."

"Ten minute limit. We'll do Rose's speech first, then I'll introduce state and county candidates."

"Congresswoman Jackson doesn't have any opposition."

"She's the top elected official at this get-together. She'll be dedicating the park during her speech after I remind the folks the Congresswoman gave us the money for it."

Uh-oh. I knew that meant I was in for a long, hot night. No doubt Winston's introduction and Rose's speech would take at least half an hour. Thirty minutes of oration to convey five minutes of information.

I had heard Congresswoman Rose Jackson speak on many occasions before she temporarily retired from Congress. A few years back she announced she would not run for re-election. She put her substantial political machine behind her chief administrative assistant in D.C., Levander Boothe, originally from Greenville. I had dealt with Levander many times over the years, and thought he was responsive and articulate. Whenever I needed to discuss something of substance with Rose's office I called Levander directly. If the call was political, I always teamed up with Lee Jones. I told Lee many times the Congresswoman had a crush on him.

To demonstrate that they have a sense of humor, the gods of politics arranged for Levander Boothe to suffer a heart attack and die three weeks before the general election, assuring the election of the only remaining candidate, Republican Buddy Wade. I knew Buddy fairly well through Jimmy Gray, my 312 pound lifelong best friend. Buddy Wade was a swashbuckling semi-retired oil man. Because of Levander's death, Buddy became the first white Congressman to represent the Mississippi Delta since reapportionment in the early eighties. To no one's surprise, Buddy Wade served only one two-year term. Rose Jackson ended her interregnum, coming out of retirement to take back her seat from the Republican interloper. Jimmy Gray said Rose Jackson beat Buddy Wade like a "rented mule," getting seventy-three per cent of the vote. Jimmy told Buddy that he suspected Rose Jackson had actually beaten him worse than the final count indicated, that some of Buddy's votes were mistakes in the voting booth or counting errors by election officials. Buddy Wade did not demand a re-count, and he wasn't interested in a re-match.

I've always gotten along fine with Rose Jackson. The downside of her re-election for me was listening to her never-ending speeches at political functions. Although Lee helped out our cause by convincing the Congresswoman not to endorse Eleanor Bernstein, I had gotten word that many of Rose's people in the district were helping Eleanor behind the scenes. The way I felt about my candidacy before Danny Thurman disappeared from the barbecue, I could not have cared less about whom the Congresswoman's people helped.

Running late as usual, Clerk Winston Moore finally introduced the Congresswoman to the adoring crowd at the barbecue. While I kept my eyes glued to Rose and a smile on my face, I tried to think about something else—the difference between a curve ball and slider, the etymology of the word *behoove,* whether quarks and down-quarks ever socialized in their tiny world—anything but what she was saying. She talked slowly, enunciating and separating each multi-syllabic word into its components, saying nothing. After a while I glanced at my watch. Ten minutes into her speech—decades to go.

I heard a dissonant commotion behind me, not typical crowd noise. Thankful for the distraction, I turned and saw Connie Thurman rushing through the crowd, people making room for her.

"Danny," Connie called out, searching the crowd. "Danny."

I moved toward Connie as fast as the crowd would allow. As I grew closer, I could see she was crying. I watched her grab every white kid close to Danny's size. She was desperate to find her son.

"Thank God," I heard her say as she rushed toward a young boy on the edge of the crowd. She pushed and shoved startled people aside as she closed in on her boy.

"Danny," she yelled, but he didn't acknowledge her.

I glanced back at the podium when the crowd erupted in applause and whistles at something Congresswoman Jackson said. Maybe Danny couldn't hear his mother with all the noise.

I was almost at her side when she elbowed her way through two gangling teens. She grabbed the little boy and jerked him around, squeezing him to her.

"Danny," I heard her cry, tears flowing down her cheeks.

When I finally got a good look at the boy my heart sank. It wasn't Danny. After running her hand through the boy's hair and pulling back to smother him in kisses, Connie realized the startled boy was not her son. The boy pushed her away and looked at her as if she were crazy.

Connie let the boy go. I rushed over and caught her as she began to collapse. As I held her, she wailed, then fainted.

I watched a solemn Circuit Clerk Winston Moore stand at the microphone to close the truncated political gathering. He asked the people to bow their heads.

"And heavenly father," he ended the prayer, "please help us bring Danny Thurman home safely this evening. Amen."

Subdued "amens" echoed here and there through what little was left of the crowd. Winston signaled the city crew to begin shutting down the public address system. Most people had begun to wander away thirty minutes earlier after the initial search of the grounds failed to turn up seven-year-old Danny Thurman, only child of Bill and Connie Thurman, who lived four blocks from the park.

I remember the feeling I had an hour earlier when I saw Connie pushing and shoving her way through the gathering shouting for Danny. I shuddered. The hair on the back of my neck bristled. Something told me Danny was not merely missing. Even though the search for Danny had not even begun, I knew for certain there would be no happy ending.

To her credit, when she saw me catch Connie as she fell out, Congresswoman Jackson immediately stopped speaking and waded into the crowd. She took Connie in her arms. When she came to, Rose Jackson spoke softly to Connie for a moment and gestured for Sheriff Jones, the Circuit Clerk, and me to join her in assuring Connie everything would be suspended while we searched for Danny. Thirty minutes later, we cancelled the remaining speeches and two minutes of fireworks.

Sheriff Lee Jones was in charge of the search, calling in all his deputies and civil defense volunteers. Bill Thurman's buddies from the fire station joined in as soon as they heard about Danny.

I saw Walton Donaldson, my thirty-two-year-old assistant district attorney, and waved him over.

"Where's Connie and Bill?" I asked.

"They took Connie home. Gayle's with her. Bill is still out looking with the other firemen."

Gayle Donaldson and Connie Thurman were close. Walton and Gayle's twin sons Nicholas and Payne played with Danny Thurman almost every day in the summer. Gayle and Connie were friends with Susan, too, and I knew without asking that my wife would already be helping Connie in some way.

Sheriff Lee Jones joined us.

"Nothing," Lee said shaking his head. "I've got men from here to the Thurman's house, checking every nook and cranny."

"Why'd Connie send Danny home to get her sweater, hot as it is?" I asked. "I don't get that."

"Bill told me she got sunburned this afternoon and when the sun started going down she got a chill," Walton said. "Bill said Danny has ridden his bicycle all over this town, sometimes by himself, sometimes with other kids. He walks from his house to the stores downtown by himself all the time. He's never had a problem or run into trouble."

"Until now," I said.

"We'll keep looking," Lee Jones said, "until we find him."

CHAPTER TWO

Twenty-three days after Danny disappeared, Walton and I were in my private office in the suite of offices in the courthouse designated as the Office of the Yaloquena County District Attorney. The "suite" consists of eight interconnecting rooms on the south side of the second floor. The décor is 1960s institutional except for my office, which Susan redecorated when I was out of town for a couple of days at a Mississippi D.A.'s Association meeting on the coast. I had finished the trial of Lester "Mule" Gardner and needed a few days away.

The rest of the offices are badly in need of refurbishing, which will never happen because the Supervisors don't have enough money to pave the county roads, much less re-decorate courthouse offices.

Walton and I were parsing the felony docket, trying to figure out which of the thirty defendants set for trial in August would insist on a jury trial and which ones would plead out. We suffered through this exercise before every jury term, debating the range of years we thought Judge Williams would approve before making the sentence recommendation part of the plea offer we made to the public defender. Except in rare cases in the state prosecution system, I believed any defense lawyer who pleaded his client guilty "in the dark," even to a lesser offense, without some kind of deal on sentencing was committing legal malpractice.

Walton tossed the list of felonies on my desk. I watched him walk to the window and stare down at the firemen playing basketball behind the fire station.

"It never gets better," Walton said, "does it?"

"Nope. Worse every year."

"And if each defendant insisted on a trial, we could dispose of how many in this term? Two?"

"Two at most."

"If the defense lawyers collaborated and refused any plea deals, our next jury term we'd have sixty felonies set for trial. Then ninety in another two months. Why don't they?"

"I've always worried about it," I said, "but I guess it hasn't happened because no lawyer's going to volunteer his client to do the maximum prison time to implement the work stoppage. Might be good for everyone else on the docket to get their cases postponed, but not for the defendant getting convicted. Defense lawyers know we can use the habitual offender statute to turn a third offense burglary into thirty years. And most of the decent lawyers want to move their cases."

Walton continued to watch the firemen. I could feel his frustration. He had been prosecuting long enough to realize the system needed to be revamped from top to bottom.

"You know," Walton said, "I can handle this felony docket without you. You ought to be out knocking on doors."

"I should be."

The phone buzzed. I listened for a moment and heard the words I thought I'd never hear.

"When?" I asked. "Where is he now?"

I gave Walton a thumbs up.

"We're on our way."

I hung up.

"What is it?" Walton asked.

"Ross Bullard shot himself in the stomach and left a note about Danny Thurman. He's at the hospital."

I was drafting Walton's coattails as he burst through the doors of the emergency entrance. We blew past the check-in desk. Sheriff Lee Jones waved at us from the hall outside one of the treatment rooms. We made a beeline for Lee.

Lee wore his dark blue Sheriff's uniform and white Stetson. He had just turned forty-nine, but with his thick torso and muscular arms, Lee looked much like he had as an All-SWAC Conference linebacker almost three decades earlier. Throughout his careers in the military and state police, physical fitness was important to him, and it showed. Lee and his wife Yancey had two teenaged daughters. I told him his teenagers caused the wrinkles starting to show in the milk chocolate skin around his eyes, but I knew it was the stress of being Sheriff. Lee Jones and I had grown close in the eight years since his first election. I admired his character and ability, and told anyone who would listen that Lee was the best-trained, most professional Sheriff in the history of Yaloquena County. Lee's peers must have agreed with me, because two years earlier he was the first black man to be elected president of the Mississippi Sheriff's Association.

"What's Bullard's status?" I asked.

"Ten minutes ago Dr. Clement stuck his head out and said as soon as they stabilize him they're taking him into the operating room."

"What did the note say?" Walton asked.

"I wrote it down, word for word." Lee pulled a small spiral notebook from his pocket. "There were three sentences. The first said 'I am sorry about Danny'; the second 'I don't know why it happened'; and the last sentence was 'The boy's body was in an old hunting camp'."

"Where is the note?" I asked.

"I took a picture of it on the floor, bagged it and gave it to Kitty. I left the pistol on the floor where Bullard dropped it after he shot himself. The note's the only thing I moved and I was careful to pick it up by the edge. I told Kitty I'd get her additional deputies over there to preserve the scene for the crime lab and hightailed it over here."

"It's an unusual suicide note," Walton said.

"Not a straight-forward confession, either," I said.

Lee shook his head. "Even though he never admitted killing Danny common sense says it's a confession. Maybe we'll find something on his computer or at his office in the bank."

"Who called 9-1-1?" Walton asked.

"He did."

"He really wanted to die, didn't he?" Walton said. "Shoots himself then calls for help. What did he tell the operator?"

"All he said was 'I'm shot'. We've got it on tape."

"Be sure to preserve the original tape," I reminded Lee, "and make a copy for us."

"How old is Ross?" Walton asked.

"Forty-three, forty-four," I said. "His wife's older. She's more like forty-eight or so. She's a CPA." I turned to Lee. "Had you questioned him in the investigation?"

"Twice," Lee said. "First time was the canvass of Whitley Drive the night Danny disappeared. Investigators checked with him again about three days ago."

"Was he a suspect?" Walton asked.

"No. He's got a clean record, never been arrested for anything. In the first canvass, he said he knew Danny from the neighborhood. He said Danny had been in the house with other neighborhood kids to look at Ross's Indian relics. He's supposed to have a big collection."

"When was that?" I asked.

"He told the investigators it was sometime in late April or early May. He said a week or two later Danny came back by himself to ask him about mowing his grass. Bullard said he told the boy he already had someone mowing this summer, but would think about him for next year."

"So," Walton said, "it's not like you were closing in on him."

"No," Lee said, "he was no more a suspect than anyone else in the neighborhood. Not sure why he did it."

"Guilt," I said. "Did your men talk to his wife?"

"No," the Sheriff said. "She wasn't at the house either time he was questioned."

"He couldn't have been feeling too guilty," Walton said. "He called 9-1-1 because he didn't want to die."

"And wait until a good defense lawyer gets hold of that note," I said. "Ross's lawyer will have a creative interpretation."

"Maybe he'll do us a favor and die," Walton said. "Any idea what old hunting camp he's talking about?"

"I didn't know Ross was a hunter," I said. "We'll have to find out what hunting camp he's gone to over the last few years. It's funny. I've always thought of Ross Bullard as a meek sort of guy, the kind you could run out of the county with a switch."

"Doesn't seem so meek now," Walton said.

"I don't think Bullard's going to die," the Sheriff said. "Dr. Clement said he had no pulse when they brought him in. Said the EMTs told him he was breathing when they picked him up at his house, but on the ride here in the ambulance they couldn't find a pulse. They were still working on him when they pulled up outside and Dr. Clement took over. Dr. Clement said they got his pulse going again in the E.R., had him breathing on his own."

"Did he make any kind of admission to the EMTs or say anything here in the E.R. about Danny?" I asked.

"No," Lee said.

"We need a deputy at his bedside around the clock," I said, "someone good so when he comes to we can get his statement."

"He'll have to be Mirandized," Walton said.

"Right," Lee said. "I'll tell my man to talk fast."

We turned around when we heard the sound of high heels behind us on the tile floor. I made eye contact with Judy Bullard, Ross's wife. Jimmy Gray told me on a morning walk weeks before that Ross and Judy were separated. I kept up with civil filings in the Clerk's office and knew no divorce paperwork had been filed.

Jules Bullard, Ross's father, followed Judy. I couldn't stand the old goat. Neither could Jimmy Gray, and Jimmy was tolerant of just about everyone. It wasn't because his bank was our bank's chief competition. We disliked Jules because he was mean and greedy, the kind of banker who had ruined a lot of folks.

Jules owned all but ten per cent of the stock of First Savings Bank. First Savings was the only financial institution in Yaloquena County besides our bank. Our late fathers, James Gray Sr. and Monroe Banks, founded Sunshine Bank. Jimmy Gray was currently CEO and owned a slightly larger percentage of common stock than I. Together we had a controlling interest, well over half of the outstanding shares. Unlike Jules, we took good care of our minority shareholders. The last time Jimmy and I discussed Jules, Jimmy said he was a "hateful, dick-nosed, avaricious son-of-a-bitch who's going to have to hire pallbearers to carry his casket."

While I was running the D.A.'s office, Jimmy Gray ran our bank, so he had more hands-on knowledge about Jules' *modus operandi* than I did. Jimmy told me many tales of Bullard's taking advantage of unsophisticated borrowers, charging them the maximum legal interest and ultimately confiscating their collateral. Jimmy said Jules didn't break any laws, as far as he knew, but what the old buzzard was doing was despicable nonetheless.

As I watched the seventy-year-old walk toward us, it seemed to me Jules the bloodsucker resembled a vulture, too. He was tall and thin, slightly stooped, and bald with a fringe of white hair. His nose was large, aquiline—his dominant feature. He wore thick, rimless glasses and behind them his eyes darted about and seemed too small for his face. In contrast, Jules' daughter-in-law Judy was good-looking—alabaster skin set off by long, straight hair more red than brown. The few times I had talked to her she seemed aloof, but pleasant enough, which was more than I could say about Jules. Jules was obsessed with money and a complete ass.

"Mean as a snake and crooked as a barrel of guts," was another thing Jimmy liked to say about Jules. Jimmy said it was odd how the title to assets used as collateral for bank loans always ended up in the name of Jules personally.

"Judy and Mr. Bullard," I said, minding my manners, "this is Sheriff Lee Jones and my first assistant Walton Donaldson."

Jules was in no mood for chit chat. He ignored my introduction.

"He's in here?" Jules asked and brushed my shoulder as he pushed open the door to the treatment room. "Ross?" he called out.

In seconds, Dr. Nathan Clement, clad in his light green scrubs and wearing blood-smeared latex gloves, shooed Jules Bullard back and stepped into the hall to talk.

"You can't come in here, Mr. Bullard," Dr. Clement said.

"Tell me how my son is."

Nathan removed his gloves and led Jules by the elbow away from the treatment room. Judy followed closely behind. Fifteen feet away, Nathan whispered and gestured to the Bullards. After a couple of minutes he walked back into the treatment room.

"We're moving him into the O.R.," Nathan said in passing.

Jules and Judy Bullard kept their distance from us. I turned, showing them my back. Looking at Jules gave me the creeps. After ten minutes, several orderlies walked quickly past us into the treatment room. A few moments later they left pushing Ross Bullard on a gurney. We stayed put, but Judy walked past us following the orderlies. Jules stopped next to me and leaned in too close to the Sheriff. It made me uncomfortable, but I was sure Lee would hold his own.

"Is Ross under arrest?" Jules said, pointing his crooked index finger at Lee.

"Not yet," Lee said.

"Stay away from him," Jules growled and turned his finger and beady eyes to me. "Both of you. He's not to be questioned."

"He's an adult," I said. "He'll have to tell us that himself. You can't speak for him unless you've been declared his legal guardian."

"You heard what I told you, Banks," Jules said, drawing close to me, invading my space. His breath was rank. "I'm telling you right now in front of witnesses he has a lawyer. I'll give you the name later. Any information you want call the lawyer."

Jules stormed off. I was grateful to have my space back, not to mention fresh air.

"Close talker," Walton said, "and asshole."

"That man's got some really stankie breath," Lee said. "I almost gagged. How's she do it?"

"The smell of his money overwhelms the halitosis," I said.

Dr. Clement and the young surgeon came out of the treatment room. The surgeon nodded to us and walked past on his way to the O.R. Nathan stopped to talk.

"It was touch and go there for a while," he said. "I didn't think we could get him stable."

"What's his prognosis?"

"Looks like the worst is over. Once we got him back breathing on his own and his pulse stronger, we tried to assess the damage the bullet did. He's bleeding internally in several places. That's why we're taking him into surgery."

"Bleeding badly?" I asked.

"I've seen a lot worse. He should make it."

"Where did the bullet enter?" I asked.

Nathan stuck his right index finger slightly below my sternum on my left side, then reached around and stuck his left index finger at a spot on my back below the rib cage and just to the left of my spine.

"It went in here," he said, tapping his right index finger, "and came out right here," putting pressure on my back. "It passed through the stomach, anterior and posterior, missing his lungs, pancreas, and aorta. It came very close to his spine and kidney," he said, "but didn't damage either one. He was lucky."

"He's going to live," I said, making no effort to hide the disappointment in my voice.

"Most likely," Nathan said and began walking.

"Thanks, Nathan. Can you give me a call after the surgery?"

"Will do. His old man's rough," Nathan said and left for the O.R.

"I'll stay here until I can set up shifts to have a deputy here all the time," Lee said, "whether Jules Bullard likes it or not."

"Okay. Walton and I are headed to Ross's house."

CHAPTER THREE

I had only taken two steps toward the exit when the E.R. door burst open. Three men were struggling to stop a large red-faced man in a fireman's uniform charging into the hospital.

"Bill," Walton yelled and joined the state policeman and two Sheriff's deputies trying to corral Danny Thurman's father. Lee Jones ran past me and plowed linebacker-style into the men, knocking his smallest deputy into the wall, sending a tray of bandages, clips, and hemostats skittering across the tile. Walton went low, grabbing Bill's lower legs and holding on while Sheriff Jones and the state trooper pushed against Bill. He fell hard on the floor. The deputies grabbed Bill's legs while Walton straddled his chest and held his head.

"Stop it, Bill," Walton said. "Stop it. Calm down."

After a moment the big fireman stopped fighting. He lay on the floor with Walton on his chest and the two deputies and trooper pressing his legs and arms against the floor. Large tears ran down Bill's cheeks and onto the tile floor. It had been a long time since I had seen a grown man in such agony.

"If I get off you," Walton said, "will you control yourself?"

Bill Thurman, eyes still closed, did not respond. I knelt down and whispered, inches from Bill's face.

"Look at me, Bill," I said. "It's Willie Mitchell. Sheriff Jones is here, too. Walton and the other men will let you up if you promise not to try to strangle Ross Thurman."

Bill took a deep breath and opened his eyes, blinking against the fluorescent light over him. After a while he said "okay" quietly. Walton climbed off Bill's chest. The deputies and trooper relaxed their holds on his legs and arms but stayed ready. They helped Bill up. Tears continued to streak through his close-cropped red and brown beard.

"All right," Bill said.

"You go with these deputies," Sheriff Jones said, gesturing to his men. "They're going to take you home and stay with you a while."

Bill picked up his hat off the floor and pulled the brim low over his eyes. He looked at me.

"Okay, but I'm still going to kill the son-of-a-bitch."

I watched Bill walk off between the two deputies. I hadn't realized how strong Bill Thurman was. He was only an inch taller but probably outweighed me by fifty pounds—fifty pounds of muscle. He wasn't fat. Bill had big shoulders, a thick chest, and a square jaw. He kept his reddish hair in a short crew cut.

"I'll make sure Bill has someone with him until he calms down," Lee said as we walked out.

I drove my silver Ford F-150 the short distance to Whitley Drive. In Sunshine, every destination was a short drive.

"Bill is one strong man," Walton said. "He's normally so mild-mannered. I've never seen him lose it like that, but I don't blame him." He turned to me. "Why don't you let me handle this from now on?"

Given the fact that I was supposed to be devoting all my time to my re-election campaign, Walton had a point.

"There's no reason for you to get down in the weeds on this one, boss. Connie and Gayle are close and Bill's a good friend of mine. My twins and Danny Thurman played together all the time. I'm not going to let anything get by me. I'll nail Ross Bullard for this."

"I know you can handle it just fine. I have no doubt of that."

"This will make up for my bailing out on Mule Gardner's trial."

I told him it wasn't his fault his wife had been rushed to the emergency room in Jackson.

"You belonged at the hospital with Gayle. That was a lot more important than trying Mule Gardner."

"I promise I'll keep you in the loop and let you know everything about the investigation. If you don't pay attention to your re-election, neither one of us will have a job."

I started to say that my losing the job would probably be the best thing for me, but I didn't. No need to spread my malaise to Walton. He had the energy and drive I had in years past. I didn't want to infect him with my chronic *ennui*.

"You can make a lot more money in your civil practice," I said.

"I know, but this is what I want to do. Let me work with the Sheriff and Kitty in the investigation and take Ross Bullard to trial. You get on with the politicking."

"All right," I said as I stopped the truck in front of Ross Bullard's home on Whitley. "I'd rather take a beating, but you're right. The case is yours. Just keep me informed. Let me take a peek inside the house and I'll leave. You can catch a ride home or back to the courthouse."

Like the other houses in the neighborhood, the Bullard home was a ranch-style brick veneer built in the sixties. The front yard was large and well-landscaped. The dense mat of St. Augustine grass was manicured, with a grouping of mature pines along one property line and a large pecan tree on the other.

"At least you won't have to deal with the Sunshine police," I told Walton as I killed the engine.

"No kidding."

Sheriff Lee Jones now ran the only law enforcement agency in Yaloquena County. Ten years ago, before Lee was elected, Mayor Johnson and I convinced the Sunshine Alderman to disband the City Police Department. We argued that it would save the city money and eliminate duplicate services. That was true, but the driving force was not fiscal. Everett and I were fed up with being embarrassed by the incompetence and dishonesty of the local cops. Every year the local paper featured at least one police department scandal. In the five years before Everett and I put them out of business, city cops were arrested on a regular basis for domestic violence, drug consumption and distribution, and the occasional armed robbery or burglary.

The City P.D. was also a constant financial drain on Sunshine. In contrast the authority of the Yaloquena Sheriff was grounded in the Mississippi Constitution. Its funding came from the state and the county, enabling the Sheriff to pay his deputies better and keep them insulated from the political whims of the dim bulbs who masqueraded as public officials in the city and county. Sunshine paid its cops a pittance, so naturally the job attracted few law-abiding applicants and none that were qualified or trained. The results were predictable.

As Walton and I walked toward the front door, Kitty Douglas stopped us on the sidewalk. FBI Special Agent Kitty Douglas was a tall brunette with olive skin and a .40 caliber Glock 23 semi-automatic in a leather holster on her right hip. She was on assignment in Yaloquena County, posted to Lee's office through an intergovernmental program to assist rural, poorly funded law enforcement offices. She was also Jake Banks' girl friend again.

We all missed Jake. I made a mental note to call Deputy Attorney General Patrick Dunwoody IV, the highest ranking non-political appointee in the Justice Department in D.C. Dunwoody was Jake's ostensible supervisor in DOJ. Last year he was good enough to speak frankly to me at the Magnolia Hotel coffee shop about Jake's organization. I hoped Dunwoody could give me enough details about the status of Jake's current mission to give Kitty, Susan and me some comfort.

"Sheriff Jones spoke to Mr. Robbie Cedars at the crime lab," Kitty said, "and asked them to send a team to process the scene. I've got deputies posted around the house. Before he left for the hospital, the Sheriff told me to make a quick walk through the rest of the house to make sure the place was secure. Other than the EMTs who took Bullard to the hospital and the Sheriff and me, no one else has been in the place."

"Good," I said.

"The Sheriff gave me Bullard's note to hold for the crime lab," she said, patting the plastic bag sticking out of her shirt pocket.

"Did y'all call Judge Williams regarding the search before you went in the house?" Walton asked. "You know she's changed the local court rules to allow phone applications for...."

"Lee called Judge Williams and got the search approved before either one of us set foot inside," she said.

"Good going," I said, patting her shoulder.

Kitty coughed a couple of times. I walked past her to the deputy guarding the front door. I cupped my palms around my eyes and looked inside. I couldn't see much.

"Walton's going to stay here and wait for the crime lab with you," I told Kitty. "I'm headed back to the courthouse."

I cranked the truck and pulled into the driveway across the street. After I backed out into Whitley, I kept my foot on the brake and watched a slow-moving Sheriff's Office patrol unit pass in front of Ross Bullard's house. As the cruiser crept by, I realized the two deputies in the front seat were the ones who helped subdue Bill Thurman at the hospital. The unit moved slowly enough for me to recognize the man in the back seat. It was Bill Thurman, staring at Ross Bullard's home.

CHAPTER FOUR

Jake Banks. London. July 28

Jake Banks sat in the front passenger seat of the beat up, rusted out VW van, itching like crazy. It was three a.m. Saturday morning. Jake and Doberman had been at it a while. Jake couldn't figure out why Dunne made the entire team wear black *thawbs.* Any black outfit would have done just as well in the intense darkness, including the black protective assault gear the team normally wore on missions. The gear was bulky but didn't itch. Jake wanted to scratch his chest but Doberman had already warned him about shaking the van.

They were in Newham borough on a crooked, deserted street named Mumford. Only six men had walked past them in the past few hours. Since Doberman told him not to talk, Jake had plenty of time to think.

Staring at the empty street, Jake decided he had been in England too long. He started feeling homesick three and a half weeks earlier on July 4. The date meant nothing in England, but it made Jake think about all the fun he used to have back home on the Fourth. Willie Mitchell would always put the MasterCraft in the oxbow lake not far from Sunshine. Even though he was four years younger, Scott tried to do everything Jake did when they skied double. Scott was as good an athlete as Jake, but not as big or strong. Jake smiled in the darkness thinking about how mad it made Scott when Jake learned to barefoot and Scott couldn't. In Jake's high school and college years there were always parties on the lake, some with parents, some without.

Jake and the rest of Dunne's team had been in England off and on for six months. It was an eye-opener for Jake. He had no idea that the England he learned about in history courses at Ole Miss no longer existed. The tiny island nation, fountainhead of western civilization for 350 years, the country that led the Industrial Revolution and dominated the world in exploration, colonization, science and discovery—was a shadow of its former self. This England would never have survived the Battle of Britain and would likely never produce another Winston Churchill. Unfettered immigration, the incredibly generous socialist-style welfare system, and an explosive immigrant birth rate had changed the streets of London forever.

Jake and the rest of David Dunne's D.O.G.s team listened to Deputy U.S. Attorney General Patrick Dunwoody talk about the metamorphosis when Dunwoody was last in London. Dunwoody was a brilliant guy, a patriot, and an Anglophile. He grew angry describing the ruination of his ancestors' country. He traced his Dunwoody roots to the Magna Carta and said his forebears were spinning in their ancient crypts. He described how Muslims from the Middle East, North Africa, and Eastern Europe began pouring into English cities in the seventies, congregating in and co-opting entire areas. The immigrants made no effort to assimilate or integrate. Eventually because of their numbers, they took control of entire boroughs in London and Birmingham. The new Balkanized London was ungovernable. Local law enforcement and natives treated some of the new Muslim conclaves as "No Go" zones, areas where no native Londoner dare venture.

Dunwoody said he couldn't understand why critics were outraged at John Cleese, the Monthy Python actor, for saying that London was no longer a British city. Cleese walked it back, but the chattering class wasn't mollified, still referring to the comment as racist and zenophobic. Dunwoody said Cleese was merely describing what he saw.

"Cleese was spot on," Dunwoody said.

Jake looked toward the driver's seat. He could barely see Doberman in the blackness inside the VW, though they were only two feet apart. Dunwoody's *thawb* didn't seem to bother him because he hadn't moved or spoken to Jake in over an hour. If Jake couldn't scratch his chest soon, he thought he might scream.

Doberman was the most effective member of D.O.G.s, not counting David Dunne. Jake felt intimidated working with him because Doberman's experience and abilities were much more advanced than his own. With the beard Doberman had grown over the last six months and his Mediterranean coloring, he could have passed for one of the *jihadists* he and Jake were staking out.

This wasn't Jake's first kill mission with Doberman. Jake knew Doberman didn't like to talk before an assault, leaving Jake alone with his thoughts, which were turning more every day to Sunshine. He missed everyone, especially Kitty. He dreamed about their time together at the duck camp a few miles north of Sunshine, just the two of them in the middle of nowhere.

Jake looked at the time. With the six hour time differential, he guessed little brother Scott was probably at a political event in D.C. with his good-looking girlfriend Donna Piersall. Jake knew a comparison of his situation with Scott's by any neutral observer would prove that Scott was much smarter than his big brother.

Jake thought about Willie Mitchell and his disappointing decision to run for re-election. Jake wondered if he would have been able to talk him out of it if he had been in Sunshine rather than London.

"Jake," Doberman whispered in the darkness. "Go over the plan again. Visualize every step. Picture yourself in the apartment house, going through the rooms one-by-one."

Jake imagined himself going through the rooms, projecting what each looked like and where it led. He wondered about Hound and Bull. They hadn't checked in with Doberman in a while.

Jake watched a car pull up in front of the rundown apartment building they were watching.

"Straight ahead," Doberman said.

"I see it."

It was a black or dark blue BMW. It stopped at the main entrance. Two men exited and opened the front door. In the dim light from inside, Jake recognized them as Khabir's lieutenants.

"Khabir's not with them," Jake whispered.

"Roger that."

Doberman picked up the radio and informed Dunne. They waited in the darkness for a decision. Khabir was the primary target, the reason for the mission. Jake thought Dunne would probably call it off. The radio popped.

"Team One advance," Dunne said, proving Jake wrong.

Doberman and Jake reached under their seats and pulled out their modified pistols with suppressors. Jake missed his Colt, but Dunne insisted on uniform weaponry for this mission. Pistols only. Identical caliber and ammunition. Both men checked their gun chambers and made sure their extra magazines were secure but accessible.

They weren't preparing to arrest the targets. They were sent to eliminate them.

"Ready Jake?"

"Let's go."

They synchronized their exit and ran in a crouch to the seedy apartment house. Pressing their backs against the front wall, they waited. Jake worked on steadying his breathing, controlling the adrenaline rush.

After a moment, Doberman signaled and they eased into the foyer. Doberman unscrewed the naked light bulb and gestured with his pistol for Jake to head upstairs.

Jake crept up the wooden steps as silently as possible, moving toward the first room. He pointed his pistol toward the ceiling and turned the door knob quietly. Jake signaled to Doberman and nodded.

It was time to kill.

CHAPTER FIVE

I finished my four-mile run and dragged myself soaking wet into Jimmy Gray's carport at six-thirty the next morning. It was hot and humid, a typical summer morning in the Delta. I normally met Jimmy after my run for his fifteen minute stroll on Monday, Wednesday, and Friday. I had called him the night before to see if he could work me in for an unscheduled fifteen minute walk.

"You do know it's Saturday," the big banker told me on the phone.

"I need to talk."

"We can talk in my house or my office or anywhere there's a working air conditioner. It's going to be hot as hell in the morning."

"I know," I said and waited.

"What time?"

"I'll be in your carport about six-thirty."

"Okay. This better be good."

"Damn it's hot," was the first thing Jimmy Gray said to me when he walked out of his kitchen door onto the carport.

"It's July."

"Yeah, but shoot. We gotta do this? It's nice and cool inside. Martha's sound asleep."

"You need the exercise," I said, starting my timer. "Let's go."

We began the walk. Jimmy was already sweating.

"Darrell Ross Bullard still unconscious?" he asked.

"Must be. Lee said he would call or text as soon as he came to. Nathan told me they might keep him sedated for a day or two after the surgery. Darrell?"

"That's his first name. Named after his grandfather. His late mother's dad. He never uses the name. Jules made him go by Ross. You think the note is enough for a conviction?"

"It depends. It will be if there's some corroborating physical evidence when we find Danny's body."

"You sure he's dead?"

"These kinds of cases, if we don't find the victim in the first few days of the investigation he's probably dead. I've had a bad feeling since the barbecue this wouldn't end well for the Thurmans."

"Nathan shouldn't have saved the bastard."

"I know, but that's what he's supposed to do."

"I wish he weren't such a good doctor. What did you want to talk to me about? Like I told you, I don't know much about Ross. I know plenty of bad stuff about the old man, but I've already told you most of that."

I dropped to one knee to tighten my shoelaces. I took my time because as slow as Jimmy Gray walked, I could catch up with him in two seconds. When I did, I noticed the back of Jimmy's shirt and couldn't help but laugh. I read it out loud.

"National Talk Like A Pirate Day. September 19. That's almost two months away. Why are you wearing it now?"

"Practice. Arrrrrgggghhh," he added, closing one eye and tilting his head. "Arrrrrgggghh. 53 days. Be here before you know it."

"Pirates around the world would kill to have your outfit. It gives you that certain look of understated elegance, that *je ne c'est quoi*. People are constantly asking me: what is it that makes Jimmy Gray so cool?"

Jimmy wore a pair of gigantic DayGlo orange nylon shorts matching the fluorescent orange writing on his shirt. Around his big round head was a luminescent orange sweat band. He wore it tilted at a rakish angle.

"Lot of pirates spoke French, you know." He ran his forefinger across his forehead and flicked the sweat at me. "Got to make your own fun in this little bitty town. Martha's searching online for an eye patch and a three-cornered hat for the big day. Yarrrrrp. You heard back from the crime lab yet?"

"Walton said they finished the house late and Robbie Cedars and his crew went on back to Jackson. Robbie said he would call today to report. I'm going to sit in on the conversation."

"I thought Walton was handling this case."

"He is. That doesn't mean I can't listen to what Robbie has to say."

"Some things you just can't change," Jimmy Gray said, shaking his big head at me. "I know what you want to talk about, the reason you dragged me out in the heat on a Saturday morning."

"What?"

"The campaign. You can't make yourself do it."

"I left Ross Bullard's house on Whitley yesterday, fully intending to get back to the office and make a few phone calls, then knock on some doors until about six last night. I never left the courthouse. The media started calling and I had to get with Lee and work up a joint statement to release to the press late yesterday. Then I coordinated with Walton and Lee to schedule a press conference for Monday."

"Walton can do all that."

"I know. Look, I'm not going to talk to the media. He's going to answer their questions. He knows what he can say, which isn't much."

"What are you doing today?"

"I thought I'd go out into the county after Walton and I talk to Robbie. Call on a few folks, put some cards out at a couple of stores."

Jimmy Gray laughed like I had said something funny.

"What?"

"You know when you first ran and knocked on every door in the city and county, you had each day mapped out months in advance. You knew what streets and roads you would cover each day and the names of the people you would call on. You had a different black church scheduled for each Sunday. Do you even have a county map or calendar marked up like you did first time around?"

"No."

"Do you have a current list of registered voters?"

"Not yet."

"Damn, Willie Mitchell. I guess the reason you called me to walk this morning is to pump you up, right? Light a fire under you? Turn this thing around? Did I leave out any clichés?"

"Get my mojo back?"

"Yeah. That's a good one."

"I seem to have a motivational problem."

"Nicely understated. The reason is you don't want the job bad enough to put out the effort it takes to run a political campaign."

"Any suggestions?"

"Yeah, I do. How about this? D.A. stands for dumb ass."

"I already know that."

"We're going to have to get you some shock treatment or something. Maybe some crystal meth out of Lee's evidence locker." Jimmy stopped walking and faced me. "It's way too late for this kind of talk. I told you before you qualified it was time to hang it up. I asked you to get Walton to run or anybody else for that matter, but you let Everett and Lee talk you into it, telling you no one can do your job like you do. You didn't listen to me. It's too late now. It's like being pregnant. There's no half-way here, no way to do this but balls to the wall. Nobody filed for the office except you and Eleanor. You drop out now and Eleanor Bernstein wins by default."

"Maybe that wouldn't be so bad."

Jimmy looked at me like I was insane.

"You've got to get off your ass and concentrate on winning this election. We've never quit on anything, partner, and this ain't the time to start. I'm going to drag the real Willie Mitchell Banks kicking and screaming out of you.

"We're going to spend this afternoon doing some planning. Go have your phone conference with Robbie Cedars, then call me and I'll meet you at your house. I'll pick up some county maps from the bank and dig out my old files on your first campaign. We'll reconstruct the planning as best we can. I'll call Buddy Wade and get him to meet with us later today. We're getting your ass in gear." His big frame was generating torrents of sweat. "That's another good one, ass in gear.

"We have a hundred days until November 6. That's plenty of time. We're going to win this election, and then you can decide what you want to do. You're not going out with a whimper."

I took a deep breath. Jimmy was right. For the first time since qualifying I committed to do what it took to win.

I took off running with a spring in my step for the first time in a week. I made the three blocks to my house and stopped at my front steps. The energy and motivation Jimmy Gray gave me had dissipated, leeching out of my pores with my sweat. I knew down deep nothing had changed. I dragged myself up to the porch, dreading the afternoon.

CHAPTER SIX

After a quick shower at home I walked into my office. Walton was already there in well-worn jeans and a red short-sleeved Polo. He held up a photocopy of Ross Bullard's handwritten note for me to see.

"Three sentences," he said. "Three crummy sentences."

"Robbie called yet?"

Walton shook his head. I took the copy of Ross's note and sat behind my desk, Walton across from me. I read the three sentences silently then read them aloud.

"I am sorry about Danny," I read. "So, we know he's talking about someone named Danny. That narrows it down."

"Saying he's sorry means nothing for us," Walton said. "Everyone in town is sorry Danny's gone. He doesn't say he killed Danny."

"But we know Ross is talking about someone named Danny. His lawyer might say he's referring to some other person named Danny who Ross has some connection to." I read the second sentence. "I don't know why it happened."

"Means nothing, evidentiary wise," Walton said. "Take it out of the context of the investigation, and it could mean thousands of things."

"I agree. The last sentence is the best for us. 'The boy's body was in an old hunting camp'."

"It's by far the most inculpatory," Walton said. "It narrows the meaning of *Danny* in the first sentence. *Danny* has to be a boy, not a man. The use of *the body* definitely indicates the boy *Danny* was dead.

"Right, and if Bullard's lawyer claims there's another Danny in Ross's life, it would have to be a dead boy named *Danny*."

"This is a confession," Walton said loudly, grabbing the copy off my desk and shaking it in the air. "No defense lawyer is going to be able to convince a jury it means anything else."

"I'm going to make myself a cup of coffee," I said. "Want one?"

"No," Walton said and walked to the window to look down on the firemen across the street. "They're lifting weights today."

I walked through the empty offices to the kitchenette in next to the bathroom. I flipped the switch on the back of the Keurig one-cup coffeemaker. Waiting for it to warm up, I had to admire Walton's passion. There was nothing more important in the makeup of a good prosecutor. Walton had it. He was good in front of a jury, too.

Walton had only recently turned thirty-two. He was in good shape. I tried for years to get him to jog with me, but he said he wasn't a runner, and preferred working out several days a week at the fitness center in the Sunshine Country Club. He was a couple of inches shorter than I, but much more muscular. Walton was built more like Jake and probably outweighed me by ten or fifteen pounds.

Walton had been my assistant district attorney for eight years. He grew up in Clarksdale, less than an hour from Sunshine. I had asked one of my law professor buddies at Ole Miss to keep an eye out for someone from the Delta who had some talent, and he put me on to Walton. I checked on Walton with some Delta folks and each one gave him a thumbs up. I offered Walton the position at the beginning of his senior year. He waited a couple of days and accepted. Walton had sat second chair for me in a slew of trials in the eight years we worked together, and had handled a lot of jury trials on his own. He had become a first-rate trial practitioner.

For the last several years I had spent more time with Walton than with Jake or Scott. Walton's mother died of cancer when he was in college. His father moved to Texas to live next door to Walton's sister. Walton opened up to me about his father. He said he was a decent provider but a difficult man to live with. Over drinks one night after a murder trial, Walton told me he wanted to be just like me in and out of the courtroom. It was one of the highest compliments I ever received.

I took a sip of my coffee and walked back to my office. When I walked into my office Walton was standing at the window flexing, admiring his muscles in the reflection.

"You thinking of joining the WWE?" I said.

Walton laughed and pointed out the window.

"I was watching the firemen pump up across the street and was checking out my guns. Not very impressive."

"It's this muscle that counts," I said, thumping my right index finger against my temple.

"I've read Bullard's note probably twenty times. It seems more ambiguous each time."

"Quit reading it then. I might have made too much of that. The jury will look at it in context. We'll be all right if we can get the slightest bit of physical evidence to prove the murder. If we don't find Danny's body, then we've got a serious uphill battle no matter what the note says. And even if we find Danny we still have to prove he suffered a violent cause of death, that he was murdered."

"I did some research online last night after the crime lab investigators left," Walton said. "Case law says we have to prove the elements of whichever murder classification we go with."

"I know the cases."

My phone rang.

"That's probably Robbie," I said and punched the speaker button. "Right on time, Robbie."

"How are you, Willie Mitchell?" the caller said.

"Good, Robbie. You?"

"Tired. I'm getting too old for these all-nighters."

"You know we appreciate what you do for us. Walton's with me and you're on speaker. It's just the two of us here."

"Hey, Walton," Robbie said. "I don't have a lot to tell you guys."

I watched Walton hang his head for a moment. When he looked up, I waggled my finger at him. I knew Robbie's m.o.

"Well, that means you do have at least something to tell us," I said. "You've always come through."

"We dusted every surface in the house and in his car in the garage. We lifted a lot of prints. Three different adult-sized and it looks like a half-dozen prints of different kids."

"Damn," I said.

"We're going to need comparison prints," Robbie said. "Any chance the Thurman boy has ever been printed?"

"I spoke to Bill Thurman this morning," Walton said. "All the firemen had their kids printed a year ago when our Sheriff had a grant from the state for something called 'Missing Kids Week'."

"Good for Lee Jones," Robbie said. "Can you get Danny's card to me down here in Jackson?"

"I've talked to the Sheriff about one of his deputies running it down there first thing Monday," Walton said. "Bullard's already admitted to deputies in the first neighborhood canvass that Danny's been in his house at least a couple of times to look at his Indian relics and asking to mow Bullard's yard to earn some money."

"Ross Bullard's not been arrested yet," I said. "We'll get you his prints as soon as he's booked."

"I'm sure most of the adult prints are his," Robbie said. "Be nice to get his wife's and anyone else's who might have spent time there."

"We'll work on that," Walton said. "Probably his father Jules."

"Anything else?" I said.

"Was this guy an anthropologist or something?"

"Bookkeeper at a bank," I said.

"He's supposed to have a museum quality collection of artifacts from the mound builders and other Indians that lived throughout the Delta," Walton said.

"Well, I can attest he has an impressive amount of Indian relics and artifacts in that house."

"What else, Robbie?" I said.

"Lots of commercial DVDs and homemade DVDs," Robbie said. "We took all of 'em. I'll get our tech guys to start going through them Monday. Your man owns some fine professional camera equipment."

"That's it?" Walton asked.

"We've got Bullard's gun and samples of his blood from the carpet. We found the bullet in the corner of the room. It's in good shape."

"That's not much help to our prosecution," Walton said. "We know Ross shot himself in his living room."

Robbie Cedars was silent for a moment. I pointed to Walton and winked. "Here it comes," I whispered.

"All right, Robbie," I said. "Give us the good stuff."

"Aw, hell, Willie Mitchell. We've been working together too long. You're taking all the fun out of this." He paused a few seconds. "Walton said something outside the house last night about the boy going home from the Fourth of July barbecue to get his mother a sweater?"

"That's right," Walton said, leaning into the phone.

"And it was light blue, right?" Robbie said.

"Yes," Walton said. "That's what the mother said in her statement."

"One of my fiber men gathered some light blue wool fiber wedged between the cushions of the couch in the living room. He said it looked like it could have come off a sweater. Any chance I could send my man up there Monday and check out the closet or drawer where Mrs. Thurman kept her blue sweater?"

"Tell him to call me first thing," Walton said. "I'll meet him over there at the Thurman's."

After Robbie signed off, Walton gave me a muted fist pump.

"If the fibers match, that will put Danny and Connie's blue sweater on Bullard's couch, which will put Danny in Ross's house the night he disappeared."

"It might," I said. "It just might."

I called Jimmy Gray before I left the courthouse. I hadn't been home long when he came in the back and barreled through the swinging door between our kitchen and dining room. He tossed a file on the dining room table and made a beeline for the guest bathroom under the stairs. The dining room table was a fine piece of furniture, like all the antiques my parents collected. My meticulous father left small envelopes taped under each piece of significance throughout the house. It wasn't until my parents were dead that I discovered the detailed descriptions of the antiques he wrote in his tiny, cramped writing style and placed in the envelope. His description of the table was "English Regency mahogany dining room table with twelve original matching chairs and sideboard circa 1800 West Sussex County."

I don't know why Monroe Banks began collecting fine antiques in 1967 after he and my mother bought the Neo-Classical Revival style house built in 1905 in which Susan and I lived. He never seemed to enjoy the furniture. I was twelve when we moved into this place and he began collecting English Regency furniture. He took pleasure in finding the pieces and cataloguing information about them, but once the piece was in the house, he never paid much attention to it. I can count on one hand the number of times I saw my parents eat at the dining room table. They never entertained and ate their meals at the worm-eaten and scarred pine table in the kitchen. My mother thought the old English furniture was pretty, and had fun on the buying trips they took to England, but it was Monroe who was the collector. By 1967, Sunshine Bank was throwing off significant profits. The furniture in the house and the buying trips were the only things my parents spent money on that might be considered an extravagance.

Jimmy Gray finished his business and walked back into the dining room. He grabbed his sturdy oak chair and placed it across from mine. Out of an abundance of caution and common sense, Jimmy Gray never sat in the mahogany dining chairs. Just for Jimmy's use, Susan kept a heavy, indestructible barrel backed oak chair in the southeast corner of the dining room. When Jimmy Gray finished dinner, or enjoyed his fifth or sixth cocktail seated at our antique table, he tended to lean back in his chair and balance his prodigious weight on the back legs of his chair, teetering dangerously. Rather than put Susan's teeth on edge whenever he sat at the dining room table, Jimmy always pulled up his solid oak chair, "Jimmy's Chair," from the corner and plopped down. It did not embarrass him one bit, and Jimmy felt free to lean back, rock, or balance in his own customized seat.

"Did you wash your hands?" I asked.

"Yes, Martha."

Jimmy rested his big arms on the table. He pored over a map of Yaloquena County on which he had marked the lines of the voting wards and precincts with a red Sharpie. I was working on my Month-At-A-Glance calendar, making notes on each date, scheduling areas of Sunshine and the county for visits.

I looked up when Susan walked through the dining room with two seven-year-old boys in swimming trunks.

"If it ain't Heckel and Jeckel," Jimmy Gray said to the boys.

"That's not our names," the smaller of the twin boys said very seriously, his brow furrowed. "It's Nicholas and Payne."

"That's right, Nicholas," Susan said. "Mr. Jimmy knows better."

"I was just picking," Jimmy said. "Come shake hands with Mr. Willie Mitchell and me."

Payne, the taller and stronger-looking of the two boys moved forward first, walking directly to me, looking me in the eye and confidently extending his hand. The slighter, shorter Nicholas followed suit reluctantly. Nicholas avoided eye contact when we shook hands. He was slightly built and seemed embarrassed.

"How are you today Nicholas?" I asked.

"All right, Mr. Banks," Nicholas said quietly.

Nicholas was the older of Walton and Gayle Donaldson's fraternal twins, even though he was smaller than his younger brother, Payne. Walton said both boys were intelligent, but Nicholas was the smarter of the two. Payne was the better athlete and more outgoing. Nicholas was bookish and introverted.

"We're going swimming at the country club," Susan said.

"Have fun, men," I said.

"Where's your pretty Mama?" Jimmy Gray asked.

"At home with baby Laura," Payne said.

"All right, boys," Susan said. "Let's get going."

Susan herded Nicholas and Payne through the heavy swinging door between the dining room and kitchen. I heard her speaking to someone in the kitchen. The door swung into the dining room and there stood Buddy Wade, former Congressman and self-made millionaire many times over in the oil and gas exploration business. Buddy was 6'3" and strong-looking for a man of sixty. His bald head was nicely tanned, and what remained of his blond hair on the side was turning gray.

"Looks like election central in here," Buddy Wade said.

"Yep," Jimmy Gray said, pointing at me. "This here's the candidate." He jabbed his index finger into his own chest. "And right here's his brain trust."

"Uh-oh," Buddy said to me. "You are in deep shit."

"Listen who's talking," Jimmy said. "If you hadn't tried so hard to join the Black Caucus you might still be our Congressman, up there in the seat of power."

"I just thought it was the thing to do. Most of my constituents were black and I was trying to get with the program." He paused. "You know, not one of those s.o.b.'s could see the humor in it."

"It's a damned shame," Jimmy said. "Seems like there ought to be at least one Caucasian in a caucus, by definition."

"My sentiments exactly," Buddy said.

"Any words of political insight you can share based on your experience in the system?" I asked.

"Yes. Never underestimate the stupidity of the voting public."

"Hear, hear," Jimmy Gray said to Buddy. "Words of wisdom. Before you get on the Willie Mitchell victory march with us, there's something you deserve to know. I'm probably going to have to have surgery before election day."

"Finally getting that lobotomy, huh?" Buddy said.

"Nope. Martha said she couldn't stand the pain any longer. She said she wouldn't have anything to do with me unless I have penile reduction surgery. Just too much to handle, she said."

I smiled and watched Buddy Wade think for a moment, scratching his chin, deadly serious.

"Let me give you the name of the surgeon that did mine."

I laughed out loud for the first time in weeks. Jimmy's body shook like a bowl of Jello as he leaned back in the Jimmy chair and roared, slapping his knee. It felt so good to laugh and break out of the *angst* I had wallowed in for the past month. As Buddy sat down with us, I felt a sense of pride and purpose. It felt good. I took a deep breath and shot the breeze with my two friends. After a while we got down to work.

At least I wasn't alone.

CHAPTER SEVEN

After a couple of hours of planning interspersed with a lot of joking and laughing, Buddy Wade and Jimmy headed to the cocktail lounge at the Sunshine Country Club. After Susan returned from taking the twins swimming, she and I were sitting at the kitchen table when the phone rang. The Sheriff said he and the Mayor needed to see me right away. He said Reverend Bobby Sanders had just left them. Everett wondered if I could join them in his office at City Hall. It was seven o'clock and hot, still plenty of sunshine. I drove the four blocks and walked into Everett's office. He and the Sheriff were sitting at a round table. They weren't smiling.

"Must be bad news," I said as I shook hands and had a seat.

"We just spent two hours with Bobby," Everett said.

"We're worried about the campaign," Lee said.

"We tried to talk some sense into Bobby," the Mayor said. "He won't listen to reason."

"I could have told you that," I said.

"I'd like to wring his little skinny neck," Lee said. "I told him the Mayor and I were only interested in what was best for Sunshine and Yaloquena County and that Eleanor Bernstein cannot do all the things you do for us. She doesn't have the experience."

"I told Bobby about your talking the federal judge up in Oxford into letting us keep our dilapidated jail open," Everett said. "Neither the city nor the county can raise the money for a new jail."

"You know what Bobby said?" Lee said. "He said you don't put anybody but black folks up in that jail anyway."

"Bobby didn't even know your office represents the School Board and the Board of Supervisors," Everett said. "We told him Eleanor didn't know the federal rules and regulations like you do. He said she was a good lawyer and could learn."

"Those knuckleheads on the School Board will run all over Eleanor," Lee said. "She's not tough enough to stop them from doing something that's going to get the school system in deeper trouble. He's got no idea this county is on its last legs, losing people and jobs every year. Bobby thinks the federal and state money spigots are going to keep gushing forever."

"Right now," the Mayor said, "food stamps and welfare checks are the only thing keeping most people around here from starving."

"It's all about race with Bobby," I said.

"That's it in a nutshell," Lee said. "Bobby kept saying that Eleanor was 'one of us' and it was about time our people had one of their own in the D.A.'s office to get some justice for a change. He called us Uncle Toms and said we were nothing but buck dancin', boot lickin', shoe shinin' minstrels doing what the white man wants. It took all the will power I had to keep from cold-cocking the little hypocrite. I told him I remembered when he was drinking and running women in juke joints every night before he claimed to be saved and became a preacher."

"What did he say to that?"

"He just laughed," Lee said. "He said there was nothing we could do to stop Eleanor from being Yaloquena's first black District Attorney. He said he had the votes and they were going to win in a landslide, that you would be the last white politician elected in Yaloquena County."

"What do you guys think?" I asked. "Are we wasting our time?"

"No," Everett said. "We can win this thing, but we've got to come up with a different strategy. What Bobby's spreading all over the county is working right now."

"He's talking about slavery and Jim Crow," Lee said, "blaming you and the other white folks in town for things your ancestors did a long time ago."

"Bottom line is," Everett said, "this community needs you in that courthouse, not Eleanor Bernstein. Bobby Sanders will be running things if she wins."

We sat for a moment. I broke the silence.

"I'm open for suggestions, men. What do you want me to do?"

"We got to be more creative," Everett said, "use your legal knowledge. For one thing I don't think she lives in Yaloquena County."

"She's had an apartment on Baker Street for years," I said. "Over there behind the softball fields. She's the indigent defender for Yaloquena and has tried more cases in our courthouse than anyone except Walton or me."

"She stays in Jackson," the Mayor said.

"Residency is almost impossible to prove. It's a question of intent. Besides," I said, "the time for filing suit to challenge a candidate on residency grounds is long gone.

"I just met with Jimmy Gray and Buddy Wade to go over some strategy. I'm going to pick up the campaigning, try to build some momentum." I stood up to leave. "You guys continue to work it with your volunteers. Let me know when you need me to be somewhere or do something in particular. We'll do the best we can, give it our best shot, and see what happens. That's all we can do."

"The last thing we asked him," Lee said, "was to back off the black-white thing, to quit talking about race and slavery and segregation and just campaign on who's the best candidate."

"The Reverend Sanders said we were whistling past the graveyard," Everett said. "He told us this election *was* all about race."

"And as he was doing his pimp walk out the office," Lee said, "I told him he was being a racist. He looked back at us over his shoulder and said 'So what? Payback's hell, ain't it'?"

CHAPTER EIGHT

Thanks to a call from Dr. Clement, Sheriff Jones, Walton, and I were waiting Monday morning in the hospital corridor outside Ross's room when the nurse opened Ross's door and said we could come in. At the same time, I saw Jules Bullard push open the swinging doors down the hall and march toward us.

"Don't go in there," Jules yelled, his beady eyes focused on the door. "I told you to stay away from my son."

A second man in a gray suit carrying a briefcase followed several paces behind him. In contrast to Jules' bald head, the second man combed his dense silver hair back from his forehead in a rigid, shoulder-length pompadour. He had to walk fast to keep up with Jules, but his hair never moved. I took one last look at Jules before I pushed open the door and walked in to see Ross.

I barely had time to notice that Ross's eyes were closed before Jules burst in and grabbed the Sheriff by the arm and spun him around. Lucky for Jules, his man quickly moved between Lee and Jules and gave Lee a card. It was then I recognized him. J.D. Silver.

"It's my information Ross Bullard has not been arrested, gentlemen," Silver said and gave Walton and me his card. "I'm J.D. Silver from Memphis and I've been retained by Ross and his father Jules. Henceforth all communication with Ross is to be directed to me. Kindly remove yourself from this room."

The hubbub in the small room caused Ross to open his eyes. He glanced around, bewildered.

"Where am I?" he croaked.

Jules rushed over and placed his hand over Ross's mouth. He bent over and whispered in his ear. Ross's eyes grew wide and he pushed his father's hand away.

"Oh God, just leave me alone," Ross said moving his head from side to side and moaning. "No. No. No. No."

I gestured to Lee and Walton that it was time to go. We walked into the hallway followed by J.D. Silver.

"Did Ross say anything before we arrived?"

"Not to us," I said, extending my hand. "I'm District Attorney Willie Mitchell Banks, this is Sheriff Lee Jones, and this is Walton Donaldson my first assistant."

"Good to meet you all," he said. "You'll have to forgive Mr. Bullard's manners. He's fairly distraught, as you might imagine."

I heard Ross say something inside the room but couldn't understand him through the door.

"From now on, please understand I'll be the only person you contact if you need some information from Ross or from his father. Just so we're clear, we'll not be making any statement or answering any questions. Is my information correct, that Ross is not under arrest?"

"That's right," I said. "Not yet."

"Then I guess our business here is finished. If you do decide to place him under arrest, please give me the courtesy of letting me know in advance and I will bring him in."

We walked out through the swinging doors.

"You know that guy?" Walton asked me.

"Not personally. I've seen him on Memphis stations, read about him in the Commercial Appeal. He's a big time criminal defense lawyer, and not just in Memphis."

"I've never heard of him," Lee said. "And with that hair, if I had seen him before I would sure have remembered."

Walton started laughing. "Like a big helmet."

"Did either of you make out what Ross was saying when we were outside in the hall? I couldn't hear it well enough to understand."

"Not me," Lee said.

"I did," Walton said. "He said 'I should be dead'." He paused a moment. "It's a shame he didn't get his wish."

We parted ways with Lee in the parking lot and climbed into my truck for the drive back to the courthouse.

"Last night at home," Walton said, "we were sitting around the supper table. Laura was in her crib. Payne had cleaned his plate but Nicholas was picking at his food. I was talking to Gayle about the case. I noticed the twins were paying close attention. So I just came out and asked them if they had ever talked to Ross Bullard in the neighborhood or gone in his house.

"Payne answered right away. He said they went over there with Danny to look at Mr. Bullard's Indian stuff. Payne said Ross really had some cool things."

"How many times?"

"They weren't sure. Payne said he thought he had gone twice. He said Nick and Danny Thurman had gone over there without him a bunch of times. Nicholas jumped up from the table told Payne to be quiet then ran to his bedroom."

"Did you talk to Nicholas?"

"I started to but Gayle told me to leave it alone. She said he had been upset since Danny disappeared, that Nick and Danny were best friends. She said last night before she could turn off the news the anchor said something about Ross being in the hospital and there was still no sign of Danny. Nick heard it all."

"What about Payne?"

"He's sad about Danny but nothing like Nick. I asked Payne myself, when it was just the two of us, if he knew how many times Danny and Nick had gone over there without him. He didn't know. I asked him if Ross ever tried to touch him or Nicholas or Danny in a bad way. He said no, that all they ever did was look at his Indian things. After Payne left the table Gayle told me the twins would have told her if Ross had tried anything. She's had many talks with them about that sort of thing."

"What's Gayle say about how Connie's doing?"

"She said Connie cries every time she's over there. Connie told her she thinks she's losing her mind."

"I imagine so. Did you talk to Peewee?"

"This afternoon. He's organizing a search of all the hunting camps in the county. The camps have to file a form with Wildlife and Fisheries describing the location and extent of their lease. He's got all those forms."

"Good. We're going to find Danny's body."

CHAPTER NINE

The next morning I was telling Walton what I knew about some of the big cases J.D. Silver had handled when Ethel Morris appeared in my office door. Ethel had been with me since I hung out a shingle in Sunshine my first year out of law school. She looked almost like her old self after surviving a bout with breast cancer, her neatly cropped white hair a vast improvement over the wigs she wore when she was in treatment.

"Peewee Bernhardt is here to see you two," Ethel said to us in her soft voice.

"Bring him in," I said. "Thanks."

Peewee walked into my office in his Mississippi Wildlife, Fisheries, and Parks uniform. He was 5'4" and weighed no more than 140 pounds fully-clothed and soaking wet. At sixty-two, Peewee was the senior enforcement agent in Yaloquena County, but rarely wrote tickets any more. I really liked Peewee's approach to the fish and game laws. Peewee considered himself more of a goodwill agent for the deer, ducks, and fish his agency worked to protect. He preferred educating hunters and fishermen and working with them rather than citing them for violations and hauling them into court for prosecution. As a result of his non-confrontational style, I knew Peewee had amassed a devoted following among the outdoorsmen all over the Delta, making him the perfect choice to head up our search for Danny Thurman out in the county.

"Thanks for coming in, Peewee," I said. "Walton is in charge of this investigation, so you'll be working with him. He'll keep me informed and I'm available as needed, but most days I'll be out and about running for re-election."

"Ten-four," Peewee said. "The head man in Jackson doesn't like us getting involved in politics. Civil service has all those rules, you know. But I'm talking you up everywhere I can, Willie Mitchell. I got to be careful, though."

"I understand," I said.

"I'll keep doing some good for you where I can. I know who I can talk to and who I can't."

After twenty-four years of working with Peewee on wildlife cases, I knew his word was his bond. Peewee spent most of his days outdoors in the woods or on the lakes and rivers in the Delta. His skin was wrinkled and leathery from the constant exposure. A lot of people thought Peewee was a drinker, but I was quick to set the record straight. His face was red and splotchy and his eyes bloodshot much of the time, all due to the sun and the elements, not alcohol. His principal vice was tobacco. He chain smoked Marlboros in his truck and in the woods. When Peewee was in the courthouse or on any other occasion where he couldn't smoke, he kept a Skoal Bandit tucked inside his lip. Peewee never used a spit cup. It made me nauseous just thinking about his swallowing tobacco juice. When I was a teenager I used Skoal a few times, regular chewing tobacco, too. Whenever I accidentally swallowed the juice, within minutes I wanted to throw up. I would sit down until the color came back to my face and the world stopped spinning. Peewee told me the juice didn't bother him a bit, claiming it kept him alert better than the Community Coffee he drank strong and black.

"I spent yesterday on the phone," Peewee told us. "I've got more volunteers than we'll need. I have a county map I've kept current over the years coloring in the location of all the major hunting camps. I called the person in charge at each camp. We start the search tomorrow."

"Great," Walton said. "Ross said in the note the hunting camp was old, so I guess we ought to focus on camps that have been in use a while, disregard the newer ones."

"Ross wasn't a hunter far as I know," Peewee said. "I've run into him searching for arrowheads and such in the woods, especially around mounds the Indians built. Since he never hunted deer or squirrels or even ducks it's curious to me why he would hide the boy's body in an old hunting camp."

Upset at his own choice of words, Peewee glanced at me. He swallowed some Skoal juice and cleared his throat.

"I didn't mean to say his body, because we don't know that Danny's dead, do we?"

I bit my tongue and let Walton respond. I needed to get used to deferring to him. It was Walton's case. I was second chair for the first time in two-and-a-half decades.

"He probably is," Walton said. "Missing this long, odds are pretty strong that Ross killed him."

"Damnation," Peewee said. "Well, it don't make any difference in the search. We have to find Danny no matter what. His folks deserve to have him buried proper. It might help them deal with their loss. You reckon the boy's buried?"

"We don't know," Walton said.

"If he ain't, there's not going to be much to find. What the coyotes and wild dogs don't get the hogs will."

I knew Peewee was right, but I cringed at hearing the words spoken. If the animals got into Danny's remains, there would be no physical evidence to prove he was murdered. On top of that, it would be an awful thing to tell Bill and Connie Thurman.

"Did you bring your map?" Walton asked.

"It's in the satchel I left at Ethel's desk."

"Let's go into my office and take a look," Walton said.

"Thanks, Peewee," I said quietly to the wildlife agent as he walked out with Walton.

I buzzed Ethel and told her to hold my calls. I pulled out the county map that Jimmy Gray gave me on Saturday and studied the rural precinct I intended to cover in the afternoon, trying to recall where the population centers were on the seldom traveled country roads. I planned to knock on doors, smile, hand out push cards, and do my best to keep my mind off Danny Thurman's missing body.

CHAPTER TEN

I wasn't very successful at keeping my mind off Danny. Early the next morning I was driving through clouds of dust following Peewee's tail lights. We were on a gravel road in the hardwood forest that extended west from Dundee County and covered twenty thousand acres in southeast Yaloquena.

"I got this feeling yesterday about a hunting camp close to the old Jennings place," Peewee said when we met in the courthouse parking lot before daylight. "Booger Temple and a dozen of the other men who lease the camp from Georgia-Pacific should already be there. He said they would get the search started at daybreak. We need to head out."

Walton rode shotgun in Peewee's dark green Wildlife and Fisheries truck. I added little value to the county-wide search of hunting camps that Peewee organized, but I wanted to show up to support the army of hunters on four-wheelers scouring the woods in search of Danny. Walton felt the same.

Peewee slowed as he approached two pickup trucks parked at a steep angle on the side of the gravel road. The tailgates were down with loading ramps in place from the truck bed to the gravel road for unloading the four-wheelers. We stopped and waited in the road. Peewee pointed out the spot where the four-wheelers entered the woods, evidenced by the small saplings and bushes crushed into the dirt by the four-wheelers, some of which weighed 750 pounds and were propelled by 75 horsepower gasoline engines.

"Listen," Peewee said, cupping his hand around his right ear. "You hear them? They're getting closer."

I didn't at first, but in a moment I heard the roar of the four-wheeler engines.

The radio on Peewee's truck crackled and emitted a loud, high-pitched burst of noise. It sounded like someone talking but I couldn't understand a single word. Peewee ran to the open truck door and grabbed his radio handset.

"That you, Booger?" Peewee said. "This is Peewee on the road next to your truck. Talk slower. Over."

"We got a pack of wild dogs on the run," Booger yelled. "We picked'em up just north of the Jennings place."

"Why are you running them? Over."

"We found them digging on the edge of our campsite and had a bunch of bones dug up when we run up on'em. The lead dog's got some kind of head in his mouth."

Chills ran up my spine.

"Which direction?" Peewee yelled into his handset.

"We're runnin' them toward the road. Just sit tight where you are."

"We hear you loud and clear," Peewee said and tossed the radio handset onto the front bench seat.

Peewee reached behind the front seat and pulled out a rifle and a pump shotgun. He tossed the shotgun to Walton and followed with a box of red twelve-gauge shells. He asked me if I wanted a rifle. I said no. Peewee loaded his bolt action thirty-aught-six Springfield rifle and chambered a round.

"Load the shotgun and get ready, Walton," Peewee said. "Mr. D.A., you hang loose and stay behind the guns. Don't know what's going to happen when those dogs hit this road."

"We're going to shoot the dogs?" Walton asked.

"Not unless we have to. If one of them dogs has the boy's head in his jaws I'm bringing it down."

We listened as the roar of the four-wheelers tearing through the trees grew closer. Peewee gestured and Walton and I followed him down the road in the direction of the engine noise. We stopped in the ditch opposite the woods and waited. I saw Walton push the shotgun safety to red. He was ready to shoot if he had to.

When I took my eyes off Walton's safety, the pack of wild dogs tore out of the woods leaping over the ditch onto the gravel road. They were running straight at us.

The lead dog skidded in the gravel when he saw us. He dug his claws into the road and turned ninety degrees, running away from the three of us, staying in the middle of the road. I only got a quick glance, but enough to know Booger was right. The lead dog had his huge jaws clamped on what looked like a head. Tattered shards of pink flesh hung from the bone and one eye bulged out of the skull above the lead dog's glistening white fangs.

"Shoot him," Peewee yelled to Walton.

Walton raised his shotgun and blasted the road in front of the dog. A violent shower of brown and orange gravel and dirt exploded in the dog's path, causing him to turn sharply away from the blast. The gruesome head tumbled from the dog's jaws and rolled to a stop in the bottom of the roadside ditch.

Booger and his men roared out of the woods and slid to a stop in the road, slinging rocks from their oversized tires.

A few paces in front of me, Walton shouldered his shotgun again when he saw one of the dogs veer from the back of the pack and run toward the mass of pink tissue and bone in the ditch. Walton fired into the ditch bank close to the severed head. The dog yelped and scrambled to rejoin the pack.

Booger and the two men with him dismounted. They nodded and walked with us to the ditch. Peewee knelt and studied the head.

"Thank God," he said. "It's a wild hog. Them dogs stripped the flesh and hide off making it look like...."

I was glad Peewee's voice trailed off and didn't finish the sentence. It was hideous to think it could have been Danny's head.

"We couldn't tell," Booger said. "We jumped them dogs when they was in the middle of fighting over bones and this here head."

"You did right," Peewee said. "It could have been something. Y'all been all through your camp?"

"Naw," Booger said, "we just got started good when we seen the dogs. We'll get on back and finish up. Tell you what though, there ain't no sign anyone's been on the logging road into our camp, and it don't look like nothing's been disturbed."

"You go on back to the camp and we'll be there directly."

Booger and his men rode their four-wheelers across the ditch and back into the woods.

"There's lots of wild hogs in these woods," Peewee said pointing to the head in the ditch. "This here's a yearling, maybe younger."

"Glad we didn't have to kill the dogs," Walton said.

"Yeah," Peewee said. "I don't like killing anything I can't eat. Those dogs got a right to live, too, even though they ain't good for much except killin' coons and possums. Maybe an occasional hog if they's enough of'em in the pack."

"Let's go on to Booger's camp," I said. "After we check it out I'd like you to bring me back to my truck."

"You had enough?"

"Yeah. I can do the Thurmans a lot more good in my office than I can out here. You guys know what you're doing. I'll leave the hunting camp search to you and your volunteers."

"I guess that's so," Peewee said, "but at least now you'll have an idea of the scope of this search we're undertaking. We might pass right by Danny's body out here in these woods and never know."

"I'll stay with Peewee," Walton said, "if that's all right with you."

"Good idea. I've got some campaigning to do this afternoon. Do your best in those woods."

"Don't you worry about this mule," Peewee said. "You just load the wagon. I'll get it done. We'll head over to Booger's and get after it."

CHAPTER ELEVEN

That afternoon I listened to Walton describe the rest of his day in the woods with Peewee. They hadn't found any trace of Danny. Neither had any of the other volunteers.

"Crime lab called about eleven this morning with good news," I said. "Robbie says the blue fibers they took from Connie's sweater drawer Monday morning at the Thurman home match the blue fibers found in Ross's couch during the search of his house Friday night."

"All right," Walton said, clenching his fist.

"And they compared Danny's known prints with sets of juvenile prints they took in the kitchen and in Ross's living room. They match."

"So we've got proof Danny was on the couch in Ross's living room with Connie's blue sweater," Walton said, standing and pacing in front of my desk. "That means he went home from the rally, got Connie's sweater, and on the way back to the park he stopped in Ross Bullard's house and sat on the couch leaving the blue fibers."

"Looks like it. We don't know why he went in the house, whether Ross lured him inside or what."

"I'm sure that's what happened."

"The bad news is there's nothing in the house the crime lab analyzed to indicate that a murder or even a struggle took place. There's no blood, hair, or anything else that would support the fact that something violent happened."

"Yeah, but we can prove Danny was there that night sitting on the couch with Connie's sweater. We've got his prints and the blue fibers. Then we establish he was never seen again and the jury can draw the obvious inference that Ross took him."

"And there's one more thing that will help," I said, "if Judge Williams will let it in. Robbie's people have looked at all the DVDs. He said they would keep the originals at the crime lab and make several dupes of each for us to prepare the case for trial and provide to the defense in discovery."

Walton sat down. "What do they show?"

"The commercial DVDs are of naked children, boys and girls."

"Jesus."

"There's no sexual activity on any of the DVDs, just collections of still shots of nude youngsters ranging in age from six or seven to ten or eleven. According to Robbie all the kids are prepubescent. There's no touching or interaction between the kids. There are no adults at all."

"Doesn't matter if there's no sexual activity. It's still a major felony to possess them. What about the non-commercial DVDs?"

"Robbie says there's only one homemade DVD," I said.

"What does it show?"

"Robbie said it's a couple of nude boys sitting on Ross's couch in his living room."

"Who are the boys?"

"Robbie says the DVD never shows their faces. Bullard taped them putting on some of his Indian artifacts, dressing like little warriors. Bastard was careful to shoot them from the neck down, nothing else."

"When will we get the copies?"

"Robbie's is sending them by courier."

I could tell from Walton's face he knew what had to be done as soon as the DVD arrived.

"I'll go by and talk to the Thurmans about it this afternoon on the way home," Walton said. "I'd like for them to see the homemade DVD as soon as possible. No sense putting it off."

"It's going to be tough for the Thurmans to watch it," I said, "but we have to know if it's Danny."

Walton and I pulled into the Thurman's driveway at ten the next morning with the DVD. Walton had visited with Bill and Connie on his way home the day before. They both told Walton they wanted to see the DVD right away. Walton and Gayle were very close to the Thurmans, so I asked him to take the lead.

Bill Thurman walked out the front door before I cut off the engine. Bill must have been standing at the window, probably pacing, waiting for us to show up.

"How's Connie this morning?" Walton asked as they shook hands.

"She's been crying."

"Maybe we should put this off," I said.

"No. No. We both want to see it. It's just that...it's been tough."

"I'm sure," Walton said quietly. "You understand there are no faces on the DVD."

"Right. You told us that yesterday."

He led us into the house. Walking behind Walton and Bill, I noted the breadth of Bill's back and shoulders. He was four inches taller than Walton and at least 35 pounds heavier, but his size alone did not account for the overwhelming brute strength Bill demonstrated at the hospital. Walton was in good condition, but if he had been by himself trying to stop Bill that day outside the E.R., the fireman would have swatted Walton aside like a bug.

Connie stood just inside the front door. She extended her hand to me and tried to smile, but the dread of the DVD viewing overcame her. Connie's lips and cheeks trembled, distorting her face. Walton took her hand and gathered her in a gentle hug. I could see her shaking as he held her. She began to sob in his arms. Bill looked away. Based on what Gayle had been telling Walton, I knew Connie had been getting little comfort from her husband. After a while, Connie's sobs quieted. She backed away from Walton and said she was ready.

I was struck by the physical change in Connie. She was always petite, but now she appeared to weigh less than a hundred pounds. She was a little over five feet, with short black hair and dark skin inherited from her ancestors in southern Italy. Before the Fourth of July I thought she was one of the prettiest, sweetest young women in town. The stress had aged her dramatically, creating dark circles under her eyes and sapping the life from her.

"I'm sorry we have to do this," Walton said.

"We know," she said, "but we want to see it."

Walton gave the DVD to Bill and followed them into the family room. Bill turned on the television and placed the disc into the player. He gave Walton the remote. The four of us stood five feet from the screen. Walton pressed play.

The nude bodies of two boys sitting on Ross Bullard's couch appeared on the screen. The camera captured the boys from their necks to their knees. Connie whimpered and slumped against Bill. Walton stopped the DVD. Bill scooped Connie up with one arm and stepped back with her to their sofa, placing her on the seat next to him. He did not put his arm around her. Walton walked quickly into the kitchen and drew Connie some water. After she rested a moment and drank half the glass, I asked her if she wanted to continue.

"Please," she said. "Danny's the one on the right."

Walton looked at Bill. He nodded and Walton hit play again. I had studied the crime lab photos of the scene and recognized Ross's living room couch. The quality of the DVD was poor, the lighting uneven and the camera unsteady at times. Walton told me had already watched the entire disc four times. The faces of the boys were never shown, but I could tell from their bodies they were around seven or eight years old. Bullard seemed to focus the camera on Danny more than the other boy, sometime zooming in on Danny and ignoring the other boy.

The most chilling aspect of the DVD was the calm, soothing voice on the tape assuring the two boys that this was the way the Indians in the Delta dressed. We watched as Bullard told the boys to put on the leather arm bands, then the loin cloths that appeared to be made of a *chamois*-type material. The disc ended a few seconds after the boys draped the loin cloths over themselves.

"That's Ross Bullard's voice," Connie said. "I recognize it."

"So do I," Bill said. "I've talked to him in the neighborhood over the years. It's definitely him."

"You're sure the boy is Danny?"

"It's Danny," Connie said. "Danny's the boy Bullard had the camera on most of the time. I know every inch of my son, and I have no doubt that's him."

"What about the other boy?"

She glanced at Bill, then Walton.

"I don't know for sure." She hesitated, then blurted. "The twins went over there, too."

"I know," Walton said and removed the DVD from the player. "Thank you for doing this. I'm sorry you had to see it."

"Anything you need us to do to help you convict this perverted s.o.b, we'll do it," Bill said.

"Anything," Connie said, tears streaming from her dark eyes.

Moments later, I backed my truck out of the Thurman's driveway and drove toward the courthouse.

"Was the other boy one of the twins?" I asked.

"It wasn't Payne, I'm sure of that," Walton said. "It could have been Nicholas, but I really can't tell. Gayle will know. When we get to the courthouse I'll drive home and show the DVD to her. She's there with the baby. The twins are at the Methodist Church Vacation Bible School until noon so this is a good time to find out."

If Gayle identified the other boy on the tape as Nicholas, Walton would have to recuse himself from the case. There was no need for me to bring up the ethical and legal problems it created for us. Walton already knew. Without Danny's body our case against Ross Bullard was already hanging by a thread. We didn't need to add to our problems. For my sake and Walton's, for Nick's sake and Gayle's, I prayed the other boy was not Nicholas Donaldson.

CHAPTER TWELVE

When Walton entered my office that afternoon, I could tell from the look on his face that my prayers had been answered.

"It's not him," Walton said.

"Thank goodness. What all did she say?"

"Gayle said neither one of the boys on the DVD is Nicholas. She said the boy on the right of the screen was broader in the chest than Nicholas. And the smaller boy on the left, the one we were worried about, she's positive it's not Nicholas. She said Nick had a lot of respiratory infections when he was a baby and his sternum is shallow and his chest more concave than the boy on the tape. She also said Nick's right nipple is larger than his left and...."

"There's no doubt in her mind?"

"No. I never noticed any of those things."

"You're not his mother," I said.

"You can imagine how relieved we both were after she viewed the DVD. Nicholas is already traumatized by Danny's disappearance. Gayle's talking about getting him some counseling. If he had been on the couch with Danny...."

"He would have had to testify," I said.

"In his current state I don't know if he could have."

"He's probably stronger than you think. Kids are resilient."

"Gayle is certain that Nicholas would have told her if Ross had done something like this to him. She said he keeps things from Payne sometimes, but he always confides in his mother. Gayle also said she recognized the voice on the DVD as Bullard. She had a few dealings with him in person at the bank involving the Junior Auxiliary account and talked on the phone with him a couple of times, too."

"What did she say about him?"

"She said Ross didn't make an impression on her one way or the other. It was just a business thing, clearing up the mess their bookkeeper made in accounting for cookbook sales. Gayle said it was like dealing with a CPA or an accountant—all business, cut and dried. She said he was pretty low-key."

After Walton left my office, I thought about his wife. Gayle was an interesting woman. Susan and she were very close. Before Laura was born, Susan and Gayle walked almost every morning. They played tennis together and took the same yoga class. We had the Donaldsons over for dinner all the time and kept the twins when they wanted to get away. Walton and I were like father and son. Gayle and Susan were like sisters. Over the course of the eight years Walton and Gayle had lived in Sunshine, Susan and I had spent thousands of hours with them. Because of the nature of small town relationships, I knew Gayle's history as well as my own.

Gayle Bannerman was born in 1980 in West Point, Mississippi, in the northern third of the state, about thirty miles west of the Alabama line. She was popular in high school, cheerleading and playing on the tennis team. She attended what everyone called "the W," Mississippi University for Women, just a few miles down the road in Columbus. She met Walton her senior year on a blind date set up by one of Walton's Mississippi State SAE brothers. They dated for a couple of months, then went their separate ways after graduation—Walton to law school at Ole Miss and Gayle to Manhattan to learn the restaurant business.

Walton went to see her in New York twice in the summer after his first year of law school. Walton told me that was when their relationship began to click. While Walton tolerated his second year of law school, Gayle worked in Coda, an upscale seafood restaurant in the theatre district in Midtown West. Walton made four trips to New York to see her that year. She came down for two football games, one in Starkville and one in Oxford, and they saw each other at Thanksgiving, Christmas, and Easter at her home in West Point.

Walton told me he liked her family. He played the Old Waverly course with her father, Lewis, and her two brothers. Gayle told Susan on one of their walks that Walton began dropping hints about getting married after he finished law school. Gayle said she was not sure at first. She was reluctant to give up her dream of opening a restaurant in Manhattan serving authentic southern food. But when Walton proposed in the fall of his final year in law school, she decided she loved him more than the restaurant business and wanted to have children with him.

Gayle told us over dinner one night they had already sent the wedding invitations when Walton accepted Willie Mitchell's offer of employment in Sunshine. The Delta was the last place Gayle wanted to settle down. Gayle said she had to decide between breaking the engagement or going through with the wedding and living in Sunshine. She couldn't bear the thought of giving up Walton so the wedding took place as scheduled. A year later the twins were born. They named their firstborn Nicholas, her maternal grandfather's name, and the second twin Payne, Walton's late mother's maiden name.

Gayle told Susan that once the twins were born, she never second-guessed her decision to marry Walton and move with him to Sunshine. She said her children meant more to her than anything she might have achieved in the restaurant industry or living in the bright lights of New York City. She treasured her family more than she ever thought possible.

Susan told me Gayle was a wonderful mother, putting her children's welfare above all else. It was one of the reasons Susan liked her so much. Susan also admired Gayle's intelligence and grit. Susan said Gayle could be plenty tough when the situation called for it.

The fact that Gayle was certain neither of the boys on the DVD was Nicholas was a welcome break in the string of setbacks Walton and I had suffered in putting our case together. Ross Bullard didn't know it, but he was fortunate as well that Nicholas wasn't on the couch with Danny. It was bad enough having Bill Thurman wanting to kill him. It would have been quite another to have Gayle Donaldson after him as well.

CHAPTER THIRTEEN

I glanced in the side mirror at the dust bank I was kicking up on the dirt and gravel lane. I slowed down as I approached the road's dead-end at Reverend Gray's church. I parked next to the red brick building on the banks of the shallow, muddy Yaloquena River. A visceral sense of nostalgia and *déjà vu* enveloped me as I studied the weathered white sign in front of the church.

Broken and faded black letters proclaimed EBENEEZER PRIMITIVE BAPTIST CHURCH, REVEREND PAUL GRAY. It would have been difficult to read had I not known the sign so well. I recalled that Ebeneezer Baptist met every third Sunday at eleven a.m. Smaller letters further down read "Sunday School 9 a.m." and proclaimed the amount of the collection the previous Sunday had been thirty-two dollars and twenty-something cents. The last digit in the cents column was gone.

It was hot. The back of my shirt and seat of my pants were wet. Before stopping at Ebeneezer Baptist, I had spent several hours getting in and out of the truck, knocking on doors in the unincorporated community of Sadie's Bend. It was impossible for me to stay cool, no matter how hard the air conditioner in my truck worked.

When I ran the first time Sadie's Bend was a vibrant place. Reverend Gray's church was one of the most successful and well-attended black Baptist churches in the county. The church anchored the rural settlement for many years, but no longer. I remembered scores of white frame homes and brick veneer homes financed through Farmer's Home Administration in Sadie's Bend. They were well-kept, full of families and prospective voters. Even then, most of Reverend Gray's churchgoers lived in Sunshine but kept allegiance to their ancestral Baptist roots by attending church and getting married in Sadie's Bend. Many generations of Sunshine voters were baptized in the shallows beside the church. Reverend Gray fully immersed the candidates in the yellow-gray waters of the languorous Yaloquena.

Reverend Paul Gray was a tall, gentle man whose light brown skin was peppered with dark freckles and moles. He was nearly twice my age when I began my first campaign. Reverend Gray did custodial work at the bank for Monroe Banks and James Gray Sr., and handyman work from time to time at their personal residences. One morning I saw him in the Sunshine Bank lobby. He invited me to speak at Ebeneezer Church.

My visit to Reverend Gray's church that Sunday morning twenty-four years ago was a revelation. I had been to black churches for funerals in Sunshine and out in the county as a child and later as a young man, but Ebeneezer Primitive was the first black church I attended as a candidate running for office. I did not know how to act.

Looking out at the muddy Yaloquena, I remembered that Sunday like it was yesterday. Reverend Gray told me the service started at eleven, so I was parked at the church fifteen minutes before eleven watching eight and ten-foot-long alligator gars, holdovers from the Cretaceous Period, roll and break the surface of the water. After ten minutes, my vehicle was still the only one around. I remembered checking my watch, panicking, thinking I must have gotten the date or the time wrong, and hoping Reverend Gray would give me a second chance. When I backed away to leave, I saw an older model Lincoln and an early-eighties Chrysler Lebaron with a white vinyl top approaching on the gravel road. I waited as the cars parked next to the church. The half-dozen passengers were dressed in their Sunday best. I pulled back into my parking spot and introduced myself to the new arrivals. Between eleven and eleven forty-five when the service finally kicked off, parishioners continue to file in until the church was almost full.

At some point before the service Reverend Gray joined me on the front steps and introduced me to his members as they arrived. He was soft-spoken and warm, a kind word for everyone. Eventually he led me into the church and walked down the center of the nave. I lingered at the back of the church, not knowing the protocol, unsure where to sit. When he reached the apse and turned, he seemed surprised to see me still standing in the back. Reverend Gray gestured to two older women dressed in white dresses, gloves, and small white hats. They led me to the front of the church, seating me in the first row directly in front of the pulpit. I felt humbled and awkward. It was clearly a seat of honor.

With his eyes closed and head bowed, Reverend Gray said an opening prayer that astounded me. It was a dramatic call to worship, complete with whole verses and psalms the preacher recited without a note. I followed Reverend Gray's lead. Whatever he did I did. He kept his eyes closed and head down during the call to worship. So did I.

Thinking back on that Sunday, I recall how moved I felt by Reverend Gray's words, not only by the prayer but also by the power and sincerity of the gentle man's voice. But there was something else. The day was an awakening for me. I had known Reverend Gray for many years. I saw him all the time in the bank, *Paul* stenciled above the shirt pocket in his khaki uniform. When he did odd jobs in our home, I tagged along. He could fix anything. I watched him do plumbing, electrical, and carpentry repairs. When I was about eight, Reverend Gray proclaimed to my father with me standing next to him that I was his official assistant for repairs in the Banks home. I remembered how proud that made me. I spent many hours listening to Reverend Gray explain at various stages of repairs what he was doing and why.

Sitting in the front row that Sunday, I saw a different Paul Gray. I marveled at his metamorphosis from handyman into the leader of his congregation, holding a position of power and respect among his flock. After the opening prayer, Reverend Gray turned the pulpit over to a large black woman in a bright flowered dress to give "the welcome." She spoke for five minutes, and was followed by another woman in a black suit and hat who gave "the agenda," referring the congregants to the mimeographed program, going over each entry. Several black-suited deacons delivered messages to the congregation, the last one leading the church in a slow, drawn-out chant of "Guide Me O Thy Great Jehovah."

I recognized some of the members who rose to the pulpit for their role in the service. I had seen them at the courthouse or around town. I never realized how different their world was on Sunday. In Ebeneezer Baptist they were free from the dominance of their white employers and white society, free to be themselves. Sitting in that front row, I felt my face grow warm with shame and guilt. It was an odd sort of guilt. I grew up in the bifurcated society of Yaloquena. I didn't create the schism between the races; my forebears did. I lived and practiced law in a divided society, and did nothing about it. Truth was, I rarely thought much about the situation, no doubt because I was on the prosperous side of the divide.

I looked up at Reverend Gray that Sunday morning and realized the grim truth. If I won the election, most of the men and women I would be prosecuting in Yaloquena County would be black. I wasn't sure at that moment if I could do anything about it except resolve to treat all people fairly, regardless of race.

Reverend Gray gave a powerful sermon that Sunday. He started preaching softly but firmly, giving a cogent and practical message. As his sermon continued, he preached more forcefully, ending with a crescendo of prayer and wiping the sweat from his face.

I put a check drawn on my campaign account for $25 dollars into the collection plate. After the sermon, Reverend Gray said a few words to the members about me and why I was in church with them that Sunday. He explained how important the position of District Attorney was to the county. He said he knew me from the time I was a boy, and said he knew I would be a "firm but fair" man in office. He opened his large palm to me and asked me to say a few words. I stood up where I was and turned to the congregation. He stopped me before I said a word.

"Willie Mitchell, join me up here," he said, gesturing to the pulpit.

I walked up the carpeted steps and stood behind the pulpit staring for a moment at the sea of black faces, young and old, some interested, others bored. I had no idea what to say, what would be appropriate. Reverend Gray saved me by asking me to explain to the congregants the office I was seeking, what the District Attorney did in the courthouse, and when the election was. I was reared Catholic, so I knew nothing about the Bible. I ended with the only quote I could recall at that moment, the passage from First Corinthians that said even if you have the "gift of prophecy" and faith but have not charity you are nothing but a "sounding brass or tinkling cymbal." I stumbled through the verse as best I could and was relieved when I noticed most parishioners were nodding and smiling.

Reverend Gray didn't stop there. He set me up with other black Baptist and AME preachers during the campaign. I attended more than a dozen black church services during that campaign, each time following the script from Ebeneezer Primitive and depositing a campaign check into the collection plate. When all the votes were counted on election night, I knew Reverend Gray had been instrumental in my electoral victory.

But that was twenty-four years ago. Sitting in my truck with the motor running and the air conditioning blowing, staring at what was left of Reverend Gray's sign, I realized how much had changed in the county since that first campaign. Three-fourths of the homes in the Sadie's Bend area were now empty, the remainder sadly neglected. It was the same with small communities all over the county. Ebeneezer Baptist had not been used for Sunday worship since Reverend Gray passed away three years earlier. My campaign trips outside Sunshine made me realize how much of rural Yaloquena County had been depopulated in the last two decades. Just like Sadie's Bend, homes were empty and dilapidated. All over the county, once active communities had been abandoned.

I was about to leave when I saw a young black man exit the front door of the red brick parsonage next to the church. I had assumed the house was unoccupied. The man walked toward the truck. I stepped out into the heat to greet him.

"Can I help you?" the young man asked.

"I'm Willie Mitchell Banks, District Attorney for Yaloquena County." I gave the young man a push card with my picture on one side and political b.s. on the other.

"Yes, sir," the young man said. "I know who you are."

He looked familiar, tall and light-skinned with a few freckles spread around his face, probably in his late twenties.

"You must be kin to Reverend Gray."

"Yes, sir. I'm his grandson. My name's David Jefferson."

"You favor him."

"Yes, sir, that's what everyone says."

"He was a fine man. He did work for my father when I was young. Your grandpa invited me to speak right here at this church and helped me win my first District Attorney election a long time ago. I'm sure you were just a baby then."

"Grandpa talked about you when he was still alive. Every time he read in the paper you won a big case he would tell me about helping you in your first campaign."

"I'm sorry he passed away. I imagine that lawsuit over the church membership had something to do with it."

"Yes, sir. My grandma Glenora said after we lost that lawsuit to Reverend Bobby Sanders' church my grandpa went down fast. She said he died of a broken heart."

"Neither Judge Williams nor I wanted that case to go to trial. We did our best to negotiate a settlement to avoid the courtroom."

"I know. I was there. Bobby Sanders and his people bullied my grandpa. He was old and feeble by that time. To tell you the truth, the trial didn't hurt him near as much as all the long-time members leaving the church after the trial was over to join Bobby Sanders' Full Gospel church in town."

"I'm sorry for your loss, David."

I pointed to the abandoned houses up and down the gravel lane. Though I already knew the answer I wanted David's take.

"What happened to all the families that used to live out here?"

"People started moving to town about when I was in junior high, mainly because the School Board closed South Yaloquena when they consolidated the county schools. The people out here wanted to live in town in the new housing projects that went up. They wanted to be closer to school. I guess they figured there was more to do in town, too. One by one they left until they just about all gone."

"You live in the parsonage?"

"Yes, sir. I keep it and the church up best I can, keep the grass mowed. Judge Williams ruled grandpa's congregation still owned the buildings."

"I'd appreciate your consideration," I said, pointing to the push card. "How about your folks? Do they vote?"

"My grandparents raised me. My mama left here when I was a little baby. She never came back."

"Well, I guess I better get going. Hope you'll go to the polls and vote for me on election day."

"I'll do more than that, Mr. Banks. I'll get as many people to vote for you as I can. I know that Bobby Sanders is behind Eleanor Bernstein. He stole my grandpa's congregation and caused him to die before his time. Bobby Sanders is up to no good in this election, I'm sure. Don't you worry, I'm with you all the way."

"Thanks, David," I said, shaking his hand. "I'm proud to have you on my team."

"Yes, sir, Mr. Banks. I know about Eleanor Bernstein, too. She's got no business being D.A. for this county." David paused. "What about Sheriff Lee Jones? Is he for you?"

"He is. Lee's one of the reasons I'm in this race."

"Good. He's a good Sheriff. I'll get in touch with him. See where I can be the most help."

I started the truck and drove away, kicking up another wall of dust. I felt a twinge of encouragement.

On the way to the paved highway, I drove past the weeds and trash accumulated in the abandoned yards of Sadie's Bend. David Jefferson was partially correct in saying the closure of the South Yaloquena school and the new housing projects in town caused the migration from Sadie's Bend to Sunshine. Those were two of the factors, but the more important truth was the people who fled to town were no longer satisfied with the slow pace and traditional values fostered in Sadie's Bend.

In the twenty-four years since the first campaign, I had watched the national culture change for the worse, Yaloquena County right along with it. Television, movies, politics and the legal system coarsened everything. Children growing up in Sadie's bend wanted to be in town where, even in tiny Sunshine, life was faster and seemed more glamorous than the simple life in the country.

I knew the awful statistics. Seventy-eight per cent of children born in Yaloquena County last year were illegitimate. The federal government's good intentions inadvertently promoted the demise of the black family. The unintended consequences of more welfare and other government benefits bestowed financial rewards on unwed mothers for giving birth. There was no longer any social stigma attached to being a single mother while still in junior high or high school. Watching what went on in my office's non-support division was depressing. We tried to collect child support, but there was little Judge Williams could do to an unemployable young man who dropped out of school at sixteen, had no income or job prospects, and nothing to do all day but hang out on the corner looking for ways to dull the pain of his bleak future.

Over the last twenty-four years I've watched race relations deteriorate as well. On the few doors I've knocked on so far in the current campaign, I've encountered more indifference or hostility at black homes than in the past. I'm sure Yaloquena County is a microcosm of the entire country. So much effort had been consumed by the federal and state governments in making up for past discrimination not only in Mississippi but all over the country, many white voters felt disenfranchised and irrelevant. And rather than close the financial disparity between the races, at least in Yaloquena, the government had just made things worse. Even with subsidized housing, food stamps, family assistance, unemployment assistance, the poor blacks were still poor and now totally dependent on the government dole. The young black sports and entertainment celebrities the Yaloquena youngsters watched on television flaunting their money, cars, and bling poured salt on the wound. It spawned jealousy and resentment.

The positive feeling David Jefferson's comments generated was gone. If by some fluke I did win re-election, I was dooming myself to another four years watching the further decline of Yaloquena County. Conditions were in place to continue the downward spiral of the local economy, culture, and education, and more ominous, the increase in antagonism between blacks and whites and the Zeitgeist of despair.

Watching the alligator gars in the muddy Yaloquena twenty-four years ago, I was full of optimism about where the county could go with an improved education system and economic prosperity. Now, things were worse, with little prospect for improvement. As I pulled from the gravel lane onto the paved road back to town, I passed one of the county's faded green solid waste collection containers. NO DEAD ANIMALS was stenciled on its battered side.

What a depressing mess.

CHAPTER FOURTEEN

The following Monday morning I walked through the dimly lit hallway on the second floor of the courthouse, unlocked the main door to the empty reception area, and headed toward my office. It was early, but Walton and Peewee Bernhardt were already seated at the long conference room table outside my office.

"You must have run early," Walton said, his voice flat.

"No good news, I take it."

"We've covered all the camps I know of," Peewee said. "There were four wheelers all over this county beginning on Wednesday of last week. By Friday night, we'd covered all of the hunting camps still in use."

"The ones still operational were easiest to check," Walton said. "Peewee got in touch with the members of each one and they did the search of their own camp."

"Makes sense," I said. "They know their lease better than anyone. If any ground was disturbed or something unusual went on they'd be the ones to recognize it."

"That's how I figured it," Peewee said. "Then this weekend, I had a smaller crew, but it was still a lot of people, and we checked out the hunting camps I know about that aren't used any more. Some of them the leases run out on and some abandoned 'cause the club broke up."

"Nothing?"

"Nary a thing," Peewee said. "I'm sure sorry."

"You did the best you could," Walton said.

"Is it possible there's a camp in the woods or on a lake or river that has been shut down for years you didn't know about?" I asked.

Peewee thought for a minute and shook his head.

"No, sir, Willie Mitchell. I pretty much know'em all going back thirty years or so. We checked every one of them the past five days. If Bullard's note is right that Danny's body is in an old hunting camp I'd have to say it ain't in Yaloquena County."

"I appreciate everything you've done, Peewee," I said, patting Peewee's back. "I know the Thurmans do, too."

"I can go back over the same areas if you want me to. The volunteers are willing."

"Do you think it would do any good?" Walton asked.

"I don't think so," Peewee said. "We've kind of run out of places to look. Somebody going on the lease would have to use the old logging roads and lanes the clubs cut through the woods. The boys all say there's no sign anyone's been there."

I turned on the light in my private office. Peewee and Walton stood in the door.

"I'm getting on to work now," Peewee said, "but if you fellas need me to do anything else, anything at all, you just let me know."

Walton shook Peewee's hand. He walked out and Walton sat down across from me, his shoulders sagging.

"Not a good way to start the week," he said.

"No. What's the latest on Bullard?"

"I spoke to Dr. Clement last night. He said he's going to discharge Ross from the hospital this afternoon."

"Time to fish or cut bait."

"Yep."

"Prepare an arrest warrant for first degree murder and let's get Lee to arrest Ross after he's discharged but before he leaves the hospital."

"Now we're talking," Walton said. "I don't think we have a choice. Body or no body, Ross abducted and killed Danny and we can't let him be walking around."

"I'll call Helmet Head and let him know."

"Who?"

"J.D. Silver."

"Oh," Walton laughed.

"It'd take hurricane force winds to move his hair. I don't know why a grown man would go around looking like that."

"He seems to be pretty full of himself."

"It goes with the territory. Every good defense lawyer I've ever been up against is a narcissist."

"Is Silver married?"

"I don't know but I seriously doubt it. Lawyers like Silver are rarely good family men. Too many hours, too much drama, too much strange offered."

"What else do you have going on today?"

"Meeting online with the campaign consultant Buddy Wade and Jimmy want me to use."

"What's his name?"

"Judice is his last name. Fast-talking coonass out of New Orleans. Supposed to be the best around. I've seen him on national T.V. a couple of times. He ran Buddy's campaign when he won."

"Buddy Wade won because Levander Boothe died. Eleanor's too lean and fit to have a heart attack."

"We're Skyping at ten this morning. I'll see what he has to say."

Walton seemed to have the weight of the world on him.

"Hey," I said. "Just do the best you can."

He gave me a weak smile and left.

CHAPTER FIFTEEN

I couldn't stand it. I was supposed to be out campaigning, but there I was, late that same afternoon, with Walton and Sheriff Jones at the hospital. They didn't need me, but I had to be there.

Willie Mitchell Banks: World's Worst Delegator.

The three of us walked out of the hospital behind two deputies escorting the manacled Ross Bullard through the automatic doors. The largest media contingent I had ever seen in Sunshine closed in on Ross and Helmet Head, jamming microphones and cameras in Ross's face. Bullard lowered his head as far as possible, jamming his chin into his chest. J.D. Silver moved in front of his client and stopped dead still with arms crossed, chin in the air.

"My name is J.D. Silver," he said, "out of Memphis, Tennessee. I am sure most of you have heard of me. I will be representing Ross Bullard in this matter. As you know by now, if you've read the press release Sheriff Jones's office distributed contemporaneously with the arrest, my client is charged with First Degree Murder in the case of the missing child Danny Thurman of Sunshine. For the record, we will be entering a not guilty plea and will move forward expeditiously to obtain the release of my client and the dismissal of these baseless charges."

At least a half-dozen print and television reporters began firing questions at Silver when he paused to take a breath. Silver waited stone-faced until they stopped asking their questions.

"As you know, there is a principle in the law that is basic to every criminal case. The prosecutor for the State must prove every element of the offense, the *corpus delicti*. In this case, my client has been charged with First Degree Murder although the most critical element of the *corpus delicti* is indisputably absent. The Sheriff and the D.A. of this county have failed to produce a dead body in this investigation, much less any proof that young Danny Thurman was murdered."

The reporters surged forward, hurling questions and jamming microphones in the lawyer's face. J.D. Silver again waited in silence until they stopped. Behind him, Bullard continued to stare at the ground.

"Now, this is what we're going to do," J.D. said. "We will make no statement other than what I just said, and you will back away and provide us an unimpeded lane to the Sheriff's transport vehicle waiting for us. If you take those few steps to allow us to get there, my client and I will walk slowly so that you can get photographs and video of the two of us that you can use in your publication or television station."

J.D. Silver waited. The reporters began to back off, clearing the way to the Sheriff's unit. J.D. whispered something to Ross, who looked up for the first time outside the hospital. He stared straight ahead and made no attempt to hide his face.

Silver strode forward with Ross in the bright camera lights and flashes. Thirty seconds later, the deputies helped Bullard into the Sheriff's transport van, which sped away from the hospital as soon as Bullard was securely inside.

J.D. Silver walked over and joined us. The reporters took hundreds of shots of the four of us standing together. They continued to pepper Silver with questions about Ross. He only answered one before leaving us to join Jules and Judy Bullard waiting in the parking lot in their black Cadillac sedan.

"What's J.D. stand for?" a reporter asked.

"J.D." the defense lawyer said over his shoulder.

CHAPTER SIXTEEN

The next morning Walton and I watched the Greenville station's coverage of the arrest on the small television I kept on the credenza behind my desk.

"You have to admire the way he controlled that mob of reporters," Walton said. "The s.o.b is charismatic."

"He's had a lot of practice. He knows the one thing the media can't stand is dead air, and he's got the guts and confidence to wait them out."

Louise Kelly, my office receptionist for the past fifteen years, walked in. She was forty-nine with dark brown skin and a short afro. She was by far the toughest woman in the office. Her job was to screen each visitor and direct them to the appropriate person in the office to handle their issue. Most people were reasonable, but it was not unusual for Louise to encounter people who were angry, confused, or insane.

"There's a forester here to see you," she said to me. "His name is Howard McCain."

"He ever been in here before?"

"No. He's from Dundee County. He says it's about the case involving Danny Thurman."

"Send him in. Thanks."

"Who is he?" Walton asked.

"No idea."

Howard McCain sat down in the hard oak chair next to Walton. Walton turned his chair so that he looked directly at the man, who was about Walton's age, average build with a well-groomed black beard.

"What can we do for you, Mr. McCain?" I asked.

"My wife and I were watching television last night and saw the story on the guy you arrested. He and his lawyer were outside the hospital and the lawyer did all the talking."

"Right," Walton said.

"I saw y'all standing behind them," Howard said to Walton. "I told my wife I had seen that guy before."

"Who?" Walton asked.

"The guy you arrested for the boy's murder. Bullard."

"Where did you see him?" I asked.

"I was cruising some timber for a client in the southern part of your county, down near the national forest. You know where the Iron Bridge is, the one crosses Chickasaw Creek not far from the county line?"

"I know the Iron Bridge," I said.

"That's where I saw him."

"What was he doing?" Walton asked.

"Standing on the bridge, looking down into the creek."

"Looking at what?" I asked. "Was he looking in the water or on the creek bank? Could you tell?"

"He was in the middle of the bridge, so I guess the water, but it could have been the rip rap the state's been putting under the bridge to shore up the foundation. There's lots of big rock there."

"Have they finished the work?" Walton asked.

"I don't know. I haven't been back. There was still a big dragline and track hoe on the creek bank that day I saw him."

"You said he was just standing there, looking down. Did you notice anything unusual about him?" I asked.

"It was unusual him being at the bridge. Nobody lives in the area. I've never run into another human being there with the exception of the MDOT bridge crew laying in that rip rap."

"When was this?" Walton asked.

"July 5."

"What time of day?" Walton asked.

"Late in the day. Maybe six-thirty or seven. Work crew was gone."

"How can you be sure of the date?" I asked.

"I keep a log book in my truck, keep my time, too, when I'm doing a timber cruise. Some companies want me to document each hour."

"How was he dressed?" Walton asked.

"It was pretty strange. Bullard had on a pair of old jeans but no shirt or shoes. I slowed down to see what he was doing and he turned to look at me."

"You got a good look at his face?" Walton asked.

"Real good. He stared a hole through me. I was going to stop and ask if he needed a ride or something but to tell you the truth I was scared to fool with the guy after I got a good look at him up close."

"Was he armed or threatening in any way?" Walton asked.

"He just had a real mean look on his face. It was painted."

"Painted?" I asked. "What color?"

"It was just stripes. He had paint stripes on his face."

"Like what kind of stripes?" Walton asked.

"You know. War paint. Stripes on his cheeks. Like Geronimo."

I called in some favors at MDOT and by nine o'clock that night, the Mississippi Department of Transportation bridge crew had returned to the Iron Bridge and were beginning the process of removing the huge rocks they had spent much of the previous month depositing on the creek bank under the bridge to shore up its foundation. The crew set up heavy duty generators powering banks of high intensity lights they used for night construction. The operators began lifting the rip rap and placing it on the high bank of the creek. Because of the generator noise and the roar of the dragline and track hoe, we had to shout to be heard.

Lee, Walton, and I stood on the bridge with a half-dozen deputies and Kitty Douglas, who wore a navy nylon vest with FBI in bright yellow on the back. Peewee Bernhardt leaned on the rail next to Bill Thurman, who was accompanied by two of his firemen buddies. We watched the crew move one big rock at a time. It was a few minutes after nine and ninety degrees. My shirt was wet. I glanced at the others. Everyone was sweating. The lights around Iron Bridge seemed intensely bright in the pitch black darkness of the national forest.

Tens, maybe hundreds of thousands of flying bugs dive bombed the high intensity lights from great heights like tiny *Kamikaze* pilots. A big one landed on the rusted bridge railing close to Peewee. He made a vee against his lips with his index and middle fingers and shot a stream of brown tobacco juice knocking the bug off the rail.

I glanced at my watch. It was going to be a long night.

I walked toward the other side of the bridge to get away from the bugs and diesel fumes for a while. Twenty feet from me, I saw Kitty doing the same, coughing as she walked. I joined her against the bridge rail opposite where we had been watching the riprap removal.

"Exhaust smoke getting to you, too?" I said.

Kitty looked at me and nodded as she coughed into her fist. I hadn't seen Kitty much since Ross Bullard shot himself. As she coughed, I noticed strands of her long brown hair were wet and stuck to her skin. There were dark circles under her eyes and she had lost weight.

"Hot night," I said. "Are you all right?"

Kitty wiped her face with a small towel.

"I've had a cold I haven't been able to shake."

"There's no reason for you to be out here tonight. Go home and get some rest. Have you seen Dr. Clement?"

"I don't want to bother him."

"Don't be silly. Promise me you'll call him tomorrow."

"I will. I didn't bring my car. I rode with the two investigators."

"Take my truck. We might be out here all night. I can get a ride in. I'll tell Lee for you."

"I'll talk to him," Kitty said, taking my keys.

I knew if she was leaving she was feeling very badly. I had watched her work with the Sheriff's office for over a year now. She was always the first to arrive and the last to leave any crime scene. Kitty was tough and in good condition and wanted all the investigative experience she could get in Yaloquena County.

Moments later Kitty drove my truck away from the bridge into the darkness. I walked back to the railing to join the rest of the men silently watching the dragline and track hoe work. There's something in the male genome that makes us fascinated with seeing heavy equipment moving tons of rock or dirt. The impulse kicks in when we're little boys and lasts a lifetime. The same chromosomal alignment makes it impossible to avoid looking at female cleavage. We're hard-wired to do it.

Around two in the morning, the MDOT dragline operator idled his machine, hung out of his cab and yelled.

"There's something down there under the rock I just moved. It's hard to tell in this light but I think maybe it's clothes."

"What did he say?" Walton asked me.

Before I could answer Bill Thurman took off running to the end of the bridge, jumped to the high creek bank, and stepped from one big rock to the other on the way to where the operator pointed.

"Stop right there, Bill" I yelled. "Don't touch anything."

"Bill," Walton shouted, "if you touch or move anything it might contaminate the evidence and hurt our case against Bullard."

Bill stopped on a big rock ten feet from the spot.

"Okay," he said loudly. "Can I stay right here?"

"Not a step closer," Walton said.

Sheriff Jones's two investigators pulled on latex gloves and began descending the bank, stepping gingerly on the rip rap. The rest of us leaned over the rail to watch the investigators' every step. When they reached the hole left by the big rock the operator had moved, one investigator squatted next to it while the other began taking photographs. The investigator on his haunches carefully placed a pack of cigarettes into the hole to provide scale for the pictures.

After a few minutes, the photographer gestured and his partner reached into the hole and with two fingers pulled out a Texas Rangers baseball cap, bright red with a large white capital T on the front. He held it up for all of us to see then put it in a plastic bag.

Ten feet away, Bill Thurman sat down on the rock behind him and lowered his head. I watched the big man's shoulders heave.

"It's Danny's cap," Bill said.

"What did he say?" Peewee asked, leaning over the bridge rail and straining to hear.

"Bill said it's Danny's cap," I said, my voice catching on the lump building in my throat. "It's Danny's cap."

CHAPTER SEVENTEEN

"What happens if you don't take it to the Grand Jury right away?" Bill Thurman asked me.

I deferred to Walton, reminding myself I was second chair.

"Judge Williams is much more likely to consider bail," Walton said. "Right after the arrest Judge Williams ordered him held without a bond. I guarantee you J.D. Silver will be filing a motion any day now asking the judge to set a bail amount and let Bullard out on bail."

"Bail?" Bill said. "No way that could happen, is it?"

Connie sniffed into her tattered wad of Kleenex.

"Much less likely if the Grand Jury indicts Bullard for First Degree Murder," Walton said. "The Grand Jury's determination that there's probable cause to believe he committed the offense would support Judge Williams keeping him in jail without bond."

"So, if you don't present it to the Grand Jury," Bill said, "Judge Williams might let the bastard out on bail."

Connie winced at Bill's choice of words. Walton continued.

"And J.D. Silver will file a Motion to Dismiss for sure."

"What is the downside of taking it to the Grand Jury now and getting his ass indicted?" Bill asked, ignoring his wife's pat on the arm.

"It starts the case heading to trial," Walton said. "There are things that will begin to happen that we cannot control. The defense will start filing motions for discovery, motions to exclude...."

"There's no telling what Silver will file," I said. "He'll want to change venue for sure."

I watched Bill's neck turn red. I didn't blame him one bit. What Silver was about to put the Thurmans through was nothing short of torture. Pure hell. The sad truth was there was little Walton and I could do about it except warn them.

"One good thing about getting an indictment," I said, "Judge Williams is not required to grant them a preliminary hearing after indictment. It becomes discretionary with her."

"What happens at a preliminary hearing?" Connie asked, her voice weak, tremulous. "Will we have to testify?"

"No. We just have to establish probable cause," Walton said, "a very light burden of proof. Unlike at trial, at the preliminary we can put on the Sheriff's investigators and they can use hearsay statements and reports to establish the elements of First Degree Murder."

I watched Bill as Connie spoke. He stared straight ahead, never turning to watch her ask the question. The tension between them was palpable. I had no choice but to add to it. It was time to lay out in detail the problems in going forward with the prosecution without finding Danny's body. I leaned into them, my palms flat on his desk. I wanted them to hear and understand every word I said.

"We haven't been able to find Danny. The Sheriff's office and Wildlife and Fisheries plus hundreds of volunteers have combed every hunting camp in the county."

"Everyone's been helpful," Bill said. "I appreciate that."

"Last Wednesday morning when the MDOT crew removed the rip rap and we found Danny's hat and Connie's blue sweater...."

"And Danny's jeans," Bill said.

"I'm not certain...," Connie said, "what I'm saying is that pair of jeans looked like the ones I bought him recently," Connie said, "but I can't be sure. I was going to sew his name on them but then he didn't come home...."

Bill turned to his wife. His eyes were angry, his fists clinched, his face even redder. I watched his jaw muscles ripple. It was exactly how he looked that day he stormed the emergency room. For the first time I realized Bill blamed Connie for Danny's disappearance.

"Now hold on just a second, Bill," I said as sternly as the situation allowed. "The fact that Connie can't positively identify those jeans as Danny's is not important. She's just being honest, which is what we want every witness to be. We don't need Connie to be absolutely certain the jeans are his if she's not comfortable saying that. They were found in the hole with the Rangers cap and the blue sweater she's positively identified as hers. Danny wrote his name under the bill of the cap. It's 100% certain it's his cap and it's Connie's sweater. When Connie testifies the jeans are the same size, style, and make as the ones she bought Danny, that's going to be enough. The jury will appreciate her honesty and will use common sense to conclude the jeans are Danny's. And one other thing—Danny's disappearance is not Connie's fault. It's not your fault, either. It's Ross Bullard's fault."

"And the crime lab," Walton added, "identified the blue sweater fibers as matching the fibers from Connie's drawer and Bullard's couch. Even though the lab found no blood or DNA evidence on the cap or the clothes, it's going to be clear to a jury that something bad happened to Danny. He didn't give up his clothes voluntarily. And Bullard put them in that hole for a reason—so they'd never be found."

"Howard McCain is going to be an excellent witness for us," I said. "He's positive he saw Ross Bullard on the Iron Bridge the night after Danny went missing. So, we've got enough to get an indictment for First Degree Murder." I leaned into them again. "But I want to be clear about this: getting a conviction that will hold up to appellate court scrutiny is going to be difficult without Danny's remains."

Tears began to stream from Connie's eyes when I said "remains." She lowered her head and sobbed into her Kleenex. Bill made no effort to comfort her. Connie was on her own. Bill scooted up in his chair and placed his large right fist on my desk.

"I saw that son-of-a-bitch J.D. Silver on television last week talking about us not being able to prove Bullard murdered him unless we find Danny," Bill said. "That makes no sense. It means Bullard gets off because he did a good job getting rid of the body. What kind of justice system do we have?"

"It defies logic but that's entirely possible," I said. "We not only have to prove that Danny's dead, we have to prove that he suffered a violent death to get a conviction."

"You have to prove he was murdered," Bill said, "that he didn't die of natural causes or by accident. I understand that. But with the note and the other evidence I don't believe a Yaloquena jury is going to cut him loose."

"I think you're right," Walton said, "but Judge Williams may order us to try it somewhere else because of all the publicity. Bill, Willie Mitchell is right. We've got to have enough evidence of a violent death to have the jury verdict upheld by an appeals court. The appellate judges won't know anything about the case except what they read in the transcript."

"And depending on what panel we get in the appellate court," I said, wanting them to know the worst, "the judges might be political hacks or just plain incompetent."

Connie dabbed her eyes and sobbed.

"What do you think we should do?" she asked between jagged breaths, her eyes fixed on her hands in her lap.

"This is for us to decide," Bill barked at her. "They've told us what the stupid law is." He paused, not bothering to consult Connie. "We elect to go to the Grand Jury with the case even though Danny's still missing. I don't want Bullard out on bail. I couldn't handle that. Not sure what I would do. I believe a jury will convict him of murder. And if some appeals court down the road cuts him loose and he gets out, I'll kill Ross Bullard myself if the law won't."

"Hold on," I said. "That kind of talk stays inside these four walls. Don't ever say that again. A threat like that can get you in a lot of trouble, and we already have enough problems with Danny's case."

"All right," Bill said. "I'll keep my mouth shut for now."

"I'm empaneling a new Grand Jury this Friday," Walton said, "and I'll present the case to them."

"How long will all that take?" Bill asked.

"We'll have him indicted for First Degree Murder by three o'clock on Friday afternoon," Walton said. "No problem."

"Then the battle begins," I said. "Silver is a really good defense lawyer, but Walton's good, too. And we're on the right side of this battle."

"Now hold on," Bill said to me. "I want you representing us in court. Walton is a friend of ours and I know he's smart and a good lawyer, but he's told me himself many times he'll never be as good as you are. He says you're the best, and if this case is going to be as hard as you say it is, don't you think Danny deserves the best?"

"I asked Willie Mitchell for this case," Walton told Bill. "He's going to have my back, but he's in the middle of a campaign. I promise I won't let you down."

Both men looked at me. Connie was in her private torture chamber, trembling every other breath, her eyes downcast. It was crunch time for me. Was I really going to tell Bill Thurman my campaign for a seventh damn term was more important than making Ross Bullard pay for what he did? Was I going to pit Walton, a good trial lawyer, against J.D. Silver, a *great* trial lawyer with unlimited resources from the Bullards? Was my political status more important than Danny?

I needed Walton's input. I glanced at him, hoping for a sign. The look on his face was not ambiguous. He knew what we had to do and nodded slightly to me, giving me the okay.

"I want both of you to know Walton is fully capable of handling this case, but now I realize he might be too close to you to be objective. So, I'll be lead counsel and handle the jury trial. Walton will be with me every step of the way, and I may have to miss a hearing or two because of the campaign. Both of us will see you and Connie through this."

Bill stood and extended his hand. His face was scarlet. He tried to thank me, but the words hung in his throat. I felt my chest constricting and my throat closing, too. I cleared my throat. I needed to stay composed for the Thurmans. Connie sobbed louder. I gestured for Bill to sit back down and wait a moment.

"A couple more things," I said. "If we don't get Bullard tried before the election and I lose, Silver will string this thing out until Eleanor Bernstein takes over as D.A."

Connie's mouth flew open.

"That ain't going to happen," Bill said. "You won't lose to her."

"There's a very good chance I will," I said.

"Bobby Sanders is preaching all over the county that it's time for a black District Attorney in Yaloquena," Walton said. "Whites make up less than 30% of the vote."

"Can you get it to trial before November?" Bill asked.

"We'll do our best. I will be out of the office a lot between now and then. Walton will have to do most of the preparation work."

"I can do that, boss."

"And it's always possible we can find Danny," I said. "Right now Peewee Bernhardt has an army of volunteer hunters searching the woods around Iron Bridge on four-wheelers because of what the forester Howard McCain told us. They'll cover every inch of a five mile radius around the bridge. They started Thursday morning. It's all heavily wooded and slow going, but Peewee said his men would stay out there until they find something."

"Peewee told me himself there's no hunting camp around Iron Bridge," Bill said, standing up again. "Said there never has been."

"We'll see what they come up with," Willie Mitchell said. "And one final thing, Bill. I've already said it once this morning. This is not Connie's fault. You have to stop acting like you think it is."

Bill stepped back, shocked that I noticed. He took a deep breath and looked over at Connie. She glanced at her husband for a second. He put his big hand on her back and guided her out. Walton escorted them into the hallway, returning after a few minutes.

"You're going to have to talk to Gayle about Bill and Connie," I said. "Make sure Gayle stays in close contact with her. You might have to talk to Bill to reinforce the point I just made. If he keeps up his attitude toward Connie it's going to make things worse. She's fragile."

"I will. And you made the right choice about first chair. You couldn't tell Bill anything else. I'm a little relieved, if you want to know the truth. I probably let my ego get out ahead of my abilities when I asked you for the case."

"You would have done fine," I said.

"You didn't tell them about double jeopardy."

"One thing at a time. Let's get past the Grand Jury. As it gets closer to trial, we'll sit them down and explain what happens if we go to trial and we lose because we can't prove Danny was murdered."

"I believe Bill will kill Ross Bullard if he gets the chance," Walton said. "I don't think there's a jury in the world that would convict him if he did."

"Let's hope we don't have to find out. I know one thing. If I were Ross Bullard I wouldn't want to be out on bond or anywhere Bill Thurman could get to me. I'd stay in jail for now."

Chapter Eighteen

I watched Susan bounce out of bed in the dim light in our bedroom and hurry into the bathroom. There was no rush, but Susan always moves fast, no matter where she's heading. When we walk for exercise together on the streets of Sunshine, I have a difficult time keeping up with her, having to run a few steps every block or two.

"That was nice," she said when she hopped back into the bed, pulling the sheet over her naked body and snuggling against me.

"You know," I told her, "some things seem to get better with age."

"Mmm-hmmm," she said. "Like you."

The bathroom plug-in provided just enough light to keep me from running into things when I got out of bed to visit the bathroom. It seemed like I had to get up more often at night since my near death experience in Jackson during the El Moro trial. I told Nathan about it, adding that the vision in my left eye seemed worse in the past few months. Nathan examined me but didn't have an explanation for either. My guess was the weeks in the hospital and months of therapy and recovery must have accelerated the aging process. The two hit men didn't kill me, but they left me with blurred vision in my left eye, a near-constant ache in my left leg, and occasional *absent* seizures. Thankfully the leg was no worse and my seizures seemed to be occurring less frequently these days.

I watched the ceiling fan turn slowly above the four-poster bed. Susan's bare skin felt good against mine. I had my arm around her and turned my head slightly to kiss the top of her head.

"I'm glad you told Bill and Connie you would try the case."

"Me, too. Did you check on Kitty?"

"She thinks she's better. Nathan's put her on some antibiotics."

"Summer colds are the worst."

"Nathan says it's more than a cold. He says her respiratory system was compromised in New Orleans when she went through that ordeal. He treated her for double pneumonia after we moved her up here."

"She's going to be okay?"

"Nathan says he'll keep an eye on it. He told her to quit exercising and stay out of the heat."

"Has she talked to Jake lately?"

"Briefly a few days ago. She doesn't tell me everything."

"Jake probably doesn't tell her much either."

"I wish Jake would just come home to Mississippi and practice law, marry Kitty and raise a family."

"I suspect Jake will do what he wants. Kitty, too. They don't think like we do about marriage and kids. Scott may be our only hope."

Susan pushed away and raised up on her elbow.

"I want a grandchild," she said and fell back onto the mattress, burrowing into my side.

"It'll happen."

"Scott called me today about your campaign."

"Did you tell him it was going just great?"

"I told him the truth. He said Skeeter said for him to get down here to help, that the Senate could get along without him for a few weeks."

"That's not necessary," Willie Mitchell said. "Scott's strategies are too sophisticated for this campaign, same as the Judice guy Jimmy and Buddy had me talk to. I'm sure Judice is good at running big campaigns but it's a waste of money to hire him for a one county election like this. Shaking hands is still the best way to campaign in Yaloquena. Scott needs to stay in D.C."

Susan was up on her elbow again.

"What's wrong?"

"Gayle told me Walton asked her to talk to Bill about the way he's treating Connie."

"Somebody needs to. I'm not sure he listened to me."

"Gayle said Walton didn't make much headway with Bill either."

"He's not rational right now."

"I understand but can't he see what effect it's having on Connie? She already feels bad enough. She's hanging on by a thread."

"Is Gayle going to talk to Bill?"

"She said she'd try to catch him at the fire station. She wanted to talk to him away from Connie."

"The twins spent a lot of time playing with Danny," I said.

"Nicholas and Danny were best friends."

"That's what Walton told me."

I wanted to get back to sleep. I moved over to my side and fluffed my pillow.

"Night," I said. "Love you."

"I love you," Susan whispered, patting my back. "Thank you for waiting for me."

"You were worth the wait. Sorry for being the way I am."

"We all do the best we can."

I took a deep breath and began to drift off, thinking about Susan's three-year sabbatical from our marriage. I was grateful she came home and sorry for the time we lost during the hiatus. I was hopeful Gayle might get Bill to let up on his wife. They needed to support each other now more than ever, especially with J.D. Silver in play. Helmet Head was about to deal them some serious misery.

CHAPTER NINETEEN

On Thursday I picked up Jimmy Gray and drove to the cake auction at the New Tabernacle Agape Church Family Center in a formerly abandoned shopping center on the four-lane running east and west in Sunshine.

"We got time for a toddy before this august gathering?" Jimmy asked, riding shotgun. "Maybe let me get a little buzz on?"

"Not hardly. No drinking on the campaign trail, especially at a church event."

"Cake auction my ass," Jimmy said. "It puzzles me how they got the nerve to put you poor suckers asking for votes in front of a bunch of people and embarrass you into bidding two hundred dollars to buy a cake with fuzzy frosting it probably took three dollars to make. It's extortion."

"So, what's your point?"

"Just sticks in my craw, that's all."

"It's not your money."

"Some of it is. You forget I'm your biggest contributor?"

"I'm not using the money you gave me for this."

Jimmy Gray laughed.

"If you have to give a speech put a little sizzle in it. Don't talk about any legal crap. Dazzle'em with your eloquence. Jazz it up."

I glanced over at big Jimmy. His face was covered with beads of sweat in spite of my truck's air conditioner blowing full blast.

"What's with all the double Zs?"

"What?" Jimmy asked.

"I've been listening to your bull shit over fifty-five years, and I know when you're messing with me. What is the double Z bit?"

"Damn," Jimmy said. "I didn't think you'd get it that quick."

"Why the Zs?"

"When I woke up this morning, I declared today "Double Z" day. I set out to use as many words with two Zs as possible and see if anyone noticed. I started at breakfast and did it all day at the bank."

"Why?"

"Hell, I don't know. Just to do it. Same reason I get fired up about National Talk Like a Pirate Day."

"How many people noticed the Zs?"

"Two. Martha over breakfast and you just now."

"What was the best double zee word you used?"

"Razzle-dazzle. I used it a lot because it was two zee words together, so I got double credit. Fuzzy and puzzling were two more I used at least once an hour."

"You are a very odd man," I said.

"Thank you. At least I've got the sense not to be a politician."

"I'm no politician."

"You can say that again."

"I worked my behind off this week. Went all over the place."

Jimmy Gray started laughing, his big body shaking the seat. I fought it, but I cracked a smile, which morphed into a chuckle, then an all-out laugh. I couldn't help it. Watching Jimmy laugh broke me up. He had been making me laugh since we were both in diapers.

"Ain't this some shit?" Jimmy asked between laughs. "Two grown men on their way to pay a small fortune for a cake we aren't going to eat."

After a few blocks I pulled into the shopping center, avoiding potholes in the long-neglected asphalt. There were forty to fifty vehicles parked haphazardly near the Agape Family Center. The parking lines on the asphalt disappeared many years ago. As Big Jimmy and I walked to the entrance the front door opened. A black youngster in a white shirt and skinny black tie welcomed us inside.

I looked around at the cavernous Family Center. The last time I stood inside the room it was an Odd Lots Dollar Store, which went out of business in the late nineties, causing the shopping center's smaller businesses that depended on the anchor store's traffic to shut down in short order. The store had been empty for a decade until the New

Tabernacle opened its doors. The rest of the shopping center was still vacant, with no prospects.

I saw Reverend Sam Lattimore gesturing for us to come to the front of the room and join the other candidates. I noticed Jimmy was open-mouthed looking around, awestruck by the size of the old facility. We walked through the rows of metal folding chairs to the riser Reverend Lattimore was using as a stage.

"Good evening, gentlemen," the preacher said as we shook hands. "We appreciate your attendance. Mr. Banks, you may be seated with the other candidates in the first row. We will be calling the race for District Attorney first. You and Ms Bernstein get to bid on a cake, then each of you will be given five minutes to speak or answer questions."

"Sounds good, Reverend Lattimore," I said.

I took a seat in the empty folding chair next to Eleanor. Jimmy sat in the row behind me. I turned and noticed three empty seats separating Jimmy from Reverend Bobby Sanders. Without smiling, Jimmy nodded to the preacher running Eleanor's campaign.

"How are you, Eleanor?" I asked quietly, shaking her hand.

"Just fine, Willie Mitchell," she said, "trying to survive in this heat."

"It ought to be illegal to have to campaign in August."

"I agree," she said.

As usual, Eleanor was dressed tastefully in a dark business suit and white blouse with ruffles in front. She was attractive, thin with dark brown skin. She displayed the same dignified mien as she did in court as the public defender for Yaloquena County. Given the nature of her indigent clients, I admired her for representing criminals with decorum and restraint under many difficult circumstances. Even though Eleanor was soft-spoken I figured she would do a decent job as district attorney if she could reverse her current default position that all deputies were corrupt bullies and all defendants deserved mercy.

I had no animosity toward Eleanor. I saved it all for Reverend Bobby Sanders, founder and spiritual leader of the Full Gospel Non-Denominational House of the Lord, the fastest growing black church in Sunshine. Bobby Sanders did not like me and made no bones about it. He had created a lot of problems for me in recent years, the latest being talking Eleanor into the race. I was certain she would never have run if Bobby Sanders hadn't jaw-boned her. She was self-funded, too, using the substantial proceeds of her part of the Gas & Go Fast civil settlement she received as co-counsel for Lester "Mule" Gardner.

Preacher Lattimore called the crowd to order and began with an opening prayer. He explained the ground rules to Eleanor and me and the dozen men and women in the first row running for positions on the Yaloquena County Board of Supervisors.

I was the only white person among the fourteen candidates. Jimmy Gray was the only white person in the audience, which I estimated to be around fifty people, not counting the politicians. The gathering was for the sole purpose of raising a few hundred dollars for the church. Nobody in the Family Center cared about the political campaigns except the candidates.

When Reverend Lattimore held up the first cake and called for bids from the candidates for District Attorney, I raised a finger.

"One hundred dollars," I said.

"One hundred twenty-five," Eleanor said quietly.

"One fifty."

"One seventy-five," she said.

"One eighty."

"Two hundred," Eleanor called out.

"Two twenty-five."

"Two fifty," she said immediately.

I decided that was enough. Reverend Lattimore called it once, twice, and a third time, and awarded the cake to Eleanor. I made a point of being the first one to clap for Eleanor. While she rose and walked to get her prize, I quickly removed a campaign check from my wallet and made it out to New Tabernacle Agape for $250.

"Would you care to make a statement to our congregation?" the preacher asked Eleanor.

"I'm Eleanor Bernstein and I'm running for District Attorney. I would appreciate your vote because I believe it's time for a change."

There were no questions. I walked to Reverend Lattimore after Eleanor took her seat. I handed the preacher my check.

"Reverend Lattimore, ladies and gentlemen of the congregation, I am sorry I missed out on the cake, but I would like to match Ms Bernstein's contribution with my check to the church for $250."

The preacher beamed and the audience clapped for me. When they stopped I told them I was their current District Attorney, had been for twenty-four years, and that I would continue my policy of being fair with everyone. I ended by asking each voter in the room to consider me when they went to the polls, then asked if there were any questions.

When Reverend Bobby Sanders stood up in the second row, I steeled myself. I knew this was trouble. Bobby was slender and as usual, wore his gray tailored suit with a stark black shirt and white collar encircling his skinny neck as if he were a Roman Catholic priest.

"One question, Mr. District Attorney," Bobby said, "about your health. Is it true that you have some kind of brain disorder that makes you pass out from time to time, even in the middle of a trial?"

The room became silent. The only sound I heard was the distant roar of the air conditioner struggling to cope with the expanse of square footage it was expected to cool. There was no whispering, no rustling of papers and campaign handouts—only quiet tension as I considered my response.

"Yes," I said, "it's true that I have a seizure disorder resulting from an attempt on my life in Jackson when I was picking a jury to try the Mexican drug smuggler who murdered Deputy Sheriff Travis Ware two years ago." I paused for effect. "Anyone here remember Travis Ware?"

Most of the adults in the audience and all of the candidates on the front row raised their hands.

"Travis was a good deputy and a friend of mine. I prosecuted the man that killed him. That's part of my job as District Attorney. My seizures occur occasionally, and last about ten minutes. They don't interfere with my job. I hope you'll consider keeping me as your District Attorney with your vote. Thank you."

I stared directly at Eleanor as I walked back to my seat. Maybe she didn't know Bobby was going to ask about the seizures. Eleanor wouldn't make eye contact with me. I gave her the benefit of the doubt.

After the first two supervisor candidates bought cakes for twenty-five dollars and spoke about their plans to transform the county if elected, I took Reverend Lattimore aside and told him I had a heavy schedule the next day and had to go. He gave me his blessing and Jimmy and I walked out.

"How about that toddy now?" Jimmy Gray said as we drove out of the New Tabernacle Agape parking lot.

"I think I'd like that. Where do you want to go? Country Club?"

"Nah. Let's run by the house and I'll fix us a couple of drinks to go. We'll ride around like we used to. With this damned campaign and the Ross Bullard case we haven't been able to spend any quality time together lately. I feel neglected."

"Sounds good, sweetheart," I said and drove to his house.

I sat in my truck in Jimmy's driveway waiting for him to make the drinks. I phoned Susan, telling her Jimmy and I were going to take a ride out in the country and I'd be home in an hour or so. She asked me how the cake auction went. I said fine.

I pushed open the passenger door when I saw him on his carport walking toward me carefully with two large Styrofoam cups.

"VT for you," Jimmy said, handing me the drink.

"Gracias."

Jimmy Gray placed his own drink in the cup holder between us before he began the multi-stage process of situating his 312 pounds comfortably in the passenger seat and buckling up. Jimmy's cup was full to the brim with bourbon and ice.

"Maybe you ought to take a sip of your drink before I start backing out, get the whiskey level below flood stage."

"Gladly," Jimmy grunted and lifted the twenty-ounce cup, careful to preserve every precious drop. He took a big sip, then another.

"Cleared for takeoff," he said.

I drove our usual route, paralleling the bayou that meandered through Sunshine, crossing the four-lane and heading out of town on the two-lane county road with no shoulders. I drove between twenty and twenty-five. We had no place to go and were in no hurry to get there.

"Since when did you switch back to bourbon?"

"My planters protested my drinking vodka, threatened to move their loans unless I switched back, so I had to take drastic action. It was a sacrifice I felt I had to make to keep our bank operations profitable."

"Good going," I said. "For the team."

"For the team," Jimmy Gray said, toasting with his cup.

"It's brave men like you that make our country great."

"Yeah," Jimmy said, taking a big sip. "I'd do it all over again."

We drove through cut over corn fields and healthy cotton fields. The cotton flowers had morphed into bolls that were now splitting open to expose the bright white fiber that was the foundation of the entire Delta economy half-a-century earlier.

"Cotton looks good," I said, sipping my vodka and tonic.

"Yeah." Jimmy took a drink. "That pissant Bobby Sanders is a piece of work ain't he?"

"I should have gotten ahead of that, should have known Bobby would bring that up at some point. I'd like to believe Eleanor had nothing to do with it, but she wouldn't look at me from that point on."

"You notice the dead silence after Bobby asked you about your seizure situation? That big old room got as quiet as a rat peeing on cotton."

"That is extremely quiet," I said.

"I say sins of omission are as bad as sins of commission. She could put a stop to crap like that if she wanted."

"She can't control Bobby. He's got a much stronger personality."

"Well, she's going to be one hell of a D.A. if that pencil-necked prick is going to be pulling her strings."

I pointed at Jimmy Gray's large neck, with its double chins and significant wattle.

"I'm proud you're no pencil-necked prick."

"Damn straight." He pointed to himself. "Now, this is a neck."

"A man's neck."

"Right on, brother. That's what I'm talking about."

We chuckled and I continued to drive slowly, bisecting the 990 acre farm I inherited from my parents. I kept it leased to the Hudson brothers to farm on quarters. We passed the Banks family cemetery on the edge of the farm where my parents and paternal grandparents were buried.

"Why don't you stop at the Gas & Go Fast when we get back to town so I can get a beer?" Jimmy said after draining the last sip of his bourbon. "All of a sudden I got a hankering for a Bud Select."

"That's not a good idea. Remember what you've always said? Beer after whiskey, might risky. Whiskey after beer, never fear."

"You got it backwards," Jimmy said. "It's beer before liquor, never sicker. Liquor before beer, never fear."

"Wrong. Bet you a quarter."

"Nah. I'd rather not resolve it. Allows me to go either way."

I put my drink in the cup holder in the console as we came into town. On the four lane heading to the Gas & Go Fast we passed the New Tabernacle Agape center. In the pock-marked parking lot I saw Eleanor shaking her finger at Bobby Sanders, fussing at him.

"Well, look at that," Jimmy said.

"Told you that was probably Bobby's doing."

"Good for her. Let's go home. No Bud Select tonight."

"It's probably best, a man in top physical condition like you."

"Yeah," he said, "my body's a fine-tuned instrument."

CHAPTER TWENTY

I looked over at J.D. Silver when he stood up at the defense table. Ross Bullard was writing furiously on a legal pad and had been since we started. I wondered what the hell he could be writing. It didn't seem to correlate with the testimony of Lee Jones on the witness stand. I thought at first Bullard might be writing questions he wanted Silver to ask the Sheriff, but after a while I realized Bullard was paying no attention to his lawyer.

Silver had a real presence in the courtroom. Plenty smart, he was not about to put Bullard on the stand for this bail hearing. When Ross said "not guilty" at the arraignment earlier in response to Judge Williams asking him how he pleaded to the charges, I figured those two words were the only ones Silver would ever allow out of Ross's mouth.

"Permission to approach the witness, Your Honor," Silver said.

"Granted," Judge Zelda Williams said. "For future reference, Mr. Silver, there's no need to ask for permission to approach in my courtroom. Feel free to approach as needed."

"Thank you, Your Honor. I will not abuse the privilege."

"I hand you a printout of my client's criminal record," Silver said to the Sheriff, "which your office so graciously provided me this morning. Could you examine it please?"

"Mr. Bullard does not have a criminal record," Lee said.

"Any record of any arrest of any kind? A traffic ticket?"

"No, sir. He's never been arrested according to the state crime information system."

"Your Honor," I said. "The State offered to stipulate that Mr. Bullard has no record. This is not necessary."

Judge Williams looked down from her elevated bench at Silver standing on the carpeted floor in front of the witness box. She was in her early fifties, attractive and dignified. Much of her hair had turned a pretty shade of gray in the last four or five years. I thought the gray contrasted nicely with her dark chocolate skin and added *gravitas* to her appearance on the bench. Unlike many other judges before whom I had practiced, she was always prepared. She read the pre-trial memoranda and filings, which accelerated the pace of every hearing or trial in her court because she knew in advance the legal issues involved.

"Mr. Donaldson is correct, Mr. Silver. No need to belabor the points the State has conceded. Sheriff Jones has testified to the contents of the note your client left and the circumstances in which he left it. He's described the findings of the crime lab regarding the blue fibers from the defendant's home and the blue sweater and red Texas Rangers hat found at the Iron Bridge, and described how each piece of evidence was found."

"Just a couple of additional questions, Your Honor," Silver said.

"Proceed."

"Has your department found the alleged victim of the murder with which my client is charged?"

"No, sir," the Sheriff said.

"So you know of no evidence at this time to the effect that seven-year-old Danny Thurman is actually dead, do you?"

"Considering the facts surrounding his disappearance the night of July 4, the events leading up to his disappearance including his appearing on a homemade videotape...."

"Non-responsive, Your Honor," Silver said interrupting.

"He asked the question," I said, "he just doesn't like the answer."

"Mr. Silver," Judge Williams said, "is this really necessary? Your client was indicted for First Degree Murder of Danny Thurman by the Yaloquena County Grand Jury one week ago today, so this combined hearing on your Motions for Bail and for a Preliminary Hearing is solely for the purpose of persuading me to exercise my discretion in regard to both bail and the preliminary hearing. Isn't that correct?"

"Yes, Your Honor," Silver said. "If I may be heard?"

Judge Williams nodded.

"I cited the *Breedlove* case originating in Wayne County in my memorandum. It was a capital case in which the defendant asked for post-indictment bail. The Mississippi Supreme Court ruled that in cases where the evidence is not strong that the defendant committed the homicide, the trial court should grant bail. In this case, there's not even proof of a death. There's no body. No *corpus delicti.*"

I heard rustling in the courtroom behind me and noticed Walton staring at the center aisle. I turned in time to see Bill Thurman's back as he walked out, his neck a bright red. Listening to Silver had made Bill angry. From Walton's expressions and gestures sitting next to me, I knew he was irritated at Silver, too. Probably best that I took back first chair. I was sure Silver counted on angering the prosecution side, goading us into mistakes fueled by anger. I had been up against good defense lawyers who did the same thing, and had learned to hold my tongue and to accept the behavior for what it was, a tactic. I figured out long ago that if you lose your temper, you lose the argument.

"Your Honor," I said, "that was *dicta* in the *Breedlove* case because the majority ultimately ruled that the matters of bail and preliminary hearing are still in the trial judge's discretion, regardless of the strength of the evidence indicating the defendant committed the homicide in question."

"I believe Mr. Banks' interpretation of *Breedlove* is correct, Mr. Silver," Judge Williams said. "Regardless of the evidence asserted by the defendant in *Breedlove,* our Supreme Court indicated it would not disturb the trial court's discretion in both matters."

"But Your Honor," Silver said before being interrupted.

"I'm ready to rule," she said. "Counsel take your seats."

"Mr. Silver," Judge Williams said, "you've offered evidence that your client has no criminal record, has a sterling work history, and has been a model citizen up to this time. You've offered to turn in his passport. All laudable points. However, as the District Attorney points out in his argument, the substantial resources of the client's family does create a serious concern in terms of the defendant's ability to flee, with or without a passport.

"Ultimately, for this Court, it comes down to this. The Grand Jury heard the case exactly one week ago, August 17, and returned an indictment for First Degree Murder. The law is clear, I believe, that it is solely within my discretion whether to grant pre-trial bail or a preliminary hearing. I am concerned that the defendant is a flight risk because of his financial resources. I might add, Mr. Silver, though there's been no testimony on this point, I believe your client to be much safer in his cell upstairs than out in the community.

"As far as the preliminary hearing, I believe that given the extensive testimony of the Sheriff this morning on all aspects of the investigation, you have had, in effect, a preliminary hearing.

"I hereby deny the defense motions for pre-trial bail and for a preliminary examination for the reasons just stated." She looked at the attorneys. "Anything else?"

"No, Your Honor," I said. "Thank you."

"I do, Your Honor," Silver said. "May I have a moment?"

"By all means," Judge Williams said.

Silver walked to the rail behind his table. Jules Bullard left his seat next to Judy on the front row behind the defense table to confer with Silver. I watched the two men whisper for a moment, and looked over the rest of the courtroom observers sitting in the pew-like oak benches the Board of Supervisors purchased in my first term as District Attorney over twenty years ago when they actually had money.

I estimated the press corps in the courtroom to be twelve to fifteen reporters, print and television, waiting to report Judge Williams' ruling and interview Silver. I had phoned the District Attorney in Memphis earlier and asked what to expect from Silver. He provided a laundry list of things Silver would do in the course of the case, including make bombastic statements to the press.

I also saw five or six women from the various courthouse departments on their breaks, including the offices of Tax Assessor, the Chancery Clerk, Board of Supervisors, and Family Services. The two firemen I noticed earlier must have left when Bill did. There were a few Sunshine retirees who were regular court watchers. I nodded to them as I waited for Silver and Bullard to finish. The last person I noticed was an attractive, well-dressed woman sitting by herself. She reminded me of Zsa Zsa Gabor.

I glanced again at Silver and Bullard whispering at the rail. I made eye contact with Judy Bullard seated behind the two men. Judy seemed to stare right through me. She had shown no emotion during the hearing and did not react to Judge Williams' ruling. I had also noticed that Ross never turned to look at his father and wife during the ninety minutes they'd been in the courtroom. Ross was engrossed in whatever he was writing. Jules was intense, as usual, and was giving Silver an earful when Judge Williams tapped her gavel. The thought of the old man's foul breath invading Silver's hair and nostrils made me cringe. Silver was earning his money.

"Mr. Silver," the Judge said.

"Coming, Your Honor," Silver said and returned to sit at the defense table. He opened the briefcase on the table in front of Ross and pulled out a stack of documents, separating them into smaller piles on the table.

"I would like to enter an objection to the Court's ruling."

"Mr. Bordelon," Judge Williams said to her Minute Clerk for the hearing, Chief Deputy Clerk of the Circuit Court Eddie Bordelon, a bald, nervous, transplanted Cajun from Acadia Parish who single-handedly kept the Clerk's office running properly, "please note in the record Mr. Silver's objection."

"Thank you, Judge Williams," Silver said. "I'd like to file now four discovery motions."

Silver collected the four originals and gave them to Eddie Bordelon, then gave Judge Williams and Walton and me copies of each.

"In addition to the discovery motions, I would like to file, in order...," Silver spent a moment organizing his documents, "Motion For Change of Venue, a Motion To Suppress various items of evidence taken from my client's home pursuant to an illegal search, including the written note seized by the State from my client's domicile, a Motion for a Psychiatric Examination, a Brady Motion for all exculpatory evidence within the possession or knowledge of the State, and a Motion to Exclude Other Crimes Evidence."

Silver provided copies to us and filed the originals with Eddie.

"Anything else, Mr. Silver?" the Judge asked.

"I dictated a few other motions yesterday that my staff was not able to prepare for filing this morning. I will be delivering those to the Circuit Clerk in the next few days and provide copies to the State."

"Very well, if there's nothing further...,"

"One final thing, Your Honor, since my client will be incarcerated until trial, I would ask that this case be expedited on the Court's docket."

"No objection," I said.

"We'll move it along fast as we can, Mr. Silver," the Judge said and banged her gavel. "Court is hereby adjourned."

Everyone stood while Judge Williams left the courtroom. As soon as the side door closed behind her, the room began to buzz with conversation and the noise of observers leaving. Walton and I collected Silver's filings and stuck them in the accordion file on the table.

I felt eyes on my back and turned to see the well-dressed woman I noticed earlier in the gallery. She stood at the rail behind me and extended her hand. I walked the two steps to the rail and shook hands.

"I'm Cheryl Diamond from Houston," she said in a pleasant, almost child-like voice. "May I speak to you, Mr. Banks?"

J.D. Silver walked behind the woman out the center aisle into the crowd of reporters in the back of the courtroom. The reporters surrounded Silver and began to ask him questions.

"Just a moment, ma'am," I said. "I need to listen to what the defense attorney is telling the reporters. They'll want to talk to me, too, after they're through with Mr. Silver. I might be a while."

"That's fine," she said. "I'll wait right here until you're through."

As I walked past her I asked her what she wanted to talk about.

"Danny Thurman," she said.

CHAPTER TWENTY-ONE

I forgot about Cheryl Diamond while I listened to J.D. Silver answer the media questions. Twenty minutes later Walton and I were in my office going over the motions Silver filed when Ethel told me a Mrs. Diamond from Houston was waiting.

"Oh, I forgot," I said. "Please bring her back, Ethel."

"Who is Mrs. Diamond?" Walton asked.

"I don't know. She stopped me after the hearing and said she wanted to talk to me about Danny. You want to sit in?"

"Maybe for a minute but I've got to get to work answering these motions and preparing some of our own. If it sounds like she knows something I'll stick around."

Cheryl Diamond walked in. Walton and I stood. I introduced her to Walton and held the back of her chair, gesturing for her to have a seat. I sat in my chair facing the two of them across the desk.

"Thank you for seeing me, Mr. Banks," she said.

"My pleasure. You said it was about Danny Thurman."

"Yes. I wanted you to know you have the right man."

"We're certain we do, Mrs. Diamond. It is Mrs., right?"

"Oh, I was married once a long time ago, but that's ancient history. Please call me Cheryl."

"If you'll call me Willie Mitchell." We both smiled. "Now tell me how you know that Ross Bullard killed Danny. Did you see or hear something on the Fourth of July that...."

"Not in the conventional sense. I just happen to know it's true."

Walton leaned back in his chair and rolled his eyes.

"You folks are going to have to excuse me," he said, "I've got all these motions to get to work on."

He quickly gathered his files and nodded to Cheryl then left.

"He thinks I'm a crackpot," she said after Walton was gone.

"He's young and in a hurry, Cheryl. Don't think anything about it."

She stood up and extended her hand to me. Instinctively I stood and extended mine. She clasped my hand in both of hers and closed her eyes. At first I thought it strange but after several seconds, I was fine with it. She let go of my hand and sat down with a peaceful smile.

"A lot of people think I'm a nut," she said. "I'm used to it."

"You ought to hear what they say about me."

Cheryl giggled like a schoolgirl. She was attractive, her platinum blond hair swept back into an elegant *chignon,* exposing her substantial and elegant diamond earrings. Her skin was radiant, healthy and pink with few wrinkles or blemishes. I guessed she was in her early to mid-sixties and slightly overweight, *full-figured* as they say on T.V.

Her three strand pearl necklace was exquisite, as were the diamonds and rubies on her hands. The white gold and platinum settings had the hallmarks of estate pieces made a century ago. From the way she carried herself and her appearance, Cheryl Diamond had plenty of money.

"How long have you been in town, Cheryl?"

"I drove in from Houston on Thursday. I'm staying at the High Cotton B&B. It's the first time I've been in the Mississippi Delta."

"It's pretty hot here this time of year."

"So is Houston," she said, "and just as humid. Driving in on the highway I expected to see some antebellum plantation homes along the road but of course I didn't. It's funny the impressions we have of places."

"No hoop skirts either," he said. "You can still find plenty of both of those in Natchez during Pilgrimage."

"I enjoyed the old homes and the Pilgrimage in Natchez many years ago," she said, "I guess I thought all of Mississippi was like that."

"No, ma'am. Nothing close to Sunshine but flat farmland as far as the eye can see. You probably drove through a lot of cotton and corn fields. Should be a good crop for our farmers this year."

As I made small talk about our crops she sat up in her chair and her smile disappeared. She had something serious to tell me—the lady was on a mission.

"I know you don't have time to chit chat," she said. "Let's talk about the case. I know Ross Bullard killed Danny Thurman."

"But you said you didn't know in the conventional sense."

"I've known since the night he went missing," she said, clutching the purse in her lap in both hands.

"Since the Fourth of July? How is that possible?"

She removed a business card from her purse and gave it to me. *Cheryl Diamond, Seer* it said in reddish-pink print, along with her contact information and address in the same bright color.

"It's fuschia," she said, "the color. Everybody asks."

"What exactly is a seer?" I asked and made a mental note for the umpteenth time to remember that fuschia is bright reddish-pink like the bougainvilleas in Cozumel.

"It's hard to explain," she said. "I sense things. They come to me from the outside. I see things, but not with my eyes."

"You're a psychic."

"I guess that's a fair description. It's the word they use most often on television and in movies. I don't like to use it because it makes me sound like a kook. Seer is a word that's been around for centuries and may be more accurate."

"The Oracle at Delphi."

"Right, but I don't want to claim to be something I'm not. I'm no oracle. I can't read minds and I don't see auras. I cannot predict the future. I do get images and messages from somewhere outside the normal range of human senses. Sometimes they come out of nowhere. Like with this case. When I'm in the presence of some people I sense things and receive information about them. It doesn't happen all the time, but on occasion it does."

"You received a message about Danny's murder on July 4?"

"I was in bed at my house in Houston, sound asleep, and all of a sudden I was wide awake. I knew something bad had happened. I pored over newspapers the next morning and got on my computer. As soon as I discovered the story about Danny Thurman, I knew he was the one. Since then, I've read everything I could about your case. When I found out Ross Bullard was arrested I started making plans to come over here."

"How did you know the message was about Danny Thurman?"

"I don't know how or why these things come to me," she shrugged, "but there's no doubt in my mind Danny was the victim."

"And Ross Bullard was the killer."

"Right. When I was in the courtroom Friday Ross Bullard walked near me. I sensed it clear as a bell. I'm sure he murdered Danny."

"I've known from the night he disappeared that Danny had been killed," I said. "Statistics say if a child is not found in the first couple of days there's a substantial probability he's dead."

"Is that why you knew he was dead that night?"

"No," Willie Mitchell said, "it wasn't the statistical probability. I just had a feeling as soon as I saw Connie, his mother, searching the crowd for him. I knew right then."

"I understand perfectly," Cheryl said. "I'd like to ask you something if you don't mind, Willie Mitchell."

"Sure."

"You don't seem as skeptical about me as most D.A.'s or law enforcement people I've had contact with on other cases. Why do you think that is?"

It was a good question. I tried to answer as best I could. It was something I had thought about for a long time, but never talked to anyone about.

"Things happen all the time that can't be explained, even with all the science and technology we have today. I believe there is some type of communication out there that doesn't rely on phones or texts. When I was in college I took a survey course on philosophy. We studied Jung's theory of collective unconsciousness. I don't know if that's relevant to how information comes to you or to other clairvoyants. I guess all I'm saying is that as smart as we modern human beings think we are, we still don't have all the answers."

Cheryl relaxed her two-handed grip on her purse and leaned back against her chair.

"For example," I said, "and this is a small thing, I can't tell you the number of times I've been thinking of someone I haven't seen in a while and they call the next day. When I was young I thought it was a coincidence, but not any more. It happens to me too often."

"It's not coincidental," she said. "You have the gift."

"Me?" I said, tapping my chest.

"I felt it the moment I met you, and when I held your hand a minute ago I knew it to be true."

"I don't think so."

"Oh, you do. Maybe it's not developed, but that's because you haven't really worked on it. You're aware of it. I can tell."

"My mother had the ability to see through people who were putting on, trying to be someone they were not," I said after a moment. "She was a remarkable judge of character. My wife Susan says I inherited that trait from her."

"I'm sure you did, but your gift is a lot stronger than that. You're an old soul. I can feel it."

"I don't think so, but thanks, I guess. Getting back to the case, do you have any sense of where we should look for Danny?"

"I'm sorry to say I don't. Driving through your county I was hoping I might get some idea, but...."

"Would it help to talk to the Thurmans?"

"I don't want to do that right now. Maybe later on."

"What did you think of the Bullards when you saw them in court?"

"I left with some very strong impressions."

"Tell me."

"Ross Bullard did kill Danny, but he's not nearly as malevolent as his father. Jules is a very sinister person."

"What about the woman?"

"She has no emotion invested in Jules or Ross, nor does she have any remorse for Danny's death. She's a sociopath."

"I knew she was cold, but I just thought she was aloof and had a superiority complex. It must have been a delightful marriage."

"There's no love there. She has no feelings for Jules, either, even though she's sleeping with him."

"How do you know that?"

"I've taken up enough of your time," she said and stood. "If you'll look at the web site on my card it has links to newspaper and magazine articles about my history with law enforcement in other jurisdictions. I've had some successes, some failures, but the messages I'm getting in this case are so strong it's not likely that I'm off base."

"What kind of fees do you charge for your services?"

"None. I don't do this for the money. My late father was a good businessman in addition to being a good heart surgeon, and I was his only heir. I will be in and out of Sunshine staying at the High Cotton until Ross Bullard goes to trial. Best way to reach me is to send a text to my cell. Even if you don't feel the need to talk to me again, I'll be back and forth between Houston and Sunshine until you put him away. I plan on being here for the whole trial, by the way."

"Thank you," I said and extended my hand.

She took my hand and pulled me into a brief hug. She cradled my hand between hers again.

"I will be thinking about you and Danny Thurman," she said. "I want to help in any way I can."

I closed the door behind Cheryl and sat down. It defied logic, but somehow I knew every single word she said was true. Even before I took a look at her web site, I knew Cheryl Diamond was the real deal.

Strange days.

CHAPTER TWENTY-TWO

Heeding Eddie Bordelon's advice, I waited until eleven to walk into Circuit Clerk Winston Moore's office. Eddie had told me in confidence that the Clerk never appeared in the office before ten, and on many days he didn't make it in until after eleven. I stopped at the front desk.

"Is Winston in?" I asked the young black girl who could not have been more than nineteen, maybe twenty.

"Yes, sir, Mr. Banks. Let me buzz him."

She picked up the phone and punched in the Clerk's number. Winston's private office was no more than twenty feet from the girl at the front desk. I heard Winston's desk phone buzz through his closed door.

"Mr. Banks is here to see you," the girl said into the phone.

Through the door I could hear Winston talking into his intercom but I wasn't able to make out what he said. It would have saved time and money if the young girl would talk to the Clerk through the door. I knew Winston could hear her. But I also knew Winston was big on protocol and liked having a secretary announce his visitors so he could let them cool their heels a bit before he opened his door.

"He'll be right with you," the girl said.

"How long have you been working here?"

"I just started this week."

There were chairs in the Clerk of Court's foyer, but I stood for a while, then walked a few steps to the civil suit register and studied the lawsuits that had been filed the last few days. The new litigation was unremarkable, mostly divorces which would inevitably result in a husband and wife attempting to make the same amount of money that had been supporting one household support two after the split. The prospects of success were not good. I did not know how young couples made it these days. I knew how much it cost Susan and me to live. With the low rate of pay for most jobs in Yaloquena, even with both parents working, how young parents coped was a mystery to me, especially if they had to pay for day care

"Mr. Moore will see you now," the girl said.

I paused for a second, reached in my inside pocket and pulled out one of my push cards.

"I know you're a voter," I told her, "and I would appreciate your consideration in November."

"Yes sir," she said taking the card after a moment's hesitation.

I continued smiling as I walked off, but I knew what her hesitation meant. I had seen it enough to know. It meant the voter knew about the election and was not supporting me.

"Have a seat, Mr. District Attorney," the Circuit Clerk said.

The Clerk left his office door open. I waited for a moment then stood and closed it. Winston wore gray slacks and a navy blue blazer, a crimson tie and matching handkerchief.

"This is a private conversation," I said, "just between you and me."

"All right. What's on your mind?"

"I saw a couple of your employees out and about last week while I was out campaigning. Both of them had bumper stickers for Eleanor on their cars."

"I can't control what they do in their personal lives."

"Theoretically that's correct," I said, "but I know you well enough to be certain that not a single one of your deputy clerks would have Eleanor's bumper sticker on her car or a sign for Eleanor in their yard if they didn't know for sure that you were okay with it."

I watched Winston squirm for a moment then come to terms with what he was about to say.

"I told my employees in a meeting last week to support whoever they wanted to in your race."

There had to be more to it than that. The normal instructions to courthouse employees would be "stay out of other people's politics." If Winston gave such permission to his employees, it was a significant breach of rural political etiquette. Winston and I were both well aware of the ramifications.

"I stayed out of your first race four years ago, Winston, and was fine with you going in unopposed this time. You and I have never had any differences. I've done a good job as District Attorney...,"

"That's a fact, Willie Mitchell. You have indeed."

"So I don't understand why you're letting this happen. People on the street see your people with those bumper stickers and they're going to assume you're with Eleanor, too."

"It hurts my heart to say this, Mr. D.A., but I am for Eleanor."

Winston Moore might not know much about civil procedure or the other protocols of his office set forth in the Mississippi statutes, but he was one hell of a popular politician. He had emceed events for every organization in Yaloquena County, and his endorsement carried a lot of weight. This was not good news for me.

"I've known Eleanor for quite some time" Winston said. "A couple of the women that work in this office are friends of hers."

"The young girl out front you just hired, I guess she's for Eleanor."

"She goes to Bobby Sanders' church. That's one thing you got going against you, D.A., Bobby's got a big congregation and getting bigger. He's out working for Eleanor full time and has most of his members talking her up."

I felt myself deflating as I sat across from Winston. The die was cast. There was nothing I could to change Winston's mind. It took some spine for the Clerk to own up to supporting Eleanor.

"Thanks for your honesty, Winston," I said, extending my hand. "All I ask is that you don't work too hard for her."

"I told her I ain't working against you, Willie Mitchell. I'm going to vote for Eleanor and so is my wife, but that's all I'm doing. I'm not going to get behind her in a big way. I told my people in that meeting they were free to do whatever they wanted in your election. That's the truth."

I nodded. He kept on.

"You know, most of my staff is black, and all women except for Eddie. I have to tell you the truth, all the women are voting for Eleanor."

"Is it a racial thing?"

"It is. The black folks that work up here in the courthouse and for that matter all over the county figure it's time to have a brother or sister in the D.A.'s office. They say it's our turn. It ain't about you or the job you done. They all know you're a good lawyer and done what you had to do with the cases that come before you."

I opened the door to leave.

"Don't take it personal, Willie Mitchell," Winston said sincerely. "It's just politics."

The meeting with Winston Moore took all the wind out of my sails. I had lunch at home with Susan. Even her chicken salad, the best in the world, had failed to make me feel better. Susan downplayed the significance of what the Circuit Clerk said. She said as long as Winston didn't get out and actively campaign for Eleanor it wouldn't make much difference. Susan reminded me campaigns have their highs and lows. Some days things looked great, other days bleak. I agreed, said she was right, and got in my truck for more campaigning.

I looked at my watch. It was one-thirty and hot as blazes. I drove slowly, thinking I might hand out cards to the merchants and their customers downtown. Popping into stores was a lazy way to catch voters—picking low-hanging fruit. The merchants, both black and white, were going to vote for me. My office collected their hot checks at no cost to them. We prosecuted shoplifters diligently and quickly. Most were under age, so their cases were heard in juvenile court.

I drove onto Main Streeet and stopped in front of a locally owned men's clothing store. Looking down the street, I counted no more than twenty cars and five pedestrians in two blocks. I kept the engine running as I looked through the window. There were no customers inside. I could see the owner Jim Dawson sitting in the back reading a newspaper. I draped my right hand over the steering wheel and slumped in my seat trying to muster the energy to go into the store. No luck.

I pulled out of the parking spot, not sure where I was going. I drifted on a southerly tack through the half-empty streets of Sunshine. My mind drifted back to Winston Moore. There was something uniquely unsettling about what Winston said. A savvy county-wide public official like Winston would not tell me he was voting for Eleanor unless he was fairly sure there would be no repercussions for his own political future. It meant Winston was confident Eleanor would beat me handily.

I blew off my afternoon plans to politick. I knew I wouldn't make a good impression on anyone. Playing hooky seemed like the thing to do. It had been a long time since I behaved irresponsibly. I continued to drive south slowly, no particular destination in mind. After a while I realized where I was headed. I picked up speed.

Twenty-five minutes later I stopped on the Iron Bridge. The MDOT bridge crew had finished shoring up the bridge supports with rip rap and concrete. The dragline and track hoe that helped uncover Danny's Rangers cap and Connie's blue sweater were gone. I stepped from my truck and walked to the railing to search for the spot where the crew had unearthed the evidence. I leaned over, my elbows on the rail. It was difficult to pick out the exact place because the hole had been covered over with a lot of additional rip rap.

After a moment I looked up. In the southern sky gigantic cumulus clouds boiled up toward the stratosphere in the afternoon heat. I heard a splash in the creek and turned.

In the shallow water below me, I saw a young albino deer with a small rack of atypical antlers. The deer seemed to spot me at the same time. We stared at one another, not moving. I was transfixed by the deer's pink eyes and bright white fur.

I had heard of albino white-tails, but never seen one. The antlers were undersized with two parallel downward tines on each side, another anomaly. I realized I was holding my breath. I exhaled slowly, trying to keep still. I felt a bead of sweat trickle down my forehead.

The deer lowered his head and drank from the creek. I would have sworn the pink eyes were still watching me, even as the deer filled his belly with water.

After a while, the deer raised his nose to the sky, winding. He seemed to take one last look at me, a long look, then turned and walked slowly away in the creek. I didn't move until the he was out of sight.

I pushed away from the rail and made my way back to the truck to return to Sunshine. As I drove away from the bridge, I thought about the odds against my seeing such a rare creature. In the context of what was going on with the election, the Ross Bullard trial, and the visit with Cheryl Diamond, I didn't know what to make of it all.

Stranger days.

CHAPTER TWENTY-THREE

J.D. Silver and I stood at our respective tables to address Judge Williams. While Silver made his point I turned and quickly surveyed the courtroom. Jules and Judy Bullard sat in the first row behind the rail on the defense side. Kitty Douglas sat across the center aisle from them behind Walton and me. Cheryl Diamond, dressed to the nines, was in the second row on our side. Bill Thurman in his fireman's uniform sat in the row behind Cheryl. There were several reporters and television crews, but no other spectators.

"It's Friday, last day of the month," J.D. Silver said to Judge Williams, "and if we're going to try this case during the court's jury term in October, I must have a more complete answer to questions thirteen and fourteen in my Motion for Bill of Particulars."

"Mr. Silver has all the information that we have, Your Honor." I gestured to Walton seated to my left. "Mr. Donaldson has worked with the Crime Lab and the Sheriff's Office and provided all documents, test results, physical evidence for inspection, everything the defense has asked for. Mr. Silver's real objective in traversing our answers is to reinforce his position on the *corpus delicti* issue."

"If I may be heard before you rule, Judge Williams? My question thirteen asks simply for information about how the victim allegedly died. When? Where? By what means? Was there a weapon? Cause of death? My alleged motive in asking for this vital information is irrelevant."

"You've made your argument, Mr. Silver," the Judge said. "I fully understand your position. We will have a separate hearing on the *corpus delicti* issue before trial. For today, I am ruling that the State's answer to thirteen and fourteen is sufficient for discovery purposes. His answer provides that Danny Thurman was abducted by the defendant at the defendant's home on the night of July 4 and thereafter the defendant caused his death and hid the boy's Texas Rangers hat, jeans, and Mrs. Thurman's blue sweater under the rocks at the Iron Bridge. Moreover, the State further states in its answer that on Friday July 27 Mr. Bullard left a note in which he refers to 'Danny' and 'the boy's body.' The State says this conclusively implicates your client in whatever happened to Danny Thurman. For the record, the Court is fully aware that Danny's body has not been recovered."

"With all due respect, Your Honor, this Court, in accepting the State's bald assertion that the victim suffered a violent death is assuming a fact for which there is no evidentiary foundation whatsoever. There's not one scintilla of proof that the victim is dead much less murdered. And until there is proof of death, there are several Mississippi Supreme Court cases that indicate that the alleged inculpatory note found in my client's house cannot be offered into evidence. Also, for the record we deny that the note is a confession or is inculpatory."

"There's no Mississippi Supreme Court case on point," I said.

"Move on to something else, Mr. Silver."

What happened next surprised me. Silver was an old pro, and had to know Judge Williams was going to rule in our favor. His reaction to the Judge's admonition was petulant. Silver plopped down in his chair, made a point of rustling papers near the microphone at his table, and fumed. Judge Williams glared at him.

"Mr. Silver?" Judge Williams said, her voice rising.

Silver got the message. He patted his sturdy silver helmet and whispered to Ross Bullard in the matching oak chair next to him. Ross was busy writing in his legal pad, oblivious to the arguments. I watched Ross interrupt his writing for a brief moment to listen to his lawyer, then right get back to his legal pad. Silver crossed his arms tightly across his chest and turned to glance at Jules and Judy Bullard sitting behind him. The old man nodded vigorously to Silver, encouraging him. Judy did not react. Helmet Head knew what he was doing. He was playing to the crowd, which in this case consisted only of Jules Bullard, the man bankrolling Silver's performance, and the media. Silver was doing his best to give the old buzzard his money's worth.

"What's next, Mr. Banks?" Judge Williams asked.

"I would like to file at this time the State's Notice of Intent to Seek the Death Penalty."

I placed a copy of the Notice that Walton had prepared on Silver's desk and gave the original to Eddie Bordelon. Silver grabbed the motion and stood, waiting for Walton to return from the Minute Clerk's desk.

"Objection to this filing, Your Honor. In order for the charge to be capital murder there must be proof of a murder."

"Your Honor," I said, my inflection making it clear I was as tired of Silver's broken record as the Judge was.

"Hold on, Mr. Banks" she said, extending her arm, palm toward me. "Overruled, Mr. Silver. The law requires the State to give you this notice. Mr. Donaldson is merely meeting the requirements of the death penalty statute."

Silver exhaled as loudly as Al Gore in a presidential debate. His microphone broadcast it throughout the courtroom. More drama for his benefactor behind him. From my many trials before Zelda, I knew Silver's antics were having the opposite effect of what Silver was trying to achieve. In her courtroom, Zelda Williams would not be intimidated.

"I am also filing this morning the State's Motion for Psychiatric Examination of the Defendant," I said.

Silver shot out of his chair. He started to object but before he said anything, he pressed his index finger against his pursed lips. I assumed Silver was trying to show the Judge that he was trying to moderate his behavior. It was all an act, and Silver was an excellent actor.

"This is outrageous," Silver finally said in a steady voice. "The State is not entitled to examine my client's mental state...."

"Unless Mr. Silver intends to assert any kind of defense based on insanity or diminished capacity in the guilt phase of the trial," I countered, "or if he intends to offer psychiatric testimony in the penalty phase of trial. It's all laid out in the motion. Mr. Silver has filed his own motion asking for a psychiatric examination. This is in the nature of a motion *in limine*, Your Honor."

"I have not entered a plea of not guilty by reason of insanity," Silver said, "nor do I presently intend to offer such testimony at any sentencing hearing. I hereby withdraw my Motion for a Psychiatric Examination that I previously filed. On further review, I don't feel it is necessary."

"Then we don't have a problem with this now," Judge Williams said calmly, "do we? Mr. Banks is giving you plenty of advance notice that if you call any witness to testify about your client's mental state he wants his expert to examine your client. He's entitled to do this, Mr. Silver. If you change your mind and decide to call a psychiatric witness, give the State enough notice so their psychiatrist can examine your client before trial."

I heard the courtroom door open behind me while Judge Williams ruled. When she finished, I turned to watch a strong-looking man in jeans, cowboy boots, a sport coat and tie walk in and take a seat in the second row behind Jules and Judy. The man was in his late forties or early fifties with dark hair, a thick mustache, and ruddy skin.

"All right, gentlemen," Judge Williams said, looking at her notes. "I believe we've disposed of all the issues relating to the discovery motions. Prior to trial, we need to schedule hearings on Mr. Silver's Motion for Change of Venue, Motion to Suppress the note and all evidence seized at the defendant's home pursuant to a search the night of July 27 and early morning hours of July 28, and...."

"Also my Motion to Exclude Evidence of Other Crimes," Silver said, and "my Brady Motion and Motion to Dismiss based on lack of *corpus delicti*."

"Right," she said. "With respect to Brady, there's no need for a hearing. Mr. Banks and Mr. Donaldson are under a continuing obligation to disclose to the defense any evidence of an exculpatory nature."

"That's the law, Your Honor," I said. "The State does not know of any evidence favorable to the defense at this time. If we become aware of any such evidence we will notify Mr. Silver immediately."

"You gentlemen consult your calendars," Judge Williams said, "and submit dates that are acceptable to both of you for the remaining pre-trial hearings. Mr. Banks knows my court schedule for the next several months, which days are set aside for criminal matters. Advise the Court which motions we can consolidate for hearing. Because the defense has asked for an expedited trial date, let's try to dispose of all motions by Friday, October 12. That will give you a week of trial preparation before we start picking the jury on October 22, the first day of my last criminal jury term for the year."

Silver and I thanked Judge Williams almost simultaneously.

"Court's adjourned," she said tapping her gavel.

She left the bench, walked down the three carpeted steps to the floor and exited the side door. I watched Silver pull Ross to his feet as the Judge walked by. As soon as the door closed, Ross plopped down and resumed writing on his pad. I turned and saw Bill Thurman leave.

"Bill's not happy again," I told Walton as he gathered our files.

"It's going to get worse," Walton said. "I'll talk to him again."

I gestured for Kitty to join me at the rail.

"You feeling better?" I asked her.

"Much," she said and coughed gently. "Dr. Clement put me on an antibiotic and told me to take it easy for a while."

"Good. Susan wants you to call her. Come meet Cheryl Diamond. She's the lady from Houston I told you about."

I motioned for Cheryl Diamond to join us.

"It's a pleasure to meet you," Cheryl said to Kitty.

"Excuse me, ladies," I said and rejoined Walton at the table.

"Who's the bulky guy in the coat and tie behind Judy Bullard?" I asked him.

Walton stopped stuffing files in his briefcase long enough to glance at the man in the second row.

"Not a clue."

"We need to find out."

Two deputies escorted Ross Bullard from the defense table. I kept my eyes on Cheryl Diamond. She stopped talking to Kitty and stared at Ross as he shuffled by. Walton and I followed Ross and the deputies out of the courtroom to the jail elevator. Lee Jones was in the hallway watching his men escort Ross. We walked over to the Sheriff.

"Did you see the stocky guy in the coat and tie in the courtroom?" I asked the Sheriff.

"Sure did. He stopped by my office this morning on his way to the courtroom, introduced himself and gave me his business card."

Lee gave me the man's card.

"Phil Myers," I read aloud. "Private investigator from Memphis." I gave the card back to Lee. "I need a copy of this."

"No problem. After the guy left my office I called the Shelby County Sheriff," Lee said. "He and I sat on a panel at a National Sheriff's Association meeting in Atlanta last year. He's a nice fellow. Anyway, I asked the Sheriff if he knew anything about Myers. He told me Phil Myers used to be with the Memphis Police Department and now does all of J.D. Silver's investigative work. The Sheriff said Myers was the chief homicide detective for Memphis P.D. when he retired."

"Did the Sheriff say he was good?" Walton asked.

"No," Lee said. "What the Sheriff said was Phil Myers is the best homicide detective in the entire state of Tennessee."

CHAPTER TWENTY-FOUR

I left Lee and Walton in the hallway. Alone in my office, clearing end-of-the-week loose ends, I thought about making some calls to lawyer friends in Memphis to ask them what they knew about Phil Myers. I checked the time— almost five o'clock on a Friday afternoon. I had two chances of catching any attorney in his office: slim and none. I left my desk and walked to the window to see if the firemen were shooting hoops. Blue smoke rose from their giant cast iron barbecue grill under a big hackberry tree behind the station, but no firemen were in sight. It was the end of a busy week and I was worn out. I heard someone whisper "Willie Mitchell." I turned and saw Cheryl Diamond.

"I'm sorry to just walk in Willie Mitchell but there was no one at the reception desk," she said. "I'm leaving for Houston tomorrow and I just wanted to speak before I left."

"Come in," I said and walked her to a chair. "The ladies up front have already gone for the day."

Instead of sitting behind my desk, I took the chair next to her.

"I know you're tired," she said and patted my arm.

"What did you think of Mr. Silver's performance this afternoon?"

"Oh, he's very dramatic, and quite a showman, but it's clear to me he's just in this for the money. He doesn't care about the Bullards at all."

"He's a formidable defense attorney."

"Oh, I think he's met his match," she said with a big smile.

"Do you have plans for the evening?"

"Not really."

"Would you join Susan and me in our home for a quiet dinner?"

"That would be lovely, but I don't want to intrude."

"You wouldn't be. There's one condition: I want to talk about something other than this trial or the election."

"Well, if you think it's all right."

I called Susan and talked to her about Cheryl coming over.

"What time?" Cheryl asked.

"How about right now? Susan said she'd love to meet you. Dinner is nothing fancy, just some grilled chicken. You can follow me there."

"Wonderful. I'll be in the parking lot."

"It'll be cocktail hour when we get to the house. Does the Seer's Union allow you to consume alcohol?"

"The rules allow a little white wine every now and then."

A few minutes later I waved at Cheryl to follow me. She drove a Town Car, solid white. It was an older model with a long, wide wheel base, a real land yacht that Lincoln stopped making in the nineties. In two minutes we pulled into the circular drive at my house.

"That's a big ride you have there, Cheryl.

"It's the smoothest riding automobile ever built. It's my road car. When I drive in Houston I have a small Lexus I zip around in. This Town Car is a 1997, the last model year. I'll drive it until the wheels fall off.

Susan walked onto the front porch to greet us.

"I am so glad you're joining us," she said to Cheryl. "Willie Mitchell has told me all about your visit with him in his office last week."

"I'm sorry for such short notice. It's very nice of you."

"The pleasure is ours, Cheryl," I said to her as I held open the front door for the ladies to enter.

It was too hot to sit on the sun porch, so Susan directed us to the living room, the most comfortable room in the house. I led Cheryl to a wing back chair.

"I'll bring out something to nibble on," Susan said.

"Let me do it. You ladies get to know one another."

I walked into the kitchen. Ina was arranging crackers on a cheese tray. I picked up the bowl of Susan's corn dip surrounded by Frito's Scoops, brought it to the ladies and took drink orders.

Back in the kitchen I fixed a Tito's vodka and tonic for Susan, poured a glass of Pinot Grigio for Cheryl, and opened a Beck's for me. Ina was still arranging the crackers. She was very slow these days but it didn't matter. She had worked for my parents then Susan and me for over forty years. She was a fixture in our home, though she only came when she felt up to it. Susan paid her the same every week regardless of how much she worked. I put the drinks on a tray.

"I'd like you to meet our guest," I said to Ina.

"I'll be there directly."

I delivered the drinks. Ina followed shortly and placed the cheese tray on the coffee table next to the corn dip.

"Ina, this is Cheryl Diamond from Houston."

Cheryl stood up and extended her hand. Ina gradually did the same and studied Cheryl a moment.

"Pleased to meet you," Ina said and turned to Susan. "I'll be headed on home now unless you need me."

"Thanks for coming today," Susan said.

Ina took one last look at Cheryl and walked back to the kitchen. After a minute, I heard the kitchen door close.

"Does she drive?" Cheryl asked.

"She does," Susan said, "and is still a careful driver. It won't be long though. She told me her vision is getting to the point where she's going to have to give it up."

"She's lived through a lot," Cheryl said.

Susan and I nodded. Ina and her late husband John worked hard all their lives and were good citizens, but her children, grandchildren, and now great-grandchildren were in and out of trouble, unable to stay in school or stick with a job. When she asked me to help them out of a jam over the years I did, but I never understood how such fine parents could produce such rudderless offspring.

"You have some lovely pieces of furniture," Cheryl said.

"Willie Mitchell's parents collected English antiques, so they get the credit for most of the furniture in the house."

"How long have you lived in Houston?" I asked.

"All my life. My father came to Houston for medical school and never left. He did a residency in cardiovascular surgery and caught the attention of the surgeons who pioneered the first heart transplant procedures in the United States. He went to work for their group after his residency and practiced until he died. He was a wonderful man."

"Is your mother still alive?" Susan asked.

"No."

"I went to your website," Susan said. "I read about the big cases you've worked on. Some of the stories of what you've done are really amazing."

"Thank you, but I've had some disappointments, too. Sometimes things don't click and I'm not much help to law enforcement."

"I think it's a wonderful gift," Susan said.

"Willie Mitchell has it," Cheryl said.

"He has something," Susan said. "His mother did, too."

"Now girls," I said, "let's not get carried away."

"It's true," Cheryl said, "I knew it the first time I met you. You've never developed it. It's like having the natural ability to play for the Astros but never picking up a bat or a glove your entire life."

"Which way are you driving home tomorrow?" I said.

"I stay on the interstates. I'll take I-55 then the Baton Rouge exit and I-10 the rest of the way home."

"I bet that Town Car rides nicely on the interstates."

"It's like floating on a cloud," Cheryl said.

"You are coming back, right?" Susan asked.

"Absolutely." Cheryl smiled like an imp and leaned toward Susan. "I have an appointment with my hairdresser and I cannot miss it. The man is an artist, and is in such demand rescheduling is getting harder and harder."

I walked to the kitchen to refill glasses.

"Thank you so much for helping us in this case," I heard Susan say. "I can tell Willie Mitchell really appreciates you."

"I admire your husband. There's a lot of substance to him."

"And I'm afraid most people don't recognize it."

"Those that count do."

I delivered round two and sat down. Cheryl's already pink cheeks had become rosier, her giggles more frequent.

"Tell me about your mother," I said.

"Oh, there's nothing to say, really."

"I think there is. You told me to work on my abilities."

"I never knew my biological parents. When I was in my thirties I began the legal process of opening my sealed adoption records in the Harris County courthouse, but never went through with it."

"Why not?" I asked.

"Willie Mitchell?" Susan said.

"No, it's all right, Susan. I haven't talked about this in a long time," Cheryl said, taking a sip of wine and placing her glass on the table. "Early in the process, when I was walking into the records office at the courthouse with my attorney I had an overwhelming feeling that it was the wrong thing to do. Something was telling me in no uncertain terms to leave it alone, that finding my natural parents would be destructive. I told the lawyer to withdraw the petition and I've never looked back on the decision."

"I've read some horror stories about children finding their birth mother then wishing they never had," Susan said.

"I try to use my gifts for good. My biological parents were enemies of the good. You may wonder how I know that. I don't know, but I am certain it is true."

Cheryl took a sip of wine and leaned back.

"What about your adoptive parents?" I asked.

"My mother was Catherine DeLaune, from an old Houston family with good social connections. My father Roger's parents were secular Jews from Boston. He had never practiced Judaism, so joining the Presbyterian Church was no problem for him. His cardiovascular surgery group was incredibly prosperous and he made some very good real estate investments ahead of population growth around Houston. Roger and Catherine were in the thick of the Houston social scene, but my mother had a problem that became an obsession: she was barren.

"Five years after they married they adopted me as a newborn. I had a very happy early childhood thanks to my father. He was kind and loving. My mother was not a warm person, and when I was six, I overheard her complaining to Roger that the fertility doctor he sent her to was a quack. She said Roger better find her a decent doctor because she was not about to go through the adoption process again for fear that they would get "another Cheryl."

"Oh, my God," Susan said. "You must have been hurt terribly."

"I was, but I hid my feelings and decided to be a perfect child from then on. I was determined to win her over."

"Did you know at that age you could sense things others couldn't?" I asked. "When did that start?"

"Mother took great pride in her roses, and I began working with her in the garden, learning and helping. One afternoon I was pulling weeds by myself, I stuck a rose thorn deep into my finger. It was a terrible pain that seemed to settle in my head. I lay on the ground between the roses and closed my eyes, hoping my head would stop hurting. It did, but it was replaced by a vision of my mother in maternity dress, her stomach swollen.

"I was seven years old and was so excited I ran and hugged my mother when she got home from shopping. I told her she would be having a baby soon, that I was so happy for her."

"What did she say?" Susan said.

"She slapped me," Cheryl said, "and told me I was a wicked child. She sent me to my room for the rest of the day."

"That was your first experience with your ability?" I asked.

"Yes. A few months later my father told me mother was expecting. I was thrilled, but my mother still kept me at arms length. She thought I was a strange creature, something to be avoided like a snake slithering through her roses. By that time I think my mother was afraid of me."

"So you have a sibling," Susan said. "Was it a boy or girl?"

"It was a boy, stillborn."

"Oh, I'm sorry," Susan said. "Let's talk about something else."

"It's up to Cheryl," I said. "This might be helpful to her."

She looked at me and smiled.

"I haven't talked about this for so many years," Cheryl said. "It does relieve me to share it, if you don't mind."

"Please go on," I said.

"When my mother was seven months along, I awoke one morning terrified. I was convinced the baby would not survive. I didn't dare tell my mother, but when father and I rode to get an ice cream cone one Saturday afternoon, I told him I was worried about the new baby and we should pray the baby would be all right. He said mother would deliver in

Houston's finest hospital with the best medical care in the world and that everything would be fine.

"Two months later, the little boy mother carried to term was delivered dead, strangled on his umbilical cord. Even worse, the rushed delivery and attempts to save the child irreparably damaged her so that she would never again conceive. When mother came home from the hospital, she was inconsolable. Even in her depressed state, she made it clear she wanted nothing to do with me. My father told me he never shared my premonition with mother. He tried to make up for her aversion to me by spending as much time as he could with me. He told me he believed I had the ability to "see" things, but cautioned me to never mention my visions to anyone if I wanted a normal life.

"My father was everything to me, and I did what he said. Two years later, when I was nine, I had a vision of a boy drowning in a swimming pool but I kept it to myself. A week later a friend had a swimming birthday party for our class and one of our classmates, Josh Plover, broke his neck diving into the pool and drowned."

"Oh, Cheryl," Susan said.

I picked up Cheryl's wine glass and took it to the kitchen. Listening to Cheryl's story was mesmerizing and I didn't want her to stop. I quickly filled her glass and returned to the living room. *In vino veritas.*

"I convinced myself my father's advice was correct and that my friends would have thought I was some kind of freak if they had known. As I grew older, my power to sense things grew much stronger and I welcomed the visions, cultivating them in my own private world. Mother treated me like a tenant in our home, but my father's love expanded to fill the void. When I was seventeen, he bought me a red Mustang convertible. I had lots of friends and suitors."

"I bet you were a pretty young girl," Susan said.

"You still are," I said to Cheryl.

"Oh, Willie Mitchell. Thank you for saying so, but I know...."

"None of us look like we did at seventeen," Susan said.

"I graduated from SMU with honors. I dated and partied like every coed except for the days I had my visions, which by that time were coming more often. Some were dream-like sequences I couldn't understand. The most jarring were the ones that seemed so real they frightened me, like watching a scary movie. Some involved people and places I didn't know. I never told anyone, not even my father.

"The summer after I graduated, I was scheduled to tour Europe with a group from SMU. A week before departure, my parents were hosting their supper club when mother suffered a fatal brain aneurysm. I cancelled my trip and stayed in Houston to be with my father. After a few months, he thanked me for supporting him during his mourning and encouraged me to get on with my life. He knew I was getting serious about a promising young Houston lawyer I met at a summer party and by Christmas my young man and I were engaged. Before the wedding, my father encouraged me to keep my visions secret, even from my husband.

"We had a wonderful society wedding and I became adept at suppressing my gift. After a year of marriage, my visions stopped altogether. Being normal was just fine with me, and we began to talk about starting a family. My husband was ambitious, and said he was being considered for partnership in his firm and thought we should wait until it happened because of the financial security it would provide. I thought he was wise, so I lived the happy life of a young Houston socialite for the next year. We went to all the right parties and became friends with so many young couples. The day before I got the call, I remember having lunch with my father at his country club. I told him I had never been happier. He beamed and hugged me tightly, whispering that I deserved all the joy that life could bring.

"I remember the day like it was yesterday. I had won a hard-fought doubles tennis match with friends and was about to start dinner when the phone in my kitchen rang. It was a woman. I remember her exact words: 'Your husband is in love with me,' the woman said. 'We started seeing each other when you were engaged and we've made love at least once a week since you've been married. He's afraid to tell you, so I will. He knows I'm making this call. He wants a divorce.'

"I screamed and said she was lying. She said it was true, that it was the reason my husband wouldn't have a child with me.

"I fainted and woke up a few minutes later on the kitchen floor. I was still sobbing when I called my husband to tell him what the awful woman said. He was quiet a moment, and stammered when he began to speak. Right then, I knew everything the woman said was true.

"I moved back in with my father, thankful I wasn't pregnant. He put me together with his personal attorney, who referred me to the best divorce attorney in Houston. My husband was in a fever to marry his girl friend, so the split was uncontested. There was no property to divide and I didn't need alimony. By that time father was a very wealthy man.

"Gradually, I withdrew from the society carousel and nurtured my abilities, reopening neural passageways grown dormant during the marriage. After a while, the visions and sensations came back stronger than ever. I know now it had been a mistake to shut them out. My father's advice was well-intentioned and I thought he was right, that I should ignore my gift in the name of normalcy. If I hadn't suppressed it, I would have known what my husband was up to and I would have recognized his lack of character before we married. Denying my abilities was unnatural; the results disastrous."

"You never re-married?" Susan asked.

"No. I dated other men, but never the right one."

She looked at me.

"My goodness," she said, "I've been talking so much I've overstayed my welcome I'm sure."

"To the contrary," I said, "I don't know when I've enjoyed a conversation more. I'll put the chicken on the grill. It won't take fifteen minutes."

"And I'll get everything together in the kitchen," Susan said.

"Let me help you Susan," Cheryl said.

In a few minutes I stood outside waiting for the grill to heat up, thinking about Cheryl's willful suppression of her authenticity during her marriage. She paid a high price for her dishonesty. I knew at my core I didn't want to win the election. I wondered what price I would pay for my own deception.

The three of us polished off the Pinot Grigio with dinner and Cheryl said it was time for her to go. She had drunk two-thirds of the bottle by herself, so I insisted on driving her home.

"Besides," I said, "I want to drive your Town Car."

Susan offered to follow but I told her I would walk home. It was only a few blocks, a ten minute stroll. I opened the passenger door for Cheryl and started the engine.

"Quiet for a fifteen-year-old car."

"Isn't it wonderful?" Cheryl said, still in the Pinot glow.

"Tell me about waking up in Houston on July 4," I said.

"You didn't want to ask me in front of Susan, did you?" she asked, looking directly at me. "I don't blame you."

"You said you had been asleep and ...."

"I bolted upright in my bed. It was about midnight and I knew something bad had happened."

"Where do you live in Houston?"

"In an older neighborhood not far from Rice. I turned on my bedside lamp because it scared me so. There was this man in my vision that night," she said, her eyes closed, concentrating, "a very primitive man with long black hair. I saw him dancing bare-chested around a fire, bending and hopping on one foot then the other. He stopped, spread his legs, bent over and popped his neck, slinging his hair in circles and figure eights over the fire. I couldn't see his face at first. I looked away from the fire and saw part of him in the corner of my eye. When I turned back I saw his face. It wasn't human. He had the head of a reptile, with black eyes and a wide, sinister grin. His bright red tongue was forked and moved in and out between long sharp teeth. It scared me to death."

"What did you think it meant?"

"I didn't know exactly, but I was certain something really bad had happened to someone. When I saw the article in the Houston Chronicle the next day about Danny Thurman disappearing I knew the creature I saw had something to do with it."

I didn't say anything.

"I know it all sounds so strange."

"Surely it's symbolic. The reptile man represents something."

"No. He's not a symbol. He's real and has something to do with Danny," she said and paused. "This thing of mine is kind of like the internet," she said. "You know how information from around the world pops up right on your computer or phone in an instant. To me, that's every bit as magical as my ability. The images come to me from somewhere out there in the cosmic ether that connects us all. Don't make fun of me, but I think of it as the outernet. I've never told anyone else that," she said, looking into my eyes.

I parked on the concrete pad for guest vehicles at the High Cotton. I gave Cheryl her keys when I opened the passenger door.

"I hate for you to have to walk back," she said.

"Don't. It's no big deal. I'll be home in a few minutes."

"Well, thank you for a lovely evening. I hope it wasn't too dismal for you and Susan."

"*Au contraire,*" I said and kissed the back of her hand. "It's been a pleasure. I'm not sure how the cosmic elements coalesced to get you here for Danny Thurman, but I know you're doing a very good thing."

She took a deep breath and smiled.

"You don't know how good it makes me feel to hear you say that." She paused. "Would you mind if I said one more thing?"

"Please."

"I knew you were an old soul the moment we met. I've been thinking about it and watching you in court today it came to me as clear as a bell."

"I'm listening."

"You are the Avenger of Blood. You've been around a very long time. Look it up. What do they say? Google it?"

"I know what it means."

"Of course you do, Willie Mitchell," she said and paused a moment. "Your energy is very protective. It makes me feel secure."

She kissed me on the cheek and said, "Thank you."

"Good night, Cheryl."

I waited until she was safely inside and walked home thinking about what she said.

CHAPTER TWENTY-FIVE

I finished my coffee watching The Weather Channel, retied my running shoes and turned on my iPod. I walked out the kitchen door, down the wooden steps and took off running. My Sauconys crunched the pea gravel in the driveway drowning out Mick Jagger's *Sympathy for the Devil* until I reached the pavement. It was earlier than usual, about five-fifteen, and dark, no hint of dawn yet on the eastern horizon.

I didn't sleep worth a damn. I did a search for Avenger of Blood as soon as I got home and spent an hour reading. Much of it I had read before. I fell asleep about ten, but woke up for my first bathroom trip about one a.m. and had trouble getting back to sleep, highly unusual for me. I put the search results out of my head and began thinking about what kind of havoc Phil Myers might wreak on the case. Unusual homicides were *de rigueur* in Memphis, a city perennially vying for the title of "Murder Capital of the U.S." Myers had probably seen more homicides in his career in Memphis than all the law enforcement professionals in north Mississippi combined. Being promoted to chief homicide detective was a major accomplishment in Memphis. It meant he had political and people skills to go along with his ability as a cop, which meant he would be an impressive witness. Even if he didn't testify, he was a formidable addition to Helmet Head's defense team.

I decided while drinking my coffee I would deviate from my normal route. Instead of crossing the four-lane and heading into the country, I wanted to run in town because there were some things wanted to check out before anyone was stirring.

It was the first day of September but there was no hint of a break from the summer's heat and humidity. According to the Weather Channel it was supposed to reach a hundred by three o'clock. I slowed down when I reached the asphalt covering Whitley Drive.

I stopped in front of Ross Bullard's house and pulled out my ear buds. Sweat dripped from my head and hands. There were no lights on. I walked toward the house in the driveway and checked the carport. No vehicles. I peeked through the plate glass window, my hands cupped around my eyes. There were no lights inside, no sign of life.

I put in my ear buds and trotted the short distance to Bill and Connie Thurman's home across the street and three houses down from Ross Bullard. The front drapes were open. I turned off my iPod when I saw Bill Thurman in the window, sitting in his La-Z-Boy watching something on television.

I moved close enough to see what was on Bill's T.V. It was a homemade video of a little kids' tee-ball game. *Damn.* Bill was watching Danny play tee-ball. My sorrow segued into dread when I saw at least a half-dozen long-necked beer bottles on the T.V. tray next to Bill. I watched Bill remove another beer from a small ice chest on the floor. He twisted the cap and threw it across the room, took a long pull from the amber bottle, then another. He turned up the bottle and drained the rest. Bill wiped his upper lip with his sleeve and sat the bottle on the T.V. tray with the other dead soldiers.

Standing on Bill's lawn in the darkness, I didn't know what I would do if something happened to Jake or Scott, but I hoped I wouldn't be knocking back a beer at five-thirty on a Saturday morning. Then again, losing Beau in the hunting accident almost killed Jimmy Gray, sending him into a multi-year depression exacerbated by heavy drinking every day until his wife Martha and I teamed up to pull him out of it.

"No telling," I mumbled as I took off running, backtracking to my next destination. Given the nature of Jake's activities, I decided I better give it some thought.

◆❖◆

That afternoon at the country club Jimmy Gray drove the cart toward the first tee. I was sharing the results of my detective work.

"I'm positive Ross's house was empty this morning, and then I saw Judy's BMW in old man Bullard's garage," I told him.

"Well, aren't you the little peeping Tom? I could have told you Jules was banging her. Has been for a while."

That ticked me off.

"How'd you know that? Why didn't you tell me?"

"Relax," Jimmy Gray said chuckling. "I only found out yesterday. The lady that cleans house for Jules is good friends with Ruthie. When Ruthie came to work she told Martha what Bullard's cleaning lady said."

"Is Ruthie sure?"

"Martha says housekeepers know everything about what goes on in the houses they tend to. They do the sheets, the bathroom, empty the trash. They know what you're up to, how much sex you're having, how much you're drinking."

"Damn. Screwing her father-in-law. How could Judy do that?"

"Same way she could marry Ross. It's all about the money. Jules has accumulated a lot of it in the course of a lifetime of beating his customers out of their assets. I'm sure Judy's telling people she's afraid to stay at home by herself with all that's going on with Bill Thurman. Some folks are stupid enough to believe that, especially the ones that don't know Jules like I do. He'd screw a snake if someone would hold the damn thing's head."

"Guess what else I saw at Jules' house?"

"No telling."

"He's got an Eleanor Bernstein sign in his yard."

"After all the land he's taken from black people in this county? That's rich. In a perfect world, that ought to win you some votes in the black community. You know he's the only banker I know who loved the Community Reinvestment Act. He saw it as an opportunity to make loans to people who weren't qualified. When they defaulted he seized their land and bought it in at the Sheriff's sale. If it was an undivided interest, he'd file a partition suit and beat the rest of the owners out of their part, too. Another *fubar* program courtesy of the federal government. It had the opposite effect from what was intended."

We arrived at the first tee box the same time as our third, former Congressman Buddy Wade. Buddy was riding solo in another cart.

"Damn," Buddy Wade said, "what pissed you guys off?"

Buddy must have noticed we weren't as jovial as usual.

"Nothing," I growled.

"When big'un here called me," Buddy Wade said pointing to Jimmy Gray, "he said no talking about politics or murder trials. We're supposed to help the candidate get some R & R out here this afternoon. At least that was the plan. Has something changed?"

"Not a thing," Jimmy said grabbing three Coors Lights from his ice chest on the back of the cart, handing one to Buddy and one to me. "Let's concentrate on golf. Dollar skins is the match. Unless your game has improved a lot, Congressman, I predict you're going to be throwing this party. Lead the way."

"All I can lose is eighteen dollars," Buddy said. "As long as oil stays above fifty dollars a barrel, I can afford it."

"It closed at one-oh-two yesterday," I said.

"Then I should be fine," Buddy said with a big grin.

Jimmy Gray took a long pull on his beer and watched Buddy swing two clubs to warm up. Buddy tossed one toward the cart, teed up his ball and prepared to hit his drive.

"You're swinging like you're sore," Jimmy said.

"I'm stiff every place but one," Buddy said.

I laughed out loud.

"Now, that's more like it, Mr. D.A.," Buddy said. "You look so much better when you're smiling."

Buddy hit his drive right down the middle.

"Well, damn," Jimmy said, "cut off my legs and call me Shorty. You been practicing."

"Hope you boys brought your wallets," Buddy said.

CHAPTER TWENTY-SIX

Walton set up a meeting for eleven in my office with Deputy Big Boy Carter after running into him in the Sheriff's office Saturday morning. Big Boy told Walton he thought we ought to know what Ross Bullard was up to in his cell.

Big Boy was the chief jailer for Sheriff Jones. He had been a deputy for five years, most of those as a jailer. Lee told me Big Boy had turned into a top hand upstairs. Before he and his wife, Takisha Carter *nee* Berry, were married Takisha was arrested for shoplifting at the Dollar General next to Big Al Anderson's Jitney Mart on the highway. She was only eighteen, but had three children and an extensive shoplifting record as a juvenile, and Lee wanted me to help make an example of Takisha to stem the rampant theft in local stores. To say it blew up in our face is an understatement. It led to a boycott, a riot, and two homicides. There was a happy ending for Takisha. She married Big Boy, the jailer, and later went to work for the state child support office in Sunshine, working on a daily basis with my non-support staff. She even started a trailer park where young unmarried mothers could start out renting then eventually own their mobile homes. She and Big Boy lived on site and provided security for the single moms.

"Morning, Mr. Banks," Big Boy said when he walked in with Walton. He was 6'4" and weighed about 260 pounds. His big hand enveloped mine when we shook, but his grip was surprisingly gentle. Big Boy folded and wedged himself into one of the oak chairs across from me. Walton sat in the other, looking like a child next to Big Boy.

"Big Boy," I said, "please tell me your first name. I've known you since you went to work for the Sheriff and if I knew it I've forgotten."

"Amos, Mr. Banks. Amos Alonzo Carter. I'd rather you call me Big Boy. That's the way my payroll checks are made out. I'm thinking of changing it legally."

"Save your money," I said. "What can you tell us about Ross?"

"That's one strange man, Mr. Banks. I just felt like you and Mr. Walton should know what all he's doing up there."

"Before you start," Walton said to him, then turned to me, "I've already made sure Big Boy hasn't questioned Bullard about the case or initiated any kind of conversation about the charges."

"Good," I said, "and if you should ever have to give a statement about any of this, we want you to be able to truthfully say neither this office nor the Sheriff's office asked you to eavesdrop or gather information from Ross."

"Yes, sir. I know the rules. The thing is that one-man cell he's in is a lonely place to live. He don't see anybody all day and a lot of times he's stopping me when I walk by just to say something, anything to see or talk to another human. His daddy ain't been up there yet and his wife's only been once and that was the first week. His lawyer don't talk to him except on days when there's a hearing."

"Maybe he shouldn't have killed Danny Thurman," Walton said.

"Oh, you right, but I try to treat everyone up there as fair as I can, no matter what they might have done."

"You have to," I said, "and I think that's the way you should run the jail. No need to be mean to the people up there. What's Ross done that you want to tell us about?"

"For one thing, he started doing pushups the first week he was there. I don't mean a few either. I mean every couple of hours seven days a week he's on that floor. He told me he was up to a hundred without stopping and was working on getting up to two hundred in a set. He does a few reps one-handed. Two weeks ago he added situps, knee bends, and other exercises, some I ain't never seen before. When he first came up there he was real slight. Now he's built up muscles like you cain't believe. He's eating everything we give him and then he buys more from the canteen and his wife sends him those supplement drinks."

"Like Ensure?" Walton asked.

"That's it."

"Watching him in court I've noticed how much he's built himself up in the five weeks he's been upstairs," Walton said.

"And he's got clothes on when you see him," Big Boy said. "He spends all day in his cell with no shirt on and just his shorts. Regular dress rules don't apply to him in isolation."

"Does he write like he does in court?" I asked.

"If he ain't doing his workouts or sleeping he's writing on those yellow tablets."

"Do you know what he's writing?" Walton asked.

"No, sir, but I hear him talking to himself a lot, mostly about his daddy." Big Boy looked around as if to make sure we were alone. "One day he stopped me. Said his daddy was sleeping with his wife. But then he said he didn't care one way or the other. He said his old man was getting more from her than he ever did."

"Not a happy family," I said.

"Ross told me his daddy drove his mother to kill herself when he was just three years old."

"That's true, about the suicide," Walton said. "I don't know about the cause, I mean, but Jules basically raised Ross by himself.

"He said the old man used to like hookers and sometimes brought them home late at night when Ross was a boy."

Walton took notes but I just listened. Every piece of information we learned about the Bullard family was troubling, but nothing Big Boy said would be relevant at trial, since we were certain Helmet Head would not put him on the witness stand.

"This is all good information," I said, "and I want you to continue to observe him, but it's important you don't ask him any questions or try to get any statements out of him. Keep us informed about the things he volunteers."

"By the way, Mr. Banks," Big Boy said, "both me and Takisha doing our best to get you some votes. We want you re-elected."

"I appreciate that," I said, "but I bet your preacher Bobby Sanders probably doesn't like it one bit."

"We don't go there anymore," he said. "We left two years ago."

"Eleanor Bernstein represented Takisha in the Dollar General shoplifting charge," Walton said. "She got her a decent deal."

"Yeah, she did, but Takisha never liked her all that much. Takisha tells me something ain't right with Eleanor."

"What did she mean by that?" I asked.

"I don't know. She didn't say."

"Keep us posted on what's going on upstairs," I said.

"One last thing, Mr. Banks," Big Boy said and stood up to leave. "Sometimes I hear him singing real low, mostly at night, kind of like a chant you hear in church. It's not any language I've ever heard. I asked him one time what he was singing in there and he said it was a song the Indians around here used in burial ceremonies a long time ago."

"He might be making that up," Walton said.

"May be," Big Boy said, "but it sounds real enough to me."

CHAPTER TWENTY-SEVEN

Two days later I was almost through with my run at six-thirty a.m., gliding easily through downtown Sunshine when I saw strobes flashing on two Sheriff's cruisers on the broad sidewalk in front of the main branch of First Savings Bank. As I neared the bank, I saw Bill Thurman face down on the concrete, two of the four deputies at the scene kneeling next to him.

I called out to make sure I didn't surprise the officers. I recognized deputy Sammy Roberts when he turned to wave to me.

"What happened?" I said.

"Bank alarm went off when Bill Thurman here tried to shoot his way through the front glass," Sammy said. "We were at the courthouse and got here in little over a minute. Bill was taking aim at the glass again when we pulled up."

"Did he resist?"

"No," Sammy said. "When he saw us he laid the gun on the sidewalk next to him and raised his hands."

"You talk to him?"

"More or less. He's so drunk he can barely stand. We laid him down on the concrete for his own safety."

I walked over to Bill and knelt beside him. His hands were cuffed behind his back.

"Help me sit him up," I said to the deputies.

We rolled Bill onto his back and pushed him to a sitting position. His face was bright red and his eyes out of focus. He reeked of alcohol and sweat. One side of his reddish-brown beard was speckled with dirt.

"Bill," I said lightly slapping his cheek, trying to get him to concentrate, "it's Willie Mitchell."

He arched his eyebrows in surprise and took a deep breath. For a moment, his eyes focused and he seemed to smile when he recognized me. The moment passed quickly and Bill's big head dropped onto his chest. The two deputies strained to hold him up.

"What do you want me to do?" Sammy asked.

"I don't think you have any choice."

"We all know what he's going through. He didn't hurt anyone."

"Take him to the courthouse and put him in the holding cell. I'll call Jules Bullard and see if he wants to press charges. Put his gun in the evidence locker until we sort this out."

"I was planning on giving the gun to the Sheriff."

"That's fine. Fill Lee in and I'll come in after a while."

I watched the deputies struggle to get Bill off the concrete and into the patrol unit and I took off running for home. I hadn't gone a hundred paces when a black Cadillac with dark tinted windows raced past me. I turned and hustled back to the bank to run interference for the deputies and Bill. There was only one black Cadillac like it in town and it belonged to Jules Bullard. I ran faster and stopped next to Jules in time to hear him yelling at Sammy Roberts.

"Do you know how much it costs to replace that front glass?" he said as he moved closer to the deputy, much too close for comfort.

Sammy Roberts was ex-military, like several of Lee's deputies. His arms were crossed, his muscles tense under his dark brown skin. Jules was in his bathrobe. I felt sorry for Sammy having to endure Jules' rant and the stench from Jules' mouth. I took Jules lightly by the arm and moved him away from Sammy. Jules looked at me as if I had struck him. He transferred his wrath to me.

"I want him in jail," Jules blurted, "and I want him terminated from the fire department."

"Hold on a minute, Mr. Bullard," I said, trying to keep my distance. "I don't blame you and I'll tell the Sheriff to throw the book at Bill Thurman if that's what you want me to do. He's guilty for sure. But before we start the criminal process against Bill, I want you to talk to J.D. Silver. Most of the people in this town are sympathetic to Bill and Connie right now, and they understand what he's going through. Considering what the Grand Jury charged Ross with doing to Danny Thurman, I'm not sure you want to give the folks in Sunshine another reason to be upset with the Bullard family just now."

Jules stepped back and thought a second. He realized I might have a very good point.

"I'm sure Lee and I can get Bill to pay for the replacement of your glass, no matter what it costs," I added. "You won't be out a dime and if you and Mr. Silver decide to accept full restitution in lieu of charging Bill, I think it would do you some good with the townspeople."

"You're not trying this case here. Silver told me he's filing to get it moved somewhere Ross can get a fair trial."

"Change of venue is hard to get in front of Judge Williams. She doesn't like to travel, and even with all the publicity, the case law puts a heavy burden on J.D. Silver to prove that the local jury venire is prejudiced against Ross."

Jules harrumphed and walked to his car. Over his shoulder, he yelled that J.D. Silver would be calling me.

"Man's got a serious oral hygiene situation," Sammy said. "We'll hold Bill without charging him for now."

"I'll be there as soon as I clean up," I said. "Thanks."

I peeked in the holding cell later that morning when I arrived at the courthouse. Bill was sleeping it off, his big forearm across his eyes to shield them from the buzzing fluorescent light overhead.

"Damned shame," Lee said behind me.

"Yeah," I said, "it is."

"This is the last thing the Thurmans need."

"Bill's drinking a good bit these days."

"Jules Bullard called here a few minutes ago. He said the last time they replaced that front glass it was twelve thousand dollars. Said current replacement cost is going to be about fifteen. Sounds high."

"That glass is at least half an inch thick, bullet proof and brick proof. There's two big sections to replace. Fifteen thousand doesn't sound unreasonable. Anyway, Bill's not in a position to complain about what old man Bullard says it's going to cost."

"I guess not."

I took the stairs up to my office. Louise gave me a note when I walked past her desk.

"Mr. Silver asked if you could call him right back."

I closed my door and called Silver. His secretary put me on hold. I reminded myself to stop calling him Helmet Head. At some point in the heat of battle I might slip up and refer to him as "Mr. Helmet Head," so I pledged to break the habit. I needed to tell Walton, too. It had gotten to the point that we never called him Silver when we were doing trial preparation, always Helmet Head.

"Has Thurman been arrested?" Silver asked immediately.

"Not yet."

"Jules does not want him charged as long as he makes full restitution."

"That's good news."

"And the old man says he wants some kind of guarantee Thurman won't do something to him or Judy."

"All I can do is talk to Bill," I said.

"I told Jules that, but he insisted I bring it up. You really think Judge Williams is going to deny my change of venue motion?"

"Not sure, but she's only granted one in the entire time she's been on the bench. The Court of Appeal has upheld her every time."

Ethel Morris stood in my door and waited, which she only did if she had something important to tell me. I signed off with Helmet Head. I mean Silver.

"What's up?" I asked.

"Lee called and said someone's already volunteered to put up the fifteen thousand. Said you'd know what he was talking about."

"That's mighty generous. Did he say who it was?"

"Your wife," Ethel said.

CHAPTER TWENTY-EIGHT

I walked in the sanctuary door of Memorial Funeral Home and was surprised to see a packed house. For big funerals, the room held over two hundred mourners in thirteen church-style pews on either side of the burgundy carpet lining the central aisle. The pews were full this night, but not with people paying their respects. I stood inside the door trying to spot Everett and Lee Jones in the crowd.

I had attended many funerals in the sanctuary and quite a few meetings of the Sunshine Voters and Civic League. The meetings and the funerals had been raucous at times. I had seen many a widow or daughter of a dearly departed "fall out" into a state of frenzy or torpor, oblivious to their surroundings. On more than a few occasions the woman overcome with grief had to be carried from the room by a phalanx of deacons and church women in white.

Everett half-stood in the second pew and waved his big hand, gesturing for me to join them. I walked toward the pulpit positioned in front of the three-tiers of choir risers on the back wall of the apse. I sat in the pew between Lee and Everett.

"Big crowd," I said.

"Bobby Sanders has packed the place," Lee said.

"We've got people here, too," the Mayor said.

"Oh, yeah?" Lee said. "They must be hiding because I sure haven't seen them."

"I got the feeling walking down the aisle that I was in enemy territory. Lots of eyes on me, not many smiles."

"You know how it is up in this chapel," Everett said.

"Full contact politics," Lee said.

I watched Lee give the evil-eye to Bobby Sanders sitting next to Eleanor Bernstein in the front row across the aisle. I didn't like Bobby Sanders for a number of reasons, but Lee Jones really disliked him. I didn't think hatred was too strong a word to describe how Lee felt. The Sheriff was a straight shooter, a man who believed in defining a problem or goal, facing facts head on and overcoming obstacles through hard work. Bobby was all about the show and talking big; substance meant nothing in his world. Jimmy Gray described Bobby Sanders as, "all hat and no cattle."

Circuit Clerk Winston Moore strode to the pulpit and introduced himself as External Vice President of the Voters and Civic League. I was glad Winston was running the show this evening. In spite of his voting for Eleanor, I knew he would be an impartial host for the event. As Winston went over the agenda in way too much detail, I cautioned myself to be patient, roll with the punches. No doubt tonight would be contentious—all political gatherings in the chapel were. I would come across better if I kept my cool, especially in the Q & A.

When it came my turn I kept my speech brief and asked if there were any questions. A young woman in her mid to late-twenties raised her hand and stood. I tried to remember where I had seen her before. When she started her question it came to me. She was Bobby Sanders' receptionist at his Full Gospel Non-Denominational House of the Lord.

"Mr. Banks," the young woman said, "your campaign material does not indicate your party affiliation. Ms Bernstein's cards say that she's a registered Democrat. Someone told me that you were a Republican, but I said that cannot be. Could you enlighten us here tonight?"

"I was a registered Democrat when I ran in 1988 for District Attorney the first time. However, I am no longer a member of any political party. I have never registered as a Republican. I guess you would consider me an Independent."

"What do you have against the Democratic Party?" she asked.

I wavered for a moment. I could have said that the office of D.A. should be independent of any party affiliation, like judges, to assure impartiality of prosecution regardless of one's political leanings. That would have been the safe thing to say, defensible, too.

"The national Democratic Party left me years ago. In my third term I found that I no longer agreed with the platform of the party so I changed my registration. I don't have anything against local Democrats. In fact, some of my closest friends downtown are Democrats."

I smiled and gestured to the Mayor and the Sheriff, who raised their hands to polite, scattered applause and chuckles. This Voters and Civic League crowd was attuned to local politics and knew Lee and Everett were supporting me. I scanned the room for another friendly face and spied David Jefferson, the late Reverend Paul Gray's grandson with whom I had a good visit at Ebeneezer Baptist in Sadie's Bend a month earlier. I did a slight wave to David, hoping he was still for me.

"Thank you for clearing that up for us," the young lady said. "I have one more question if I may."

"Go right ahead," I said.

"There's been a lot of coverage in the local paper about the young white boy who went missing on the Fourth of July. I read that you've conducted county-wide searches and have gone to great lengths to try and find the boy."

"Yes," I said, "and we've arrested Ross Bullard and the Grand Jury has charged him with capital murder. We anticipate the trial starting in late October."

"Are you still searching for the boy?"

"We haven't given up. We follow up on any leads we get."

"Have you or the Sheriff done anything to find Latoya Means, the nine-year-old black girl who has been missing now for over a year?"

I had never heard the name and had no idea what she was talking about. I glanced at Lee, who shrugged his shoulders and raised his eyebrows in an "I'm totally in the dark, too" gesture.

"I'm sorry," I said, "I am not familiar with Latoya Means."

"And why is that?"

"I'm not aware of any missing black child."

"Is that because she's black and not as important as the white boy whose Daddy is a fireman?"

"That has nothing to do with it."

"This county has spent Lord knows how much money searching for the little white boy but you and the Sheriff haven't spent five minutes trying find Latoya Means."

The audience began to stir. Murmurs grew into chatter that Winston tried to quell. I watched a man in the back of the chapel stand and point at me.

"It's just like when you put Takisha Berry in jail for shoplifting," he yelled, "and that white man Al Anderson never spent the first night behind bars for driving drunk and killing a young child. There's two kinds of justice at our courthouse, the easy kind for white people, the hard kind for black folks."

In spite of Everett's claim that we had supporters in the house, it did seem to me that Bobby Sanders had packed the entire chapel with his people. The noise increased in intensity as several attendees stood simultaneously to voice grievances against me. I tried but couldn't understand what they were saying. But from the looks on their faces, they seemed pretty upset with whatever I had done.

Winston stood next to me at the podium and tried to quiet the crowd, to no avail. I looked down at the candidates for county supervisor who were waiting their turn to speak about the office they were seeking. They kept their heads down trying to avoid the verbal shrapnel coming at me from many directions. I glanced over at Bobby Sanders and Eleanor. Bobby was beaming, proud of the storm he unleashed. Eleanor never looked in my direction, but I could tell she was embarrassed.

Lee and Everett left their seats to stand on either side of me. Dozens of attendees were pointing at me and yelling. I did a quick survey of the racial makeup in the chapel. I was the only white person there.

Uh-oh. Blood in the water.

"I think we've done all the good we can here," I said to Lee.

"Time to boogie, Willie Mitchell," Lee said. "Let's go out the back door. Mayor, you cover us."

Lee grabbed the back of my upper arm and walked me over the choir risers into a short hallway and into the back parking lot which, thank God, was deserted. Just like in the movies, we hopped into Lee's huge black Tahoe with Yaloquena Sheriff on the doors and took off.

"Who the hell is Latoya Means?" I asked.

"I don't know, but I'm going to start trying to find out first thing in the morning."

"It could have been worse," I said.

"Ignorant asses," he said. "I'd like to shove my fist through Bobby Sanders' face."

"He's a man of the cloth, Lee."

"He's a crooked little shitass is what he is," Lee said, gripping the steering wheel so hard his dark knuckles turned gray.

As Lee sped off into the darkness, I noted for future gatherings how important it was in Sunshine politics to have a well-armed former All-Conference linebacker on your side.

CHAPTER TWENTY-NINE

Walton and I were hunkered down in my private office doing the final prep work for the hearings on Silver's Motion for Change of Venue and his Motion to Exclude Evidence of Other Crimes. We were due in court before Judge Williams in twenty minutes. I looked up when I heard a light knock on the door. It was Lee Jones.

"Can I see you for a minute?" he asked me.

"Talk fast."

I motioned the Sheriff in. The Mayor walked in, too.

"Before you start, did that tip about Latoya Means pan out?"

"Sure did," Lee said. "Latoya Means is no missing girl. And she's not nine; she's fourteen. It was a civil suit, divorce and custody. Judge Williams awarded custody of Latoya to her mother and Latoya took off, ended up in Chicago with her daddy's people, who have filed suit in Cook County trying to get jurisdiction. As usual, Bobby Sanders stirs up crap with no facts to back him up. It was all a big lie."

"No harm done," I said. "Those folks in that chapel weren't going to vote for me no matter what. What did you two need to talk to me about that can't wait?"

"It's about the election," Lee said. "Something's come up."

"And it's a bombshell," Everett said.

"David Jefferson," Lee said, "you know, Reverend Paul Gray's grandson, was at the Voters and Civic League meeting last Friday."

"I saw him," I said. "He was the only person in the audience other than you two who didn't want to string me up."

"After I dropped you off at home I got a call from my dispatcher saying David wanted me to meet him at my office. I spent thirty minutes with him, just David and me with the door closed."

"What did he tell you?" I asked.

"He showed me some photographs of Eleanor Bernstein. He's got a bunch. He gave me this one."

Lee opened a manila folder held at his side and pulled out a five by seven black and white print of Eleanor Bernstein and a partially clad Asian woman on a balcony locked in a passionate embrace, kissing. I pushed the photograph over to Walton. He studied it a moment and put it in front of me, tapping on the Asian.

"That's the woman who came to the El Moro trial in Jackson a couple of years back to watch Eleanor work. They walked in together."

"You ought to see some of the other pictures," Everett said. "They make this one here look real tame."

"How did David get these pictures?" I asked.

"He wouldn't say," Lee said.

"What's he plan on doing with these?" I asked.

"That's what we're here about, why we interrupted," Lee said. "He wants to get copies of these out all over town."

"What do you think about this, Mayor?" I asked.

"Like I say, it's a game-changer. Black community in town and out in the county are one hundred per cent against gay marriage, and they're not big on gay relationships either. If the voters find out Eleanor's got a girl friend, they're not going to vote for her, no matter how bad Bobby says you are."

"Lee?"

"Mayor's right. This might be our only shot. Things aren't looking so good for us right now."

I looked at Lee and the Mayor.

"Do you two think it's the right thing to do, us getting behind something like this, putting it out there?"

"No," Lee said, "I don't, but people have a right to know."

"You think people have a right to know about Eleanor's sexual preference and about her partner? Or is this more about us winning?"

Everett looked down at his big feet, hands behind his back. I half-expected him to start drawing lines in the carpet with the toe of his shoe. I could tell Lee's heart wasn't in this either. I waited for a moment.

"We knew you weren't going to go for this," Lee said.

"And I'm glad," the Mayor said. "I don't want any part of it."

"Lee?" I asked.

"Me either. I don't care if Eleanor's a lesbian. I don't want to see this stuff all over the county. Politics is nasty enough as it is."

"We just got excited about beating Bobby Sanders at his own game," Everett said. "We thought you needed to know about it. I'm telling you, if this got out..."

"If I learn that someone in my campaign is spreading this trash around for the public to see, I'll withdraw from the race. I'd rather lose the election than be involved in exposing Eleanor's private life."

"Willie Mitchell," Walton said. "We need to get to court."

"You two corral David and talk some sense to him," I said, giving the photograph back to Lee. "Tell him if he puts this out I'm going to back out of the race. Tell him it's against the law or whatever you need to in order to suppress this garbage. Walton and I are headed to the courtroom."

◆❖◆

J.D. Silver and Ross Bullard were already seated at the defense table when Walton and I walked through the rail. I nodded to Deputy Clerk Eddie Bordelon who whispered to the older, overweight deputy acting as the Judge's bailiff for the hearing.

Less than a minute later, the bailiff opened the side door and called the court to order. Judge Williams walked quickly past the bailiff and up the steps to take her seat behind the bench.

"Gentlemen," she said, "I believe we have two motions to hear this morning, Change of Venue and Motion to Exclude some digital or videotape exhibits found in the search of the defendant's house."

"That's correct, Your Honor," I said.

"Mr. Silver," she said, "I have studied the report of Mr. Granger's polling firm wherein they provide charts and graphs to demonstrate the number of Yaloquena citizens polled who knew of this case, had formed an opinion, et cetera."

"Yes, Your Honor," he said. "I have Mr. Granger in court this morning and plan to call him to testify about aspects of the poll."

"Is that really necessary?" she asked.

"Your Honor, I believe it is in order...."

"Is his testimony going to offer the same conclusions as the written report?" she asked.

"Yes, Your Honor."

"Well, I can assure you I am aware of Mr. Granger's reputation in the state for running an excellent public opinion and polling firm. Mr. Granger has testified in the courtroom before, and I know he is highly credentialed and respected. However, Mr. Silver, I've read the report twice and some parts of it three and four times, so I don't need Mr. Granger's testimony unless he has changed his mind about his findings."

I knew where Zelda was going with this. I had seen her do it before.

"But, Your Honor," Silver said.

"The way I interpret the findings," she said, "the Granger report says that seventy per cent of the persons polled had heard about the Thurman case, and that well over half of those had concluded Ross Bullard was guilty. So, Mr. Silver, it seems to me all we have to do is have enough prospective jurors in the venire so that we can exclude the thirty-five to forty per cent who have already made up their mind. I plan to shield the prospects who have not formed an opinion so they won't be tainted by the others. We will have more than enough impartial prospects left to get a jury seated."

"Mr. Granger's report concludes my client cannot get a fair and impartial jury panel in Yaloquena County."

"That's what Mr. Granger concluded the last time he polled Yaloquena County in anticipation of jury selection. In that case I ruled just like I am ruling this morning, and I was upheld by the Supreme Court." Zelda turned to me. "Mr. Banks, would you like to be heard?"

"No, Your Honor, I believe this Court is correct," I said, quitting while ahead.

"Very well," Judge Williams said, "it is the decision of this court on the venue issue today that I will defer ruling on the motion until jury selection and if responses during *voir dire* indicate that the entire venire is predisposed to convict Mr. Bullard before they hear the evidence, I will grant the venue change at that time. I may add, Mr. Silver, this is what I have done on previous venue motions and have been affirmed. A public opinion poll is no substitute for asking prospective jurors directly and listening to their responses."

"To which ruling I strenuously object," Silver said, "and assign error. I would like to say also that I am shocked that this court will not permit my witness Mr. Granger to take the stand."

I watched Judge Williams' right eyebrow slightly arch, wrinkling her brown forehead. Silver shouldn't have said it like that.

"Mr. Silver," Zelda said, "let's get one thing straight from the outset. I run my courtroom the way I see fit. You said your witnesses' testimony would not vary from his report, which is in evidence. I will read thoroughly everything you file, Mr. Silver, but I will not let you call a witness whose testimony will be repetitious and a waste of this court's time. If that shocks you, be prepared for more, because I'll let you put on all evidence that I deem relevant, but I will not allow you to grandstand for the media in my courtroom and further taint the venire. Are we clear on this?"

I could tell Helmet Head was not accustomed to being spoken to in that fashion. He was used to having rural county judges fawn, roll over, and give the famous J.D. Silver anything he wanted, because they rarely had a lawyer of Silver's reputation in their courtrooms. I was proud of Zelda, and not just because she ruled in my favor.

"Yes, Your Honor," Silver said with appropriate deference this time.

"Let's move on to the DVD issue. I've read your memoranda on the legal principles involved."

"May I be heard, Your Honor?" Silver said, trying to get ahead of Judge Williams to keep her from ruling like she did on the venue issue.

"Very well, Mr. Silver. You have the initial burden."

"Your Honor, it is our position that all eight DVDs were seized illegally pursuant to a defective warrant and that they should be suppressed not only in this case but also in any subsequent prosecution involving the DVDs."

"Let's focus on that issue. Mr. Banks?"

"The warrant was issued pursuant to facts discovered at the defendant's home on Whitley Drive by officers brought there by Ross Bullard's 911 call. There was ample probable cause."

"Mr. Silver, do you have any quarrel with the time line of events of the afternoon and evening of July 27 as set forth in the State's brief?"

"No, Your Honor. Those times are correct."

"I know I am now reviewing the legal basis of a warrant I personally approved, so I may be unable to be absolutely impartial, Mr. Silver, but I cannot imagine a clearer demonstration of probable cause. The defendant himself invited law enforcement..."

"No, Your Honor," Silver said, "the 911 call was for medical assistance, not an invitation to the Sheriff to ransack the house."

"But when the EMTs saw the note next to the defendant weren't they obligated to call the Sheriff's office in light of the fact that Danny Thurman had been missing for twenty-three days, and the note referred to "Danny," a child who lived on the same street as the defendant?"

I rose to argue and noticed Ross Bullard writing on his pad just as intensely as he had at the arraignment. The scenario was the same: Ross seemingly oblivious at the defense table engrossed in his legal tablet; Jules in the first row behind the defense, his beady eyes darting, concentrating on each word and ready to pounce; Judy seated next to Jules looking bored with the whole thing. Their investigator Phil Myers sat in the second row, paying close attention.

"Your Honor," I said, "I intend to call three witnesses who were first on the scene to establish the events of July 27."

"Are the DVDs to be offered into evidence today?"

"Yes, Your Honor. Mr. Cedars at the crime lab has the originals in his vault but he has provided duplicates to my office. I intend to offer the duplicates in connection with the testimony today with leave to substitute the originals at trial."

"Subject to my continuing and general objection," Silver said, "I have no problem with what the State proposes."

"I intend to view the DVDs at some point this morning," she said.

"Before we get to the testimony Mr. Banks intends to offer, I would like to state that I object to all eight DVDs being introduced today or at trial for the following reasons: first, the warrant was not issued on probable cause; second, the tapes are irrelevant to the charge of first degree murder, and..."

I could not believe Silver was arguing with a straight face that all the DVDs were irrelevant to the murder, since the homemade DVD showed the murder victim naked on the couch in the defendant's living room. Not a good strategy. He was burning credibility with Zelda.

"...third, these DVDs are evidence of another alleged crime and highly prejudicial, and as such not admissible in this capital murder trial."

"Other crimes evidence is admissible to show motive, system, or intent," I said, "and the relevance of the DVDs to the defendant's guilt is obvious, his obsession with naked children, in this case including the victim Danny Thurman."

"All right," Judge Williams said, "these arguments are all set out in your briefs. Let's get to the testimony. And gentlemen, we will finish this testimony today."

I heard Connie quietly begin to cry in the audience behind me when I said "naked children" and mentioned Danny's name. I needed her testimony to identify Danny on the homemade DVD and hoped she could keep it together for the duration of the hearing.

I called the EMTs, Kitty, and Lee Jones to establish what happened after Ross's 911 call. I kept my questions to a minimum. On cross, Silver's reaction to my witnesses' answers was more dramatic than called for on several occasions. Walton had prepared all the witnesses well, and they handled Silver's questions without difficulty.

We broke for lunch at noon. When the deputies took Ross from the courtroom, I noticed he gave a note to the bailiff. I mentioned it to Walton and asked him to question the bailiff about it later in the day.

At one-thirty, court reconvened and I called Connie Thurman to the stand. She raised her small right hand to be sworn. I noticed a slight tremor. The ordeal was continuing to take a toll on Connie. She had lost more weight and the circles under her eyes were larger and darker. She was no longer vivacious and full of life. She was in agony. I hated to put her through it, but she was the only person that could identify Danny as one of the naked boys on the tape.

Over the noon hour Eddie Bordelon had supervised setting up the monitor and DVD player. He did as I suggested and placed the monitor so that only Judge Williams and the court personnel could see the screen. I was sure Silver had viewed his copies of the DVDs and I wanted to see as little of the content as possible. There was no need for the spectators in the courtroom to see the naked children. At the trial, the jurors would have to watch the DVDs, especially the one of Danny.

My goal was to keep Connie on the witness stand as short a time as possible. I sped through questions about her background and family and got to the heart of the matter.

"Now, Connie, you've already seen the DVD that I am about to show you, have you not?"

"Yes, sir," she said.

"The DVD is queued up so that you will see the critical portion and not have to look at all of it like you did before. Can you do that for me?"

She nodded and dabbed her nose with a Kleenex.

"You'll have to respond out loud for the recording equipment."

"Yes," she said, her voice shaking.

Walton used the remote to start the DVD. I stood in front of the Judge's bench to see the monitor. When the picture of the two naked boys on the sofa appeared, I gestured for Walton to stop.

"Do you recognize either one of the boys on the couch?"

"Yes," she said. "The one on the right is Danny."

"Are you sure?"

"Without a doubt. That's my son."

"What about the voice on the DVD?"

"That's Ross Bullard. I know his voice from the neighborhood and from some dealings I had with him at the bank."

Connie was more composed than I expected. Walton had worked with her during the week, going over the exact questions with the DVD in front of her. The practice paid off. I sat down. Silver took his time, looking at his notes.

"Mr. Silver?" Judge Williams said.

"Just a couple of questions for Mrs. Thurman," he said.

"Let's get on with it."

"Does your son have any distinguishing marks...no, strike that," he said. "Never mind that question, Mrs. Thurman. Have you been in many of the homes in your neighborhood?"

"Yes," she said.

"For social visits, I imagine?"

"Yes."

"What about Ross Bullard's home?"

"Yes, once."

"What for?"

"To ask them to join our neighborhood watch program."

"When was that?"

"This past Spring."

"Which month?"

"I'm not sure. Late April or maybe early May."

"Have you been in the home at any other time?"

"No."

"When you were there about neighborhood watch, did you talk to the defendant Ross Bullard?"

"No, sir. I spoke to Mrs. Bullard. Judy."

"Your Honor," Silver said, "I would ask that the DVD be turned back on to show the image that the District Attorney asked Mrs. Thurman about."

Walton pointed the remote and walked over to make sure the monitor showed the two naked boys on the couch.

"You're sure the boy on the right is your son?" Silver asked.

Connie glanced quickly at the monitor then down at her hands folded in her lap. "Yes."

"What about the other boy?"

"I don't know who that is."

"Do you recognize the sofa they are sitting on?"

"Yes. That's the sofa in the Bullard's living room. I saw it when I talked to Judy."

"But you don't know the other child?"

"No, sir. I don't."

"Okay. I believe that's all the questions I have."

"You may step down," Zelda told Connie.

Connie was so relieved her knees buckled and she almost fell when she left the witness stand. Walton and I jumped to help but she recovered her balance. I nodded encouragement as she walked past to take her seat behind us.

"I'm going to take a brief recess to view the DVDs in chambers," Judge Williams said. "According to my notes, there are seven commercial DVDs and one homemade DVD, and all have been introduced into evidence today, subject to the defense objection, is that correct?"

"Correct, Your Honor," I said. "It would take some time..."

"I'm not going to look at the entirety of the DVDs, just enough of each to verify the content," she said and adjourned court. Walton followed the Judge and bailiff out the side door.

I was surprised when only thirty minutes later in my office Ethel told me Judge Williams was ready. I joined Walton at prosecution table.

"I almost forgot. Did you talk to the bailiff about the note?"

"It was something for Judy Bullard."

"Tell the bailiff not to do that again."

When Judge Williams walked in the side door, I could tell from the look on her face she was mightily disturbed.

"I've reviewed all of the DVDs," she said. "I reviewed the portions of the briefs related to their suppression and am ready to rule unless you gentlemen have more evidence to offer."

I shook my head and glanced at Helmet Head. His massive block of hair moved from side to side. We were both ready.

"The DVDs present two separate issues. First, the homemade DVD with Danny Thurman, as identified by Mrs.

Thurman today, naked on the couch in the Ross Bullard home is very relevant to the charge of capital murder. It establishes the defendant not only knew the victim but had spent time with him in intimate circumstances. There is nothing cited in the defense brief that persuades this Court that the DVD was improperly obtained. Therefore, the homemade DVD is admissible at the trial of this matter."

"To which ruling I strenuously object," Silver said.

"Noted," she said. "With respect to the seven commercial DVDs, the State concedes that they are evidence of another crime, to-wit: possession of child pornography, a serious felony. The State argues that these seven DVDs are admissible to show motive, system, and intent, and that their probative value in this capital murder charge outweighs their prejudicial effect."

I began to get a sinking feeling.

"These seven DVDs are relevant to show the defendant's propensity to involve himself with naked children, but Mr. Banks," Zelda looked at me for an extended moment, "I cannot imagine anything being more prejudicial to a defendant in a murder case involving a seven-year-old victim. The DVDs are so offensive and abhorrent, they would predispose any jury to convict the defendant, no matter what the other evidence showed. Therefore, the seven commercial DVDs are inadmissible at the capital murder trial. The prejudicial effect of these seven DVDs far outweighs their probative value. However, Mr. Banks, you may choose to pursue separately the felonies involved in the defendant's possession of the seven DVDs. The seven DVDs would certainly be admissible in the prosecution of the defendant for illegal possession of child pornography. In my opinion, there is no significant issue with the warrant and the search of the defendant's home that resulted in the discovery of the seven DVDs. Any questions, gentlemen?"

"Just to confirm the hearing on motions next Friday," I said, seeing no reason to beat a dead horse.

"The motion to dismiss the charge on the *corpus delicti* issue and the motion to suppress the note," the Judge said.

"Correct, Your Honor," Silver said.

"Have all other pre-trial issues been resolved?" she asked.

"Yes, Your Honor," I said, "only those two remain."

"I've set aside the entire day next Friday to hear the final two motions. And gentlemen, I take it we are still set to begin picking the jury five weeks from this coming Monday, is that correct?"

"Unless the Court rules in my favor next Friday," Silver said.

Judge Williams ignored Helmet Head's comment.

"The State will be ready to start jury selection October 22," I said.

"Court's adjourned," Zelda said.

Walton and I stood for the Judge's exit. I heard someone cough behind me. I turned and saw Kitty. Sitting next to her was Cheryl Diamond. I hadn't heard either of them come in. I looked for Connie and Bill. I wanted to speak briefly with them but they already left.

I sat back down with Walton and whispered.

"If I were Helmet Head, I would be doing everything I could to find out the name of the other boy on the tape."

"Lee hasn't been able to. I don't know what Helmet Head's investigator could do differently," Walton said.

"We need to ask Lee to do more work in the neighborhood. Maybe someone has seen kids going in there."

"Lee said everyone in a two block radius has been asked that question and no one's seen anything that might help us."

"What about Nicholas and Payne? Would they know of any other kids that Danny played with who might have been there?"

"Gayle says she's asked the twins several times when they were together, and she's asked them when she's been alone with each one. She says sometimes they'll tell her something when the other twin is not there. She says they don't know who the other boy on the DVD is."

"I want you and Gayle to make a list of all the white boys around Danny's age in Sunshine."

"Question each one?"

"Not yet. Just rule out the ones it can't be. The boy has to be the general size and build of the kid on the tape. You could eliminate all the fat boys, for example."

"I'm on it."

"I guarantee you Phil Myers is doing the same thing," I said.

CHAPTER THIRTY

Cheryl Diamond was waiting for me in my reception area. I checked briefly with Louise and Ethel for my messages then gestured for Cheryl to follow me into my private office. I closed the door and gave her a light hug.

"Welcome back, Cheryl."

"Thank you, Willie Mitchell."

"I see you kept your hair appointment."

"Still a blonde," she said patting her updo.

"How long were you in the courtroom today?"

"I walked in when Judge Williams reconvened after seeing the DVDs. She seemed very upset at having to watch them."

"I could tell. It's a sordid mess. Makes you uneasy about being in the same room as Ross Bullard."

"I enjoyed seeing Kitty again. I sat with her in court today."

"Kitty's great."

"She's not well, though."

"She's had a bad cold she can't shake."

"Well, I know you're busy, and I appreciate your seeing me. There's something I want to tell you."

"I have something to ask you, too. You go first."

"When I first saw the Bullards in court, I sensed Jules was the more evil of the two. I know Ross killed Danny, but I sensed confusion more than anything else when he walked by me. Since then I've seen him in dreams and I've thought about him. Seeing him today confirmed it. It's not confusion I sensed."

"What is it then?"

"He's changing. Right before our eyes."

"Into what?"

"It's a matter of the degree of evil. He's undergoing some kind of grotesque metamorphosis. He's not the same person today he was the first time I saw him. "

"His affect is different. I've noticed that."

"He is more self-confident than before. He's not nearly as jittery, and not as obsessed with what his father thinks."

"Interesting," I said.

"I don't think this information helps you in the trial, but I wanted to share it with you."

"You never know," I said. "It might. He's still consumed with his writing. It's as if he's not paying attention to the court proceedings."

"Oh, I don't think Ross Bullard misses a thing. He's very bright, you know. The writing is part of his evolution. I'm sure of that."

"Thank you for your thoughts. Whenever you sense something, please tell me. By the way, the first time we met you told me Jules was having his way with Judy. We've had it confirmed from a couple of sources. You knew before we did."

"That one was easy. Watching the Bullards today, I'm most concerned about what Ross is becoming. In the process of getting stronger he's becoming more malevolent."

"Can you get a feel for what he's writing?"

"I know it's very personal."

"I want to ask you if you will do something for me, and we need to keep this just between the two of us."

"I'll do anything to help."

"I want you to put all your abilities to work to help us find Danny Thurman's body. I'm afraid this case is not going to end well if we don't."

Ten minutes after Cheryl left Walton came in.

"I've been talking to Phil Myers," Walton said. "He'd like to introduce himself to you."

"Bring him in."

Phil Myers walked in with his hand extended. He was a couple of inches shorter than I and stocky, with a ruddy drinker's complexion, dark moustache beginning to gray, and intense, protruding eyes. After we exchanged introductions, I asked him to sit down.

"Whenever I work a case," Myers said, "I like to let the Sheriff and the D.A. know who I am and who I'm working for. I like to keep everything above board."

"I appreciate that," I said. "I'm aware of your background."

"I worked up many a homicide in Memphis and spent a lot of time with the D.A. getting cases ready for trial and in the courtroom. When I finished putting in my twenty-five years on the force I didn't want to sit around the house, so I got licensed and started taking on private work."

"Working to defend the people you used to put away," I said.

"It's not all defense work. I take on cases for plenty of prosecutors in Tennessee, especially smaller jurisdictions where the D.A. doesn't have full-time investigators. They hire me to help on the tough ones."

"I don't think I could do defense work," Walton said.

"All I do is investigate, dig out the facts," Myers said. "My attitude is I'm hired to find out things. I present what I find to whoever is paying my tab. I don't try to color things one way or the other. I tell them going in I'm going to discover what I can and give it to them straight, no matter if it seems to help or hurt. I don't twist the facts for anybody. They don't like what I find, it's all confidential and privileged. They can burn my report if they want to."

"Kind of like lawyers," I said, "who represent someone they know is guilty. Everyone is entitled to a defense in our system."

"I don't care," Walton said, "I couldn't defend someone I knew was guilty, like J.D. Silver is doing."

"He's just doing his job," Myers said to Walton, "making a paycheck like me. His is bigger, but don't think he feels all warm and fuzzy sitting next to a guy like Ross Bullard. Wait until you get as old as your boss and me," Myers said. "You'll see that everything's not always black and white. More like gray, huh Willie Mitchell? Kind of like my hair's getting."

"Mine, too," I said, liking Myers more than I expected. "Glad you came in, Phil, and hope you don't do too much damage to us."

"That's not my intention," he said, standing to leave. "Not at all. I just turn over rocks and see what's under'em. I don't make up anything. If it hurts your case, you'll hear about it in court. If it helps you, you'll never know about it unless the man that hired me tells you."

"I don't trust that guy," Walton said after Myers left.

"He's a cop," I said, "who made chief detective and retired with honors. That means he's not only a good investigator, he's a good politician."

"Like I said," Walton said. "Untrustworthy *per se.*"

"Do me a favor," I said, "ask Lee to put at least one extra man in the courtroom to watch Bill. I'm afraid he's going to erupt in there one day. I'm sure he got mad when Zelda suppressed the seven DVDs."

"I could tell he was pissed. The other day he asked me how our laws got so screwed up. I mean common sense says if you have a guy infatuated with naked children, willing to commit a felony just to look at them, isn't that extremely relevant in the prosecution of the same guy for doing something to a seven-year-old? A seven-year-old that he persuaded to strip down on his own couch?"

"Same way in a burglary prosecution. I think the best evidence against a guy for burglary is that he was convicted of burglary two or three times before. It shows he's a burglar."

"But unless they're relevant to prove his m.o.," Walton said, "the previous burglary convictions are inadmissible."

"Unless the s.o.b. gets on the witness stand," I said. "But they never do if they have priors."

"You're right about Bill," Walton said after a moment. "I'll go talk to Lee about the extra security right now."

CHAPTER THIRTY-ONE

Lee Jones parked his black Tahoe in front of Mrs. Gilbert's house on Whitley Drive. Walton and I got out and stood in the middle of the street waiting for the Sheriff to get off the phone. We were about a hundred feet from Ross's property line. Like all the houses on Whitley, Mrs. Gilbert's was a brick ranch with a big front yard. Only one home separated Mrs. Gilbert and Ross. It was owned by Mr. James McCullough, a widower who spent April to late October at his home in Cashiers, North Carolina with his girl friend. According to Lee's investigators, Mr. McCullough told them he had been in North Carolina since mid-April and wouldn't return to Sunshine this year until November.

The Thurman's home was across the street, several houses further away from town. I traced Danny's probable route on July 4. He would have had to pass by Mrs. Gilbert's home, then Mr. McCullough's, then Ross's house on the way to town to deliver the blue sweater to Connie.

Mrs. Gilbert told the Sheriff's investigators she had not seen Danny in the late afternoon of July 4. In fact, she told them twice, in both neighborhood canvasses. This morning, one day before the most important pre-trial hearing in State vs. Ross Bullard, Mrs. Gilbert called the Sheriff and told him she now remembered seeing Danny that day.

I had made two campaign appearances on Sunday, one at Mount Olive B.C., a black church in town, deep in the quarters, and the other at a white Pentecostal church on the outskirts of town. The Pentecostal preacher had hair that rivaled Helmet Head's. Monday through Wednesday I campaigned in a half-dozen unincorporated communities in the county. This morning, Thursday, I was about to head out with push cards to knock on doors in town when Lee called me with the news about Mrs. Gilbert's new recollection. Lee, Walton, and I arrived at Whitley to interview Mrs. Gilbert within fifteen minutes of her call. It was a relief to be off the campaign trail and back on Danny's case.

Mrs. Gilbert answered the door in her housecoat and slippers. She was in her seventies, thin and ghostly. She led us into the kitchen where we took seats around the small table in her breakfast nook next to the kitchen. She asked if we wanted coffee. I eyed the dirty dishes on the kitchen counter and the remainder of beans and chicken bones in several Meals on Wheels Styrofoam containers and declined her offer. So did Lee and Walton. After the usual niceties, Lee got to the point.

"What caused you to remember seeing Danny on July 4, Mrs. Gilbert, when you told my investigators earlier you hadn't?"

She turned her head to look out the window. Scratching her head and smoothing gray hair that needed washing, she began to tremble.

"Am I in trouble?" she asked, almost in tears.

"No, ma'am," I said. "Not at all. We are just curious about what triggered your memory."

"The nice man, the investigator with the moustache, he stopped by day before yesterday in the afternoon and drank coffee with me. He said he was a detective with the Memphis police department."

I was certain Myers had described his status accurately, but in a way that would be confusing to Mrs. Gilbert. It wouldn't be difficult. He may have obfuscated, but I knew he didn't lie. Myers was too much of a professional and too smart to impersonate an officer.

"And he asked you if you saw Danny Thurman that day?" I asked.

"He asked me to think about everything I did that day, starting in the morning and up to the time I heard Danny was missing. It was the way he asked me about things, it was different from the others. And all of a sudden it came to me. I did see Danny."

"Can you tell us what you remember now?" I said.

"I remember it was late in the afternoon, but still daylight. I was sitting in my chair in the living room looking out at the street. Mr. Gilbert and I used to sit there and watch the neighbors go by, before he passed away last year."

She took the hem of her housecoat and dabbed her eyes. "Anyway, I saw Danny walk in front of my house heading toward town."

"How was he dressed?" Lee asked.

"I don't recall. The man from Memphis asked me that, too. I just don't know. Like a little boy, I guess. I do remember that he was carrying a blue sweater over his shoulder and I couldn't imagine why because it was so hot."

"Did you see where he went after he walked past your house?" Walton asked. "Did he stop at the Bullard house?"

She shook her head. She had no idea.

"Did you see Ross Bullard on the Fourth?" Lee asked.

"No," she said. "I hardly ever saw him in the neighborhood."

"Did you see anyone else on the street that day?" I asked.

"That man who does yard work sometimes in the neighborhood. He's one of those Blakes from Dundee County."

"Ronnie Blake?" Lee asked.

"I think so," she said.

Lee looked at me. The name put me on full alert, too.

"What time did you see Ronnie Blake?" I asked.

"I don't know. Like I told the detective the other day, I think it was earlier, before I saw Danny, but I'm not sure."

"Did you see him talk to Danny that day?" Lee asked.

"No, not that I recall."

"Had you ever seen him talking to Danny?" I asked.

"I don't think so."

Her tremors were getting worse. I had to ask her something that I knew was going to increase her agitation. I was almost certain I knew her answer, but I had to hear her say it.

"Mrs. Gilbert," I said, "when Mr. Gilbert was alive, did the two of you have a glass of wine or a cocktail in the late afternoons looking out the picture window at the street."

"Every day," she said. "It was our quiet time together." She dabbed her eyes again with her housecoat. "I miss him so much."

"I'm sure you do," I said, "and we're sorry for your loss. We're sorry to bother you with all these questions, too, but it's important."

"I understand. The boy is gone."

"Right. Even though Mr. Gilbert has passed on, I imagine you enjoy having a cocktail or two and sitting by the window, reminiscing about him even now."

She nodded. "I do. Every day."

"Were you having your cocktail when you saw Danny that day carrying the blue sweater?"

"Yes."

"Is that why you had trouble remembering?" I asked.

"Yes," she said, trembling. "I'm so embarrassed."

"That's all right," I said. "When did you have your first drink on the Fourth of July?"

"In the morning. Sometimes I have to have it in the morning." She wiped her eyes. "When I do, I just keep going all day."

"What do you drink?" I asked.

"Bourbon," she said with her head down.

"And water and ice?"

"No," she said, her head still down. "Just bourbon."

"And when the Memphis detective was here day before yesterday," I asked, "had you been drinking that day?"

"I woke up Tuesday morning and didn't feel well, so I had a drink first thing." She paused and wrung her hands. "He came in the afternoon and started asking his questions the way he did, and that's why I think I finally remembered seeing Danny."

"Because you were drinking on July Fourth?" I asked.

"Yes," she nodded, teary-eyed. "All day, just like Tuesday."

"Who is Ronnie Blake?" Walton asked as soon as we got into Lee's Tahoe to return to the courthouse.

"A convicted sex-offender," Lee said.

"A pedophile," I added. "Young boys."

CHAPTER THIRTY-TWO

I walked through the rail to the prosecution table. Walton had already organized and spread out our files and notes, prepping for the argument. I scanned the table as a butterfly flitted through my peritoneum. The hearing this morning was by far the most critical event of the prosecution, and even after twenty-four years of trying cases, I still get butterflies. It's not an overstatement to say that if we didn't win on the *corpus delicti* issue or if Judge Williams suppressed the note, this case was over until Danny's remains were discovered.

Walton and I had already batted around ways to broach the subject with Bill and Connie. Bill insisted on swift prosecution without Danny's body and I didn't blame him one bit. But that was before the hearing today. I told Walton that if we lost either of the motions, we had to make Bill listen to reason. Ross would have to be released and the prosecution of Ross Bullard would have to wait.

The defendant shuffled in behind us between two deputies. The shackles stopped rattling right behind me. Walton and I turned.

"Just so you'll know," Ross said to us, not whispering, "Jules has been screwing her for years and it doesn't bother me one bit."

One of the deputies told him to shut up, grabbed his arm and pulled him toward the defense table. I glanced at Cheryl Diamond in the first row behind me. She was shaking her head. She looked at me and mouthed: "Yes, it does," just as Helmet Head, Jules, and Judy walked through the back door and down the center aisle towards us.

"Why don't you tell Jules what his boy just said," Walton whispered to me, "in the spirit of full disclosure."

"Jules is old, but he probably already knows he's sleeping with Judy," I whispered back. "I wish we could tell the jury."

"If we get that far," he said.

Judge Williams walked into the courtroom and took the bench.

"Gentlemen," Zelda said, "we're here on two motions today, a Motion to Dismiss on the *corpus delicti* issue, and the other a Motion to Suppress the note found next to the defendant by the EMTs."

"That's correct, Your Honor," I said.

"Seems to me," the Judge said, "these are flip sides of the same coin. Do you gentlemen agree?"

"Just about, Judge Williams," Silver said jumping to his feet.

"Based on my reading of your brief, Mr. Silver, you assert that the search warrant was issued without probable cause and everything seized at the scene, including the note, should be excluded, but that is secondary to your primary argument for suppression."

"That's correct, Your Honor. I have cited cases from Texas, Louisiana, and Alabama which hold that a defendant's inculpatory statement regarding a homicide cannot be introduced into evidence until there is independent proof that the victim was murdered."

"And Mr. Donaldson and I have cited cases in our brief," I said quickly, "from Tennessee, Arkansas and North Carolina which hold that a defendant's confession or admission can be considered alongside all other facts to establish that the defendant was murdered. In other words, the *corpus delicti* does not have to be proven by other evidence before the confession is introduced into evidence."

"And both of you agree in your briefs that the issue is *res nova* in the State of Mississippi."

Silver and I said yes. The precise question had never been faced by the Mississippi Supreme Court.

"As I see it," Zelda said, "the central issue in both motions is this: can the state prove the elements of murder without considering the defendant's note? Mr. Silver argues that there's no independent proof that Danny Thurman was murdered, so the note cannot be introduced. Mr. Banks argues that the note can be introduced and considered with all the other circumstances of the case to prove the elements of capital murder."

"The Court has precisely summarized the issue," Silver said.

"And regardless of how I rule, the Supreme Court of our state will ultimately decide this, do you agree?"

"In all likelihood," I said.

"I presumed we would have testimony this morning," Judge Williams said, "but after reading your briefs, there's really no need for any witnesses, is there? A copy of the note is attached to the State's filings."

"No need for testimony, Your Honor," Silver said, "but I would like to be heard briefly."

"Very well. Proceed."

"This Honorable Court is now aware of the facts the State intends to prove in support of its contention that young Danny Thurman was murdered. Without admitting the validity of any of the following litany, and solely for the purpose of this argument, the State claims as follows: they can establish that he disappeared on July 4; that he hasn't been found since; that his hat and probably his jeans were found under a rock at Iron Bridge with his mother's blue sweater; that a fiber from the sweater matches a fiber found in the sofa in Mr. Bullard's living room; that Danny's fingerprints were discovered in the Bullard home; that he was videotaped nude by the defendant in the defendant's home. Taken all the foregoing as fact, Your Honor, there is still no proof of murder. There's no blood on any of the evidence; there's no cause of death. There's only the note, and even the note doesn't indicate the victim was murdered. The only possible reference to death is the phrase 'the boy's body.' Still, even with the note, there's no evidence Danny was murdered."

I showed no reaction, but Helmet Head was making a powerful argument. Even if Zelda ruled in my favor, the Court of Appeal could very easily agree with the logic of Silver's argument and the case law from Texas, Louisiana, and Alabama. I glanced down at my notes and heard movement behind me. I turned in time to see Bill Thurman leaving the courtroom, like he did at the last hearing.

"Mr. Banks," Judge Williams said, "I've read your brief and am ready to rule unless you want to be heard."

I knew Zelda well enough to know nothing I said would make the slightest bit of difference. She made up her mind before she took the bench this morning.

"I have been researching the *corpus delicti* issue since arraignment in this case," she said. "I am familiar with the cases counsel cite from other jurisdictions. Although it is a close question, I believe the defendant's note may be considered alongside all other evidence in the case to establish the elements of the crime of capital murder. It's said that hard cases make bad law, but I believe this approach is fair to both sides and allows the jury to consider the totality of the circumstances surrounding the homicide. For the reasons stated, I find that the note is admissible and that there is sufficient evidence of the *corpus delicti* to allow this case to go to the jury on the charge of capital murder.

"This concludes all pre-trial matters, and we will begin picking the jury on Monday, October 22, four weeks from this Monday. Court is adjourned."

I stood while Zelda left the courtroom. Walton smiled weakly. He congratulated me, but was more subdued than usual.

"Your briefs and research won it," I said to him. "I didn't have to say anything this morning. Let's get a copy of the venire for October 22 as soon as Eddie has it ready. Why don't you and Lee start going over it as soon as you can."

Walton nodded and gathered the files. I turned to talk to Helmet Head but he, Jules, and Judy were already gone. At the defense table, Ross looked up from his tablet long enough to wink at me.

CHAPTER THIRTY-THREE

"Thank y'all for coming in this morning," I said. "Walton and I want to make sure you understand what's at stake if we continue on this path to trial October 22."

"Has something changed?" Connie asked, her eyes wide with fear.

I had hoped Connie would have gradually learned to cope with Danny's disappearance, but she was as apprehensive and fragile as ever. Bill glared at her when she asked the question. No wonder she was still a basket case; her husband continued to blame her.

"We won the motions you were worried about," Bill said. "I don't see what the problem is."

"The problem is," Walton said, "we haven't found Danny."

"Judge Williams ruled in our favor," I said, "so we can get the note into evidence along with everything else, but..."

"No jury's going to cut that bastard loose," Bill said, raising his voice. "All you have to do is look at the son of a bitch...."

Connie patted Bill's arm. He jerked it away.

"I know," I said, "I think we can win with a local jury. Jules Bullard is not well-liked and Ross's behavior in court works in our favor. All our evidence is circumstantial, but juries like circumstantial evidence. It's like solving a puzzle. They like to figure it out."

"Making the conviction stick at the appellate level is the problem," Walton said. "Even if the jury convicts him, we must have a strong enough case so that the Court of Appeal doesn't reverse it."

"We already told you we want to go forward with the case," Bill said. "I don't understand."

"We're in a different posture now," I said. "You elected to go forward at the Grand Jury stage, and we did. He's indicted and we've survived Silver's motions. Now, the stakes are higher. If we go to trial and the jury decides there's not enough evidence, if they acquit him we can never try him again for murder, even if we find Danny and it's obvious he was murdered."

"Even if Ross left his business card with the remains. The legal principle is known as double jeopardy," Walton said. "It's in the constitution. He cannot be tried twice for the same crime."

"The jury's going to convict him," Bill repeated.

He appeared to be listening but was not hearing what we said. It was a phenomenon I had dealt with many times in meeting with the families of victims. Denial is a powerful state of mind.

"Okay, let's assume he's convicted but the appellate court overturns the conviction," I said. "Let's say they agree with Silver on the *corpus delicti* issue or they rule that the note should not have been admitted."

"Then you try him again," Bill said.

"Not necessarily," Walton said, "it's possible the double jeopardy issue could still come into play. The judges on the appeals court could enter an order of acquittal at the appellate level, ruling there was insufficient evidence as a matter of law."

"After that happens," I said, "if some deer hunter comes across Danny's body during gun season, which is only a few weeks away, there's nothing we can do to Bullard."

"You still have him on the child pornography," Connie said.

"That's nothing," Bill snapped. "Ten years for killing Danny."

"What do you think we should do?" Connie said, her voice trembling. "You and Walton know what's best."

"We're going to trial," Bill said, "on capital murder."

"I think we should wait," Walton said.

I wasn't expecting that. Walton didn't look at me before he said it, which was a breach of our informal protocol. When we met with families of victims, Walton and I normally didn't make a recommendation unless we had discussed it beforehand, or we had reached a meeting of the minds during the family conference. Over the course of our eight years prosecuting together, Walton and I communicated effectively with nods and body language.

"The advantage to waiting," I said, "is we'll be certain of a conviction and have a shot at the death penalty."

"Can you guarantee Ross will stay in jail?" Bill asked.

"No," I said, "in fact I'm sure he will be allowed out on bail. If we ask for a continuance, Silver will sense weakness and push hard for the trial date to stick, in which case we might have to dismiss the indictment."

"Does that mean he gets off?" Connie asked.

"No," Walton said, "no jeopardy attaches. We can re-indict him at any time and start over."

"And if we dismiss this indictment and never find Danny?" Bill said. "He gets away with it?"

"We could prosecute him on the child pornography charges and hope he stays in prison until we locate your son's remains," I said.

"I think that's what we should do," Walton said.

"Well," I countered, "we'll do what you want us to. We've laid out the pros and cons, and if you think...."

"If you dismiss the murder indictment and go with the pornography," Bill said, "Silver is going to claim some mental illness or something and it'll take forever to get him to trial."

"Not that long," Walton said.

"But when the murder charge is dropped he gets bail, doesn't he?"

I didn't blame Bill for sneering at the impotence of the system. It was a crappy hand the Thurmans had been dealt. The rules of criminal procedure protecting the rights of the accused were stacked against them. I agreed with Bill. It wasn't fair.

"More than likely," I said.

Connie jumped when Bill slammed his open palm on my desk. He stood and pointed at me.

"I'm not agreeing to anything where Bullard gets to walk free. If he gets out, I ain't guaranteeing you I won't kill him. I know I'm not supposed to say that, but it's the truth."

Connie began to sob. Bill pursed his lips. His decision was made.

"We want to go to trial on October 22 on the charge of murder. If he gets off, or if some higher court lets him go, we'll deal with that later best we can. Right now, I can't live with the thought of Ross Bullard walking the streets a free man." He barked at Connie. "Let's go."

The Thurmans left and I closed the door. I sat back down behind my desk and looked at Walton.

"You want to tell me what you were doing just now?"

Chapter Thirty-Four

"That was different," Kitty said when she sat down across from me.

It was almost noon. She looked thin, almost gaunt.

"I knew it would be. I was about to leave for lunch. You want to join Susan and me at the house? We haven't seen enough of you lately."

"Thanks but I've got to interview Mr. and Mrs. Garzarelli at their store in Sunny Acres at 12:30."

"I heard they got robbed again yesterday evening."

"The Sheriff said he thinks it's the sixth time."

"That's just since Lee's been in office," I said.

"Why do they stay open in that same spot, right in the middle of the worst part of town?"

"They've run that little grocery store since I was a kid, same location. It's all they know. They've always lived in the back of the store. You hardly ever see them out. I don't think she drives."

"They never had any children?"

"No. In the old days, they ran tabs for people in the neighborhood. Let them pay when they could. Sunny Acres started as a blue collar starter subdivision in the fifties and transitioned gradually to an all black area. At first it was working black families, good people, then those folks moved to better neighborhoods and a lot of the houses became Section Eight rentals and things went down from there."

"I'll say."

"Tell me about your morning with Cheryl."

"I picked her up at 7:30, like you arranged. She insisted we go in her old Lincoln."

"At least you had a smooth ride."

"It was like driving a Hovercraft," she said, "floating on air. All the bumps and ridges on the county road just smoothed out. Compared to my little BMW...." She began to chuckle, which turned into a coughing jag that lasted a few moments.

"Have you been to see Nathan again?"

"I have," she said, clearing her throat, "and he started me on a stronger antibiotic. I've been trying to take it easy. Cheryl told me this morning I needed to see a specialist."

"We're all concerned."

"I had this before. I'll get over it. It just takes a little time."

"Tell me about Iron Bridge."

"I'm glad you told me something about Cheryl. She's...unusual. Kind of hard to talk to."

"Different generation."

"Different planet. But she's very nice. She spent a lot of time studying the Yaloquena map you gave her. She asked me about Jake, wanted to know our plans."

"What did you say?"

"I said I missed him. Did you tell her about New Orleans?"

"Pretty sure I didn't."

"Well, out of the blue she asked me to tell her about my scars."

Two years earlier, when Kitty was assigned to the FBI office in New Orleans, she worked on the federal investigation of Ignacio Torres and his gang Los Cuervos running guns after Katrina to Mexican cartels. Jake had waggled a transfer to the New Orleans U.S. Attorney's office to follow Kitty. He worked the case as a prosecutor. The gangsters almost killed them both.

Kitty was viciously attacked in her apartment in Faubourg Marigny and left for dead. It took four hundred stitches to repair the knife wounds, cuts, and slices below her breasts and above her *mons pubis*. Susan and I had never seen it, but Jake told us Kitty had scar tissue galore around her mid-section. Kitty told Jake she would never have remedial plastic surgery. The scars would remind her she had been a victim once, but never again. Jake told us he didn't mind Kitty's scars. He had his own. The same gangsters took him hostage and tortured him, carving a ragged "L" running from his left shoulder to his elbow along with the letter "C"; the wings of a crow in flight across his chest topped with a jagged eye suggestive of the Egyptian

Eye of Ra above the wings. Kitty's attackers were not so symbolic; they just sliced and diced.

Susan and I brought Kitty into our home in Sunshine to recuperate. Buddy Wade, Jimmy Gray, and I leaned on Senator Skeeter Sumrall to use his influence with DOJ and the FBI to get Kitty temporarily assigned to Sheriff Jones on a special intergovernmental program.

"How would she have known about my scars?"

"She's a remarkably talented psychic. That's the only explanation. Did she sense anything at the bridge?"

"Not that she told me. We got there about nine and I stopped on the bridge near the rail overlooking the spot where Danny's hat and jeans were found. She got out and stood at the rail with me. I pointed out where in the rip rap the big rocks were removed and where I thought the clothing was found.

"She held the bridge rail with both hands and closed her eyes for several minutes. I moved down the rail a few yards to give Cheryl some space. After a couple of minutes, I noticed something moving in the woods toward us. Cheryl heard it, too. We watched this deer step out of the trees onto a sandbar on the edge of the creek. It was white."

"I saw it a month ago when I rode down there. It's an albino whitetail. Very rare. Pink eyes and white fur. Did you notice its antlers?"

"They were strange-looking. I've seen lots of dead deer in the Sheriff's parking lot. The deputies like to bring them in the back of their trucks for everyone to see what great hunters they are. I've never seen antlers like on this white deer this morning."

"Wildlife people call them atypical antlers. When I saw him he didn't seem frightened of me."

"He just stood there real calmly and stared at us. He drank from the creek, looked at us like he was studying us and took his time walking back into the woods. Seeing him was worth the trip for me even if Cheryl didn't come up with anything."

"Did she ever get off the bridge?"

"No, and we weren't there long. After we saw the deer she seemed spooked and was ready to go. She slept on the way back."

"You sure she was sleeping?"
"Her eyes were closed. I assumed she was asleep."
Maybe not, I hoped. Maybe not.

CHAPTER THIRTY-FIVE

I studied J.D. Silver's hair when he turned to remove a legal pad from his briefcase. I didn't want him catching me staring. This day the helmet was heavily sprayed with something more potent—maybe industrial-strength lacquer. It fascinated me because I knew he had to look in the mirror or see himself being interviewed on television and think "Man, that looks good."

My question was: how he could think that? I wondered the same about those almost-bald men who wear a tight little ponytail, their remaining hair pulled taut as a bowstring to gather enough for the tail.

But then, perhaps I was misjudging him. Maybe the helmet was his *schtick*, something to set him apart from the other lawyers around Memphis hustling criminal and p.i. cases. Maybe he looked in the mirror and knew the helmet looked goofy but had to wear it because it had become his trademark.

I was surprised when Silver called me to set up this meeting. Negotiating is usually part of every criminal prosecution, but I didn't expect Silver to broach the subject so soon in Ross's case.

"You understand I'm not here with any authority," Silver said. "My client doesn't know I'm doing this and wouldn't like it if he did. It's something I have to explore to satisfy myself. This is all off the record and hypothetical. Consider it in the nature of a proffer."

"This discussion stays between us," I said.

"There's no question we've got a problem on the DVDs," he said. "That's a strict liability crime these days."

"Up to ten years on each count, eight counts."

"No judge would give consecutive sentences on these facts. The DVDs were discovered at the same time in the same location. It's all one event, probably acquired by him at the same time. I'm saying probably."

"Not the homemade one."

"Okay, just for these purposes, let's say the judge will treat the seven as one transaction, give concurrent sentences. Let's pretend the homemade DVD is a separate transaction. You're still looking at ten and ten consecutive, total of twenty years, max."

"Then there's the capital murder."

"You know Judge Williams was wrong on the admission of the note. There's no way the appellate court will uphold it. You're wasting your time going to trial. Without the note you have nothing."

I let Silver's comment hang there.

"Anyway," he said, "I know you must have pressure on you from the family to try Ross for murder as quickly as possible, but unless you find the boy before trial you're taking a big chance putting on such a weak case."

"It was enough for the Grand Jury."

"Grand Jury, big deal. Like kissing your sister. Tell you what, I could recommend my client plead guilty on the DVDs and get, say, a total of fifteen years."

"What about the homicide?"

"He's not going to plead to any grade of homicide."

"So you're offering fifteen in the state system, which means he's parole eligible in five."

"Something like that."

"We're asking for the death penalty and you want me to agree to five, is that right?"

"It's a place to start."

"I'm not going to mention this hypothetical meeting to the Thurmans," I said.

"We might be able to talk about a little more time."

"Unless Ross Bullard is willing to plead to some homicide charge in addition to the child porn and is willing to do a large amount of time, say forty or fifty years, I'm not going to bring it up to the family."

"He may walk on murder if the *corpus delicti* ruling goes my way."

"They know that."

"Then we might as well saddle up and try it," Silver said. "Ross Bullard is not going to plead to a homicide."

"I figured that from the start. What's he writing, by the way?"

"I don't know. I asked him several times and he wouldn't tell me. Keeps his pad situated so I can't read it."

"He's pretty intense about it."

"I'll say something else, just between you and me," Silver said, leaning forward. "The little son-of-a-bitch seems to be having a lot better time in that courtroom than the rest of us."

Helmet Head shook my hand and left. I would have given anything to find out what possessed him to make such a ridiculous offer, but I didn't have time to think about it because Ethel Morris appeared in my doorway to announce that Cheryl Diamond was there to see me.

I walked around my desk and gave Cheryl a hug. She sat down and patted the arm on the wooden armchair next to her. I took the cue. She rested her hand on my forearm. I didn't mind a bit. There was something childlike in Cheryl's demeanor, a kind of innocence. I had grown fond of Cheryl and admired her courage. It wasn't easy going around telling hard-edged law enforcement and skeptical prosecutors about her gift and explaining how she might help them.

"I heard you two ladies saw the albino deer at the Iron Bridge."

"Yes, we did. It was magnificent, an ethereal experience."

"I told Kitty yesterday that I was down there a month ago, almost to the day, and saw him."

"I know. It doesn't surprise me that you saw him."

"Why do you say that?"

"Deer are nocturnal, are they not?"

"Generally."

"And albino deer are an anomaly?"

"Definitely rare."

"What would be the odds of you seeing the white deer at the bridge and then a month later Kitty and I driving down there and seeing him as well?"

I shrugged.

"It's more than a coincidence. When you saw him was it very quiet? Did he make any noise?"

I thought for a moment and said no. I waited for her to explain.

"I'm returning to Houston tomorrow, but I'll be back for the trial. I plan on being here every day, from start to finish."

"Sorry for your change of plans. I'm glad you're going to be here for the trial, but I was hoping you'd stick around and see what you can learn about the boy's whereabouts. I understand if you have to get home."

"No, you don't understand, Willie Mitchell. I know where Danny Thurman's remains are."

"Where?"

"He's somewhere around Iron Bridge. That's where Ross Bullard hid his hat and jeans and Connie's sweater, and that's where he hid the boy's body."

"How do you know?"

"That albino deer is communicating with us."

I sat back in the chair. She squeezed my forearm.

"The deer is telling us to come back. Danny is somewhere around that bridge. There's no doubt in my mind."

I walked around my desk and pulled out the county map, spreading it in front of us.

"Here's the bridge," I said. "Do you see anything...?"

"No. I've already studied the map you gave me. There's nothing around the bridge that tells me anything."

"Maybe you could walk through the woods with...."

"No," she said, frightened at the suggestion.

"Is there something keeping you from doing that?"

"I can't go any deeper along that creek or those woods," she said. "And I don't mind admitting I'm afraid."

"What is it down there that scares you?"

"The thing that killed Danny. It's something to do with the dancing man with the reptile face."

We both knew Ross Bullard killed Danny. Cheryl was making no sense, but I left it alone because she was upset. Whatever she feared was real to her, and that's all that mattered.

"All right. Let me ask you what kind of radius do you think...?"

"I wish I knew," she said. "I'm sorry I can't be more specific. If you find that white deer, if you can track him somehow he'll lead you to Danny's body. What I'm saying is true. Please believe me."

I grabbed the phone and called Walton. I told him to find Peewee Bernhardt and the two of them get to my office a.s.a.p.

"Thank you," I said to Cheryl.

"Call me when you find Danny," she said. "If I don't hear from you, I'll be back for the trial."

She walked quickly out of the office. Something at Iron Bridge had scared her back to Houston.

CHAPTER THIRTY-SIX

I lay in bed watching Susan undress, one of my life's underrated pleasures. She wore a red top today, so underneath it she sported a red bra, in compliance with one of her many apparel rules. Another is her panties must always match her bra, hence the red panties. The lingerie was apparently new because it was cut nicely to accentuate her lovely figure. The panties rode low on her hips with smaller than usual triangles front and back. The bra pushed her breasts up and in, showcasing delectable *décolletage*.

Needless to say, watching her in the mirror in our bathroom through the open door was more than a treat. It was exhilarating. I felt the stirring that always presaged contact, so I joined her in the bathroom wearing nothing but my boxer-briefs. I stood behind her, pressing myself against her, looking over her shoulder into the mirror.

"Well," she said, "I thought you were off in another world thinking about the trial or the election."

"I was. Something came up."

"I can tell."

I dropped my boxer-briefs.

"My goodness," she said. "We should do something about that."

I *was* preoccupied earlier. Until I saw her undressing in the bathroom I was thinking about the second unsuccessful search around Iron Bridge for Danny Thurman's body. I met with Peewee and Walton right after Cheryl Diamond left my office to return to Houston. Peewee was eager to try another search around Iron Bridge. Walton thought it was a wild goose chase. He was not impressed with Cheryl's feeling that Danny was somewhere around the bridge. He reminded me of the investigations we read about where Cheryl had been wrong. I asked him what we had to lose. His answer was not persuasive, especially in light of Peewee's urging that we do another search.

Peewee was a trooper. He met with a dozen of his volunteers who had re-upped. One of the men was a civil engineer. He created twelve grids using existing surveys of the Iron Bridge area. Peewee assigned each search team four grids and the order in which the team's grids were to be searched. The result was that each grid was searched by one two-man team, then searched again by a different team. They stayed at it a solid week, starting the last Sunday in September and ending the following Saturday.

They didn't find Danny. The teams found a lot of interesting Indian relics: spear points, arrowheads, and dart points made from agate, jasper, and petrified wood. The search wasn't a total loss for the volunteers. Some hauled off pickup truck loads of heart pine fatwood rich with resin to use in their fireplaces at home. One team encountered a half-acre area covered with good-sized petrified logs. Peewee said the half-acre was so remote and difficult to access the logs probably had not been seen by human eyes in over a thousand years.

I was surprised that the infrared cameras Peewee set up around the corn and oat feeders in every other grid did not record the albino deer. In spite of Cheryl's vision I knew from the outset finding Danny was a long shot, but I was certain the white deer be would recorded. Based on the two sightings in the creek at Iron Bridge, Peewee said the albino had to be living in the area. Peewee was excited to hear about the albino because he had only seen two in his lifetime in the woods. He said his sightings were in the 1980s and neither of the deer he saw had atypical antlers. Peewee had been confident he would catch the albino on camera, and was puzzled when he didn't.

Walton did not come right out and tell me "I told you so." He did concede there was no harm in the second Iron Bridge search. He said he thought we should postpone the trial. I asked him if he had talked to the Thurmans about it again. He said he had talked to Connie but Bill wouldn't discuss it.

I was glad I was no longer preoccupied when Susan turned around in the bathroom and kissed me. I watched in the mirror as she unsnapped her bra behind her back with ease.

"You're so much better at that than I am," I whispered in her ear.

"Practice."

"I'm willing to put in the time it takes to get better."

"Hush," she said and kissed me again

The red lingerie dropped on top of my boxer-briefs on the bathroom floor and I led Susan to our bed. Later, I was on my back with my left arm behind my head on the pillow, my right arm around Susan, her head resting against my shoulder.

"That was a really good idea," she said.

"You were asking for it."

"What do you mean?"

"Standing there in your new bra and panties. That's like waving a red cape in front of an angry bull."

"That reminds me. If I got you one of those matador suits with the skin tight pants, would you wear it? I bet I could find one online."

I could tell she was grinning from the sound of her voice.

"A suit of lights? Sure. I'd wear it in here. Just for you though."

"Hmmm," she said.

"If you make me play matador I'll have to stick you with a dart."

"One of those feathered things? You wouldn't."

"That's what a matador does."

"Where would you get one?"

"I already own one and keep it ready at all times. I never go anywhere without it. It doesn't have feathers, but it's deadly."

"You can say that again," she said and bit my shoulder.

"Careful," I said. "That's my cape twirling arm."

She giggled and I kissed the top of her head. We lay quiet for a while. I relished the tranquility.

"Thirteen days until jury selection," I said.

"Four weeks to the election, but you'll be tied up with Ross Bullard until the day we vote," she said.

"Probably."

"Are you going to be upset if you lose the race?"

"I'm not sure. I'd be more upset about Bullard going free."

She rolled off me and walked naked into the bathroom. I watched her, enjoying every moment. I hated to lose at anything, but I think my answer was right about the election. I had resigned myself to Eleanor's victory. Bobby Sanders was campaigning relentlessly with Eleanor, who was unencumbered with clients. The Indigent Defender Board had brought in a lawyer to take over Eleanor's defense work on a temporary basis, so Eleanor was out campaigning every day. I received reports on her whereabouts from Everett and Lee. I told them I had committed to the Thurmans and was not going back on my word. The Mayor and Sheriff said they understood but their drooping shoulders and sad eyes sent me a clear message: Ross Bullard would most likely be my last capital murder case in Yaloquena County.

I closed my eyes and thought about life after the D.A.'s office. I couldn't see myself in private practice and I sure as hell was not going to start defending the people I had prosecuted for twenty-four years. Susan and I didn't need the money.

What exactly would I do if I lost?

I imagined a few scenarios but not many because I drifted off and was sound asleep within a couple of minutes. The next thing I heard was an awful noise. It kept on until I felt Susan move and say hello in a dusky voice. I turned my back to her and hoped whatever it was would go away.

"Is this important?" she said.

"Give me your name again," she added and shook me.

"What?" I said.

"It's someone named John Mordano. He says it's about the Bullard case. He has some information about Danny."

I threw the covers back and grabbed the note pad and pen I kept on my bedside table. I turned on the lamp. Susan gave me the phone.

"This is Willie Mitchell Banks. Who is this?"

I wrote down his name, his address in Germantown, a Memphis suburb southeast of downtown, and his phone number. He didn't hesitate giving me his personal information, so I assumed it was real.

"Tell me what you know," I said.

"The missing boy, Danny Thurman, I saw him."

My stomach tightened. I gestured to Susan to go pick up the other phone and listen. I needed a witness. I waited until she picked up.

"How do you know it was Danny Thurman?"

"I'm a truck driver," Mordano said, "and I saw the flyers posted in truck stops along I-40 and I-55. I studied the boy's picture like I do all missing kid photos, just in case."

"Where is it you think you saw Danny?"

"At this big Flying J truck stop on the 440 Loop south of Nashville. He was with a man who looked to be about fifty-five, maybe sixty."

"When was this?"

"Night before last."

"Why'd you wait to call?"

"Same reason I didn't talk to the man at the truck stop. I had to think about it, make sure I saw what I thought I saw. They were leaving as I came in and they walked by me. I only saw them for a second or two. By the time I realized it was the boy on the poster and put two-and-two together, they were gone."

"Why didn't you call local troopers or cops?"

"I couldn't remember the boy's name. I figured I was on my way home to Memphis and I'd look at one of the flyers and get the name and number of who to call."

"Did you notify anyone else?"

"I called the number on the flyer. The boy's parents."

"My God," I said.

"They told me to call you. Gave me your number."

"All right, Mr. Mordano, I need you to be at my office first thing in the morning. Can you do that?"

"I guess so. I'm between runs. You pay mileage?"

"Yes," I said calmly, hiding my disgust at the question. "Nine a.m. at my office in the courthouse. Will you be there?"

"Yes, sir, if you think it's important."

"Very much so. And by the way, if you don't show up, I'll get the local Sheriff and the Mississippi and Tennessee State Police to bring you in as a material witness. That's a promise."

"Yes, sir. I'll get there somehow."

I threw on my clothes, slipped into some deck shoes and started down the stairs, passing Susan coming up.

"Where are you going?" she asked.

"The Thurmans," I said. "Call Walton. Tell him to meet me."

Within ten minutes I pulled into the Thurman's driveway. Bill was agitated, pacing on his sidewalk with a beer in his hand.

"Hey, Bill," I said, gently removing the longneck from his hand. "We don't need this right now. I want you focused and in control. This solves nothing, just makes matters worse."

"All right," he said.

I looked past Bill through the picture window at Connie on the couch. For the first time since July 4, she looked excited, hopeful.

I dreaded having to tell her the call from John Mordano was bull shit. There was no way he saw their son. Danny Thurman was dead. I was going to tell Bill and Connie as tactfully and gently as possible that Mordano was probably some kind of crackpot and they shouldn't get their hopes up. I would assure them that Walton and I would get to the bottom of it in the morning when we talked to Mordano. If there was anything to it, we'd get on it right away.

"Go sit with Connie," I told Bill as Walton pulled up.

Bill went inside and I met Walton on the grass in the darkness.

"We need to lower their expectations," I said.

"I know. This guy's got to be a fraud or a whack-job."

"We'll know in the morning. I'm going to call Silver and Judge Williams first thing to set up a meeting in chambers to let the defense know about this."

"Why?"

"It's Brady material."

"No, it's not. This guy's a loon. We're not obligated to tell Silver about this crap."

I'm sure shock registered on my face, but it was so dark in the Thurman's front yard Walton couldn't see it.

"This information is about as exculpatory as evidence can get," I said, "and Brady imposes a standing duty to notify the other side."

"It's not exculpatory. What if the guy claimed he saw Danny abducted by aliens? I guess we'd have to tell them that, too?"

"Forget Brady for now," I said. "We've got to make sure Bill and Connie don't believe this guy. We'll talk tomorrow about disclosure."

We joined the Thurmans in their living room. I closed the curtains on the big window and began talking. It took almost an hour, but Walton and I eventually returned Connie to the tearful, wretched state in which she had lived since Danny disappeared. We also managed to destroy Bill's joy and restore his festering rage against Ross Bullard.

After skillfully dismantling the Thurman's briefly resurrected hope, Walton and I left, mission accomplished. Driving home, I had never felt such sadness. The Thurmans lost their son. Now they had to endure the insults of our legal system. It just wasn't fair.

CHAPTER THIRTY-SEVEN

I usually call defense attorneys to let them know in advance what I intend to bring up *in camera* with the Judge. Not this time. I wanted to gauge Helmet Head's reaction in the Judge's chambers when I told her about the late night call.

John Mordano had shown up in my office on time. I moved the meeting to the conference room because I wanted the Sheriff, Walton, and Kitty there to hear Mordano's story. The four of us sat and listened to Mordano repeat what he told me on the phone. For ninety minutes we asked him questions, but he provided no new details. His statement was spare and conclusory: "Two days ago when I walked into the Flying J truck stop on the 440 loop south of Nashville, a man in his fifties walked past me with Danny Thurman. I recognized the boy from flyers I had seen at various truck stops. I didn't call right away because I wanted to be sure it was the same boy, and I needed the phone number from one of the flyers."

He gave a vague description of the man with Danny, had no idea what type of vehicle they were in or where they were headed. Mordano appeared younger to me than he sounded on the phone. He was swarthy, heavy set with dark hair. He remained unflappable when Walton or I conducted our unofficial cross-examination, as if it were no big deal to him. He reminded me of a mobster who had been questioned on many occasions by law enforcement. Everything was routine, old hat.

Kitty asked him if he had ever been a witness in any kind of criminal or civil trial before, but started coughing before Mordano could answer. She excused herself as her mild cough became a croupy, jagged hack that sounded painful to me. I heard her cough through the closed door as she walked down the hall away from us, the sound diminishing as the separation grew. I asked Mordano to answer her question. He said his only brush with the legal system was in a case where Silver represented him. I told Mordano to stick around until about three p.m. because the Judge or J.D. Silver would want to talk to him.

When Mordano left the conference room, Lee walked out, too, promising to use all the resources available to him in the state and federal systems to find out what he could about John Mordano.

"You still think this isn't Brady material?" I said.

"I don't think we should disclose it, but you're the boss. What's wrong with Kitty? Her cough is getting worse."

"She's had a respiratory infection that won't go away and she's too stubborn to take care of herself properly."

I picked up the phone as Walton left. I called Susan, told her about Kitty, and asked her to come get her at the Sheriff's office and drag her physically if necessary to see Dr. Clement. She said she was on her way. I got Lee on the phone and asked him to give Kitty a direct order to go with Susan, thinking her FBI chain of command training might be a good way to force her to see Nathan. I spent the rest of the morning boning up on Motion In Limine procedures in the criminal code and finding cases to support my contention that Judge Williams had the discretion to grant the relief that I would request at the conference in three hours.

That afternoon, J.D. Silver walked into Judge Williams' reception area only a minute or two before the two o'clock start time. He asked me what the conference was about just as Judge Williams' receptionist told us the Judge was ready. I pointed Silver toward her chambers and walked in with Walton.

"It's your meeting, Mr. Banks," Judge Williams said.

The three of us sat across from Judge Williams. I laid it out for her just as it happened, the call the night before, the trip to the Thurmans, the interrogation of John Mordano this morning. I kept my eyes on Judge Williams as I spoke and was confident she recognized the charade for what it was. I cautioned myself to stay calm during Helmet Head's theatrics.

"This puts the case in an entirely new light," he said.

"It is a red herring, Your Honor. Mordano didn't see Danny Thurman. Danny's dead. Look at Bullard's note. He says he's sorry about Danny and the boy's body was near an old hunting camp. Is Mr. Silver suggesting the note means nothing?"

"I am not suggesting anything—I am asserting this sighting is the very reason other jurisdictions require proof of murder, a dead body, before any so-called inculpatory statements by the defendant can be introduced into evidence."

Judge Williams looked at me.

"I want to ask Mr. Silver in the Court's presence if he had anything to do with this."

"Absolutely not," he said, doing his best to look offended.

"Let me ask you another question, Mr. Silver. Do you know John Mordano?"

"I represented him years ago."

Judge Williams zeroed in on Silver.

"More details, Mr. Silver."

"It was a criminal case. He was arrested on some trumped up charges and I got them dismissed."

"What were the charges?" she asked.

"Mail fraud, criminal and civil RICO. The U.S. Attorney in Memphis had a vendetta against Mr. Mordano because of his association with some friends of his who were connected to...."

"Have you talked to Mr. Mordano about this case?" she asked.

"No, Your Honor, and I will swear to that under oath. I haven't spoken to him in years, either in person or on the phone."

"Have you had any communication with him, written, oral, or through third parties?" I asked.

"None at all."

"Has Phil Myers talked to him?"

"Not to my knowledge."

"If Mr. Myers is available, Your Honor, I would like to take his statement under oath."

"I strongly object to that," Silver said. "Mr. Myers is my investigator and everything he has worked on in this case is privileged as work product. I would not expect this Court to allow me to take a sworn statement from Assistant District Attorney Donaldson or any of the State's investigators."

"I believe Your Honor has the right to determine whether there is any hint of subornation of perjury with respect to Mordano. What Mordano has stated about seeing Danny is patently false. Everyone in this room knows Danny is dead. Just as this Court determined that the prejudicial effect of the seven commercial DVDs outweighed their probative value, I suggest that this Court make the same determination regarding this false testimony. It is highly prejudicial."

Judge Williams looked at her weekly docket calendar.

"We're going to hear what Mr. Mordano and Mr. Myers have to say tomorrow morning, October 12, at nine a.m. Mr. Banks, I would like you to ask Chief Deputy Clerk Mr. Bordelon to issue a subpoena immediately for Mr. Mordano and Mr. Myers, requiring their presence tomorrow morning at this hearing. Will you coordinate with Sheriff Jones and ask him to serve these two gentlemen this morning?"

Walton stood. "I'll go downstairs and see to it right now," he said.

"You can raise your work product or any other privilege objections in the morning, Mr. Silver. And a word to the wise, I better not find anything untoward in all this."

"I'm sure you won't, Your Honor," Silver said.

"I'll see you both tomorrow."

Silver and I walked down the narrow passage from the Judge's office to the main hallway. Neither of us said a word.

CHAPTER THIRTY-EIGHT

The Mordano hearing did not go well. Mordano took the stand and told the same story. His description of the sighting continued to be devoid of meaningful detail. Cross-examination on what he saw at the Flying J was uneventful, with Mordano playing stupid ("I don't know,") or forgetful ("I don't recall.") My burden of proof at the hearing put me at an extreme disadvantage—it's impossible to prove a negative. I could offer no evidence to rebut Mordano's bald assertion that he saw Danny. I could argue that Mordano was mistaken, emphasize his connection with Silver, imply collusion, but I had no witnesses of my own. The only sure-fire way to rebut Mordano's testimony was to prove Danny was dead.

Every aspect of my case against Ross Bullard eventually circled back to the same critical weakness: no dead body. I had no direct evidence of death, let alone a violent homicide. Without it, my entire rebuttal of Mordano's testimony amounted to a big "Oh, yeah?" Worthless.

Ninety per cent of my questions to Mordano focused on his relationship to Silver and Myers. He acknowledged that Silver had done a masterful job defending him the fraud and RICO charges five years earlier, but denied owing Silver any money. He denied that he came forward to ingratiate himself in any way with Silver or Myers. After he said "I saw what I saw" for the fifth time, I quit counting.

Phil Myers was a pro. I asked him how many times he testified in murder cases in Memphis. His answer was "hundreds." It was evident, too. He answered my questions using as few words as possible. He volunteered nothing. If the question could be answered in one word, that's what I got. He testified that to his knowledge J.D. Silver had no contact with Mordano and neither had he, that Mordano's declaration was as surprising to Myers and Silver as it was to us.

Down deep I knew the whole thing was a lie. I knew Mordano's story was made out of whole cloth, and that Silver and Myers had something to do with it, even if there had been no communication or provable *quid pro quo*. The problem was I could prove nothing. Judge Williams' ruling was no surprise.

I could tell she was reluctant but felt she had no choice. In a capital murder case, to deny the defense a witness who claims to have vital information on the central issue was out of the question, no matter how implausible the testimony. In the absence of proof that Silver or Myers somehow orchestrated Mordano's testimony, I had to agree with Zelda. There was only one way she could rule. I would have to destroy Mordano's credibility with the jury on cross-examination.

One encouraging thing about the hearing was the continuing evolution of Ross Bullard. He paid scant attention to Jules and Judy and would grin and chuckle at inappropriate times, detached from what was occurring in the hearing. Ross seemed physically bigger, and definitely more assertive. Big Boy had seen Walton in the courthouse and told him Ross was continuing his workouts. He continued his manic writing at the defense table next to Helmet Head. I had to wonder how many legal pads the man had gone through. Dozens by now.

I wondered what Jules thought about cuckolding his only child. The old man did manage to smirk at me a couple of times during Mordano's time on the stand as if Silver were hitting a home run with the trucker's testimony. Judy looked bored, as usual. I was sick of looking at the Bullards and dreaded the thought of being in the same room with them for the duration of the trial, at least two weeks.

I planned on leaving the office in the afternoon to knock on some doors and hand out push cards. Tonight was the big "debate" with Eleanor Bernstein at the Honorable Rose Jackson Civic Center in the park the Congresswoman funded for Sunshine. "Civic Center" was a misnomer. This was no arena. It was a small brick veneer building with a pitched roof, a kitchen and bathroom, and an open area with room for about a hundred folding chairs. A condition attached to the construction grant specified that the "Civic

Center" building had to be available to various civic and non-profit organizations for free. Since a consortium of black churches was sponsoring the "debate," it fell within the grant guidelines. It wasn't a "debate," either. Each of us would be given ten minutes to speak and another ten minutes to answer questions from the audience, not from our opponent. Some debate.

When I was walking toward the main door of the courthouse on my way out to do some politicking, I saw Bobby Sanders escorting three elderly black women into the Chancery Clerk's office. The ladies smiled and waved at me, then tottered inside to vote for Eleanor Bernstein. I didn't recognize any of them and was fairly positive they didn't know who I was. Early voting was underway, and the Mayor and Lee Jones told me the Reverend Sanders was bringing scores of elderly but still mobile voters from nursing homes and assisted living homes to vote. He was using one of his extra-length Full Gospel House of the Lord white vans, making multiple trips a day. Everett told me that Eleanor had three paid vote haulers doing the same thing, using their private vehicles. It was all perfectly legal under Mississippi's voting laws as long as the payments to the vote haulers were listed on the campaign finance reports candidates were supposed to file. Under the law the vote haulers were to provide transportation only, but everyone in politics knew the haulers made sure every person they transported voted "right." Bobby Sanders wasn't giving a free ride to anyone who might vote for me. It was a crude trade: a ride for a vote. The vote haulers for hire did the same thing. Eleanor wasn't paying them to haul my voters.

I knew I shouldn't. I knew I was going to be sorry. No matter. I couldn't help myself. I waited for Bobby to walk back into the hallway from the Clerk's office. He was not permitted to be there when the ladies voted. He flashed a big grin when he saw me. We shook hands.

"Mr. District Attorney," he said.

"Getting your early voters to the polls, I see."

"Helping the elderly exercise their rights. I feel it's my civic duty."

"Did any of those ladies indicate they were voting for me?" I said.

"Not that I recall," he said, "but it's a free country."

We both laughed. I felt awkward, but Bobby seemed at ease.

"I hope you're not taking this personally," he said. "The way I see it, this is the American way. Exercising our hard fought right to vote in a free and fair election, competition among qualified candidates. I say let the best man, or woman, win."

"Aw Bobby, come on. It's obvious you don't care for me. Or is it all white people in general?"

Bobby stopped smiling. He seemed to stand taller.

"That's a good question. Sounds like you been talking to your boys Lee and Everett about me."

"I didn't have to. It's been this way between us a long time."

He thought for a moment.

"It's true I think it's time to have an African-American as District Attorney. We make up three-fourths of the county population. Having a D.A. from one-fourth of the people don't seem to make much sense. We're the majority, so we should decide who's going to be in office."

"So it is about race. It's your folks' turn."

"That's part of it. I think Eleanor is a good lawyer and I know she'll be more understanding of our people."

"You think I haven't been fair to blacks?"

"I think you might have tried, in your own way, but it's just human nature. You got land and money, so you going to take care of people like you that's got the wealth."

"And it turns out all those kind of people in the county are white."

"All we poor blacks got is the vote. That's why I'm here today."

"For what it's worth, Bobby, I've treated everyone the same, black or white, victim or defendant. Did you ever think that 80% of the crime victims in this county are black, too? Don't they deserve some justice? You can't just focus on the black defendants." I paused. Nothing I said made any impact. "I'm sure you don't believe anything I say."

"It ain't what I believe," he said, raising his voice. "It's the facts. You let Little Al go free even though he ran over and killed a beautiful black child, Dee Johnson, and him being drunk as Cooter Brown."

"Not true. I didn't let him go. The Johnson family asked me to go along with what their lawyer was asking. They wanted a civil settlement."

"McKinley Owens doing fifteen years for getting justice for Dee."

"Fifteen years on two counts of manslaughter is lenient treatment," I said. "He's responsible for the deaths of two people, white people."

"And they both needed killing."

"Your animosity goes back further than that, Bobby. You had it in for me before Takisha Berry was ever arrested. All I want is the truth. What is it?"

He thought for a moment, making his decision.

"All right. I'm going to give it to you straight. Before I was led by God to become a pastor, I ran the roads in this county. I'm sure Lee's told you about me in the clubs with whiskey and women. Back in those dark days, I had a good friend by the name of Levarius Washington. That name ring a bell?"

"Sure. I prosecuted him for murdering his wife. He's in Parchman for life. That was six or seven years ago."

"That's right. Well he was a good friend of mine, and a good man."

"You saying he didn't kill Dollie?"

"That ain't what I'm saying. I'm saying the man's blood was up. She wasn't paying him any attention and had put him out of the house, wouldn't let him see his kids. I was with him the afternoon before it happened. He was out of his mind with grief."

"It's true they were separated. I remember the facts. He was drinking all the time, staying out all night. She was working a full day at the hospital and taking care of the two children by herself."

"She wouldn't let him even be around his own kids."

"Dollie's mother, who's raising the kids now, said he was drunk whenever he came around."

"That's just her talking. What I'm saying is he did it, but he wasn't in his right mind and don't deserve to spend the rest of his life cooped up like an animal. You heard the phrase 'heat of passion'?"

"Levarius Washington hid in the bushes with a shotgun outside their house and when Dollie came home from working a double shift at the hospital he shot her with double-aught buckshot in the chest, and as she lay on her back on their sidewalk he shot her again, this time in the head. Dollie's mother couldn't even open the casket at her service. I went to the funeral, Bobby. Did you?"

"The man is sorry for what happened. He deserved to be punished, and is doing his time like a man. The way you set it up, he got to do forty years before he even come up for parole."

"I only wish I could have prosecuted him for the death of the baby she was carrying in her womb."

"He told me that baby wasn't his."

I knew I was going to kick myself for talking to the stupid bastard. I decided I should walk away before I said or did something I would regret. There was no reasoning with the Reverend Bobby Sanders.

"When Eleanor gets in she's going to help Levarius get an earlier parole hearing," he said as I walked off. "She understands the quality of mercy, which you don't."

"It's about time we got some justice," Bobby said raising his voice to preacher volume, getting the attention of the other people in the main hallway. "Been a long time comin' for us around here."

I kept my mouth shut and kept walking. I didn't dare turn around.

CHAPTER THIRTY-NINE

If you've never experienced the jury selection process in a death penalty case, consider yourself lucky. I've picked "death qualified" juries on probably ten occasions over the last twenty-four years, and let me assure you it is a grueling, tedious process. Without a strong judge, it can become an endurance contest. Fortunately, Zelda Williams had been on the bench in at least four capital cases with me, and she knew what it took to keep the process moving. She was willing to make the parties and jury prospects put in long days. Fatigue seemed to make the selection go faster. Zelda also asked the entire jury venire a lot of the qualifying questions and stopped lawyers from repeating them. She allowed both sides to give a two-minute *voir dire* "opening" statement to the crowded courtroom, describing just enough of the case from their perspective to make their later questioning less repetitious.

The courtroom was already packed with people when I arrived. I stopped inside the door for a moment and scanned the jury prospects in the gallery. Three quarters of them were overweight. Every year our jurors get bigger. I'm not sure how fat humans can get before they explode, but some folks I saw that morning seemed to be testing the limits of their skin's elasticity.

Walton sat at our table organizing the trial material. It was ten minutes before nine. In the front row behind the prosecution table were Connie and Bill, Cheryl Diamond, and Sheriff Lee Jones.

Kitty Douglas wasn't in court. She was scheduled to see Dr. Clement again and if she hadn't improved, Nathan told me he was going to do his best to admit her to the hospital.

J.D. Silver stood with arms crossed at the defense table, rocking back and forth on his heels, facing the jury prospects. He was nodding and smiling as he made eye contact, wooing the prospects. His grand bonnet of gray hair was resplendent in its rigidity, not one hair out of place.

Lovebirds Jules and Judy sat in the first row behind the defense table next to Phil Myers, whose shirt collar and tie were much too tight for his large neck.

When I sat down with Walton I heard the side door open again. In walked an unshackled Ross Bullard accompanied by only one deputy. Ross wore khaki slacks and a blue button-down shirt. Case law and local rules made it clear the jury prospects could not see the defendant in jail clothes, handcuffs, or shackles. To make certain Ross couldn't make a run for it and to protect him from Bill Thurman, Lee had plenty of plainclothes and uniformed officers spread throughout the courtroom.

Ross's newly developed muscles made the shirt fit tight. His hair was much longer than when he worked in the bank. Under his arm he carried a slender leather file tote. To people in the courtroom seeing him the first time, I'm sure he appeared normal.

Ross walked past Silver without speaking, sat down and pulled two new legal tablets and a pen from his tote. He began to write.

The bailiff called the courtroom to order and Zelda took the bench. She looked over the two hundred faces in front of her and smiled. I counted thirty jury prospects standing along the back and side walls.

"Good morning, ladies and gentlemen. I apologize to those of you who are standing. I will move this along as quickly as possible and hope that in the next hour or so there will be plenty of seats available. The first thing I'd like to do is give you the general qualifications you must have to serve...."

I zoned out, leaving it to Walton to pay close attention. Twenty of the two hundred formed a line in front of the bench and took turns whispering to Zelda why they didn't meet the age or literacy requirements, or explaining they had a felony record or chronic physical infirmity. Zelda told us in chambers she thought it would take us a week to pick the jury. She made it clear that we were not to exceed her expectations.

Zelda dismissed all but two of the twenty. She then told the venire that the name of the case was State of Mississippi versus Darrell Ross Bullard and involved the alleged murder of the juvenile Danny Thurman of Sunshine on or about July 4. She asked if anyone in the courtroom had heard of the case.

I turned to watch the majority of prospective jurors raise their hands. I studied the others. It never ceased to amaze me how many of our citizens could be oblivious to such a high-profile case involving the death of a child in their own town and county. Nevertheless there they were, sitting in blissful ignorance with arms down, looking around at all the others raising their hands, wondering why they didn't get the memo. Zelda's next question would cause a lot of the raised hands to drop.

"How many of you with your hands raised have formed an opinion about the guilt or innocence of the defendant Darrell Ross Bullard?"

Sixty per cent of the hands dropped. I knew from experience a good number of those who lowered their hands were not telling the truth. They either wanted to be on the jury, or they had a vague feeling they weren't supposed to have an opinion because our laws proclaimed that every defendant was presumed innocent.

"All right," Zelda said, "this is for those of you who have an opinion. You may lower your hands, but when Mr. Bordelon gets to your row, raise it again. He will write down your juror number and then I want you to wait outside in the hallway until I call you back in."

Chief Deputy Clerk Eddie Bordelon, the bald, transplanted Cajun who single-handedly kept things running in the Circuit Clerk's office and in the courtroom, had been with the jury prospects for an hour before Judge Williams took the bench, calling the roll and giving each a pre-assigned number. Eddie was a bundle of nerves, but efficient.

"Each of you who hasn't heard of the case or has no opinion may leave for the day. Mr. Bordelon has given you the phone number for you to call after four p.m. today to learn if you are to return at nine in the morning or at a later time. You will have to come back after the attorneys and I have had a chance to question the folks here who remain. I remind you that you should ignore anything in the newspaper or on radio and television about this trial. Do not discuss the case with anyone."

The bailiff gestured for everyone to leave except the fifty or so who claimed to have an opinion about the case. While they filed out, Judge Williams gestured for Silver and me to approach. She cupped her hand over the microphone and whispered.

"Doesn't look like Mr. Granger's poll was all that accurate, Mr. Silver. Lots of people in Yaloquena County don't read the paper or listen to the radio. Some don't have television."

"I have the right to question each of them about what they might have heard," Silver said. "I'm not withdrawing my Motion for Change of Venue."

"I didn't expect you to withdraw it," she said. "I just wanted you to have an idea of what kind of jury pool you were dealing with."

I glanced at Silver when he took his seat. He didn't seem troubled by what he had seen. Why should he? From the defense side in a criminal case, the dumber the juror the better. Easier to influence them with theatrics and illogical arguments. I was accustomed to poorly educated jurors who were unaware of anything except what affected them and their family within their small sphere of existence. All these prospects were voters, too, what the national media euphemistically referred to as "low information voters."

I scanned the prospects again, trying to locate the dumbest of the lot. There were many contenders, but I settled on the morbidly obese white man in denim overalls in the third row. His eyes, the windows to his soul, seemed to let in very little light. I reminded myself that his vote in the November 6 contest counted just as much as mine.

The election was in fifteen days. I would be in court for at least ten of those. My prospects for losing both this trial and the election seemed to be increasing exponentially.

CHAPTER FORTY

We spent all day Tuesday and half of Wednesday with testimony of prospective jurors who claimed to have formed an opinion about the defendant's guilt or innocence. Judge Williams did a good job limiting the amount of time each prospect was on the stand. She kept Helmet Head in check and we moved quickly through this part of the venire.

I suspected that some of the prospects, the more intelligent ones, knew exactly what they were doing when they said they had followed the case in the Courier and already decided Ross Bullard was guilty. They knew it would end their jury duty. It was my loss, but how could I blame them? Who would voluntarily endure a couple of weeks of misery, especially if they were needed at work or home? Judge Williams explained early Tuesday morning that those chosen for the jury would be sequestered, i.e., put up in a crummy local motel with other jurors for the duration of the trial, starting immediately upon their selection. It's incredible what our legal system asks of these prospective jurors in a capital murder case. As soon as the prospect is selected, isolation begins immediately. The bailiff or another deputy calls their house, has someone pack a bag with clothes and toiletries and bring it to the courthouse. During the remainder of jury selection, the juror may not sit in court listening to other prospects and is confined in our ancient courthouse to the Grand Jury room, unable to read the paper, watch television, or discuss the trial with the other jurors who passed muster with Helmet Head and me.

Wednesday at one-thirty, with the vetting of the opinionated jurors completed, Judge Williams denied Silver's Motion for Change of Venue and we started the process of getting a "death qualified" jury from the 122 remaining prospects.

"The charge in this case is capital murder. If you are chosen to serve on this jury," she said from the bench, "you will be asked to consider the death penalty as a sentence if the State proves the elements of capital murder beyond a reasonable doubt. Do any of you feel that you are unable under any circumstances to consider voting for the death penalty for religious, moral, personal, or any other reasons? If so, please raise your hand and keep it raised until Mr. Bordelon notes your number on his list."

I did a quick count. Seventy-seven of the prospects raised their hands, leaving about forty-five remaining of the original two hundred. Of the seventy-seven prospects against the death penalty under any circumstances, I estimated sixty were black. The numbers were about what I expected based on my experiences in jury selection in the other Yaloquena capital murder cases. In my first four terms, white jury prospects were in favor of the death penalty at least two to one. Now, whites split almost evenly on the issue.

Neither Helmet Head nor I could rehabilitate any of the seventy-seven prospects, except for one older black man who had misunderstood the question. Zelda ended up releasing him anyway because his hearing was so bad he wouldn't have been able to understand the testimony. Of the forty-five prospects left standing, twenty-five were black. We started questioning these prospects at about three o'clock on Thursday afternoon and worked until seven. Silver used half of his twelve peremptory challenges, all against white prospects. I guarded my twelve because I wanted to get a jury from the forty-five and was afraid if I used all my challenges we would run out of prospects.

The jury that was finally selected to hear the Ross Bullard case was split racially, four black women and two black men; five white women and one white man. Because Bullard was white, I felt the racial makeup of the jurors wasn't critical, especially since all twelve were "death qualified." They said under oath they could impose the death penalty if the facts warranted it. Defense lawyers contend that a "death qualified" jury is pro-prosecution. They are correct.

Ross Bullard must have filled a dozen legal pads during jury selection. Jules sat in the first row every day. Judy showed up on Wednesday and Thursday, then skipped

Friday. Phil Myers was in and out, meeting with Silver and Jules during breaks.

Cheryl Diamond sat behind me from Wednesday on. She told me she enjoyed studying the people on the jury venire and confided that she thought all of my selections were good except for one she couldn't read, the short, red-faced older white man, P. O. Harrington. My first question to him was to ask what the initials stood for. He begrudgingly muttered "Pearl Ocie" so I was careful to call him "Mr. P.O." during the remainder of my questioning. I told Cheryl I thought P.O. would be fine. Lee Jones looked in occasionally, sometimes giving us additional information about a prospective juror. We had gone over the venire list several times with him the week before trial.

I thought it odd that Silver didn't have a jury consultant. Jules Bullard could certainly afford one.

We finished picking the jury Saturday afternoon, and Judge Williams ordered opening statements to begin promptly at nine a.m. Monday morning.

I left the courthouse at about three o'clock Saturday and looked at my text messages as I walked to the truck. When I read the text from Susan I began to walk faster.

Dr. Clement had just transferred Kitty into I.C.U. and put her on a ventilator.

CHAPTER FORTY-ONE

When I turned the corner and entered the corridor to I.C.U. I saw Susan and Dr. Clement talking quietly in the hallway. Susan hugged me when I joined them. I knew the news wasn't good.

"What's happened?" I asked, shaking Nathan's hand.

"She's gotten progressively worse this week," he said. "When Susan brought her into my clinic last Friday I recommended to Kitty that she let me admit her immediately for some tests."

"She wouldn't hear of that," Susan said. "I practically begged her."

"I gave her a shot and a strong antibiotic to take four times a day and told her she had to get some rest and come back to see me Monday."

"I tried to get her to stay at our house," Susan said, "but Kitty insisted on staying at the camp. She said she'd be more comfortable in her own place."

"She didn't get any better over the weekend," Dr. Clement said, "and when she came in with Susan on Monday I admitted her."

"Right," I said, "Susan told me all about that, that Kitty was so weak on Monday she did what you said. Now she's in I.C.U.?"

"Best I can tell Kitty's had a walking pneumonia for several weeks. She thought she could work through it. With her history, it wasn't possible. Two years ago she developed pneumonia in the New Orleans hospital after the attack. This is her third bout with it since I began taking care of her. Her lungs are severely compromised and prone to infection. The pulmonologist that comes here from Jackson one day a week saw her yesterday. He recommended the respirator and I.C.U. He said if she's not better by Monday we need to ship her to Jackson."

"Has anyone told the Sheriff?" I asked.

"He just left," Susan said.

"What about Jake?" I asked Nathan.

"I wouldn't just yet," he said. "Let's see what happens in the next couple of days. The respirator and the new antibiotic drip the pulmonologist started ought to have her feeling better soon."

"Is there anything else...?"

"You've got enough on your plate right now, Willie Mitchell," Dr. Clement said. "Let me worry about Kitty. I'll do all I can to get her well."

"You go home and get some rest," Susan said. "I'm going to sit with Kitty. I'll be there after a while."

I left the hospital and drove toward the campaign office Jimmy Gray set up for me in an empty storefront he owned downtown. It was four o'clock when I walked in. There were yard signs stapled to wooden stakes leaning against the wall, a stack of bumper stickers and push cards on one counter, and a sign up sheet for volunteers on another. The Mayor was behind a desk working the phones with several members of his extended family. Lee Jones was huddled in the corner with a half-dozen volunteers explaining the rules of transporting voters to the courthouse for early voting. I recognized one of the haulers—David Jefferson, the grandson of the late Reverend Paul Gray of Ebeneezer Primitive. I was glad to see David was willing to support the campaign even though I vetoed the use of the photos of Eleanor and her friend.

Standing inside the front door, an immense wave of guilt came over me. Scores of volunteers were doing the heavy lifting for me, working hard for my re-election while I sat in the courtroom.

Given my state of mind, I knew it was good for the campaign that I was no longer down in the weeds directing every move. In fact, I hadn't been paying attention at all. When Jimmy Gray or Lee or Everett called me at the end of the day the past week with information about the race, I felt oddly detached. It was as if they were telling me about some stranger's campaign in another state. And since Walton was doing all the research, witness preparation, and pleadings in State vs. Ross Bullard, I felt like I wasn't giving the Thurmans one hundred per cent. By my usual standards, I was half-assing the two major events occupying my life.

I turned when I heard the bell above the front door jingle. Jimmy Gray and Buddy Wade walked in.

"Well, shut my mouth," Jimmy said grabbing my hand.

"Been reading about your trial in the paper," Buddy said, "and watching the nightly summary on the local news."

"Sorry I'm not here to help, guys."

"If you ask me, and Jimmy never does, your face on the six o'clock news every night talking about the trial and on the front page of the local paper is the kind of political advertising you can't buy. I think you're doing lots more for your re-election than we can do out here."

"Just don't lose," Jimmy said, "or if you see you're going to lose, stretch it out so the verdict's not in until after November 6."

"I'll do my best," I said.

Jimmy lowered his voice.

"Lee told us about Kitty. Is she going to be all right?"

"Nathan thinks so. He says if she's not out of the woods by Monday he's sending her to Jackson."

"I'll say a prayer for her," Jimmy said.

"Better let me," Buddy said. "I'm sure the Man upstairs has the red ass at you from listening to your bull shit."

"Speaking of that," Jimmy said, "Martha said our housekeeper told her Jules and Judy have been arguing a good bit. Said Judy stayed in her own house a couple of nights this week."

"Wonder what that's about," I said.

"It's either about Ross or money, one or the other," Jimmy said.

"Maybe both," Buddy said looking at his watch. "Anybody besides me ready for a cocktail?"

"You two go ahead," I said. "I'm headed home to wait for Susan. She's still at the hospital."

"You're the one needs a drink," Jimmy said. "We'll meet you at your house."

"Might do you some good," Buddy said.

CHAPTER FORTY-TWO

Five minutes after Judge Williams took the bench at nine sharp the following Monday, twelve jurors and two alternates were led in the side door by the bailiff. Zelda welcomed the jurors, thanked them for their service, and apologized for disrupting their lives. I planned on doing that in my opening if she hadn't. She asked Silver and me if we had any final motions or housecleaning matters to tend to before opening statements.

"I amended my witness list last week to add two names, Your Honor," Silver said, "and gave notice to the State."

"We added those two names as well," I said.

Irma Gilbert and Ronnie Blake were the two names, both unearthed by Phil Myers. I chose not to object to Helmet Head's late additions to his witness list, opting to name the same two as potential State witnesses. I would wait to see how my case unfolded before deciding to call them as my witnesses. It might work out better to wait for Silver to call them so I could get them on cross. Judge Williams repeated what she told the jurors in *voir dire*: we were starting the guilt phase of the capital case and if they found the defendant guilty, we would begin the sentencing phase immediately. She told the jurors what opening statements were and nodded to me.

I closed my trial binder and walked to the podium. The two jurors in the center of the first row were less than five feet from me. I took my time opening the binder, using the silence to get their attention. At no time during the trial would the jurors pay more attention to my words. They were fresh from a day and a half of rest and eager to listen to something interesting. I looked at each uplifted face and paused again.

"I am going to prove to you beyond a reasonable doubt that the defendant Ross Bullard caused seven-year-old Danny Thurman to disappear, then caused his death. In a moment I'll summarize what I expect to prove to you in this trial, but first I would like to ask you to do something for me in this case." I paused. "Please do not reward Ross Bullard for successfully getting rid of Danny's Thurman's body."

"Objection," Helmet Head barked. "The State is exceeding the scope...."

"Dial it back, Mr. Banks," she cautioned me. "Lay out your case and save that kind of remark for closing."

"Very well, Your Honor," I said.

I noticed two jurors nod when I asked the question. One was P.O. Harrington, the strong-willed banty rooster of a man whom I fully expected to be the foreman of the twelve. I didn't understand why Silver allowed him on the jury. Maybe there was something about P.O. I didn't know. I continued with my opening, going over the testimony and exhibits I intended to share with them and what the evidence would show. I chose not to refer to Bullard's note because I would later refer to it as "his confession" and mentioning the defendant's confession in an opening statement before it was introduced into evidence warranted a mistrial. I kept my opening to less than twenty minutes.

"I thank you for your service as well," I said finally. "I know what a hardship it is to all of you. After you've heard the testimony, I will stand before you again and ask you to return a verdict of guilty of capital murder."

I sat down to watch Helmet Head smile his way to the podium. Walton and I were ready to take notes. I looked over Walton's head at Ross Bullard. As usual, he was in his own world, writing up a storm. Behind him Jules and Judy sat with Phil Myers. Cheryl Diamond and Lee sat right behind me, Bill and Connie in the second row.

"*Corpus Delicti,*" Silver boomed, causing several jurors to jump. "That's a fancy, legalistic way of saying something real simple." Helmet Head was trying to sound folksy, and doing a decent job of it. "All it means is 'the body of the crime.' And it doesn't mean the body of the alleged victim in this case. No, siree Bob. It means the elements of the crime charged, in this case, the elements of capital murder. The only element that's important in this case, ladies and gentlemen, is that the State, represented by Mr. Banks, must prove that Danny Thurman was murdered." He paused a moment. "It's not enough to prove young Danny disappeared on July 4, which he did, and it's not enough to prove he's never been found, which he hasn't. Mr. Banks has to put witnesses on that stand..." he pointed then walked from the podium to the witness stand and patted the chair, "and they have to prove to you number one," he held up one finger, "that Danny is dead, and two," he held up two, "that young Danny was murdered.

"I submit to you ladies and gentlemen there will be no proof of either one or two," he said, showing the fingers again.

"My client will not testify in this trial. I want to tell you that up front. As you acknowledged in my questioning each of you last week, our constitution gives each of us to right to choose not to testify, and our Supreme Court has ruled many times that my client's silence cannot be held against him. There can be a lot of reasons why a defendant may choose not to testify."

I scooted up in my chair, ready to object if he took this too far.

"You can think of many reasons I'm sure. Some people are not able to express themselves very well. Maybe it's fear or nerves."

Silver quickly moved on so I throttled back. I wrote down as much of his opening as I could. I had to admit Helmet Head made a good presentation. He was charismatic, an excellent communicator, but I did think he went on a little long. He could have stopped after saying I had to prove Danny was murdered. He was right, of course, and without a body, I was fighting an uphill battle.

I called Lee Jones as my first witness. I used him to build the overview of the case, beginning with the July 4 disappearance and proceeding through the investigation, the search for Danny, the Ross Bullard 911 call and discovery of the note he left about Danny, the hospital stay, the arrest, the discovery of Danny's jeans and Rangers cap and Connie's blue sweater at the Iron Bridge where a witness saw Bullard the day after Danny went missing. I asked him to explain to the jury the importance of chain of custody in handling the evidence and how the items were accounted for in this case.

From my seat at the prosecution table, the Sheriff loomed large. The witness chair was elevated and Lee was a big man with big shoulders, a broad and thick chest. He was an impressive witness in his dress uniform, turning to face the jury at critical junctures. Lee had a presence about him and in my experience, a powerful impact on juries. He was honest and truthful, traits which came across in his testimony. With the problems I had proving my case, the credibility of Lee Jones was a valuable asset, cutting across all demographic lines.

Leaving it in its clear plastic sleeve, I asked Lee to identify the note Ross left at the scene of his attempted suicide. Silver objected, but Zelda cut him off, reminding him she had already ruled on the note's admissibility in the pre-trial hearing. After I offered it into evidence I asked Lee to read the three sentences. He swiveled slightly to face the jurors and read slowly.

"I am sorry about Danny. I don't know why it happened. The boy's body was in an old hunting camp."

I watched the jurors as Lee read "the confession." It was the first time they heard what Ross wrote as he prepared to shoot himself. The impact was palpable on the jury. The words cut through all the obfuscation Silver had thrown at them during *voir dire* and his opening. Here were the words of the defendant. His meaning was clear. Ross had killed Danny and disposed of the body. Common sense allowed no other explanation of the note's meaning. I pretended to look through my files for a moment to allow the impact of Ross's own words to sink in. When I looked up, most of the jurors were staring at Ross, who continued to write on his legal pad as if none of Lee's testimony had anything to do with him. P.O. Harrington crossed his arms against his chest and stared darts at Ross, his face growing redder by the second.

Silver was deferential to the Sheriff and made it clear he had no problem with the Sheriff's investigation. He wasted no time getting to the heart of his defense.

"Sheriff Jones, I'm sure you've testified in many homicide cases in your two terms as Sheriff of Yaloquena."

"Yes, sir."

"And in those many murder trials, I'm sure you testified about the cause of the victim's death, or related the coroner's findings and the results of other forensic tests, did you not?"

"Yes, sir."

"With respect to the alleged victim in this case, what was the cause of Danny Thurman's death?"

"We don't know the exact cause, Mr. Silver."

"Do you know for a fact that he is dead?"

"Yes."

"Then please tell the jury how he died."

After Lee explained that based on his experience and all the facts and circumstances of the case, he was certain Danny Thurman was dead, Silver asked the question in a slightly different way. I objected.

"I think you can move on now, Mr. Silver," Judge Williams said.

Silver left his table and stopped in front of Lee.

"Who is the coroner of Yaloquena County?"

"Alphonse Revels."

"Is it a function of his office to issue a coroner's report on the suspicious death of any citizen of Yaloquena?"

"Yes, sir."

Silver walked back to his table, opened a file, pulled out a sheet of paper and gave it to the Sheriff.

"Sheriff Jones, would you please take a look at the coroner's report in this case from the office of Coroner Alphonse Revels?"

"This is a blank piece of paper," Lee said.

"Precisely," Silver said and made a big show of retrieving the piece of blank paper, waving it in front of the jury, wadding it into a ball and tossing it into the trash can next to Deputy Clerk Eddie Bordelon's chair. Silver picked up Ross's "suicide" note from the evidence table.

"Would you show me, Sheriff Jones, where in this note it says that my client murdered Danny Thurman?"

Lee glanced at the note. "He says in here he's sorry about Danny and says the boy's body was in an old hunting camp. To me, it's clear he's saying Danny is dead and he's describing where he left his body."

"Show me in the note where it says that Ross Bullard killed Danny."

"It doesn't say those exact words."

"Show me where it says Danny was murdered."

"It says he's dead."

"Does it say how he died?"

"No. I wouldn't expect it to."

"Now, Sheriff Jones, you've testified briefly about the county-wide search for Danny's body around all the hunting camps known to exist in your county, correct?"

"Yes, sir."

"And in spite of a well-organized and thorough search of all such camps, no body was found, is that correct?"

"That's right."

"And the area around Iron Bridge where the cap, jeans, and sweater were found, it was searched twice, was it not?"

"Yes, sir."

"The last search around Iron Bridge lasted over a week?"

"Yes, sir."

"And if the contents of this note were accurate, you should have found Danny's body, isn't that true?"

"Not necessarily. It's hard to cover every inch of these areas. They're covered with briars and thick underbrush sometimes. There's no guarantee we didn't overlook the body somehow."

"One last question. In your experience in the military, with the state police, and as Sheriff for eight years, have you ever know someone to confess to something they didn't do?"

Lee thought for a minute.

"I guess I've had cranks call in on different cases, saying they had something to do with a crime, but nothing serious like this."

"Nonetheless, you're aware are you not, that in many high-profile homicide investigations it's not unusual for someone to walk in and tell the police or deputies that they committed the murder."

"I am aware of that kind of thing occurring, but I've never been personally involved in a murder case where it happened."

"Nothing further."

"One additional question," I said. "Sheriff Jones, without going into detail, was there other evidence your investigation uncovered that supported your interpretation of the defendant's note?"

"Yes, sir."

"That's all I have," I said, saving questions about the corroborating physical evidence for subsequent witnesses.

Lee had been on the stand for three and a half hours, not counting the hour for lunch. Maybe I was too optimistic, but after Lee stepped down, I felt good about my chances with this jury. Lee was such a good witness. The jurors' reaction to Ross's note was stronger than I expected. As in all jury trials, there would be highs and lows for me; my optimism would wax and wane, depending on the witness. Ultimately, the final outcome would be a test case that would end up in the Mississippi Supreme Court: common sense versus the lack of physical evidence of murder.

In spite of technological advances, I firmly believe that Americans are dumber than they were when I was young. I base my conclusion on what I see on television and cable, the national and local news, poll results, reality television and the citizens I interact with in the courthouse on a daily basis. I hoped my twelve jurors had enough common sense left to convict Bullard.

It was a little after three p.m. when I called the most articulate of the EMTs who arrived at the scene on Whitley after Ross's 911 call. I would have used Kitty for part of this testimony if she weren't in the hospital. Susan promised to text me when Dr. Clement made a decision after getting the morning's test results, but I hadn't heard from her. No news was good news. The EMT's testimony was straightforward, a chronological recitation of what they found at Bullard's house when they arrived, what they did, and how they left the scene. Silver had no questions.

It was after four o'clock when I finished with the EMT. I only had time for one more witness so instead of calling Peewee Bernhardt, whose testimony would take several hours, I called Howard McCain, the independent forester who saw Bullard on Iron Bridge the day after Danny disappeared. McCain took the stand. His black beard was closely trimmed and he wore a dark green open-collared shirt with his timber consultant logo above the pocket. I took him quickly through his background and had him describe his work for clients, emphasizing his need for accurate time sheets and logs. I asked him about his activities on July 5, what he was doing at Iron Bridge, and what he saw.

"And the person you saw late that day on the bridge, do you see him in court today?"

For dramatic effect, I stopped McCain before he answered.

"Excuse me, Your Honor, for purposes of this identification, I would ask the Court to direct the defendant to stand up and look at the witness so the witness can see his face."

Silver nudged Bullard. Bullard glared at Silver. The nerve of Helmet Head interrupting him in the middle of his writing something earth-shattering.

"Mr. Bullard," Judge Williams said, "would you please stand?"

Bullard stood at his table and reluctantly looked up at the Judge. Howard McCain took his time looking at Ross.

"Yes sir, that's him standing at the defense table. Ross Bullard is definitely the man I saw on Iron Bridge on July 5."

I could not have orchestrated it better. McCain was a powerful witness because he had no connection to anyone involved and no reason to lie. He had the date and time well-documented, too. I had him explain that he saw Bullard on television being walked out of the hospital with his lawyer and recognized him, and only then came to my office to tell me about seeing Bullard on Iron Bridge.

"Did Mr. Bullard look that day like he appears in court?"

"No, sir. It's the same man, but he was different. He didn't have on a shirt and he had paint on his face."

"What kind of paint?"

"It was different colors, in stripes on his cheeks and forehead like Indian war paint."

It was bizarre testimony. It created an eerie silence in the courtroom. At that moment, everyone knew Ross was a freak of some sort, entirely capable of the heinous murder of a seven-year-old. It confirmed what any normal, functioning person would have already gathered watching Ross write like a maniac while on trial for his life.

"Did you stop and talk to him that day?"

"No, sir. I slowed down on the bridge, curious because there's never anyone down that way. I was going to stop and ask him if I could help him with something but the way he looked at me was so scary, I decided to keep on going past him."

"When you first saw Ross Bullard on the bridge what was he doing?"

"He was leaning against the rail staring down at the riprap lining the creek. It would have been the east rail because I was headed north at that point."

"Final question, Mr. McCain, and only if you know the answer. Are you aware which side of the Iron Bridge the victim's cap and jeans were found?"

"Objection," Silver said, "no foundation laid."

"I'll withdraw it, Your Honor. Thank you Mr. McCain."

"Mr. McCain," Silver said, "are you familiar with the Iron Bridge area as being rich in Indian arrowheads and pots and the like?"

"Yes, sir. I'm told it's all kind of Native American artifacts and mounds in the woods around Iron Bridge."

"Have you personally hunted for any in the area?"

"No, sir, but I've heard there's plenty of people that do."

I watched Silver. He began to ask another question, but decided that was enough for Mr. McCain.

Judge Williams looked up at the clock on the wall behind her.

"This may be a good place to stop for the day," she said.

We all waited for the deputy to remove the jury. Zelda adjourned with a light tap of her gavel and exited the side door. I turned to watch the spectators file out and saw Cheryl Diamond at the rail.

"I'd like to talk to you please," she whispered.

I asked her to meet me in my office. I talked to Walton for a moment and helped him gather our files. By the time I made it down the hall, everyone was gone except Ethel Morris, who looked very tired. Ethel gave me several phone messages, one of which was from Jimmy Gray. I asked her if Susan had called. Ethel said she hadn't, which gave me some hope. Susan would have called if they had transferred Kitty to Jackson. Ethel said Jimmy asked me to call him as soon as court was adjourned. I told Ethel good night, closed the door behind her and joined Cheryl in my private office.

"I was wrong about Mr. Harrington," Cheryl said. "He's coming in loud and clear now. He is ready to vote guilty and is not going to change his mind. I noticed the other jurors seem to defer to him."

"I think he'll be the foreman," I said. "I cannot imagine why Silver kept him on the jury."

"There's something between Jules Bullard and Mr. Harrington, a relationship of some kind."

"How do you think we did with our witnesses today?"

"I think it went very well. It was a smart thing to ask the jurors not to reward Ross for successfully disposing of Danny's body."

"Good. Thanks for...."

"That's not why I wanted to see you."

"Okay."

"It's Ross Bullard. He's like a volcano ready to erupt. I don't know what he's going to do in there, but it's going to be dramatic. I can feel it. I just wanted you to be ready for anything."

"All right, Cheryl. Thanks. See you tomorrow."

I led her out of the office. Having a defendant go berserk in the courtroom would not be a first for me. Physical attacks on witnesses or attorneys, screaming fits, and fainting spells—I had seen them all. I figured I could take whatever Ross Bullard could dish out. I sent Susan a text asking her to call me, and phoned the big'un, Jimmy Gray.

"It's about time you called," he said.

"I've been kind of tied up."

"Can you swing by the campaign office on your way home?"

"Sure. What's up?"

"I'd rather tell you in person."

CHAPTER FORTY-THREE

I woke with a start and looked at my clock radio. *Three a.m.* Wide awake. I mean *wide* awake.

The other side of the bed was empty. Susan was staying with Kitty in the hospital in Jackson. I had finally reached Susan after I got home the night before. She said she didn't call or text because she knew I was in the middle of important testimony. She said she rode with Kitty in the ambulance to Jackson, leaving Sunshine about three in the afternoon. Susan said the pulmonologists started working on her as soon as she arrived in the Jackson I.C.U. They were testing Kitty's blood gases every hour and were concerned about restoring her lung functions. The doctors told Susan they had hoped to let her breathe on her own but decided they couldn't until her respiratory acidosis abated. I told Susan it sounded like Kitty wasn't responding to the treatment, but Susan gave me some encouragement.

"The doctors are optimistic. As soon as her oxygen intake and CO_2 discharge stabilize they're pretty sure her lungs will bounce back and start to operate on their own again. She's young and strong. I'll call you when they tell me something."

Going by the campaign office to see what Jimmy wanted with me after Monday's testimony was anticlimactic. He was exercised about Mayor Everett's report that Bobby Sanders was already putting money out on the streets and spreading promises of half-pints next Tuesday to the know-nothings who hung out on the corner all day in the quarters. Every day was the same for them. They didn't work, so their Mondays were the same as their Saturdays. They had nothing to do and nowhere to go, but they were all registered to vote. If there were a poster showing "low information voters," these folks would have been on it.

"Money on the street is nothing new, Jimmy," I said.

"It's a shame," Lee Jones said to Jimmy, "but that's the way it's been done around here for years. When I ran it was the same thing. Shiloh Matthews put out more Old Charter half-pints than there were registered voters in some precincts. Didn't help him any. They drank his whiskey and stayed home or voted for me."

"But hell, it's against the law," Jimmy said.

"Nothing we can do about it," I said.

"Why the hell not? You're the D.A. and Lee's the Sheriff."

"The A.G.'s office has unofficially taken over enforcement of election fraud," I said, "and they test the political winds before they do anything. The conventional wisdom in Jackson is Eleanor's a shoo-in, so the A.G.'s going to look the other way."

"And if we do something," Lee said, "it looks like we're abusing our power to get Willie Mitchell re-elected. It'd make some people mad."

"So we do nothing? The election's a week from tomorrow."

"I can send some patrol units around, kind of drop a hint here and there we're looking for vote buying and illegal vote hauling," Lee said, "but these people who're taking the money or the whiskey, they've got nothing to lose."

"Everett and Lee have people canvassing right now in the black community," I told Jimmy, "doing it the legal way. We just have to energize people to vote for me."

"Anyone who's out there taking what Bobby's giving is not going to vote for Willie Mitchell anyway," Lee said. "Good people know it's wrong."

"What a shitty business you guys are in," Jimmy Gray said.

I drove home from the campaign headquarters, made a smoked turkey sandwich, spoke to Susan about Kitty, and read myself to sleep. I was sleeping well until three o'clock, when my eyes popped wide open. After I realized I was up for good, I sat on the side of the bed on full alert. It was as if I had already drunk my two cups of coffee. I'm not sure how or why, but I knew what I needed to do. I reached for the phone.

"Hello," she said.

"Did I wake you?"

"No. I wasn't asleep."

"How long have you been up?"

"Ten minutes."

"I need a big favor," I said.

"I know."

I paused for a moment.

"I need you to take a ride with me."

"I'm almost dressed. I can be ready in about five minutes."

"I'll call you when I'm close."

"No need. I'll be waiting outside at the street close to the guest parking pad."

I put on jeans and boots and a long-sleeved knit shirt. I hustled down the stairs and outside to my truck. In less than three minutes I was at the High Cotton Bed & Breakfast. Cheryl Diamond stood in the grassy median by the street. I put the truck in park and hopped out to open the passenger door.

"Good morning," she said, and "thank you" as I shut her door.

I headed south, stopping at the twenty-four hour convenience store on the edge of town to get a large black coffee for me and a bottled water for Cheryl. In the bright lights of the store's canopy I could tell Cheryl had rushed getting ready. She wore no jewelry except diamond earrings and little makeup, just some rouge and lipstick, but her platinum-blonde updo was fixed. She wore a light gray New Balance warm up suit and pink Nike sneakers.

"You always get up so early?" I asked.

"Never. I usually sleep until six-thirty or seven."

"But not this time."

"I knew you needed my help. I was expecting your call."

I didn't quite know how to respond. It was obvious we woke up at the same time. When she answered the phone I knew she hadn't been asleep. It wasn't a coincidence.

"Tell me the latest on Kitty," she said when we got back onto the highway heading south. I told her everything Susan had shared with me the night before.

"Do you mind if I use your mirror?"

She pulled down the visor and opened the mirror. I glanced over a couple of times. In the weak light in the visor she studied her appearance. She patted and fluffed her hair and pulled a small makeup pouch from her purse to touch up. Even in her pink Nikes and her gray workout suit, and in spite of only ten minutes to get ready, she looked elegantly put together at three-thirty in the morning.

We continued south in the darkness on the county road toward the Iron Bridge. I realized she'd never asked me where we were headed.

"Do you know where we're going?" I asked.

"The Iron Bridge."

I noticed her voice shook slightly when she said it. She wasn't as enthusiastic as she was when I picked her up. To change the subject I volunteered the order of the witnesses I planned to call beginning in about five and a half hours when the trial resumed.

"I'm not going to be able to do this," she said, interrupting me.

"I'll be with you the whole time."

She reached into her purse and pulled out a Kleenex.

"I'm sorry I'm such a baby," she said dabbing her eyes. "When I get frightened like this I'm no good for anything. I thought I would be all right. But as we get closer...."

I pulled off the road onto a small, gravel parking area in front of a small maintenance shed owned by the national forestry service.

"What is it about the reptile man that frightens you?"

"I don't know," she snapped.

I waited for a moment. Cheryl's eyes were closed. She turned her head from side to side and whimpered.

"Danny's down there," she said, "and that thing is guarding him. If I go down there it will come after me. It warned me when I went with Kitty. That's why I left for Houston the next day."

"Don't be upset," I said, turning around in the parking area and heading north. "We're driving back to Sunshine."

We rode in silence in the darkness. I was relying heavily on a woman I had known for just a short while. Everything I knew about Cheryl was based on what she told me, what I read on her website, and my own feelings and intuition. I began to question her stability—and my judgment.

CHAPTER FORTY-FOUR

Judge Williams began promptly at nine. I called Peewee Bernhardt to the stand as a defensive move. His search parties never uncovered the body, so he couldn't move the evidentiary burden forward for me, but I wanted to establish through Peewee how much effort was expended searching the hunting camps and surrounding areas in order to blunt Silver's assertion that if Danny were out there he would have been found. It was important to get Peewee to explain that in spite of the thoroughness of the search, finding a body in such large, heavily wooded parts of the county was difficult at best.

Even though I had been awake since three, I didn't feel tired. Perhaps it was because I was on edge. The best part of my case was now behind me. What I put before the jury Monday was compelling—Lee's testimony, Ross's suicide note, and forester Howard McCain's startling testimony about Bullard in war paint at the bridge where the clothing was found.

I asked Peewee to describe in detail how the searches were conducted around the hunting camps all over Yaloquena. I had him explain how the camp around Iron Bridge had been divided into sectors and searched twice in the most recent attempt to find Danny. I finished by asking him the most critical fact I needed Peewee to nail down.

"Now Agent Bernhardt," I said, "even though the searches were thorough, can you say for certain that Danny's body is not somewhere in an old hunting camp as the defendant said in his note?"

"No, I cannot, Mr. Banks. The body probably is out there."

"Then why didn't you find Danny?"

"There's a lot of woods to cover around each of those camps. There's gulleys, hills, creeks, bogs and swamps that don't show up on the map. You look at a map and it looks like you could cover the whole area real easy. But the map don't show the features of the terrain or the briars or dense thickets of trees."

"One more thing, Mr. Bernhardt. In your searches did you consider whether the child was buried or not."

"Oh, yes, sir. That was important. If he was buried, his remains that is, we'd might have seen recently disturbed soil. That was one of the main things we looked for. If he wasn't buried...."

"Go ahead, Agent Bernhardt."

"I hate to say it but there's coyotes, wildcats, feral hogs and packs of wild dogs out in the woods we searched. If Danny had been laid on top of the ground, those scavengers would have gotten to him and we wouldn't have found anything but bones scattered all over the place. We looked for human bones but nobody found any."

I didn't leave much for Helmet Head, and he only asked a few questions of Peewee.

"Isn't it possible, Mr. Bernhardt, that you didn't find any remains because the body wasn't placed in an old hunting camp at all, in spite of what the note says?"

"Anything is possible, Mr. Silver, but Ross said in his note that's where he put the boy's body. I figure he knows."

Cha-Ching. The perfect answer. Way to go, Peewee.

"And if in fact Danny Thurman was not murdered and is not dead, wouldn't that be another reason why...," Silver paused and tapped his right index finger against his lips, "never mind, Mr. Bernhardt. Your Honor, I withdraw the question and have nothing further for this witness."

It was a shrewd move for Helmet Head. He knew Peewee would probably zing him again by citing the note, so he asked only part of the question and stopped. The jurors could fill in the blank themselves with the obvious answer.

I called Robbie Cedars from the crime lab and kept him on the stand the rest of the morning and an hour in the afternoon. He established what few forensic results we had: Danny's fingerprints in Ross's home; Danny's DNA matching a hair stuck in the Ranger's cap found at Iron Bridge; the distinctive blue fibers from the sweater matching fibers from Connie's closet and the fibers found in Ross Bullard's sofa. He identified the homemade DVD I handed him as the same one his men found at Ross Bullard's home.

My last set of questions involved the lab's handwriting expert's analysis of Bullard's note and comparison with known examples of Ross's handwriting I had subpoenaed from the bank. Walton had provided the report of the handwriting expert in discovery. Silver never contested the expert's conclusion that it was Ross's handwriting on the note the EMT found by Ross the night he shot himself.

Silver asked Robbie questions about what his crime scene investigators failed to find at the scene: any evidence of a homicide such as blood, hair, and bone fragments. I didn't object until he started grandstanding, asking if Robbie had seen a coroner's report and what was the cause of Danny's death.

"Mr. Cedars," Silver said, "can you tell the jury exactly when Danny Thurman's fingerprints were left in my client's home?"

"No, sir," Robbie said. "We have no way of knowing."

"And isn't it true that depending on the surface, the quality of the prints and a number of other factors, fingerprints may remain on a surface for many, many months?"

"Yes."

"And the blue fibers from the sweater found in the sofa. You've testified about when you found them, the night of July 4. Do you have any idea when those blue fibers were wedged or placed there?"

"No, sir, not really."

"Like the fingerprints, is it possible the blue fibers were left in the sofa weeks or even many months before their discovery?"

"Yes, it's possible."

"And the homemade DVD you've identified, do you know when that was made?"

"No, sir. We couldn't find anything on the disk to prove the date."

Silver finished with Robbie Cedars and I put Bill Thurman on the stand briefly. I asked him to describe what happened the evening of the disappearance, why Danny went home for the sweater, and what efforts he undertook to find Danny that night and later. I asked him to identify Danny's Ranger's cap and jeans and Connie's sweater. I

Michael Henry

knew he would get emotional. That's why I did it. It's awful to see a mother cry over the death of a child, and Connie would do plenty of that. It's even more gut-wrenching to see a big, strong man break down in tears over his son's death. When Bill wept on the stand, I noticed at least three, maybe four jurors wiping their eyes. As I expected, Silver had no questions.

Connie was my last witness of the day. I wanted to finish with Connie because I knew her testimony identifying Danny as one of the naked boys on Ross's homemade DVD would be moving and powerful. I wanted the DVD to be one of the last things the jurors saw before they were taken to supper and then to their motel rooms.

Connie was tearful and shaky at times, but she held up better than I expected. I moved quickly through the events of July 4 at the political barbecue. I had her identify Danny's cap and jeans and her sweater. I held up the disk and asked her if she had seen its contents. She said Bill and she had seen it in her home with Walton and me.

It was four o'clock when I asked Judge Williams for a recess so Deputy Clerk Eddie Bordelon and Walton could set up the monitors for the jurors. Ten minutes later, we reconvened. Eddie dimmed the courtroom lights and Walton started the player with a remote. Only the jurors could see the monitors.

I studied the jurors as they watched the DVD. Their eyes were glued to the monitors. I listened to Ross's soothing voice instructing the boys. He told them exactly what to do every step of the way. When the boys sat naked on the sofa before they put on the loin cloths, most of the jurors looked away from the monitors after a second or two. They didn't want to see any more of Ross's home movie.

It was one of those courtroom moments I would long remember. Total silence except for Ross's voice. No one in the gallery made a sound. When Walton turned off the player and the lights came up, I glanced over at the defense table. Ross was busy writing; Silver wore his poker face. The jurors appeared mortified; most looked down at their hands. Mr. Harrington glared at Ross Bullard and J.D. Silver.

I asked Connie if one of the boys was her son. She said "the one on the right" was Danny. I asked her how she knew. She went into details about Danny's chest, his genitals, his navel, and the lack of symmetry in his nipples—things only a mother would know.

She said she had no idea who the other boy on the DVD was. Connie said they made an attempt to find out, questioning the parents of Danny's friends, exhausting every possibility.

I was winding down and noticed Judge Williams looking up at the clock on the wall. When I finished questioning Connie, Helmet Head stood and said he didn't anticipate any lengthy cross of Mrs. Thurman, but it was getting late and fatigue was setting in.

"I'm not as young as I once was," Helmet Head said chuckling.

His smile was the only one evident in the courtroom. Zelda adjourned court and released the jury. After the Judge left the bench, I looked up at Connie still on the witness stand. I gave her a friendly nod. She had done very well, but I had a nagging feeling Helmet Head knew something I didn't.

CHAPTER FORTY-FIVE

Helmet Head began gently questioning Connie Wednesday morning. Ten minutes in, he asked if she had anything to add to the testimony she gave the day before. Connie perked up. I could tell she was thinking that Silver was wrapping up, her ordeal ending.

"No, sir," she said with relief. "I don't think so." She turned to Judge Williams. "Before I forget, Your Honor, I wanted to ask if after the trial is over I could get Danny's baseball cap back?"

"You may talk to Mr. Banks about that later, Mrs. Thurman. He will explain how that works."

"I am very sorry for your loss, Mrs. Thurman," Silver continued, "and I know testifying about the circumstances surrounding Danny's disappearance must be extremely difficult. Last night, when you were home, did you think about the answers you gave to Mr. Banks in this courtroom yesterday?"

"A little, I guess."

"And there's no additional information you want to provide to the jury that might be relevant to the case?"

I stood to object but Judge Williams beat me to it.

"Are you going somewhere with this, Mr. Silver? If so, please get on with it."

"Mrs. Thurman, do you recall testifying at a pre-trial hearing in this case and my asking you if you had ever been inside Ross Bullard's home?"

"Yes," she said. "I stated I was there in April or May but I didn't see Mr. Bullard that day. I talked to Judy Bullard about our neighborhood watch program and asked them to join."

"Were you ever in the Bullard home at any other time?"

"No, sir."

I watched Silver pretend to go through his notes for a minute. He stood up from his seat and walked to within two feet of Connie, careful not to block any juror's view of the witness.

"Are you sure that's true, Mrs. Thurman?"

His tone was innocent, not accusatory, as if he were just trying to help jog her memory.

"I'm fairly certain," she said.

"Very well," he said and went back to his seat.

"Have you ever solicited donations in your neighborhood in connection with fund raisers for your son's school?"

Connie didn't answer. I recognized the look on her face. Silver's question unearthed a memory she had forgotten or repressed. Connie knew she had made a very serious mistake. Her eyes grew wide, then her mouth, which she covered. Connie began to shake like a leaf. I stood up at my table. There's was nothing I could object to, but I wanted to help.

"Your Honor," I said.

"No recess," Silver boomed. "The Court will kindly direct the witness to answer my question."

His voice was cold as ice. I sat down. Walton bowed his head. We had been over this many times with Connie. She told us about the neighborhood watch visit in the Bullard home and said that was the only time. From the look of terror I knew Connie hadn't lied, but it was going to be a costly lapse.

"Mrs. Thurman," Judge Williams said. "you must answer."

"I forgot," she blurted and burst into tears.

Judge Williams called a five minute recess for Connie to pull herself together, directing the bailiff to take Connie to the lounge the court reporters and other women court personnel used next to the Judge's chambers. Silver asked for a bench conference.

"Your Honor," he said in a forceful whisper, "I do not want the State woodshedding Mrs. Thurman during this break. This is a critical time in my...."

"We won't talk to the witness, Your Honor," I volunteered. "In fact, Mr. Donaldson and I will stay in the courtroom."

"Let's all stay," Zelda said.

There is nothing more awkward than sitting in court with the jury in the box, the judge on the bench, and no witness in the chair. The jurors are not permitted to talk to one another so they generally stare at the lawyers and occasionally into the gallery.

Time passed slowly, but after a few minutes the bailiff returned and whispered to the Judge. She nodded and he brought Connie back to the stand.

Out of the corner of my eye I caught Phil Myers standing at the rail to get Silver's attention. Silver joined Myers at the rail and listened as Myers whispered. Helmet Head began to glare at me and left the rail, gesturing for me to join him at the bench. He leaned close to Zelda.

"I'm told someone from the State did confer with Mrs. Thurman during the break."

"What?" I said. "Walton and I were here the entire time."

"A woman," Silver said.

I was relieved. It was probably Ethel from my office offering solace to Connie, helping her get control. Ethel knew better than to discuss Connie's testimony.

"Judge, it's probably one of my staff trying to help. I'll...."

"No, it's not," Silver said.

He turned to Phil Myers who was pointing at the back door of the courtroom. I saw Walton's wife Gayle walk in.

"Mrs. Donaldson," Judge Williams said, "please approach."

"Judge Williams," I whispered, "Gayle and Mrs. Thurman are best friends. I'm sure she was...."

Zelda held up her palm so I stopped. Gayle appeared on the riser between Silver and me.

"Yes, Judge Williams?" Gayle said.

"Did you confer with Mrs. Thurman just now during the break?"

"Yes, ma'am. I was in the back of the courtroom when she broke down testifying and I thought I could help calm her down."

"Did you talk to her about the case?"

"Oh, no, Judge Williams. Not at all. I was there just for support."

"Satisfied, Mr. Silver?" Zelda said.

Silver nodded. We returned to our tables. Gayle took a seat on the front row behind me next to Cheryl Diamond.

"Ready to proceed, Mrs. Thurman?" Zelda asked.

Connie nodded.

"Ask your question again, Mr. Silver," the Judge said.

"Have you ever solicited donations in your neighborhood to raise money for your son's school?"

"Yes," Connie whispered, her head down, eyes on her lap.

Eddie Bordelon gestured to the Judge.

"You'll have to speak up, Mrs. Thurman, for the equipment."

"Yes," Connie said, this time too loudly. "For the renovation fund.

"And when was this visit?"

"I'm not sure. It was before the neighborhood watch time."

"February of this year?"

"It could have been."

"Do you recall if it was cold that day?"

"I think so. I guess it would have been."

"Was the defendant in his home?"

"No," Connie said, continuing to look down. "Just Judy."

"Do you remember where you talked to Judy?"

"In their living room."

"Do you remember where you sat that day?"

"I'm not sure."

"Isn't it a fact that you sat on the Bullard's sofa, the one shown on the DVD the jurors watched?"

"I could have."

"So, you're saying you might have sat on the sofa that day in February and asked Judy Bullard for a donation, is that right?"

Connie nodded.

"You'll have to speak," the Judge said.

"Yes."

"And do you recall if you wore a jacket or coat or sweater as you sat on the couch talking to Judy Bullard that day, Mrs. Thurman?"

Connie shrugged and began to cry.

"Isn't it a fact that you wore your blue sweater that day on the sofa, Mrs. Thurman, the same blue sweater found at Iron Bridge, the same blue sweater whose fibers were snagged on that couch and later recovered by the crime lab?"

My stomach knotted. It was a compound question but I saw no need to object. If what he said in his question was true, Silver had scored a major coup, casting doubt on the pivotal forensic evidence in our case. I heard commotion behind me. I turned to watch Bill Thurman storm out of the courtroom, almost tripping over two other spectators on his row as he climbed over them in a hurry to leave. In the seat next to me Walton focused on his wife in the front row. Judge Williams banged her gavel and in a moment the courtroom grew quiet again.

"Mrs. Thurman?" Zelda said.

"I may have," Connie said. "I don't know."

"May have what, Mrs. Thurman?" Silver said.

"I may have worn the blue sweater that day. I don't remember."

"And if you did, isn't it possible that the blue sweater fibers Mr. Cedars referred to as having been found in the sofa were deposited by you that day in February when you were in the Bullard home?"

"I guess so," Connie managed to say.

"Thank you," Silver said. "I'd like to draw your attention now to the DVD that Mr. Banks and Mr. Donaldson played for the jury. There were two boys shown on the couch, is that correct?"

"Yes."

"You testified the boy on screen right was your son Danny. Can you tell the jury who the other boy is?"

"No," she said. "I don't know."

"Are you sure?" Silver asked.

I could not remember anything like this occurring in any other trial during my twenty-four years as District Attorney. I had no control over what was about to happen. Connie's testimony was already a disaster, and Silver was about to drop the other shoe. I glanced to my left at Walton. He was staring at Connie, watching her implode.

Connie shrugged. "I don't know," was what I thought she said.

"Isn't the other boy Nicholas Donaldson?" Silver bellowed and spun around to point at Walton. "The son of Assistant District Attorney Walton Donaldson and his wife seated on the front row right behind him."

Just as each person in the courtroom gasped at the accusation, Ross Bullard bounced out of his chair, leapt onto Walton and grabbed him around the neck.

"I told you it was your son," Ross screamed, "sweet little Nicholas."

Deputy Sheriff Sammy Roberts in plain clothes left his seat on the second row, jumped over the rail and barreled into Ross, taking him to the floor.

"They all knew it was Nicholas," Ross screamed while Sammy Roberts pressed Ross's head into the carpet. "The Thurmans and Donaldsons. It's all a big cover up, a conspiracy to hide the truth. Willie Mitchell's in on it, too."

I heard a whump and turned to see Connie in a heap on the floor by the witness stand.

CHAPTER FORTY-SIX

Judge Williams stayed remarkably calm while Ross was being subdued after his attack on Walton. She ordered the bailiff to remove the jury while Deputy Sammy Roberts and the other courtroom security kept Ross pinned to the floor. Once she was assured the jury was safely tucked away in the Grand Jury room, she ordered the deputies to shackle Ross and drag him if necessary to the jail upstairs. Once Ross was gone, Zelda ordered all members of the gallery to leave except for Judy and Jules Bullard, Phil Myers, Gayle Donaldson, Sheriff Jones and two deputies working courtroom security. I approached the bench and asked her to exempt Cheryl Diamond as well and she did.

I continued to cradle Connie's head until the EMTs arrived. Judge Williams told them to take her into the Judge's chambers and determine her condition. When the side door closed behind the EMTs and Connie, I walked to join Walton leaning against the jury box.

"Hold on, Mr. Banks," the Judge said. "Take your seat at the prosecution table. Mr. Donaldson, you sit in the jury box for now. Mr. Banks, I want to hear from Mr. Donaldson on the record before you talk to him. We're going to convene a hearing right now on what has occurred in this courtroom today and determine the implications for this trial."

"There's no way this court can proceed with this jury," Silver said. "I demand a mistrial and the immediate release of my client on bond pending the new trial."

"Not so fast, Mr. Silver," she said. "It seems to me much of this has been orchestrated by your client for that very reason. If I can see a path to continue on with this trial I will do so. It's not my wish to reward the defendant's behavior with the relief he obviously wants. Take your seat at the defense table."

"My client has the constitutional right to be present at any hearing involving the disposition of his case," Silver sputtered.

She looked down at me.

"Regrettably," Your Honor, "I must agree with Mr. Silver."

"Very well. Sheriff Jones. Have your men gag and shackle the defendant and bring him back into this courtroom so we can begin. Check with the bailiff and confirm that all jurors are sequestered in the Grand Jury room before you bring Mr. Bullard into the hallway. Make sure they don't see him."

"Objection to the shackling and gagging of my client."

"Mr. Bordelon," she said to her clerk, "note defense's objection."

Ten minutes later, Lee Jones, Sammy Roberts, and two other deputies half-carried Ross Bullard into the courtroom and sat him at the defense table.

"Mr. Bullard," Judge Williams said, "you're going to remain shackled, hands and feet, until this hearing is over. If you assure me you can sit there without saying anything, I will order the gag removed. If you say anything, I'll direct the deputies to gag you again. Understood?"

Bullard nodded his head vigorously. Judge Williams gestured to Deputy Roberts to remove the gag. She turned to Walton in the jury box.

"Take the stand, Mr. Donaldson. Swear him in, Mr. Clerk. Mrs. Donaldson, walk through the rail and take a seat in the jury box."

Walton raised his right hand and swore to tell the truth. He sat in the witness chair. He looked me briefly, then averted his eyes.

"This is how we will proceed, Zelda said. "I will ask Mr. Donaldson questions then you two will have the opportunity to do the same."

"Mr. Donaldson, do you know what the defendant was talking about when he said he told you the second boy was your son Nicholas?"

"At one of the pre-trial hearings, the bailiff gave me a note. He said Ross Bullard had asked him to give the message to me."

"Which bailiff?" she asked.

"Elbert Pickett."

"What did the note say?"

"It said 'I miss Nicholas'."

Judge Williams looked at Ross with disgust. I already knew Ross Bullard was an evil bastard, so I was more focused on the fact that Walton lied to me when I asked him about the note five weeks earlier during the change of venue hearing.

"What did you do with the note Mr. Pickett gave you?"

"I still have it. It's locked in the glove box in my truck with the other one he slipped into my notes during another court appearance."

"What did the second one say?"

Walton pursed his lips and looked down at his hands.

"It said 'Nicholas was sweeter than Danny'."

Walton didn't lie to me about the second note. He just neglected to tell me it existed. The first thing I considered was whether the notes had evidentiary value in the trial. Could they have been used against Ross had I known about them? Probably not. The first one didn't mention Danny. The second one mentioned Danny but it's not inculpatory. I was satisfied I wouldn't have offered them into evidence. I listened to Zelda begin questioning Walton about the second issue that concerned me.

"Did you tell Mr. Banks or anyone involved in this trial?"

"No, Your Honor."

"Did you mention to notes to anyone?"

"My wife," he said glancing in the direction of the jury box. "I had shown my wife the DVD when we first got it back from the crime lab. I was worried that the other boy might be Nicholas. They were good friends, Nick and Danny. She said she was positive it was not Nicholas on the DVD. When I got the first note from Bullard, I told her about it and asked her again if she was positive it wasn't Nick on the DVD. She said she knew her son and it wasn't him."

"Did you tell her about the second note?"

"I did. She said it didn't matter what Bullard said in the second note, that the boy on the DVD wasn't Nick."

I leaned back in my chair, more sympathetic to Walton. The notes weren't evidentiary. He questioned his wife repeatedly about the boy on the DVD. If the content of the notes became public, and I knew in our small town it eventually would, Nicholas would be stigmatized for the rest of his life as another little boy molested by Ross Bullard. Kids at school would tease him whether it was true or not.

"As you sit there today, Mr. Donaldson," Zelda said, "do you know if the second boy on the tape is Nicholas?"

"I do not know. My wife insists that it isn't."

"Any questions for Mr. Donaldson?" she asked us.

I shook my head. Silver said he had a couple.

"Mr. Donaldson," Silver said, "did you ever communicate orally or in writing or by any other means with my client?"

"No, sir."

"Didn't you recognize your obligation as an officer of this Court to notify the Judge...."

"Hold on, Mr. Silver," she said, "you're getting into my territory. Let me worry about Mr. Donaldson's obligation to this Court. Anything else?"

Walton stepped down and walked toward me at our table. I shook my head slightly and pointed to the jury box. He took a seat next to his wife. Walton was off the case. He could no longer sit with me nor would I consult with him in any manner about the proceedings.

"Take the stand and be sworn, Mrs. Donaldson," Zelda said.

Gayle took the witness chair and Eddie Bordelon administered the oath. Before she asked the first question, Zelda gestured for Eddie to approach. She whispered to him and he walked out the side door. A few moments later, Eddie returned ahead of Connie Thurman and the EMTs.

"Have a seat on the front row, Mrs. Thurman. You folks from the hospital continue to monitor her."

Connie was ashen, so limp I was surprised she could sit up. Gayle, in contrast, did not appear scared or intimidated on the witness stand.

"First of all, Mrs. Donaldson, when you talked to Mrs. Thurman earlier today after her difficulties on the witness stand, did you talk to her about the trial, Danny, or your son?"

"No, Your Honor. What I told you before was the truth."

"Were you in court when the defendant jumped on your husband and made the claim that the Thurmans, you and your husband, and the District Attorney all knew it was Nicholas on the DVD and conspired to conceal that fact?"

"I was here, yes ma'am."

"Is it true?"

"No, ma'am," she said and glared at Ross. "He's a liar and a coward, and an evil little vermin."

Judge Williams cleared her throat. I glanced back at Jules and Judy. Judy was reading a magazine of some kind. Jules appeared to be giving the evil eye to Gayle. Silver was all business, making notes of Gayle's testimony. Ross had resumed writing on his legal pad.

"Mrs. Donaldson, if I do not get to the bottom of this with you, I'm going to have to put Mrs. Thurman back on the witness stand. She's in no condition to withstand much more stress, but if you force me to question her to get to the truth I will."

Gayle sat there a moment. She remained defiant.

"All right, Judge Williams," she said, "I'll tell you exactly what happened and if you decide to put me in jail so be it. I'd do it again if I had the chance."

"Proceed," Zelda said.

"As soon as I saw the DVD I knew it was Nicholas on the left of the screen. No doubt in my mind. But I was not going to let Ross Bullard drag my son through the mud, scar him for life. He had already killed Danny. It was time to put a stop to his reign of terror, this ineffective legal system be damned. For the first time in our marriage I lied to my husband and told him it wasn't Nick, and I made Connie promise she would never tell anyone the other boy was Nick. I'm responsible for Connie saying she didn't know who it was, so if there's anyone to be punished with something let it be me and not Connie. I did it."

Undaunted, Gayle leaned back in the witness chair.

"All right, gentlemen," Zelda said, "our little hearing is over. Mr. Silver, I am denying your motion for a mistrial. We will reconvene first thing in the morning and proceed with the next witness. Did you intend to put Mrs. Thurman back on the stand, Mr. Silver?"

"I believe I must, Your Honor. I need her to confirm that it is in fact Nicholas Donaldson on the DVD with Danny Thurman."

"Your Honor," I said, "in light of Mrs. Donaldson's testimony the State will stipulate that the other child on the DVD is Nicholas Donaldson."

"That's not sufficient," Silver protested. "I intend to prove the conspiracy between Mrs. Thurman and Mrs. Donaldson to present a falsehood to the jury and this Court with respect to the identity of the other child."

"No, sir," Judge Williams said. "You will do no such thing. I hereby rule that the suppression of the identity of the second child by Mrs. Thurman and Mrs. Donaldson is irrelevant in these proceedings. I will instruct the jury in the morning that they are to accept as a fact that the second boy on the DVD is Nicholas Donaldson, the son of Walton and Gayle, and that Mr. Banks and Mr. Donaldson were unaware of the fact.

"I will instruct them to ignore the disturbance in court this morning, that everything has been resolved, and they are not to consider today's events in their deliberations."

"To which ruling I strongly object, Your Honor," Silver said. "No matter how you instruct the jury, you cannot unring that bell. This Court is committing reversible error."

"Everything is on the record, Mr. Silver. You'll have your opportunity with the appellate court if there is a conviction. If the jury doesn't convict, then none of what happened today matters. Mr. Donaldson, I will be sending a transcript of this hearing to the State Bar Association Ethics Board for them to handle as they see fit. Your participation in this trial is over and I think it advisable that you not sit in as a spectator, either. Court is adjourned until nine a.m. tomorrow."

After Zelda left, I started toward Walton in the jury box. Before I reached him, he pointed to the back of the courtroom. I turned around to see Dr. Clement walking toward me. We shook hands.

"What are you doing here, Nathan?"

"It's time to call Jake."

CHAPTER FORTY-SEVEN

I left Sunshine and sped toward Yazoo City, expecting to arrive at the hospital in Jackson before two p.m. Cheryl Diamond appeared at my side when I spoke to Nathan in the courtroom and insisted she accompany me to the hospital. I was in such a dither I didn't know if it was a good idea or not, but I didn't resist.

It turned out Cheryl had gone to see Nathan about Kitty the week before he put her in the hospital. Cheryl had told him that Kitty was much too ill to be working and needed treatment immediately.

"I should have insisted earlier," Cheryl said. "I knew the first time I met her that she was extremely sick."

I would have gotten off sooner after Zelda dismissed the trial for the day but it took some time to reach Deputy Attorney General Patrick Dunwoody in D.C. I explained the circumstances and told him Dr. Clement said time was of the essence. Dunwoody said he would personally see to it that Jake was on a military flight home within hours.

We drove under low overcast skies through the cotton fields of Humphreys County, barren save for bent and broken brown stalks dangling gossamer wisps left by giant mechanical pickers.

"Kind of gloomy," Cheryl said staring at the flat fields.

"Late fall and winter are not very pretty in the Delta," I said, "unless you like flat vistas and broken stems as far as the eye can see." She hadn't brought up the fiasco this morning so I did. "You were right about Bullard."

"But not specific enough to help you. I was shocked when he jumped on Mr. Donaldson."

"I've been trying cases a long time and I've never had a case blow up on me like this."

"After this morning the jury is with you even more than ever."

"I'm not sure," I said, "Connie could have easily left those fibers in the couch in February."

"That's not going to matter. Neither is Bullard's claim of a cover up between the Donaldsons and the Thurmans about the identity of the second boy on the DVD."

I glanced over at Cheryl. She seemed very certain.

"Believe me, Willie Mitchell, the main thing those jurors will take away from this morning is that Ross Bullard is fully capable of violent behavior. You don't even have to mention it yourself. They saw it."

"I hope you're right."

"I'm sorry I was so frightened on our trip south Tuesday morning."

"It's all right," I said. "You tried."

We drove in silence for a while, passing a dead deer on the gravel shoulder.

"Kitty has to pull through," I said. "I can't believe this is happening to her. She's so young."

Cheryl said nothing.

"You're not optimistic," I said.

"Not really, Willie Mitchell," she said and wiped her eyes with a Kleenex she retrieved from her purse.

"Do you ever see your ex-husband in Houston?"

"No."

"Are he and the other woman still together?"

"I don't know and have no interest. I learned everything I needed to about my husband from the telephone call I told you and Susan about."

I took the loop encircling Jackson and approached the exit for I-20 East. I noticed a large billboard west of us proclaiming ALLIGATOR SWAMP TOUR in Morgan City, Louisiana. The smiling gator on the sign wore men's clothes and stood on its hind legs pointing to a cartoonish wooden boat in a swamp with alligators surrounding it. I checked to see if Cheryl noticed. She stared at the alligator man on the billboard until the ramp led us east.

I took my exit and stopped at the first traffic light on the surface street that led to the hospital. My cell phone buzzed. It was Susan.

"Hurry," she said.

CHAPTER FORTY-EIGHT

Jake Banks. Over The Atlantic. November 1

The sound of Jake's book hitting the floor woke him from a deep sleep. He looked around the room trying to figure out where he was. Sleep had been at a premium the last two weeks, with surveillance duty or missions almost every night. He was bone-tired. He saw two neatly made beds next to him and remembered he was inside a military transport on the way home. He had fallen asleep in one of the two bunk rooms on the upper deck of the aircraft where the crew normally slept.

Jake sat on the edge of the bunk and picked up his book, Bill Bryson's A SHORT HISTORY OF NEARLY EVERYTHING, a five-star recommendation from Willie Mitchell. He looked at his watch, made a quick calculation, and re-set it to 2:30 Memphis time. He'd been flying for six hours, and estimated another four hours flight time based on what the crew told him after takeoff, putting him at the Tennessee air base at about 6:30 a.m.

As usual, Dunne gave Jake as little information as possible. Dunne told Jake he was needed at home, that Kitty was sick in the hospital. Jake was glad to go home to see her, but he didn't think it was the real reason Dunne was shipping him out of England. He thought it much more likely there was too much heat on the team resulting from the mission four days earlier in which Jake dispatched one of the top ten targets in Operation Camelot, Yousef Khabir. For all Jake knew, Bull and Hound were also headed back stateside for a cooling off period. Doberman had assimilated so deeply into the borough he was in no danger, and David Dunne never personally entered Newham in daylight hours. Dunne implied he had information that Jake might have been seen before the Khabir operation, but Jake knew he wasn't getting the real story from Dunne. Jake was an operative and did what he was told.

Theirs not to reason why, theirs but to do and die.

Military transports were Jake's least favorite means of travel, especially overseas, but as transports went, the C-5 Galaxy was top of the line. It was huge and comfortable. Jake had been in a C-130 several times in the last two years, but this was his first ride in a C-5. He met the crew before takeoff, a bunch of good old boys, Tennessee National Air National Guardsmen of the 164th Airlift Wing out of Memphis. That's where the C-5 was headed, non-stop. Jake hung out with the crew the first hour of the flight but they kept trying to find out who he was and what he had been doing. He couldn't tell them his team was waging a silent war on the streets of London fighting the intramural terrorism of a *jihadist* group aimed at imposing Sharia on secular Muslims in the boroughs they controlled, then exporting their success to other boroughs then to the U.S. After a while Jake grew tired of dodging the crew's questions and said he had to get some sleep, which was the truth. He had five hours of shut eye under his belt and planned on getting more.

He washed his hands and face in the bathroom and unbuttoned the top two buttons of his shirt to check the bandage on the minor wound he sustained on the Khabir mission. Khabir had not gone down easily. Jake stared into the mirror at the slight trace of blood staining the gauze on his chest. He decided to redress it at the end of the flight.

Jake lay down in his bunk and began reading about British explorers and their remarkable expeditions almost two centuries ago. As fascinating as their stories were, he was still sleep-deprived. He started nodding off and put down the book.

Jake closed his eyes and pictured the C-5 landing in Tennessee. In seconds he was sound asleep.

Chapter Forty-Nine

Cheryl Diamond and I arrived in the I.C.U. waiting room in the Jackson hospital a little after two o'clock. We were the only people there. The receptionist told us someone would be right in to see us, but after waiting for ten minutes, I pushed open the door and peeked down the hallway. At the opposite end, about a hundred feet from us, there were several doctors gathered. When one of them moved from the huddle, I saw Susan.

"Let's go down there where Susan is," I told Cheryl.

"You go," Cheryl said. "I'm not family."

I thought it an odd thing to say, but Cheryl had already sat down. She shooed me out the door with a flip of her hand. I walked quietly down the hallway and gave a discreet wave to Susan, who left the doctors and walked toward me. When we drew close I could tell she was crying.

"She's gone," Susan said.

I took her into my arms and held her while she cried into my chest. After a moment I drew back slightly. I knew Susan wasn't saying they had moved Kitty to another ward. Stunned is not a strong enough word to describe how I felt. It could not be. Death did not come for someone as young and vibrant as Kitty. There had to be some mistake.

"What do you mean?" I asked.

"I mean Kitty died."

"Damn," I said and pulled Susan back against my chest.

A spasm erupted somewhere inside my diaphragm and lodged like a brick in my throat. Susan shook. Tears filled my eyes. I held Susan tighter and choked on the emotion inside me trying to get out. For a moment I had no idea what to do. Susan took my hand and led me back to the doctors. She said their names but I didn't know what they were. We did shake hands, I remember that. What they said in quiet tones made no sense to me, or at least it wasn't registering. I do remember them saying Kitty had acute respiratory distress syndrome then using the acronym ARDS which I googled later.

"Her brain function stopped completely thirty minutes ago," Susan said crying. "They're going to take her off the ventilator."

"There's nothing else you can do?" I asked one of the white coats in front of me. "She can't be resuscitated?"

The three of them shook their heads almost simultaneously, as if they choreographed it before I arrived. That was another thing, when I look back on it. The docs were so young. The oldest of the three could not have been more than forty-five. That was irrelevant, of course, just an observation apropos of nothing.

Susan, Cheryl, and I sat in the waiting room for a while until we were joined by a young woman in a business suit with a clip board. There were a lot of questions we couldn't answer. Kitty's next of kin was her mother, currently residing in a mental institution in Tacoma oblivious to her identity and the universe. As far as Susan and I knew, based on what Kitty had shared with us over the past three years, there was no one else.

"Kitty told me we were the closest thing she had to a family," Susan said and started crying again.

So did I. Cheryl didn't. She sat quietly. Apparently she had known Kitty's time was up well before I did. I looked at Cheryl in a new light there in the waiting room. What a burden to know something this awful before everyone else. It took a good bit of self-control and strength for Cheryl to keep her presumed knowledge about Kitty to herself. I guessed Cheryl had probably learned through trial and error not to say anything. After all, she might have been wrong.

The young lady with the clipboard moved on to the nitty-gritty. Susan had given the admission desk Kitty's group insurance card when they arrived Monday. The lady needed more details. Who would claim the body? How and when would it be moved from the hospital morgue? I had to think for a moment to give her the real name and number of the funeral director in Sunshine who would handle the "arrangements." Jimmy Gray and I always called him Concrete Head, the nickname Jimmy gave him when we were teenagers growing up in Sunshine. I assumed we'd bury her in the Banks family cemetery in a wooded corner of our 990 acre farm, if it was all right with Jake and Susan.

I left Susan and Cheryl and walked on a concrete deck adjacent to the reception area to call Patrick Dunwoody. He said he was sorry to hear about Kitty and that Jake could not be reached, but was due to land at the Tennessee Air National Guard base inside Memphis International Airport at around 6:30 in the morning. When I relayed the information to Susan, she suggested that I drive home, get some sleep and get up early enough to pick up Jake in Memphis. Susan said she and Cheryl would tie up all the loose ends at the hospital and talk to the funeral director about transporting Kitty to Sunshine.

"I've got to be in the courtroom at nine," I said. "Walton's been ordered off the case by Judge Williams."

"I know," Susan said. "Cheryl told me what happened this morning while you were out on the terrace talking to Dunwoody. If Jake lands on schedule, you'll be back in Sunshine in time."

"I hate to break the news to Jake," I said.

"He needs to hear it from you," Susan said, "and no one else. He'll have time to come to grips with it on the drive back to Sunshine."

Cheryl nodded in agreement.

"You go on now," Susan said, "there's nothing more you can do here. Cheryl and I will stay here as long as it takes."

It was a lonely, miserable drive home. I got there about six, heated some leftovers in the microwave and ate at the pine table in the kitchen. I was in no mood to eat but I had to. I needed to get some sleep, too. That would be a challenge as well. I grabbed a note pad and made notes while I chewed. Unless Silver was willing to ignore what Zelda told him this morning, Connie Thurman's testimony was over. I decided to bite the bullet and call Irma Gilbert and Ronnie Black as my last witnesses. If I didn't get in front of their testimony Silver would make a big deal of calling them himself. Better the jury hears it first with me doing the questioning. Helmet Head would have to call that son-of-a-bitch John Mordano, the lying long distance trucker. I wanted him on cross.

CHAPTER FIFTY

I fell asleep reading about ten, I guess, woke up when Susan got in about midnight, and slept until 2:30. I managed to stay in bed for another hour, my mind jumping from one thing to another. At 3:30 I showered, dressed, and tiptoed down the stairs to drink a cup of coffee. I poured my second into a twenty-ounce Styrofoam go cup and got in my F-150. Getting on the highway before daylight on a road trip, a big coffee in my hand, was something I usually enjoyed no matter where I was going. Not today.

It was dark and uncomfortable, about sixty-eight degrees and humid. I set my trip odometer to zero. I had plenty of time to get to Memphis International and figure out how to get access to the National Guard airbase. Dunwoody said he would make a call so they would be expecting me. He said they would have no record of Jake at the base or on the flight and suggested I refrain from asking for him by name.

I checked my watch and noticed the date. November 1. *El Dia de los Muertos.* The Day of the Dead. I made the sign of the cross.

I followed signs inside the airport to the Air National Guard unit. It was easier than I thought it would be. I went through a low-key security check and was shown a corridor where I could sit and watch the passengers from the C-5 arrive.

It was only a few minutes after six when I spotted Jake trailing the flight crew into the small National Guard terminal. I waved him over. He was surprised to see me.

"What are you doing here?" he asked with a big grin, shaking my hand vigorously and sharing a discreet man hug the way we always did.

"Thought you might need a ride."

"I was going to rent a car, but this is great."

"Long flight?"

"Not bad. I slept most of the way. I'm really enjoying the Bryson book. Those Brits were amazing people."

"I knew you'd like it."

"I want to go right to the hospital when we get to Sunshine, if that's all right."

I nodded and led him out of the terminal to the truck. He tossed his duffel into the bed of the truck and was about to open the door when I stopped him.

"I need to tell you something, Jake."

"Tell me in the truck. Let's go."

"It's Kitty."

Jake stopped moving.

"She died yesterday."

It hit him hard. He grabbed the edge of the truck bed with both hands and leaned against it. I put my hand on his shoulder and he turned to face me.

"How did that happen?"

"She had been fighting pneumonia for several weeks and wouldn't slow down. Dr. Clement tried to get her into the hospital sooner but she wouldn't hear of it until she got so weak she couldn't get out of bed. Nathan treated her but her lungs started to fail. He sent her to Jackson to their pulmonology unit and, well, they tried but...."

"Damn her hard head," he said and slammed his palm against the side of the truck.

Tears rolled down Jake's cheeks. I took him into my arms and gave him a real hug, the first time since he was a kid, and held him for a minute. I heard him sniff hard. He backed away, wiping his eyes with the back of his hand.

"Let's go," he said and got into the truck.

We rode in silence for a long time. I took U.S. Highway 61 south toward Clarksdale, paralleling the Mississippi, at times no more than a few miles east of the river. In every community we drove through there were Blues Trail markers about a famous son who played or sang the blues. Jake stared out his window or through the windshield for much of the ride, occasionally wiping his eyes. I figured when he wanted to talk he would let me know.

"Where will we bury her?" he asked.

"I thought in our family cemetery."

He nodded. It made sense. Poor Kitty had nowhere else to go. We were the only people who cared about her.

"She could never catch a break," he said.

"She met you."

Jake shrugged.

"She never fully recovered from what Brujo's men did to her," he said. "Physically she was never the same."

"That's what Nathan said. Her lungs were weak."

"When's the funeral?"

"I don't know. Your mother did all the arrangements." I paused. "I know this sucks, son, but I've got to be in court at nine."

"Ross Bullard," he said. "Kitty told me the few times I got to talk to her. I hope you fry the bastard. Just drop me off at the house."

"I'm sure you're mother's got breakfast ready for you." I gave him my cell phone. "Why don't you call her?"

When Susan answered Jake said a few words and listened. He started crying again and so did I.

CHAPTER FIFTY-ONE

I made it to my office with time to spare. I gathered my files and notes and did a quick review of the summary of Irma Gilbert and Ronnie Blake's statements that Walton had prepared in advance of trial. I looked up when I heard a light knock on the door jamb and saw Walton. It wasn't the usual Walton, full of vinegar and aggression, brimming with confidence. It was a humbler version.

"Sorry about Kitty," he said. "Gayle and I couldn't believe it. It doesn't seem real."

"I just picked up Jake. He's at the house."

"I'll call him after a while."

He stood silently for a moment. I knew he was trying to get his arms around the elephant standing between us.

"I apologize for what happened," he said.

"I've had a good bit of time in the truck by myself since yesterday morning, Walton. I'm not sure I would have done things any differently."

He perked up.

"Except for one thing," I said. "You should have told me. We've been working side-by-side for eight years and I'm disappointed you didn't feel like you could come to me with it so we could face it together."

"I didn't want to put you in the bind I was in. I was praying the whole thing would just go away. I know now that was stupid."

"Ethics Board is not going to do anything. If you're worrying about that, put it out of your mind. I'll go with you if there's a hearing, but I know several of the guys on the Board. You'll be all right there."

"Thanks," he said and took a deep breath.

"Worst thing to come out of it is I don't have you in there with me."

I picked up my files and put my arm around Walton's shoulder.

"Next time, partner, just remember this: you can trust me with your life. I will never let you down."

Within a couple of minutes I was at the prosecution table. While the bailiff brought in the jury I turned to acknowledge my team behind me in the front row. I winked at Cheryl and nodded to Lee Jones. To my left, J.D. Silver was dressed in an expensive navy blue suit. He patted his formidable helmet. Ross was writing like a madman, his sweet, adoring wife and doting father sitting behind him, supporting him all the way.

The Bullards. What a lovely family. It's good to be back with them.

Silver announced to Judge Williams he had no further questions for Mrs. Thurman. Zelda addressed the jury about the brouhaha the day before, cautioning them to put it out of their minds, assuring them it was irrelevant. She told them about the stipulation.

"The parties agree and you may accept as a fact, ladies and gentlemen, that the boy sitting next to Danny Thurman on the sofa as shown on the DVD is Nicholas Donaldson, the son of Assistant District Attorney Walton Donaldson and his wife Gayle. To avoid any appearance of a conflict of interest, Mr. Donaldson will not participate in the remainder of the trial. I am instructing you now that these facts should not be considered in favor or against the State or the defendant."

I tried to put myself in the place of one of the jurors, imagining what he or she might be thinking: "Judge Williams, do you really expect me to act like nothing happened yesterday? I mean, come on. Ross jumps on Walton and screams about a giant conspiracy. The other jurors and I are supposed to forget all about that when we're deliberating? Hell, we've already talked about it in the Grand Jury room where we were stuck for almost two hours yesterday morning, totally in the dark while you guys were in here sorting it out."

I was reminded of one of my favorite New Yorker cartoons of all time. One juror leans over and whispers to another: "I'm not striking that from my record."

I called Irma Gilbert to the stand. It didn't seem possible, but she was more pallid and wraith-like than when we spoke to her in her home. And, she had the shakes. I thought she might faint when she took the oath so I stood behind her when she climbed the two steps to the witness chair. If she fell she would shatter into a thousand pieces.

I took her through the preliminaries, showing her a chart of the homes on Whitley that Walton had prepared. She seemed confused at first, then got her bearings and correctly identified the houses in the neighborhood. I had her repeat to the jury what she told Lee, Walton, and me in her home about what happened on July 4, how she had seen Danny carrying the blue sweater that day, walking toward town. I also asked her about Ronnie Blake, whom she had seen working in the neighborhood the day Danny disappeared. I confirmed that she hadn't seen Ronnie Blake talking to Danny.

I asked her about her drinking as gently as I could. Her alcoholism diminished the reliability of her testimony and I wanted the jury to hear it from me rather than Silver. I caught a break when Silver asked her if she really couldn't be sure what she saw that day because of the amount of bourbon she had drunk.

"I know I drink too much since my husband died, but I'm sure I saw Danny Thurman with the blue sweater walk in front of my window on the evening of the Fourth of July," she said. "I wasn't seeing things."

Ronnie Blake was next. He was a grizzled redneck of indeterminate age from somewhere out in the county. Ronnie sported a three-day growth of white whiskers and wore dingy denim bib overalls. He was wiry, kind of raw-boned with weathered skin and lots of hard miles. If I hadn't already known his vital stats, I could not have guessed his age within ten years. He could have ranged in age from thirty-five to fifty-five. In spite of his off-putting appearance and sex-offender status, he turned out to be a decent witness and didn't damage our case as much as he could have.

I asked him to tell the jury about his sex offender record. He didn't seem embarrassed and told them he pleaded guilty to a sex offense with a young boy and that he did hard time for it. He said he knew who Danny Thurman was from doing yard work for different people on Whitley Drive.

He said he had never had any communication with Danny except to say hello and had never been alone with the boy. He said he knew because of his record it was only a matter of time before the cops talked to him about Danny, but he didn't have anything to do with it.

When Silver asked him if he was aware that pedophiles like him were never cured and they were chronic repeat offenders, Ronnie said he didn't know any other pedophiles so he couldn't say. He said he didn't have internet or cable T.V. and could barely read, so he didn't know much of anything about what was going on in the world. He said he knew one thing: he had nothing to do with Danny going missing.

I couldn't shoo away a random thought that popped in my head about the intersection of Ronnie's life and mine. It seemed Ronnie Blake would have been a perfect juror for this trial had he not had the minor complication of being a convicted sex offender. In Yaloquena County, my ancestral home where I spent my entire professional career, the majority of citizens knew very little about most things and it didn't seem to bother them. In five days, this unknowing, bird-brained electorate would decide my political fate. Had Ronnie not been convicted of a felony years ago, he would have probably voted. But then I had a lot of room to talk about Yaloquena bird-brains. I voluntarily put myself at their mercy by qualifying for office again. No one held a gun to my head. I did it anyway, knowing I didn't want to. So I ask you, who was I to call anyone in Yaloquena County stupid?

CHAPTER FIFTY-TWO

"The State rests, Your Honor," I said with the sense of relief I always felt when I said those words.

I had finished putting on my witnesses and introducing my exhibits. It hadn't been pretty, but it was over. All that was left for me to do was cross-examine and make my closing argument. Both were a lot more fun than calling my witnesses and putting on my case. Judge Williams asked Silver if he was ready to call his first witness. He asked for a short break, which I thought was reasonable. After Judge Williams and the jury went out, I went to the corner of the courtroom to the left of the bench, faced the wall and called Susan.

"How's Jake?" I asked.

"He's still in shock. Walton came over this morning and they've been talking. They're riding out to the duck camp now."

Walton was three years older than Jake but they were good buddies, deer and duck hunting together when Jake was home during open seasons. Walton was the only guy in Sunshine Jake hung out with on his visits to Sunshine, which I was certain would become fewer and farther between now that Kitty was gone.

"We're going to have a small graveside service Saturday morning at the family cemetery," Susan said. "I talked to Father Bayani and he's agreed to do it. Lee is coming, Martha and Jimmy Gray, Nathan and Karen. I talked to Scott this morning. He said he'd be here." She paused. "How's the trial going?"

"Silver's about to put on his first witness," I said and saw the bailiff walk in the side door and give me a nod. "Judge is coming back. I'll be home during the noon break."

Moments later, Helmet Head called Judy Bullard to the stand. I watched her being sworn. She was stylish, good-looking, and well-educated, a fish out of water in Sunshine. Her skin was pale with just a hint of a freckle or two. She wore her reddish hair long and straight and looked me right in the eyes with her cold blue eyes when she sat in the witness chair. Judy seemed like a big-city girl; one tough cookie.

After some initial questions about her background and education, Silver asked about her marital history, touching briefly on her divorce from her first husband, her move to Sunshine to work for an accounting firm, her marriage to Ross. She said she and Ross had planned on having a child at some point.

I knew that was a whopper. I couldn't prove it, but I was certain Judy and Ross did not have the kind of sex life that might lead to pregnancy. I'd bet a dollar to a dime whatever they had was unusual.

Silver had coached Judy well. She turned to address the jurors with her answers when it was appropriate, like when he asked her about Connie Thurman asking for a donation for Danny's school in February. She had it all down pat. Connie was there on the sofa in her blue sweater, the same one the State had introduced into evidence on Monday. They had a nice visit and Connie left. Yes, Danny had been in the house on several occasions, sometimes to look at Ross's Indian artifact collection with other boys, and on a couple of other occasions to talk to Ross about mowing their grass. She said she saw him in the neighborhood on occasion and he seemed to be a nice, polite little boy.

Judy testified she was out of town on business the entire week in July when Danny disappeared. She said she returned home Friday, July 6 and everything was normal at their house. Silver then touched on a number of issues because he had to. He didn't want me bringing them out for the first time on cross. Judy said she knew nothing about the DVD of the two boys on the couch. When Mr. Silver told her about it she was shocked because that was a side of Ross she had never seen. Yes, they had some difficult periods in their marriage "like everyone does" and she and Ross had separated for a short while in May but had resolved things and she moved back in with Ross in early June.

Judy said she was aware of Ross getting into "costume" from time to time for his Indian studies and yes, she had seen him with "war paint" on once or twice and she thought his reenactments were very interesting and creative. She likened what Ross did to the Civil War re-enactors who dressed in authentic Union and Confederate uniforms and recreated Civil War battles around the South.

Judy told the jury Ross was a good husband and provider, that he was honest and conscientious, got along well with everyone at work, and had never been in trouble, not even a speeding ticket. Judy recounted Ross's community involvement in different projects and said he was always doing things to improve Sunshine.

"You've told the jury that your husband is an honest man, Mrs. Bullard," Silver said, "but has he ever lied to you?"

She pretended to think for a moment.

"Once," she told the jury, "he confessed to me that he had and affair with a co-worker."

"What did you do in response?"

"Like any wife, I was upset. I talked to Mr. Bullard, Ross's father, who has always been supportive. We determined it wasn't true. Ross had not been involved with the woman."

"Why would he confess to something like that when it wasn't true?"

"I don't know," Judy said, "but he did it on other occasions."

I didn't intervene even though I knew what Judy was going to recount was hearsay. Silver had come up with a way to explain the note.

"What other occasions?" Helmet Head asked, looking my way, expecting an objection.

"When he was younger. Before we were married."

Silver studied me for a moment. "Nothing further for Mrs. Bullard at this time, Your Honor."

It meant Helmet Head was going to call the old man as a witness. He was on the pre-trial list, but I wasn't sure until that moment Silver would take the chance of putting Jules on the stand.

Before I started with Judy, I turned to see if Bill and Connie Thurman were in the courtroom. They weren't in court during my examination of Mrs. Gilbert and Ronnie

Blake but I thought they may have shown up during Judy's direct testimony. I didn't see them.

"Good morning, Mrs. Bullard," I said, "are you currently having sexual relations with Mr. Jules Bullard?"

Chapter Fifty-Three

Ross Bullard seemed oblivious to his attorney objecting at the top of his lungs and demanding a mistrial. Judge Williams calmed Silver down at a sidebar. I said the defense had opened the door to this line of questioning when Judy testified that Ross was a good husband but they had some problems in their marriage and were separated in May. I watched Ross at the defense table while I told Zelda that Judy's testimony about Ross's false claim of an affair put their marital relations squarely at issue. Ross paid no attention to what I said.

"But not Jules Bullard's personal life," Silver said in a stage whisper, "it's totally irrelevant and prejudicial."

"Judy Bullard has been living in Jules Bullard's home since Ross shot himself on July 27, Your Honor," I said.

I watched Zelda's eyebrows rise. I knew at that point she was going to let me ask Judy about her relationship with Jules. I couldn't prove they were having sex, but I could ask Judy about it. The jury had seen the two of them together for almost two weeks. I was sure the thought had crossed at least one juror's mind. If it hadn't my question would plant a seed that might undermine Judy's testimony. Ross continued to frolic in his own world at the defense table, writing and thinking, paying no attention to anything going on in the courtroom.

"No, I am not," Judy said when we finally got back underway.

"Where are you currently sleeping?"

"At my father-in-law's home. After Ross shot himself I couldn't bear to stay at home by myself. Then it became a matter of security, with what Bill Thurman was doing. I was scared he might hurt me or do something to our home on Whitley, and Mr. Bullard was gracious enough to allow me to stay in his guest room at his home. I feel safer there."

"You said in your testimony you and Ross planned on a family. Ross is forty-four and you are forty-eight, isn't that correct?"

"Yes."

"Isn't forty-eight a little old to have your first child?

"Not with modern medical advances. I am pre-menopausal and many professional women my age are conceiving these days and delivering healthy children."

"Would you say you and Ross had a normal sex life for a married couple your age?"

"Objection," Silver said. "No foundation laid for what Mr. Banks considers normal. Also irrelevant."

"I'll allow it," Judge Williams said.

"Yes, we did," Judy said.

"Vaginal intercourse?"

Judy rolled her eyes. "Yes."

"How often?"

"Your honor," Silver said.

"Mr. Banks?" Zelda said, nudging me to move on.

"Just a couple of more, Your Honor." I paused. "Just to make sure I heard you correctly, Mrs. Bullard...," I pointed at Ross who was angrily striking out something he had written, "it is your testimony that you and the defendant had a normal sex life?"

"Yes."

"And you were totally unaware of his interest in young boys?"

"Objection," Silver said, "assumes a fact not in evidence."

"I'll withdraw the question," I said and took a moment to look at the jurors. No need to push for an answer. "Nothing further."

Silver had no re-direct, a sure sign he didn't want Judy exposed to any more cross-examination. Judy took her seat on the front row and picked up the magazine she was reading before she took the stand. My questions hadn't ruffled her one bit. Silver called Jules to the stand.

Jules looked down on me with disgust as he passed my table on his way to be sworn. As soon as he sat down, he fixed his beady eyes on me, daring me to take on someone my own size. I knew Jules was a tough old bird with no conscience and would be a difficult witness. Gayle

Donaldson lied on the stand to protect Nicholas. I had no doubt Jules would do or say anything to save Ross. Ross's conviction would reflect badly on Jules, First Savings Bank, and ultimately Jules' finances. His black heart was with his money, not his son.

While Silver took Jules through softball background questions about Ross's upbringing, I glanced over at Ross. For the first time in nine days in the courtroom, Ross was paying attention. He was taking notes on a new legal pad and what he was writing correlated to his father's testimony. Ross paid close attention when Jules talked about Ross's mother's suicide when Ross was three. Ross smirked when Jules described the devastating effect it had on both of them.

After twenty excruciating minutes listening to Jules talk about his career and Ross's spotless record as a child and an adult, I had to endure Jules' description of Ross as a vital part of the First Savings Bank, an institution that has done so much for Sunshine and Yaloquena County. Finally, Silver got to something relevant. Jules denied an inappropriate relationship with Judy with all the shock he could muster at such a disgusting suggestion, much of it directed at me.

"Mr. Bullard," Helmet Head said, "You were in court and heard your daughter-in-law describe your son's false confession to an extra-marital affair, did you not?"

"Yes."

"She said that you and she investigated and found it wasn't true."

"Yes. That's correct."

"Had Ross ever done something like this before?"

"Yes. When he first started driving he claimed he was responsible for a dent in my car, a dent that was quite expensive to repair, I might add. It turned out that one of our bank customers came in the following day and told me she had accidentally struck my car in the bank parking lot the previous week and had neglected to tell me. I think her conscience bothered her, Mr. Silver, and her insurance paid for the damage."

"Any other similar episodes?"

"In his late teens he tried to take responsibility for impregnating a young lady. His claim turned out to be false. About five years ago there was an accounting discrepancy in the bank and Ross volunteered to the bank examiners that he was responsible. The examiners looked into it and determined that a teller had been out of balance on several occasions and had changed her totals to cover up the missing money. When confronted she admitted it and I dismissed her. Ross had nothing to do with it.

"And of course when Ross was young, there were several instances where he tried to take the blame for an occurrence, I don't remember all the details."

"Did you ever take him for counseling?"

"No. Ross was a normal child. I attributed the false confessions to the guilt he felt about his mother's death, guilt that I shared. We both felt we had let his mother down somehow. Ross was so young at the time she left us, it's a miracle he turned out as well as he did."

I suppressed the urge to guffaw. Young Ross had really turned out great, making seven-year-olds undress on his sofa and recording them; keeping a cache of DVDs showing nude children; abducting and killing Danny Thurman. I had to hand it to Helmet Head, whether he came up with this false confession scenario or just used what Jules and Judy concocted, he had put Ross's alleged mental defect out there for the jury to think about without having a psychiatrist testify, which would have allowed me to hire a shrink to examine Ross.

Jules said he was out of town on July 4 and 5, and was unaware the Thurman boy had gone missing until the morning of July 6. He said Ross was at work as usual that Friday morning.

"Do you know what your son was doing on July 4?"

"It was a bank holiday and Ross was hunting for Indian artifacts around the Iron Bridge area. He told me earlier that week he wanted Thursday off to complete an extensive search he had planned beginning early Wednesday, the Fourth of July."

It was hearsay but I didn't object. Jules was sharp enough to get it in one way or the other and I didn't want the jury to think Jules' bogus testimony was something I was concerned about.

"Tell me about his relics," Silver said.

"I am told it is one of the finest private collections of pre-Columbian Native-American artifacts in the entire country. The Marksville Cultures and Hopewellians were mound-builders in this area of the Mississippi Delta. They were ancestors of the Cherokees. Ross is one of the premier experts in the South on these ancient societies and is fluent in their rituals."

Silver asked Jules about the two boys on the DVD. Jules said he could see how someone might think it was inappropriate, but he was certain there was an innocent explanation. He said Ross was enthusiastic in re-enacting the ancient rituals and insisted on authenticity. Jules said he assumed this dressing ritual involving the two boys was just part of re-living the ancient culture and nothing more.

"Do you know Ronnie Blake?"

"I know who he is."

"Have you ever seen him in Ross's neighborhood?"

"Yes. Ross and I are close. He and Judy are the only family I have. Before July I spent many a morning or afternoon at their home on Whitley and saw Ronnie Blake doing yard work at some of the houses."

"Did you know he was a convicted pedophile?"

"Yes."

"Did you ever see him talking to any children in the neighborhood?"

"Yes. On at least two separate occasions, maybe three, I saw him conversing with young Danny Thurman."

"Mr. Blake testified he only said hello to the boy."

"That's not true. I saw them talking and laughing together. I thought it was inappropriate."

"Did you tell anyone about what you saw?"

"No. If his parents didn't see fit to keep him away from someone like Ronnie Blake, I didn't think it was my place to do anything."

What a complete ass.

I looked at P.O. Harrington in the jury box. His face was redder than usual. P.O. and two of the other jurors looked away when Jules was spinning his yarns about Ross's

Hopewellian dressing ritual with the boys, his compulsion to confess to things he didn't do, and finally "the Ronnie Blake did it" theory. I felt confident the jury knew Jules was lying so I didn't object. Let the old buzzard keep talking. Silver knew he couldn't put Ross on the stand so he was using Judy and Jules to trot out their made-up stories to explain why Ross wasn't guilty. I couldn't rebut the things they were claiming and Silver knew it.

I thought Jules' condescension and arrogance was off-putting for everyone in the courtroom. I saw no need to cross-examine him extensively but did have a few questions.

"Mr. Bullard, prior to July of this year, had Ross ever confessed to a homicide or a child abduction?"

"Of course not."

"Had he ever shot himself and left a written statement when he made the other false confessions you described earlier?"

"No," he said and tried to stare a hole through me.

"Had Ross ever shown you the DVD of the two nude boys on his couch and described it as a re-enactment of a Hopewellian ritual?"

Jules stared at me in disgust. He didn't answer.

"Mr. Bullard?" Judge Williams said.

"That's all right, Your Honor. I think I know the answer."

Silver's next witness was John Mordano, the long-distance trucker who just happened to recognize Danny with a man at the truck stop south of Nashville. Sitting in the witness chair, Mordano looked like a cast member of *The Sopranos.* Silver walked him through his story, which Mordano related just as he had on the late night phone call to me, in my office, and at the pre-trial hearing. There wasn't much detail, just his assertion that he recognized Danny at the truck stop when he walked past him with an older man. Mordano was calm and matter-of-fact during his testimony, as if this sort of thing happened to him all the time. When I got Mordano on cross I asked him a few questions to point out the implausibility of his positive identification of a seven-year-old boy he saw in passing, a boy he only knew from a flyer.

"I know what I saw and it was him," Mordano said calmly.

I asked him why he waited so long to call authorities. He gave the same answer he had given before: "I wanted to be sure and I needed the phone number off the poster."

I went into his relationship with Silver. Helmet Head was careful to bring out on direct that Mordano was a former client, that Silver had succeeded in getting federal charges against him dismissed, that he didn't owe Silver any money nor was he obligated to him in any manner.

"When was the last time you spoke to Mr. Silver," I asked.

"Long time ago," he said.

"And to Mr. Myers?"

"The same. He was still a cop when Mr. Silver got me off the charges, but I talked to him a couple of years ago."

"What about?"

"Nothing important. Just talk."

"And it's your testimony you did not have any conversation with Mr. Silver or Mr. Myers about Danny Thurman until after your late night telephone call to me?"

"That's right. Since then I talked to both of them. They wanted to know what I saw, all the details, you know, just like you did."

I asked him about the fraud and RICO charges on which Silver represented him but getting him to provide details was like pulling teeth. Prior to trial Lee, Kitty, and Walton had tried to get information from the U.S. Attorney and FBI in Memphis but there had been a lot of turnover and the investigators and lawyers involved were no longer there. I did ask Mordano what he thought the odds were that the same lawyer, J.D. Silver, who represented him on the federal charges would end up representing the man charged in the death of Danny Thurman, the young man Mordano claimed to have seen.

"I don't know," was all he said.

When Mordano stepped down Judge Williams looked at the courtroom clock.

"It's getting late," she said. "Do you plan on calling another witness today, Mr. Silver?"

Helmet Head turned around to look at Jules and Judy, then leaned down to whisper to Ross who ignored him. Ross had paid no attention to the testimony of Mordano, ostensibly his most critical defense witness. He chose instead to resume writing on his legal pad like a man possessed.

"The defense rests, Your Honor," Silver said.

CHAPTER FIFTY-FOUR

After Silver rested his case I spent thirty minutes alone in my office organizing, making one or two word notes for each point I wanted to cover in my closing. Judge Williams told us in chambers she wouldn't place a time limit on us because it was a capital case, but suggested that one hour was the limit of jurors' attention spans. I thought it was less than that, more like twenty minutes in my experience, which I would not exceed.

Susan and Cheryl Diamond were sitting at the weathered pine kitchen table when I made it home. The table was covered with cakes, casseroles, and meat and vegetable trays. The Sunshine mourning and visitation ritual was underway. Most of our friends and acquaintances never had a conversation with Kitty, but they all knew who Kitty was and her relationship to Jake and our family. In Sunshine, the entire community mourned a death.

"Gayle brought this Italian cream cake," Susan said pointing. "She said to tell you she was very sorry for lying about Nicholas."

I shrugged and sat down.

"It probably didn't matter," I said. "The entire trial has been one screw-up after another. I've never been through one like this."

"You've never gone up against someone like the Bullards," Cheryl said. "But you shouldn't worry. The jury didn't believe Judy or Jules. And it's obvious Jules has a low opinion of the jurors' intelligence."

I didn't tell Cheryl that was something Jules and I shared. She probably already knew.

"And John Mordano had Mafia written all over him," Cheryl said.

"Where's Jake?" I asked.

"He's still out at the duck camp," Susan said.

"I'm going to drive out there as soon as I change," I said. "Would you fix me a sandwich to go?"

"I think that's a good idea," Susan said. "Jimmy Gray wants to meet with you tonight. I told him you'd be with Jake."

"I'll call him."

Ten minutes later I walked down the stairs in my jeans and boots. Cheryl stood at the foot of the stairs.

"There's something I want you to know, something I saw today when Jules was on the witness stand."

I knew she meant "sensed."

"When he testified, this hideous black miasmic cloud billowed out of his mouth. It was a tarry kind of smoke, like when tires burn. I had to close my eyes."

I stood there a moment, two steps above her.

"When I opened them again it was gone."

"What do you think...?"

"You know what it means, Willie Mitchell. He is an evil man, rotting from within."

I drove my truck north to our duck camp, wolfing down the roast beef sandwich Susan made me. She sent along two thick sandwiches and a big slice of cake for Jake. I called Jimmy Gray while I had cell service. He said the Mayor and Sheriff insisted we have a meeting at campaign headquarters tonight. I told him I was going to be at the duck camp with Jake.

"How about nine o'clock?" Jimmy said. "It's important."

I told Jimmy I'd be there and continued to drive on the state highway toward the camp. I turned west onto the dirt road that snaked around low-lying bogs to our duck camp, a cabin of rough-hewn cypress planks sitting on wooden piers on the edge of a forty acre black water pond. It had been more than a decade since I sat in our blind in the middle of the pond hidden by cypress trees in below freezing conditions shooting at mallards, teals, and wood ducks. Jake and Scott hunted the place when they were young, but neither had hunted it since they graduated from Ole Miss. When Kitty first arrived in Sunshine, as soon as she was well enough to live on her own she took up residence in our duck camp to recuperate from the trauma she suffered in New Orleans. It was supposed to be temporary, but she ended up making it her home the entire time she was in Yaloquena County. When Jake was home he spent most of his time at the camp with Kitty. She said she liked the isolation the camp provided. With her FBI training and skill with a pistol, she wasn't afraid to stay by herself. She told me it was so quiet out there she could always hear when someone approached.

By the time I parked at the duck camp the sun was setting behind the cypress trees. I saw Jake sitting in the swing on the porch. I sat with him and gave him the paper bag his mother sent.

"It's roast beef sandwiches and a big piece of Italian cream cake."

"Your favorite," Jake said.

"Gayle made it."

"Walton was out here until about four." He opened the screen door. "You want a Coke Zero? Kitty's got a whole case in the fridge."

"No, thanks."

When he sat back down in the swing I asked if he was all right.

"I guess," he said opening the aluminum foil to take a bite. "To tell you the truth, I don't know what to feel right now."

"I understand."

"How's London?"

"Different. Not getting to do a lot of sightseeing."

"I bet."

"I'm leaving Saturday after the service."

"Back to England?"

"Yeah," he nodded. "I don't know what else to do."

We drifted back and forth in the swing. Crickets and bullfrogs tuned up around us, but there were no lightning bugs. This time of year, the little slow-flying blinkers had been shot down by crop dusters strafing the cotton fields with defoliants. Winds carried the deadly mist beyond the crop rows, sometimes blanketing our camp and pond.

"How's the election going?" Jake asked after a few moments.

"Pretty badly," I said.

"Just as well. You've done about all you can do in Sunshine."

"Doesn't seem to get any better."

"I don't know why you and Mom stay here."

"I'm not sure," I said, "but everyone has to be somewhere."

"Walton told me all about the trial. What a cluster."

"It's been a tough fight with a short stick. The die was cast when Bill Thurman demanded we go to trial right away."

"Walton told me about Gayle lying to him about Nicholas on the tape and the notes Ross sent him."

"How did he seem to you?"

"Embarrassed about how badly he screwed up. He felt like he let you down. He's not angry at Gayle."

"He was put in a tough spot."

"Now he's trying to figure out how to deal with Nicholas. I told him they all needed to go to a family counselor, including Gayle and Payne."

"Pretty good advice," I said.

"Easy to advise other people."

"But hard to give them the right advice. Most people just run their mouths and say whatever pops in their heads."

"I know what you mean," Jake said. "I try to like people, but they're all so fuckin' stupid."

I looked at him for a moment expecting to see a smile. It was a Jimmy Gray phrase Jake, Scott, and I adopted years ago. Finally, there it was, a slight upturn at his mouth's edge. Jake would get through this.

"This Ross Bullard trial shows how screwed up our legal system is. You know it doesn't work anymore, don't you?"

"There's times it doesn't."

"It's why Kitty's dead. Her lungs were never the same."

"Those two guys got what was coming to them."

"Yeah," Jake said, "but it wasn't the legal system that finally delivered justice to those bastards."

Jake never told me he was the man who single-handedly hunted down and killed the two members of Los Cuervos in New Orleans who had attacked Kitty. I knew he did, though, and was proud of him. The criminal justice system in New Orleans was rendered inoperable by Katrina and ensuing NOPD scandals and had never recovered. If Jake hadn't killed the two gangsters, they would have never been caught. They would have taken more innocent lives.

Jake's system worked a lot better than mine.

We sat in the swing until it was full dark. Jake didn't say much and neither did I. We both knew there was nothing to discuss. It felt good being with him, though. It would take some time for Jake to heal. He was right to go back to work, to stay busy and focused while his subconscious worked on healing his emotional suffering.

"Scott's coming in tomorrow," he said after a while. "Be good to see Donna and him."

"Jimmy Gray says I have to meet with him and Everett and Lee tonight at campaign headquarters."

"You go on," he said. "Tell Mom I'm staying out here tonight. I'll be in first thing in the morning for breakfast."

"You sure?"

I could barely see him nodding in the darkness on the porch.

"See you tomorrow," he said.

CHAPTER FIFTY-FIVE

I walked into my campaign headquarters a little before nine. Jimmy Gray, Lee Jones, and Everett Johnson sat around a table and Congressman Buddy Wade leaned against a counter. No one was smiling.

"This doesn't look good," I said.

"Have a seat, Willie Mitchell," Jimmy said.

"How is Jake?" Lee asked.

"He seemed better this evening. I just came from the camp."

"We're all sad about Kitty, Willie Mitchell," Jimmy said. "I hate to bother you with this now but we need to make a decision."

"Things aren't going so well I take it."

"No," Jimmy said.

"I've been moving around all week," the Mayor said, "listening to people, asking a few questions. Black folks are voting for Eleanor. There's no other way to put it. They don't have anything against you, it's just they want a black lawyer as district attorney."

"Like Winston told me a few weeks ago," I said, "it's nothing personal. It's just politics."

"That's it in a nutshell," Lee Jones said. "Makes no sense unless you look at it just in terms of race. People out there are telling me 'it's time for a change,' but I know what they mean is they're for Eleanor just because she's black. Most of them don't even know her."

"It's an irresistible force," Buddy Wade said. "When Rose Jackson beat me like a red-headed stepchild the early voters turned out just like they're doing in your race."

"Bobby Sanders has really ginned up the support for her," Jimmy Gray said. "We've looked at the early voter lists and figure she's way out in front."

"And election day results go the same way as early and absentee voting," Everett said. "That's been my experience."

"So what do we need to decide tonight?" I asked. "We've known the odds were against us."

"It's about money," Jimmy Gray said.

"Bobby's starting to get the money out there on the street," Everett said. "I'm hearing about it from all directions."

"Me, too," Lee said.

"So what Lee and Everett want to know," Buddy Wade said, "is whether you're going to put money out to compete with Bobby's."

I looked around the room.

"Who thinks I should?"

No one raised a hand.

"Who thinks I shouldn't because it's a lost cause?"

All four raised their hands.

"Who thinks I shouldn't because it's morally repugnant?"

I raised my hand. At first I was alone, then Buddy raised his; then Jimmy Gray, then Lee and Everett.

"All right," I said. "We're no doubt going to lose the election, but we'll be taking the high road."

"You know something?" Jimmy Gray said. "You're right. You are the world's worst politician."

"Thank you," I said.

CHAPTER FIFTY-SIX

It was five minutes to nine. I sat at the prosecution table thinking about what I was going to say to the jurors. Helmet Head was studying his notes; Ross was writing. Behind them Jules was staring as if trying to put a hex on me. Judy was reading Vogue.

Cheryl and Lee Jones sat behind me in the first row. Earlier I had seen Jake take a seat in the back of the courtroom. There was no sign of Bill or Connie again and it worried me. Walton left the courthouse at eight to check on the Thurmans but didn't make it back before I left for the courtroom. Before he left I asked Walton how he and Gayle were doing. He said they were working on seeing somebody together first, then with the twins. Walton said talking to Jake helped put everything in perspective.

I wrote the date at the top of my legal pad in big letters: November 2. I had never closed out a trial on All Souls Day, the day on which everyone is supposed to pray for the souls in purgatory to make it into heaven, according to the nuns who taught in my elementary school. Purgatory is no cake walk, but it's much better than limbo. The nuns said people in limbo, primarily infants who died before they could be baptized into the Roman Catholic faith, could never enter heaven. Even in the second grade I thought getting sent to limbo was cruel. It made for an extremely long afterlife for someone who didn't do anything wrong. It was at that point in my religious education I knew the sisters were pulling my leg. No way God would punish an innocent baby like that. By the ripe old age of seven, I figured out the God I prayed to was the original Good Guy and wouldn't banish a little baby to day care for eternity. After the baloney about limbo, I took everything else the nuns said with a grain of salt.

Zelda took the bench and the bailiff brought in the jurors. Their mood seemed lighter, probably because the end was in sight. She asked Silver and me if there was anything to tend to before we started. We said no and she briefly explained to the jury what closing argument was.

"Mr. Banks," she said.

I stood at the podium that Eddie Bordelon had moved in front of the jury box. I didn't try to add any drama to what the jurors had to decide. Deliberating in a capital murder case is dramatic enough. I moved quickly through the evidence. There wasn't much of it to go over. I used the remote to show the naked boys on the DVD but only for a couple of seconds. No one wanted to see that image any more. I urged the jurors to use their common sense when viewing all the facts and circumstances. When I saw P.O. Harrington moving his red face up and down in time to my argument, I sprinted to the finish. By then I was certain he was going to be the foreman and I knew he was with me.

Helmet Head put on a show. He was eloquent and emotional. At times he reminded me of the Reverend Bobby Sanders. There was even a tear, maybe two. I knew his performance was for Jules, the man paying the fare. I stopped counting after the sixth time he reminded the jurors that there was no body and no proof of death let alone proof of murder. Silver had an excellent legal case, a case that would pique the interest of the law clerks who wrote the opinions for the judges on the court of appeal. Helmet Head's problem was he had a client the jury had observed for two weeks. That alone was enough for the jury to convict, because Ross's behavior was so very bizarre. Unfortunately, his antics would not be reflected on the cold appellate record. To the judges on the Court of Appeal, Ross Bullard would just be a name.

I struggled to stay focused when Zelda started reading the jury instructions. Silver and I had butted heads for several days in the Judge's chambers during breaks in the testimony, arguing over the exact wording of the instructions. I glanced at the jurors five minutes into Zelda's reading. Some had already stopped paying attention. Fifteen minutes later, when the bailiff took the jury out to begin deliberating, I reminded myself it only took one not guilty vote in a capital case to hang the jury and cause a mistrial. Just one.

The deputies escorted Ross from his table. I looked up as he walked by. He smiled and winked at me. I shook my head—the wink was a good example of something that won't be on the record.

I turned and shook hands with Lee Jones at the rail. It was a tradition the Sheriff and I maintained. Cheryl joined us and told me how well I had argued. Over her head I saw Jake jabbing his finger in a southerly direction and knew he meant he'd see me in my office.

Moments later I walked in as Jake was visiting with Ethel, Louise, and Walton in the reception area. The mood was odd. The ladies had known Jake since he was a child and were glad to see him, but the circumstances were somber.

"I spoke to Connie," Walton said.

I gestured for Jake and Walton to join me in my private office.

"Connie said she can't show her face in the courtroom after lying about Nicholas on the DVD," Walton said. "She said Bill was really angry with her, said she screwed up the case. I told her everything was fine, that it was more Gayle's fault than hers."

"What about Bill?" I asked. "You talk to him?"

"I waited around but he didn't show. Connie said he's been drinking, coming and going all hours of the day and night."

"You can't really blame him," Jake said. "I didn't see any of the trial but I listened to Silver's argument in there. It's been two years since I practiced law but I'm pretty sure if this jury finds Bullard guilty you're going to have a hard time making the conviction stick."

"I tried the case I had. That's all I could do."

"Legally," Jake said.

Chapter Fifty-Seven

We gathered a little before ten a.m. Saturday morning inside what was left of the wrought iron fence surrounding the Banks family cemetery in a corner of our 990 acres. Thieves had taken all of the gates and much of the fence. I knew they were selling the ornate metal work to scrap yards based solely on its weight for pennies on the dollar. Susan and I had priced replacement wrought iron and learned that the high quality artistic designs we lost could not be replicated these days at any price. There simply were no artisans capable of making it. The dimwits who took it knew nothing of the aesthetic value of what they were destroying. They were only concerned with its heft.

My parents' and grandparents' tombstones were intact, but some of the stones for my collateral relatives had been broken and pushed over. I tried to maintain the cemetery but it was a tough fight with the vandals and looters having a distinct advantage. No one lived close enough to the cemetery to keep an eye on it for me. I had it bush hogged and mowed from April to October of each year. I could trim the grass and weeds but I could not prevent the cemetery's continuing degradation.

After closing arguments and instructions the jury got the Bullard case at eleven a.m. Friday. The bailiff said they had lunch and started deliberating about one p.m. They finished the day at five and were taken to the all-you-can-eat fried catfish place on the four lane and later to their motel cells. Sheriff Jones kept a patrol unit at the motel all night to keep outsiders away and make sure the jurors stayed in their rooms. The motel phones were disabled and the television cable was rigged to block all channels except for a sports cable network and two movie channels. Dangerous prison inmates had access to more entertainment than Ross Bullard's jurors.

While the jurors were incarcerated in their rooms, the visitation to mourn Kitty started at the house at six-thirty.

Jake and Susan decided her body would remain at the funeral home until it was transported to the family cemetery for burial. Susan had called to invite the small number of people who were close to Kitty to drop by Friday night.

Our youngest son Scott and his girl friend Donna Piersall arrived from D.C. in the afternoon. It was good feeling to have our family together, even though it was to mourn the death of one of its *de facto* members. Scott and Donna were a striking couple. He was twenty-four and handsome, built like Susan at 5'10', slender with blond hair. Donna was the same age. She was a beautiful young woman from Charleston with long, straight brown hair, a gorgeous smile and dimples. She and Scott were political junkies. Donna worked as an aide for the junior Senator from South Carolina and Scott for Mississippi Senator Skeeter Sumrall. Skeeter was a friend of mine and even closer to Jimmy Gray and Buddy Wade. Skeeter had called me early in my campaign and offered to let Scott leave D.C. and come to Sunshine to help with my campaign, but I said no thanks. No need to subject Scott to the mess I had gotten myself into.

I loved watching Jake and Scott talking quietly at the house. Though Jake was almost five years older, they were close. By the time he was in the eighth grade, Scott thought he ought to be able to do what Jake did. Scott was competitive, especially in athletics, and wanted to run as fast and jump as high as his brother. Jake was taller, stronger, and tougher, and would always be, though he admitted that Scott was better athletically at some things. Jake used his strength to knock people over; Scott would figure out a way around them. Jake was a bull, Scott a panther. They were both smart. Jake was direct. He saw things in black and white. Scott was more tactful and sly, a natural politician.

All the people that mattered to Kitty came by the house Friday night: Jimmy and Martha Gray; the Sheriff and his wife Yancey; Buddy Wade and his current girl friend, Ramona, a tall short-haired blond with a pretty face and, like Buddy, a checkered marital history; Deputy Sammy Roberts and his wife June; Dr. Nathan and Karen Clement; our longtime housekeeper Ina; Walton and Gayle

Donaldson; Ethel Morris and Louise Kelly from the office; Mayor Everett Johnson and his wife Gladys; and Cheryl Diamond, who helped Susan and Ina in the kitchen.

Like all Delta wakes, the visitation morphed into a subdued cocktail party. I had put out plenty of liquor, wine, and beer, and everyone except Ina and Cheryl had a few. Our visitors had kind things to say about Kitty to Jake and to Susan, to whom Kitty had become like the daughter she never had. Nathan took care of Kitty's medical needs, but it was Susan and Ina who nursed Kitty back to health when she arrived in our home from New Orleans. Susan started Kitty on short walks that led eventually to long, meandering treks around Sunshine, talking all the while. Susan and I wanted Jake and Kitty to marry, but they never got around to it.

After everyone left, Jake, Scott and Donna, and Susan and I finished cleaning up and sat around the old pine table in the kitchen telling stories about Jake and Scott growing up. It was fun for Donna to hear them for the first time. For the rest of us, reliving the happy times was a poultice for our sorrow.

At the cemetery Saturday morning Lee told me the jurors had breakfast and were taken to the courthouse to resume deliberating at eight. I had no idea how long it might take for them to come to a unanimous decision, and I made no attempt to handicap it. I didn't know if a long or short deliberation worked for or against me. I gave up long ago trying to generalize about such things. Jury deliberations were like snowflakes—each one was different.

Father Bayani, the local Catholic priest from the Philippines, conducted the graveside service. It was brief and dignified. He was new in Sunshine, sent by the diocese to replace Father Danilo, also a Philippino. Sunshine was considered a mission parish and for the past twenty years had been pastored by priests born in Asia. I was sure the irony of local Catholics being ministered by priests from former colonies of western powers was lost on most parishioners.

Susan and I were standing with Scott and Donna when I saw Lee pull his radio from his belt and walk away to talk. When he came back he told me the jury was ready to report.

Adrenaline shot through my system like an electric current. I asked Lee if I could ride in with him, made my apologies to the others and looked for Jake. He was by himself standing over the open grave staring down at Kitty's casket.

"Jake," I said, "I have to go. The jury is back."

"Go ahead," he said looking at his watch. "I'm going to swing by the house for a minute then I'm headed back to Memphis."

"You can't stay a little bit longer?"

"I could, Daddy, but Dunne needs me in London. I feel useless here, at loose ends. I'll come back for a good, long visit when we're through with the mission."

"You know how long that will be?"

"No idea."

I looked at my son for a moment. There was nothing more to say.

"Stay safe, Jake," I said and hugged him, patting him on the back. His arm and shoulder muscles were hard as a rock.

"I'm sure you convicted him, Dad. And don't worry about what happens next Tuesday. You'll be better off if you lose the election."

"I think we're going to have the chance to see if you're right," I said and walked off to join Lee at his shiny black Tahoe.

CHAPTER FIFTY-EIGHT

I followed the Sheriff up the stairs and into the hallway leading to the courtroom. One of his deputies stood at the main entrance gesturing for us to step on it. We hustled down the hall and into court. The entire cast of characters, including the jury, was in place. I stood at the prosecution table.

"Your Honor, I'm sorry. I was...."

"I know where you were, Mr. Banks. There's no problem. The jury has been seated for less than a minute and I knew you were on your way." She turned to the jury. "Ladies and gentlemen of the jury, have you selected a foreperson?"

"Yes, ma'am, Your Honor," P.O. Harrington stood and proclaimed in a loud voice, "and I am it."

I said a silent prayer of thanksgiving.

"Has the jury reached a verdict?" she asked P.O.

"We have, Judge Williams."

"Mr. Clerk," she said to Eddie Bordelon, "will you retrieve the written verdict for the Court to examine?"

Eddie walked quickly to get the one page verdict sheet. He gave it to the Judge who read it over for a moment, then handed it back to Eddie, who returned it to P.O. to read.

"Mr. Harrington," she said, "how does the jury find?"

"We the jury," P.O. said loudly, his face glowing, "find the defendant, Darrell Ross Bullard, guilty of capital murder."

I relaxed for the first time in a while. I glanced at Helmet Head. He didn't seem surprised or disappointed. Ross continued to write on his legal pad. I wasn't sure he had been listening. Behind him, Jules was livid but in control. Judy sat stone-faced. I turned further to see the reaction from my team. Cheryl Diamond beamed. Lee smiled.

"Would you like the jury to be polled, Mr. Silver?" Zelda asked.

"Judge, you can just ask the panel if they were unanimous. There's no need to poll each juror."

Zelda asked if each juror agreed and all twelve nodded.

"Just to be on the safe side," she said, "if any one of you twelve jurors did not vote guilty of capital murder, please raise your hand."

Not one of the jurors did.

"As I explained to you before we started the guilt phase," she said, "we now move into the penalty phase, where the State and the Defense will call witnesses...."

"Excuse me, Your Honor," P.O. said standing up in the box. "Your Honor" came out *"Yore Honor."* "We've already talked about what penalty we want."

"Mr. Harrington, your discussion of penalty was premature...."

"I'd like to hear what the jury has to say," J.D. Silver said.

"Very well. Go ahead, Mr. Harrington."

"What we decided is if Ross Bullard will take the Sheriff and the D.A. to the spot where he put Danny Thurman's body we'll recommend life imprisonment instead of death."

P.O. pronounced it *"putt"* instead of "put."

Silver stood and objected, asking for a judgment of acquittal notwithstanding the verdict. The crowd noise behind me had risen from a murmur to a loud buzz, and Zelda banged her gavel for a minute or two before there was enough quiet to proceed. P.O. Harrington caught my eye and smiled, nodding then winking at me with his crimson eyelid.

In the midst of the uproar in the courtroom, I tried to put my finger on what had changed about me. In the previous twenty-four years, through countless jury trials of murderers and other vicious felons, no one had ever winked at me. Beginning yesterday I was now getting a wink a day. I decided to wait a few days before I declared it a trend.

Zelda asked the bailiff to take the jury back to the deliberation room. After they were gone, she asked us how we wanted to proceed.

"I propose we start the penalty phase Monday morning at nine," I said to the Judge. "I believe everyone could use some rest."

"I concur," Silver said.

"Mr. Banks, how long do you anticipate yours will take?"

"Probably just the morning, Judge Williams."

"About three days," Helmet Head said, "maybe less."

"Let's bring the jury back in and we'll adjourn until Monday morning," she said and gestured to Lee to inform the bailiff.

Within five minutes the jury was seated in the box.

"Ladies and gentlemen of the jury, we have finished for the day. I will ask the deputies to return you to your motel and we will start fresh Monday morning with testimony in the penalty phase."

"Judge Williams," P.O. said standing. "They ain't none of us wants to go back to that motel. I was running a bluff a minute ago about him taking us to the body. I took a poll in the jury room and there's only two people, me and one other, that wants the death penalty. Ten of us ain't going to vote for it period, no matter what. It has a lot to do with Danny not being found. Without the boy's body, ten of us on this jury ain't going to give the death penalty, no matter what the evidence is we're going to hear next week."

"Your Honor," I said, "the State is willing to accept the jury's position as stated by Mr. Harrington. I see no need to put the jury through the sentencing phase and will not object to this Court entering a sentence of life imprisonment at this time."

"Though it's highly irregular," Helmet Head said, "the Defense concurs with Mr. Banks."

"I was sure you would, Mr. Silver," Zelda said with a slight smile.

"We would waive any requirements for a pre-sentence report or recommendation," Silver said, "and agree to be sentenced this morning, since the statute mandates what this court must impose."

"Very well. Mr. Silver, stand with your client, if he doesn't mind my interrupting whatever he's doing down there."

Silver tugged on Ross's arm, pulling him to his feet. Zelda sentenced Ross to life imprisonment with no probation, parole, or suspension of sentence, and directed the Sheriff's deputies to escort him to the jail upstairs. She thanked the jury for their service and dismissed them. I stood and shook hands with each juror as he or she stepped from the jury box. They were all very happy to be going home.

Zelda adjourned court. I stepped toward Silver and took Ross's seat next to the lawyer.

"Why in the world did y'all keep P.O. Harrington?"

Helmet Head turned around to make sure Jules wasn't within earshot. He leaned over to me and whispered.

"Mr. Buffalo Breath insisted I take him. He said he made Harrington's sister a loan years ago to save her house and fifty-five acres from being foreclosed on. He said Harrington and his sister were very close and he was certain P.O. loved him."

"She ended up losing the home anyway," I said. "The interest rate Jules charged her was way above the going rate. He sold the loan for a pot full of money in the secondary market. The final holder of the note, a bank out of Michigan, ended up foreclosing a couple of years later, took the property and evicted P.O.'s sister. She came to see me about it but I told her I couldn't represent her. I looked at the documents and told her I didn't think there was anything she could do to save the place. Before she left my office that day she called Jules a blood sucker." I paused. "But Jules was right about one thing. P.O. and his sister are very close."

"I'm glad P.O.'s sister loves him," Silver said. "I'll be filing several motions Monday morning," he said. "I'm correct on the *corpus delicti* issue. Judge Williams is going to be reversed. Then there's the conduct of the jury, the sentencing nonsense. There's the perjury by Mrs. Thurman and Mrs. Donaldson, your Assistant's involvement, and the free-for-all in front of the jury. This verdict will be overturned."

"You may be right," I said, "I really never expected to get this far."

CHAPTER FIFTY-NINE

It was noon Sunday, twenty-four hours since P.O.'s *tour de force* performance in the jury box. How I wished I could have been a fly on the wall and watched the choleric Pearl Ocie Harrington direct the other jurors during deliberations. After the jury verdict and sentence, I had media interviews Saturday for several hours. I made it home about three o'clock. I knew State vs. Darrell Ross Bullard was far from over, but winning this first round felt good.

Scott told me at the house that Jake spent thirty minutes alone with Susan immediately after the interment then took off for Memphis in a Sheriff's unit chauffeured by Deputy Sammy Roberts, courtesy of Lee Jones. Susan spent an hour by herself on the sun porch after Jake left, according to Scott, then joined Scott and Donna for a lunch of visitation leftovers at the kitchen table.

Susan was napping when I walked in our bedroom to change. I was still jazzed from the jury verdict and knew if I stayed around the house someone would call me with some election b.s. I gently woke Susan with a kiss on her forehead and talked her into going to Jimmy Gray's gazebo for a picnic with Scott and Donna.

It was an hour drive northwest of Sunshine to the three thousand acres of wetlands adjoining the Mississippi River Jimmy Gray owned. He bought it for a song in the early eighties and built a winding gravel road that followed the land ridges to the river. When I wanted total isolation, this is where I came. We unloaded our wine and picnic supplies at the crude gazebo Jimmy's caretaker built out of hand-hewn cypress planks on the private levee overlooking the river.

The four of us sat in redwood deck chairs and sipped a Georges De Bouef Pinot Noir. I reminded Scott their annual Beaujolais Nouveau would be available in three weeks. Scott said he had already ordered some from his favorite D.C. liquor store. Donna was astounded at the traffic on the river, especially the sight of a tug pushing twenty-one fully-loaded barges against the current, three barges wide, seven long.

"How does the tug captain keep them in line?" Donna asked.

No one knew. We talked about Jake. Susan said she was satisfied after their brief conversation at home that Jake was in London doing what he thought he had to do, something important in the grand scheme of things. Scott told Susan the people who should worry about Jake were the ones he was sent to fight. Scott implied he knew a little about what Jake was up to, that he was fighting in a necessary cause. When the mosquitoes started swarming as the sun dipped lower, we packed our things and headed back to Sunshine.

I slept soundly that night. Scott and Donna left after breakfast to catch their flight back to D.C. Susan wanted to go to church, so I accompanied her, daydreaming during the sermon about my life after the D.A.'s office, the idea of which was beginning to appeal to me. I realized Ross Bullard would probably be my last murder trial. The new D.A. Eleanor Bernstein would be representing the State on appeal. More than likely she was inheriting a losing hand.

It felt good to go out with a bang.

For lunch we foraged through the leftovers from Friday night again. I was about to cut myself a piece of Italian cream cake for dessert when the Mayor knocked on the kitchen door and walked in.

"Have a seat, Everoot," I said, imitating Jimmy Gray, who never called him Everett. "We've got plenty of groceries."

"No, thanks," Everett said standing by the door. "I need you to come with me, Willie Mitchell."

"I thought we had thrown in the towel," I said.

"We did, but someone has thrown it back to us."

I left with Everett in his big black BMW. As he drove out of my circular pea gravel driveway he gave me a half-dozen sheets of copy paper. I turned them over one-by-one—six different shots of Eleanor Bernstein in scorching hot sexual congress with her Asian lesbian lover. The black and white photographs had been reproduced on cheap copy paper, but the quality was good. Eleanor's identity was unmistakable, the acts themselves creative and provocative.

"David Jefferson has people giving these out in every black church in the city and county this morning. They gave out a pile of them at juke joints and honky tonks starting about midnight. They stuck them on the windshields of people's cars in driveways and parking lots all over town while people were sleeping. Everybody's talking about it."

I turned the pictures face down and tossed them on the back seat.

"After Lee and I came to your office with the one photograph six or seven weeks ago I made David promise he wouldn't use these pictures."

"We've got to do something about this," I said.

"Like what? The cat's out of the bag."

The Mayor pulled into the Sheriff's parking area beside the courthouse and stopped next to Lee's Tahoe. We walked inside. Lee was sitting behind his desk.

"I just got off the phone with Bobby Sanders," Lee said. "He wants David Jefferson and his friends arrested. I took a look at the Sheriff's Association Handbook and I can't see any law that applies."

"It's not criminal," I said. "Eleanor's got a civil claim I imagine, but I'm not sure she would win a lawsuit for defamation because truth is a defense. Invasion of privacy cases in Mississippi are rare, and because she's running for office she would be considered a 'public figure' and fair game for garbage like this."

"I would have thought putting out naked pictures of somebody without their permission would be against the law." Everett pronounced "naked," *nekkid.*

"Any idea what the public reaction is so far?" I asked. "I hope there's some kind of backlash. Maybe this won't make any difference."

Everett looked at Lee.

"I don't know what Lee's heard," the Mayor said, "but the reaction out there is exactly what I said it would be when we talked about this the first time."

"It may be a dirty trick," Lee said, "but Everett's right. People around here are angry with Eleanor. They feel like she hasn't been honest with them."

"Plain and simple they just don't like gays," Everett said. "They'll vote for one if they stay in the closet, but once it's out in the open like this, they ain't no way."

"No one's mad at us about this?" I asked. "It's no secret David's part of our campaign, even if he went rogue."

"Naw, Willie Mitchell," the Mayor said. "They're mad at your opponent for being a lesbian."

"Mayor's right," Lee said. "This thing's turned on a dime."

"It's too late to put something in the paper," Everett said, "telling people this is Eleanor's private business and has no place in an election. You'd be wasting your money. It won't mean a thing to any black voters who've seen these photographs."

"And based on the feedback I'm getting from all over, every black voter in Yaloquena County has seen 'em," Lee said, standing to shake my hand. "Like it or not, you're going to win a seventh term."

Everett and I left. He dropped me at the house where Jimmy Gray and Buddy Wade were waiting for me on the front porch.

"It's seventy-five degrees and I've got a cooler full of ice cold Michelob Ultras. What say we go play golf, Mr. Seven-Term D.A?"

"I will," I said, "but only if you wipe that grin off your face. I'll meet you out there. Let me talk to Susan a minute."

Susan was sitting at the kitchen table reading the Sunday paper.

"Walton called me," she said. "He told me about the pictures."

"Sorry," I said.

"Walton said you told them a month-and-a-half ago you'd drop out of the race if they went public with them."

"Lee and Everett didn't do it."

"That's what Walton told me. I've met David Jefferson. He seems like a nice young man. I never would have guessed he'd do this."

"He's bitter as hell about Bobby Sanders stealing his grandfather's congregation. He loved Reverend Gray like his father and said he would have lived a lot longer if his church hadn't shut down."

"You ought to call Eleanor."

"I am. Everett said she's not in town today. I'll call her cell later. Jimmy and Buddy want me to play golf."

"That's better than sitting around moping with me. It's a perfect day outside. Try not to think about Kitty, Ross Bullard, or the election."

"That's the plan."

I took the stairs two at a time, changed into shorts and a knit shirt, came back down and put my arm around Susan. She had moved with her paper to the sofa in the living room.

"Good picture of you in the Memphis paper," she said.

"I'm gone," I said, kissing the top of her head.

"After Tuesday, let's go somewhere, get away for a few days."

"I'm in. How about the coast?"

"Walton said the election's as good as over, but I just can't see you serving out another term. We need to talk about what we're going to do. I'm not sure I want to stay here anymore."

"I'm not either. Let's wait a few weeks until we get over the shock of everything and make a decision. Right now, I don't know what to do."

I started for the door. She said the same words she always did.

"Hope you make a hole in one."

CHAPTER SIXTY

The pro had already loaded my bag and shoes on a cart. He said my partners were waiting for me on the first tee. I floored the accelerator in the battered Ez Go electric cart and drove as fast as it would take me, which was pretty slow. I wasn't sure we could afford it, but it was time for Sunshine Country Club to lease a new fleet.

Jimmy, Buddy, and Lee Jones were ready to play.

"I didn't know you were playing, Sheriff," I said.

"Since we're celebrating your re-election and your courtroom victory I thought Lee ought to join us," Jimmy Gray said. "I called Everoot, too, but he turned me down."

"You ever seen Everett swing a golf club?" Lee said. "The Mayor's swing is worse than Charles Barkley's."

"I don't believe that's possible," Buddy Wade said.

"Let's play," Jimmy said. "Me and Buddy against you two."

"Can you wait for me to put on my shoes and take a few practice swings?"

"No," Jimmy said, going down on one knee to place his tee in the ground. "You don't need any warming up. Three dollar Nassau."

I tied my shoe laces and watched Jimmy Gray struggle to raise his big frame off the grass. He hit his drive down the middle, walked to his cart, grabbed an Ultra out of the ice chest and gave it to me as he popped the top.

"Time to unwind, partner," he said.

Jimmy insisted we drink a beer a hole for the first three to loosen up. I have to admit it was the most fun I had in many, many months. There's nothing Jimmy Gray won't say, and all of it's funny. Buddy's a hoot, too, and listening to those two clowns play off of each other was hilarious. I birdied the first two holes. Jimmy beat my par on number three by sinking a thirty-foot putt for a bird. Lee and I were one-up standing on the fourth tee when I saw the pro headed our way in his work cart loaded with tools and chemicals.

"Susan wants you to call her at home," he said.

Jimmy and I had a strict rule against phones on the course. The pro knew it and offered his. I punched in the number and walked off the tee box to talk. Moments later, I gave the phone back to the pro and walked toward my cart.

"Susan said Bill and Connie Thurman are at the house to see me. She says I ought to come home."

"That's a serious buzz kill," Buddy Wade said.

"I'll go with you," Lee said.

"There's no need for both of us," I said. "You stay."

I shook hands with Lee and Buddy, but Jimmy Gray brushed my hand aside and pulled me in for a bear hug.

"Go do your duty, Mr. D.A.," Jimmy said. "You always do."

I pulled off my golf shoes on the ride in and turned in the cart. The Country Club was on the outskirts of Sunshine, so it took every bit of ten minutes to get home. The Thurmans and Susan were on the porch.

"We asked Susan to let you enjoy yourself," Connie said.

"No matter," I said, "I have plenty of golf ahead of me."

I was struck by how much better they looked. Bill had cleaned himself up, shaving off his reddish-brown beard. His eyes were clear for the first time in a while.

"We came by to thank you, Willie Mitchell," Bill said pumping my hand. "I know I've been hard to handle and probably hurt the case more than helped it."

"We're just so grateful," Connie said.

Her eyes were filling with tears, but it was unlike the crying I had witnessed over the last four months. These were tears of gratitude. The light was back in her eyes and she was pretty again.

"It's not over," I said. "This is just the first step of a long legal journey. We've got a tough row to hoe with the appellate courts and I want you to be ready for some setbacks."

"We know," Bill said. "It was important to us that the local people on the jury stayed behind us on this. I'm glad we went to trial and didn't wait to find Danny, no matter what else happens down the road."

We sat and talked on the porch for thirty minutes. Susan was right to get me off the course. Seeing the weight of the world partially lifted off the Thurmans reminded me of the good I could do as a prosecutor. Now Bill and Connie could begin to mourn the loss of their son, start the grieving process. Bill's understandable fury at Ross Bullard and his misguided anger at Connie had interfered with his coming to terms with Danny's death.

"Thanks for calling me," I told Susan after the Thurmans left.

"I knew it would do you some good to see them. It's like a dark cloud has been lifted from all of us."

"It's not over."

"I know, but at least the good guys are in the lead for a while."

"I need to do one more thing."

"Call Eleanor?"

I nodded went inside and called her cell. I thought it unlikely she would answer, but she did.

"Hey, Eleanor," I said. "I didn't think you'd pick up."

"I wouldn't have but I saw it was you."

"I'm sorry about those pictures. Lee and Everett showed them to me six weeks ago and I told them to bury those things."

"I know. Everett called me this morning. He said you told him to tell David Jefferson that you'd withdraw from the race if he used them."

"Are you in town?"

"No. And I'm never coming back, either."

I took a deep breath. I didn't blame her. With her intelligence and education, her legal abilities and dignified manner, she stuck out in Sunshine like a sore thumb. Other than Zelda Williams, there was no black woman in town like Eleanor. The canons prevented her from socializing with the Judge, and her natural reticence made it hard for her to make friends, to be one of the girls. The disgraceful exposure of her private life over the previous thirteen hours made her situation in Sunshine untenable. Pulling up stakes was the right thing for her to do.

"I hate to hear that, Eleanor, but I understand. You know David Jefferson was really after Bobby Sanders. You are collateral damage. It's Sunshine's loss."

"I don't know why I let Bobby Sanders talk me into it. I've never wanted to be a District Attorney."

It may have been a first: a hard-fought, nasty political campaign in a race where neither candidate wanted the job.

"He's a salesman, Eleanor."

"I owe you an apology for Bobby bringing up your seizure condition at the cake auction. I told him it was none of our concern but he did it anyway. I almost quit right then."

That was good to hear.

"And that ambush at the funeral home chapel where the house was packed against you, that was another thing he did without telling me," she said. "I was so embarrassed at how they acted."

"I've been through worse."

"And I want to thank you for how you treated me over the years, Willie Mitchell. I was right out of law school when I got the Yaloquena public defender appointment and you were nice to me from day one. You always treated me like a professional, with respect. I didn't get that in other jurisdictions. In all our years litigating against each other you never told me something that wasn't true, and you always kept your word."

"Nice of you to say, Eleanor. I always admired how you handled your job, too. I know it wasn't easy."

"One last thing about the election," she said.

"The votes haven't been counted yet."

"No, they haven't, but after today I won't have that many to count. Even Bobby Sanders told me an hour ago it was all over with. He said all our workers have quit and told him they're voting for Willie Mitchell."

"I'm sorry."

"That's all right," she said, "I'm actually relieved. I'm tired of living a double life. It's time for me to be honest with people and if they don't like who I am, that's their business."

"It's their problem, not yours."

"The thing I wanted to say about the election is this. If I had been white you would have trounced me. It wouldn't have been close."

"Call me if you ever need anything, Eleanor. I mean that."

"I might need a job reference down here in Jackson."

"Just say the word."

I walked into the kitchen.

"That must have gone well," Susan said.

"She's okay. Said some nice things. Made me feel good."

"You're on a roll," she said, "first the Thurmans and now Eleanor."

"Yes," I said, sticking my thumbs under my arms, all fingers pointing to the ceiling, "I am really something."

She patted the chair next to her.

"Sit right here, handsome, and let me tell you what a great lover you are, too."

Chapter Sixty-One

Cheryl Diamond stopped by the house at 7:30 on her way out of town. I was in the kitchen watching Susan fix breakfast. Susan insisted Cheryl eat with us before she got on the road. She looked great, dolled up in a Kelly green silk suit with rhinestone buttons, and seemed as happy about Ross's conviction as I was.

"You're mighty dressed up for a drive to Houston," I said.

"I always try to look nice when I travel," she said. "These days people don't seem to care how they look."

"That's an understatement," Susan said.

"You know, Cheryl," I said, "you're the prettiest psychic I know."

She giggled. "I bet I'm the only one you know, too."

"Why don't you let me take that big boat of yours to the service station and get the tires and everything checked out?"

"Oh, thanks but I've already seen to that. There's a full service gas station downtown. They looked at my tires and everything under the hood, filled it up and washed it. I've gotten to know the attendants since I've been here and they're very nice to me. It's like going back in time."

"There's a lot of that around here," Susan said.

"You didn't jog this morning?" Cheryl asked.

"I was lazy."

Cheryl caught Susan in a wry smile as she put Cheryl's plate in front of her.

"Or maybe busy doing something else," Cheryl said with a wink.

There it was. The third day in a row. Winking at me *was* a trend. Thank goodness it was a woman doing the winking this time.

"You two were made for one another," Cheryl said. "You are very blessed."

"I think so," Susan said. "Willie Mitchell is a lucky man."

"I admit it," I said laughing.

"You both are lucky," Cheryl said.

She finished breakfast and I walked her to her Town Car, opening the driver's door for her.

"You know the Bullards aren't through with you," she said. "They're going to be trouble for everyone until this is over."

"Our case has problems. The conviction may be reversed."

"I'm not talking about legal trouble." She paused. "You be careful, Willie Mitchell. Don't let your guard down."

"I'll keep that in mind, but just because the trial is over doesn't mean you can't come back to see us, Cheryl. You're a friend now."

"You work on your gift," she said with a smile. "Toodles."

She pulled out of the driveway. I didn't envy her long drive home. I finished my cup of coffee at the pine table with Susan and got dressed for work. When I walked into the office Walton was waiting.

"I called your cell," he said.

"It was off."

"J.D. Silver filed four motions as soon as Eddie opened the doors to the Clerk's office, A Motion to Set Aside the Verdict; a Motion for a New Trial; a Motion for an Expedited Appeal; and a Motion for Post-Conviction Bail."

"Have you read them?"

Walton nodded. I could tell he was worried.

"It all sounds so bad when you read it," he said, "what happened in the trial. It's not just the *corpus delicti* issue, it's...."

"Prosecutorial misconduct, I'm sure."

"That's all through there. He claims we knew Connie and Gayle were perjuring themselves, that I had an obligation to tell the Court about the notes Bullard sent me, that I goaded him into jumping on me, saying that was my fault, too."

Nothing Walton told me was a surprise except for two things: the Motion for Post-Conviction Bail, which was a bad idea for everyone involved, especially Ross Bullard, and the speed with which Silver prepared and filed the motions. The fact that he filed them two days after the conviction told me Jules was shelling out big bucks.

I took our copies of the four motions into my private office and told Ethel and Louise I didn't want to be disturbed for a while. I read each filing and the legal memoranda in support. The documents were well-crafted, well-researched and compelling. I didn't know how many lawyers or paralegals Silver had on staff, but the filings had not been thrown together in a couple of days. Silver anticipated the jury verdict and was loaded for bear for the appeal. I should have expected this. His defense was a legal one—the elements of murder cannot be proven where there is no body and no evidence whatsoever of a violent death. That's why he didn't object to an accelerated trial date. He counted on losing at the trial court level. Silver wanted to get to the arena where the law counted more than the facts. Ross Bullard would just be another defendant to the appellate judges. None of his bizarre behavior would be apparent from the transcript.

Silver's brief writer cited all the leading cases from the jurisdictions surrounding Mississippi on the issue of the admissibility of the combination suicide note and confession before proof of murder was established. Since the issue was *res nova* in Mississippi the case was guaranteed to pique the interest of the Court of Appeal, especially the judges who actually read the briefs and were interested in the law. I wasn't sure how many of those kind of judges were left on the appellate bench. State judges were elected by popular vote, a process that resulted in the elevation of a number of lightweight political hacks to the court. Then again, patronage and the spoils system determined which judges were appointed by the President to the federal bench, so the federal method of judicial selection wasn't much better. And federal judges were appointed for life—an incredibly bad idea. My only hope in the Bullard appeal was that the panel that ultimately heard the case had law clerks who favored prosecutors. I wouldn't find out which panel would hear the case until after Zelda ruled on the four motions at the trial court level.

I analyzed which of the motions would require an evidentiary hearing and decided none of them did. The motions for a new trial and to set aside the verdict sought the same relief. The same trial errors were alleged. Silver could have combined the two and saved a lot of paper. Maybe he was charging Jules by the pound. The motion for an expedited appeal required no evidence, just allegations of irreparable harm to the defense if the Circuit Clerk took the usual four months to get the record ready to send up. Transcription of the two weeks of jury selection and trial testimony by the court reporter would account for most of the delay.

The most problematic to me of the four motions was the Motion for Post-Conviction Bail. Now I understood why Silver took so much time in the pre-trial bail hearing. There was already a record of everything Zelda or the appellate court needed to make a bail determination—the defendant's prior criminal record and work history, his financial assets, his ability to take flight, his roots in the community. The fact of his conviction of capital murder would be added to the list but everything else was already there in black and white. In Silver's motion he offered to turn in Ross's passport; have an independent third party supervise and approve any withdrawal of money from Ross's bank accounts and any credit card charge of over two hundred dollars; remain within the borders of Mississippi unless obtaining court approval of travel; and finally to submit to wearing a GPS wireless tracking device at the Bullard's expense.

I buzzed Ethel and had her ask Walton to join me. I gave him the motions and supporting documents.

"You've got a lot of work to do," I said.

"Best briefs I've ever seen," Walton said.

"You need to let Bill and Connie know what's going on. It wouldn't hurt to make them a copy of everything, let them know what we're up against."

"I spoke to Eddie. He said Silver's paralegal wanted Judge Williams to set a hearing on the motions within forty-eight hours. Eddie's going to meet with the Judge as soon as she gets in this morning."

"Go ahead and prepare answers to each motion. You've already done most of the research on the critical issues."

"I'll get right on it."

"You should be well-rested," I said, "since you took that week's vacation in the middle of the trial."

"I only missed three days, boss."

"Who's counting?" I said. "If Zelda hasn't already set a hearing date ask her to wait until Wednesday at least."

"Yeah," Walton said, "tomorrow's your big day. Lee told me it's going to be a landslide."

"What a gratifying win," I said. "It doesn't matter what kind of job I've done in this office, apparently the key to my victory is they have no pictures of me naked with a goat."

"Good thing you burned them all," Walton said.

"I never liked that goat anyway. Too needy."

CHAPTER SIXTY-TWO

I jogged before daybreak and was dressed by the time the polls opened at seven. Jimmy Gray and I rode around to different polling places to make sure everything was running smoothly. After the fourth precinct we covered, it was clear we were wasting our time.

Voting was light, the machines were working fine, and there were no problems reported by the precinct workers. Three-fourths of the voters we saw were white, which wasn't unusual. In Yaloquena County black voters tended to vote later in the day than whites. I called Lee and Everett. Each said he was seeing the same thing. Everett said almost all of the Eleanor Bernstein signs and posters in the areas he canvassed had been taken down and my signs put up. No doubt these were deep- thinking principled voters who decided after much deliberation that I had done an excellent job as D.A. after all.

Jimmy Gray dropped me off at the courthouse and I spent the rest of the day in my office, catching up on work that had piled up during two weeks in trial. Walton was in and out asking my opinion about his responses to Helmet Head's motions. Sometimes he was upbeat, other times depressed, depending on how he assessed the probable outcome of the motions and the appeal based on the legal issue he was working on at the time.

When the polls closed we had a campaign representative at each precinct call in the vote tallies the chief election worker pulled off the machines. Within thirty minutes our poll watchers had called into headquarters with their precinct totals. Jimmy Gray entered them into a spreadsheet on his iPad. With all precincts reporting, I had seventy per cent of the vote. Turnout was thirty-four per cent. A lot of disenchanted Eleanor voters chose to stay home.

Another smashing victory by the world's worst politician. I took a silent, solemn oath it would be the last election. I had learned my lesson.

Susan and I hung around headquarters for an hour, thanking the workers, celebrating with Cokes, Sprites, and a victory cake. We had some laughs with man mountain Jimmy Gray, Buddy Wade, Lee and Everett. I claimed fatigue and walked to my truck with Susan. At the edge of the building I saw David Jefferson. Susan and I stopped.

"David," I said. "Thanks for the work you did on the campaign."

"Yes, sir, Mr. Banks."

"I wish you hadn't distributed those pictures of Eleanor."

"Yes, sir. I knew you didn't want me to. Mayor Johnson all but threatened me if I let anyone see them. He told me what you said."

"But you did it anyway."

"I didn't feel like I had a choice. Might as well have Satan himself in the courthouse as someone controlled by Bobby Sanders. He claims to be holy but he's just the opposite. The Bible says how Eleanor lives is a sin, too. Bobby Sanders and Eleanor would never have gotten as far as they did if my grandfather was still on this earth."

"Good night, David," I said and walked Susan to the truck.

Finally, there it was. Clarity at last. David Jefferson had just articulated the reason I let myself be talked into running by Lee and Everett. We all knew the Reverend Sanders would be pulling Eleanor's strings. Bobby's corrupt ideas of justice would prevail in Yaloquena County. He had proven to us time and time again that he would stir up racial hatred and class warfare to achieve his goals. He would have used the power of the D.A.'s office to make the existing bad situation much worse. I didn't mind giving up the job, but I couldn't give it up to someone controlled by Reverend Bobby Sanders.

"In his mind he did the right thing," Susan said as we drove toward home. "I can see it from his point of view."

"Who knows, maybe he did?"

Susan looked at me, puzzled for a moment.

"Let's move somewhere else," she said. "No matter how hard you work it makes no difference around here. I miss Jake and Scott."

"You have some place in mind?"

"Any city or town where people read books, there's a decent newspaper, a movie theater and a restaurant or two. Some place where the schools actually teach kids something and where no fifteen-year-old girls we know are having babies."

"It may be time to go," I said. "It just may be."

CHAPTER SIXTY-THREE

When I entered the main floor of the courthouse Wednesday morning, each person I ran into pretended to be thrilled about the election results. Apparently their support of Eleanor had been a mirage—they were actually for me all along. Circuit Clerk Winston Moore pumped my hand and patted me on the back. I laughed and went along with all the revisionist history of the prior ninety days. I decided there was no reason to dwell on the recent unpleasantness with Winston and the others. Even though I had won, I knew I would not be in the courthouse much longer.

I made it to my office upstairs. Walton told me he had our answers to Helmet Head's motions ready for my signature along with the briefs in support of each. I read and signed the documents. Walton went downstairs to file the originals with Eddie Bordelon. He hand-delivered copies to Judge Williams and e-mailed scanned copies to J.D. Silver. In the afternoon Eddie called to let us know that Zelda set the hearings for ten o'clock the next morning.

◆❖◆

I sat alone at the prosecution table Thursday morning waiting for Judge Williams to begin the hearing on the motions. Zelda had sent word that Walton could observe the proceedings in court but could not participate or sit inside the rail. He took a seat next to Lee Jones in the middle of the gallery behind me.

What a difference a few days made. During the trial, you could have cut the tension with a knife. No longer. The courtroom was peaceful, and empty except for Silver and Ross at the defense table, Judy and Jules Bullard in the first row behind them, Lee Jones and Walton and three print media reporters. I glanced at the vacant jury box and thought briefly about Pearl Ocie Harrington, my new hero. I made a mental note to call him later and ask him to come by the office for a cup of coffee.

Zelda took the bench and complimented Silver and me on our conduct during the trial in spite of the numerous difficult moments. She said she had read all four motions, the State's answers, and the briefs in support and against the motions.

"Unless I have missed something," she said, "there's no need for any testimony this morning, is there?"

"No, Your Honor," Silver said, now accustomed to Zelda's avoidance of live testimony whenever possible.

"The first two, to set aside the verdict and for a new trial, are asking for the same relief and cite the same trial errors, are they not?"

"Essentially, Your Honor," Silver said.

"Unless you feel the need to add to the arguments you set forth in the motions and briefs, Mr. Silver, I don't need to hear from you or Mr. Banks on these first two." She paused and looked down at documents on the bench. "Actually, it's the first three. Mr. Banks, you have no objection to an expedited appeal, do you?"

"None at all, Your Honor."

"Mr. Silver, I've instructed the court reporter to put aside all of her other work and prepare the transcript of *voir dire* and the trial in this matter. Mr. Bordelon says he will have the record together and ready to forward to the Court of Appeal as soon as he receives the transcript. It seems to me it's going to be up to the appellate court as to whether they will be flexible and waive the normal delays."

"Yes, Your Honor. I've spoken to the appellate court and they're expecting the case."

I looked over at Helmet Head. He noticed.

"Of course I meant to say *the Clerk* of the appellate court. I spoke with him yesterday."

"Which brings us to the Motion for Post-Conviction Bail," Zelda said, "which is an unusual request following a capital murder conviction, Mr. Silver."

"It's an unusual conviction, Your Honor," he said. "There's no need for additional testimony or evidence for the court to consider bail at this time."

"There's the fact of a unanimous jury verdict," I said.

"Correct," Silver said. "And I would like to reiterate at this time the conditions we suggest in our motion, Judge

Williams. Mr. Bullard will turn in his passport, agree to close supervision of his financial assets, stay within the State of Mississippi unless authorized by this Court to travel outside its borders, and to wear a state of the art tracking device at the sole cost of the defendant."

"Your Honor, the State strongly opposes post-conviction bail. Feelings in the community are still running high...."

She held up her palm. I stopped talking.

"Mr. Silver, the Court is impressed with your offer, but I cannot in good conscience allow Mr. Bullard out on bond while his conviction is being appealed. The jury was convinced of his guilt beyond a reasonable doubt, and regardless of your representations, your client's behavior in the courtroom is the best evidence of your inability to control him.

"Incorporating by reference all the testimony and exhibits in the pre-trial bail hearing, I remain convinced that Ross Bullard is a flight risk due to his family's substantial assets. I also find that he is a danger to the community and that this community is a danger to him. The Motion for Post-Conviction Bail is hereby denied.

"I will do my part to expedite the appeal process for you, Mr. Silver, as I have stated. Let the record reflect I also deny your Motions to Set Aside the Verdict and for a New Trial."

"To which rulings the Defense objects, Your Honor," Silver said, opening his briefcase on the table and removing a multi-page document.

"I am filing at this time a notice of my intention to take writs immediately to the Court of Appeal on this Court's denial of my bail motion. Here is my original notice with memorandum in support."

Helmet Head dropped a copy on my table, gave the original to Eddie Bordelon and a copy to Zelda.

"More paper, Mr. Silver?" she asked.

"Just being thorough, Judge."

Judge Williams adjourned court and walked out. A shackled Ross Bullard walked behind me between two deputies. He had been subdued during the hearing, gazing out the window instead of writing incessantly. Maybe his *magnum opus* was complete. I gestured for Walton and Lee to join me inside the rail.

"You've got more work to do," I told Walton and gave him the writ notice and memorandum.

"There can't be anything new to research," Walton said. "I'll get on it right away."

"Ross sure was laid back," Lee said.

"Silver's been in contact with the Court of Appeal," I said.

"Just the Clerk," Walton said.

"Oh, yeah. I'm sure it was just the Clerk," I said. "Don't look now, boys, but we're about to get sandbagged."

CHAPTER SIXTY-FOUR

I spent the rest of Thursday on the phone and online checking J.D. Silver's political donations catalogued in the campaign reports section of the Secretary of State's website. It wasn't as bad as I thought—it was worse. Helmet Head had given a significant amount to every judge on the Court of Appeal and not just recently. There were some judges to whom he had contributed heavily for the last three election cycles. Each contribution was under the limit and therefore perfectly legal.

I had given each judge nothing. It was a matter of principle to me. I had a sinking feeling my principles were about to cost me.

"These judges get contributions from all over," Walton said Friday morning when we discussed it. "I don't think it means that much."

"It means all the judges on our Court of Appeal know who J.D. Silver is and they know he's a deep pocket for more contributions when they come up for re-election. Believe me, if they can do it without causing themselves any political damage, they're going to accommodate Helmet Head any way they can.

"It's human nature. Tell you something else. Silver has probably *schmoozed* the Clerk from time to time, maybe given him a gallon of single malt scotch at Christmas or bought him a big meal at an expensive restaurant. The Clerk and the judges talk. They know I'm not going to contribute toward their re-election. The influence Silver buys with his contributions is subtle. There's no blatant *quid pro quo*. His representation of a client would never be discussed openly.

"There's lots of decisions that can go either way, Walton. You know that's true. Take the issue of letting in Ross's confession prior to proof of the *corpus delicti*. Silver cited cases from three neighboring states that support Silver's position. We cited states that agreed with us. The panel can rule in Silver's favor or ours and justify the decision with plenty of precedent."

I looked past Walton at Ethel in the doorway.

"It's the Clerk from the Court of Appeal," she said. "He's faxing us an order and wanted to make sure he had our fax number."

"Bring us two copies when it comes," I said.

Ten minutes later Walton and I finished reading our copies of the fax. I was disappointed; Walton was in shock. The three-judge panel had reversed Zelda on her post-conviction bail ruling, citing the lack of proof of a violent death to satisfy the elements of capital murder and the "grave and deeply disturbing" allegations of perjury and prosecutorial misconduct during the trial.

"Pending the resolution of these significant issues on appeal and considering the substantial likelihood that all or part of the Appellant's requested relief will be granted," the panel stated in its ruling, "the incarceration of the defendant while the appeal is pending is insupportable."

The panel ordered Judge Williams to impose the four conditions Silver suggested in his Motion for Post-Conviction Bail and to set Ross's bond at one million dollars cash, an amount Jules could easily post.

"They glossed over the bail issues and focused on *corpus delicti*," Walton said, "and whether the jury should have been able to see the confession."

"Silver used the Motion for Post-Conviction Bail as a Trojan Horse," I said, "to woodshed the judges on his position that we presented no proof of death, no proof of a murder, and to show what a circus the trial turned out to be."

"They're going to reverse the conviction."

"Never know," I said. "But Silver's certainly got their attention."

That afternoon at four o'clock Ross Bullard walked out of the courthouse, free on bond. Jules had pledged $250,000 certificates of deposit from four different commercial banks in North Mississippi. The Sheriff walked into my office.

"He's out?" I asked.

"Sure is. The old man showed up in his Cadillac, but Ross wouldn't ride with him. Ross called a cab to pick him up along with the two cardboard boxes of legal pads he's filled. He told Big Boy upstairs he was moving back into his house on Whitley."

"Walton needs to get word to Connie and Bill."

"I saw him in the hallway. He's on his way. And I've got two men in a cruiser parked on Whitley between Ross's house and the Thurmans."

"Can you have deputies there around the clock?"

"We're setting up the shifts now. How long will it be before the Court of Appeal decides his case?"

"Many months," I said. "Maybe a year."

"And he gets to do whatever he wants during that time?"

"As long as he complies with the conditions of bail."

"This is not going to work," Lee said as he left. "I can't keep men there around the clock for a year."

In an hour we had a taste of how difficult it was going to be to keep the peace. Lee called me at home.

"You're not going to believe this, Willie Mitchell," Lee said.

"Yes, I will."

"My deputies were watching the front of his house and the crazy bastard walked outside into his front yard."

"Well, he has been in a cell over four months."

"Right, but it's how he looked. They said he's wearing some kind of weird pants with leather fringe, no shoes, and no shirt. You know he's got all those muscles now.

"Did he cause any trouble?"

"No. He just stood out there a while and went back inside."

"Did Bill see him?"

"The deputies didn't know. No one came out of the Thurman house."

"Just watch him as closely as you can. I'll call Silver. Maybe he can ask Jules to get Ross to use his back yard when he wants fresh air."

"Things were easier when he was in my jail."

"I know. Court of Appeal says he can walk around Sunshine all he wants as long as he follows the conditions they set."

"They don't know much about the trouble this causes for us, do they?"

"No, Lee. And they don't care."

CHAPTER SIXTY-FIVE

The next day was Saturday. Deputies said Ross stayed inside the entire day. They said Jules knocked on the door at seven p.m. and when Ross came to the door he and Jules got into a screaming match. Jules walked off with Ross shaking his fist at the old man. The deputies on the Saturday night shift said there were periodic flashes of light inside Ross's house. Ross never showed his face on Sunday.

Lee Jones called my office Monday morning about ten. I rode to the First Savings Bank downtown branch with him. Lee said the head of operations, Billy Fitzpatrick, wanted to talk to us about Ross.

We walked into Billy's office. He closed the door behind us and offered us a seat. Billy was in his early fifties. He wore tortoise shell glasses. His hair was thinning and turning gray. I had known him since we were youngsters.

"How are things, Billy?" I said.

"I've been better. Ross was in the bank this weekend."

"Are you sure?" Lee asked.

"No one saw him, but when we opened this morning one of the ladies buzzed me and asked me to meet her in Ross's office. When I got there it was obvious someone had gone through Ross's drawers and left a mess on his desk. Upstairs where we keep the loan department files and foreclosure files there were filing cabinets left open and files scattered.

"Could it have been someone other than Ross?" I asked.

"No. Ross has the only key to his desk drawers. He has access to the loan and foreclosure files, too. We keep them locked. And whoever did this has a key to the main door and knows how to disengage the alarm system. Ross is one of four people in the bank that knows the alarm code. The other three are Jules, Ginny Webster, and me. Ginny was out of town this weekend. I'm sure it's Ross."

"Can you tell if anything is missing?" I asked.

"We'll have to go through each file. That'll take a good bit of time."

"Have you told Mr. Bullard?" Lee asked.

Billy said no and averted his eyes. I knew he was afraid to tell Jules because the old man would go ballistic and probably blame Billy. Billy and every other First Savings Bank employee were deathly afraid of Jules Bullard. Jules' management style was to avoid personal relationships with his employees. Bank officers at Sunshine Bank we hired away from Jules said he ruled his bank by fear and fiat.

"Has Jules fired or suspended Ross?" I asked.

"No," Billy said. "He's still on the payroll just like always." He paused. "He's still got his job and his keys and there's nothing I can do to keep Ross out of the bank."

I got the feeling Billy was rehearsing his lines before he saw Jules.

"Where is Jules?" I asked.

"He's in Arkansas. Supposed to be back this afternoon."

"What about Judy?" I asked. "Is she with Jules?"

"He didn't tell me but that's what I heard," Billy said. "Supposedly they drove to Hot Springs Sunday morning."

"I'm sure it was a bank meeting," Lee said.

"I don't think so," Billy said without smiling.

We left the bank and walked toward Lee's Tahoe.

"Ross must have gone out the back door sometime this weekend and climbed his backyard fence," I said.

"If he went at night no one would see him. The two men on Whitley are there to protect Ross from Bill Thurman. I don't have the manpower to put men behind the house."

"I know. Just do the best you can."

I sat in Lee's Tahoe thinking about the situation. I knew it was not going to end well. It was only a matter of time.

◆❖◆

When Lee and I returned to the courthouse, Deputy Sammy Roberts was waiting for us next to Lee's reserved parking spot.

"Ross ran an errand this morning," Sammy said.

"What?" Lee said.

"The deputies watching him said a taxi showed up about nine-thirty and picked up Ross and his two boxes of legal pads. They followed the cab to the Kwik Kopy. Ross had the cabbie wait while he brought the boxes inside. He was in the store about thirty minutes. He walked out without the boxes and the taxi took him back to Whitley. He's been in his house ever since."

Lee turned to me. "Could we have a look at those legal pads?"

"We'd have to get a subpoena," I said. "There are privacy issues involved and we'd have to make a *prima facie* case showing relevance to some issue in the trial before Judge Williams would let us see them."

Lee and Sammy Roberts gave me the same look.

"Yeah, I know, but it's the system we have to work with. Got to play by the rules."

"Did he cause any problems?" Lee asked Sammy.

"No, sir." Sammy paused a second. "There was one thing."

"Go ahead," Lee said.

"The men said Kwik Kopy has one of those signs that says "No Shoes, No Shirt, No Service."

"And?" Lee said.

"Kwik Kopy didn't enforce it against Ross Bullard."

CHAPTER SIXTY-SIX

I got a late start Thursday morning. It was after eight when I ended my four-mile run at Jimmy Gray's house to join him for his morning exercise. In an effort to keep Jimmy from gaining any more weight and in hopes of extending his life a month or two, we walked for fifteen minutes every Tuesday, Thursday, and Saturday.

"I don't guess you walked any while I was in trial, huh?"

"As I recall one of us was busy getting you re-elected. I can't do everything for your skinny ass and exercise, too."

"I understand."

"Now see if you can keep up."

We walked four blocks and turned onto Walton's street. As we neared his home, Walton walked out the front door and waited for us on his front lawn. I picked up the pace when I saw him. Jimmy was sweating, huffing and puffing.

"I called and Susan told me you two were walking," Walton said. "I need you to look at something."

We walked inside. Gayle was fuming on the couch. Jimmy and I followed Walton into his son's bedroom. Jimmy stood next to me, trying to normalize his breathing. Walton pulled out an old suitcase from under the lower bunk bed.

"This is Nick's room," Walton said as he opened the case.

There were at least fifty arrowheads, each one in a glassine envelope and neatly labeled. Walton sat on the lower bunk.

"After Gayle took Nick and Payne to school this morning, I tore this room apart," Walton said. "The thing is, there's no way Nick found these himself. And it's not his writing on the labels."

I knew immediately where the arrowheads came from.

"Why'd you search the room this morning?" I asked.

"I've been worried since Ross got out last Friday," Walton said, "so I've been staying up late and rising early in the morning, ready for anything. This morning at first light I saw the bare-chested son-of-a-bitch sneaking away through our next-door-neighbor's bushes, but I got outside too late to catch him."

"Were you armed?" I asked, knowing the answer.

"Damned right I was. I've had my shotgun loaded and handy ever since Bullard got out. So anyway, I walked around the side of the house and found this sitting on Nick's window sill. I figured Nicholas had more of them stashed somewhere."

He stood up, reached in his pocket and handed me an envelope. I looked inside. There was a spear point, much larger than an arrowhead.

"Looks like flint," I said.

"It is," Jimmy Gray said examining it. "It's valuable."

"You want to charge Ross with something?" I asked.

"Like what? Trespassing? We convicted him of murder and still can't keep him in jail."

"People in this town are scared of Ross," Jimmy said. "Maybe someone will shoot him."

"We should be so lucky," Walton said.

"It doesn't need to be you," I told him. "And you and Gayle ought to have a talk with Nicholas."

"How's Bill doing since Ross got out?" Jimmy asked.

"Not good," Walton said.

CHAPTER SIXTY-SEVEN

When I got home after the walk I told Susan about the flint spear point on Nicholas's window sill and the cache of arrowheads. I mentioned the tension I felt in the Donaldson home that morning, with Gayle in a stew on the couch and Walton with his shotgun close at hand, ready to shoot Ross at the slightest provocation.

Susan picked up the phone and called Gayle. She suggested that Gayle and Walton drive over to Greenwood on Friday, catch a movie and eat dinner at Lusco's. Maybe spend the night at the Alluvian. Susan said she would keep baby Laura on Friday and pick up the twins from school. She and I would take the kids to McDonald's for supper and they could spend the night with us.

"That was thoughtful," I said when she hung up. "Are they going to take you up on it?"

"Yes. Gayle asked Walton while we were on the phone."

"Good. They need a break."

"She's on pins and needles. I could tell it in her voice."

"You want me to come home early?"

"No. I'll bring them over here after school. Laura will need a nap and the twins can do their homework at the kitchen table."

I took Susan in my arms.

"You're a sweet lady," I said, "beautiful, too."

It was four-thirty Friday. I was ready to call it a day. Louise buzzed me to pick up. When she said Cheryl Diamond was on the phone, I knew in my gut something was wrong.

"He's out, isn't he, Willie Mitchell?"

Her voice was shaking. She was terrified.

"He's been out on bond since last Friday."

"I knew it," she screamed. "Go home, Willie Mitchell. Go home right now."

I bounded out of my office, down the steps and into my truck. I drove home as fast as I could, skidding in the pea gravel in my circular drive. I burst through the front door and yelled.

"Susan? Susan?"

Silence.

I ran into the kitchen. There was a note under the salt shaker on the scarred pine table.

"We're at Gayle's. Boys needed computers to do homework. McD's at 5:30."

I ran out the front door and threw gravel everywhere when I roared out of the driveway. I pulled my Springfield .45 caliber semi-automatic out of the glove compartment, made sure the magazine was full and chambered a round. I was at Walton's house in less than ninety seconds. I jumped out of the truck. The front door was wide open.

Susan lay on the carpet in front of the television in Walton's den. There was an ancient Indian war club next to her on the floor. Ross Bullard stood over Susan, his metamorphosis complete.

His head was shaved except for a Mohawk strip down the center. Two large hawk feathers hung next to his left ear, tethered to his Mohawk with a leather cord. His face, head, and neck were striped red, white, and black. There were vivid designs and symbols on his muscular chest and arms.

Ross cocked his head to the side, moving the two hawk feathers out of his field of vision. His eyes were wide and fierce.

"I came for Nicholas," Ross said.

He picked up the war club.

"Drop the club," I said and aimed my pistol at his heart.

He started toward me.

"Put it down, Ross."

Ross stopped but still held the club.

"Put it...down."

My voice seemed odd to me, slower and deeper than usual. The words reverberated in my head. Ross raised the war club high and took a step. I aimed at Ross's chest and began to squeeze the trigger.

My finger stopped moving. I tried harder, but I could not pull the trigger. Darkness moved across my eyes and I could not move. I recognized what was happening. I was descending into the void, becoming nothing. I hadn't been there in a while, but I knew once it started, I could not stop it. I couldn't see Ross. I couldn't see Susan. Out of the blackness I heard a gunshot. After the second shot, I knew nothing, felt nothing. I was no longer there.

I don't know how long my seizure lasted. When I came to, I was unable to move. Lee Jones had his arm around me on Walton's couch. On the carpet in front of the television, EMTs were working on Susan.

Lee held a pistol in his free hand, resting in his lap. I didn't recognize the gun. It wasn't mine; it wasn't Lee's. Jules Bullard slumped in a stuffed chair in the corner. In front of him on the floor was a bloody sheet covering something. Through the picture window I saw flashing blue and white strobes.

That's all I remember.

Chapter Sixty-Eight

The day after Ross Bullard died I remember looking out the window in Susan's hospital room. The sky was beautiful, a deep, uninterrupted blue. A rare high pressure system had moved over the Delta bringing drier air and cooler temperatures.

I was going to shoot Ross. I remember trying to squeeze the trigger. I'm told Jules Bullard rushed into Walton's house just as Ross was raising the war club to bring it down hard on my skull. He had done the same thing to Susan. Jules told Lee I seemed frozen in place, my gun pointed at Ross. Jules shot his own boy twice. It turned out that all those muscles Ross had built up in jail were still no match for a bullet. Lee told me that Jules said he had been carrying a pistol since an encounter with Ross the day after he got out. I told Lee I wished I had been the one to shoot Ross. I knew I wasn't supposed to kill him, my being the District Attorney and all, but I would have if my seizure hadn't interrupted things.

Susan was the hero of the day. Little Payne Donaldson said when Susan saw Ross walking up the sidewalk she gave Payne the baby and told them to take Laura out the back door and walk to our house. She told them to stay off the streets. Nicholas told her they knew how to go through backyards to get to our home. She told the twins to hide upstairs in her closet with Laura until she came for them. Payne said they took turns carrying Laura and made it to our house as fast as they could. The last thing Payne heard in his own backyard was Susan telling Ross to go away and leave the Donaldsons alone.

It turned out that Nicholas had spent more time with Ross and his relics than anyone thought. When Lee and Robbie Cedars' crime scene specialists searched Ross's home on Whitley after the shooting, they discovered Ross had drawn primitive symbols on every wall in the house, and had built a shrine of sorts to Danny Thurman and Nicholas, using his artifacts and crude pictorials.

Walton and Gayle said they were getting Nicholas into counseling. I told them to get someone good; he was going to need a lot of help sorting out his relationship with Ross and the death of his best friend.

Nathan was at the hospital when the EMTs brought Susan in. He ordered a number of diagnostic tests and later told me she had a concussion but no skull fracture or brain damage.

I was alone in the room with her when she regained consciousness. I held her for a few moments and told her how much I loved her. When she smiled at me I called the nurses' station. Nathan and a squad of nurses came in and tended to her. I retreated to a corner and watched.

What a relief it was to hear Susan answer Nathan's simple questions. After Nathan told me Susan was going to be fine but he was going to keep her there overnight just to be safe, I asked him to have the orderlies bring me a cot. I spent the night there. The cot was wasted because I didn't sleep. I passed the hours listening to Susan breathe, thankful for it.

CHAPTER SIXTY-NINE

Saturday evening after Ross's death, I was sitting at the kitchen table boring out one of the small black wormholes with a straightened paper clip when Cheryl Diamond called. It was nine o'clock.

"How is Susan doing, Willie Mitchell?"

"She's going to be all right. Nathan says she has to take it easy for a while. She's upstairs asleep. How is Houston?"

"I'm in Sunshine."

"Since when?"

"I drove in this afternoon. Is it too late for me to come over?"

"No. I'm awake. I haven't been sleeping very well since the thing with Ross. Come through the kitchen door."

Ten minutes later Cheryl sat across from me at the old pine table.

"This is a nice surprise," I said.

"I decided I had some unfinished business over here."

I knew what she was talking about.

"Danny?"

"Yes," she said, "Danny."

After a moment I asked her if she ever thought about her philandering ex-husband.

"Not much."

"You've lived by yourself a long time."

"There's a reason. If I'm true to myself I am a very odd duck. That's how I came into this world. I would have seen through my husband at the beginning if I hadn't tried to be someone I wasn't. But that's all water under the bridge."

I sat quietly.

"I'd like to help you find Danny now."

I had already noticed Cheryl's hiking boots under the table. Her hair and makeup were fixed, but she wore no jewelry. Her North Face jacket was lined and waterproof with a pair of leather gloves sticking out of a pocket. She was ready for the woods.

"I bought two big lights at Wal-Mart and extra batteries," she said. "They're in my trunk."

"You want to go now?"

"I do."

"You don't want to wait until tomorrow morning?"

"No. I feel like we should go right now."

"If you're frightened, I don't think..."

"I'm not. The reptile man is dead and gone."

"All right," I said. "I'm not sleeping much anyway. Let me get my boots on."

Minutes later Cheryl and I walked out the kitchen door. I retrieved my pistol, holster, and an extra magazine from my truck. Cheryl sat in the passenger seat of her Town Car.

"We could take my truck," I said.

"I think we should go in my Town Car. You drive."

I pulled out of the driveway. We glided south in the big Lincoln along city streets to the highway out of town. Thirty minutes later we were close to the Iron Bridge. It was pitch black on the road. Cheryl sniffed. In the green glow of the dashboard lights I saw her wipe her eyes.

"I'm so sorry I couldn't do it before, Willie Mitchell. If I had, you would have found Danny's body before trial. Ross would have been convicted and never gotten out of jail on bond. Susan would not have been hurt."

"Maybe."

"I was so frightened. I know it makes no sense."

"Waking up on July Fourth knowing something bad had happened somewhere makes no sense, either. Nor does your calling me from Houston to tell me to get home before Ross attacked Susan."

"Susan wasn't at home."

"Pretty close. You have to listen to your instincts. I believe in you."

I parked the Town Car on the bridge and popped the trunk. I put on my holster, checked my pistol and chambered a round. I grabbed the lights from the trunk, tested them, and opened the door for Cheryl.

"Ready?"

"Okay," she said after taking a deep breath.

I led her off the bridge and down the right descending bank of the creek. October and November had been dry, so I knew following the creek bed was the most efficient way to access the area that Peewee had searched three times. There was no moon and the woods were incredibly dark. Our search would be limited to the reach of our lights. Cheryl stayed right behind me, clutching my jacket at times. The creek bottom was sandy and mostly dry, making the walking easier than trying to navigate through the trees and brush.

I stopped to let Cheryl rest a moment. When we began walking again I scanned the area in front of us. Among the trees I saw the eyes of an animal reflecting my light. I whispered to Cheryl and pointed where I had seen the eyes. Whatever it was it was gone.

"Let's get up on the bank," Cheryl said.

I searched for the easiest way out of the creek. In less than a hundred feet I spotted a dry tributary with a more gradual slope. I held Cheryl's hand and we climbed out slowly. While Cheryl caught her breath I did a three-sixty with my light. A couple of hundred feet in front of us along the edge of the creek my light caught the eyes again.

"Did you see that?"

"Go toward the eyes," she said.

I took her hand and walked to the spot. We looked in the creek and all around but saw nothing. In the process I noticed a change in the topography. It seemed out of place. Just north of the creek bank where we stood there was an upslope that defied the natural rise and fall of the ridges in the woods.

"Let's go up there," Cheryl said.

We walked up the hill a hundred feet or so. I shined my light around us. It was a mesa of some kind, thick with pines and oaks.

"See how this flattens out around here?"

"Find the center," she said.

I led her by the hand to what I thought was the middle of the mesa. It was hard to tell because of the trees and briars.

"Turn off your light," she said as she turned hers off.

We stood in the darkness. It was quiet, eerie. Below me I heard something walking through the leaves. I took Cheryl's hand and we walked quietly toward the sound. On the edge of the mesa I turned on my light and shined it down the hill we had climbed.

Fifty feet down the slope, a white deer stared into my light. I saw the atypical antlers and two parallel dropped tines on each side. It was the same albino I had seen from the bridge three months earlier.

"It's here for Danny," Cheryl whispered behind me.

We walked down the slope toward the deer. He watched us for a few steps then walked down the hill to the creek bank. He was in no hurry. We followed him to the tributary we had used to exit the big creek. He disappeared into the main creek bed and we tried to keep him in sight.

"Let's stop here for a while," Cheryl said.

We were in the creek bed directly below the hill. I shined my light in every direction to get oriented. When I focused the beam up the hill toward the mesa, it came to me. This was no natural hill. It was a mound built thousands of years ago by Native Americans. I turned the light into the creek ahead of us and saw the albino deer only ten feet from us, standing perfectly still, staring at us.

Cheryl pulled my arm causing my light to shine into the bank. When I turned it back toward the deer he was gone.

"This is where he wants us," Cheryl said. "Danny's here."

I searched the creek bank with my light and saw nothing.

"I don't see anything," I whispered.

Cheryl shined her light on a limestone outcropping on the edge of the creek between us and the mound.

"There," she said.

I got as close as I could and shined my light all around the limestone. Under the stone in the creek bank was a hole large enough for a man to crawl through. I backed away to figure out the best way to get to it. Cheryl pointed her light at smaller pieces of rock lodged in the bank.

"Steps," she said.

I studied them for a moment and decided it might work. I worked my way up to the hole and stuck my right hand and the light in the hole, holding on to the ledge with my left.

"It's a cave," I said. "I see drawings on the wall."

"Can you get in?"

"I think so."

I went in head first, crawling on my stomach, pulling myself along with my elbows, my light ahead of me. I recognized a mild stench—the smell of human decay.

Once I crawled to the bottom of the cave I shined my light around and was surprised at the size of it. Water running through the limestone strata for millions of years had carved the chamber out of the sedimentary rock. The floor was strewn with arrowheads and spear points made of rock, flint, and obsidian. There were a lot of pots, some broken, others intact. On the walls were red and orange pictographs of men with spears chasing four-footed animals of various sizes. Others showed the hunters celebrating the kill and butchering the animals. On the cave ceiling above me was a faded red circle with radiating lines, maybe symbolizing the sun. The ancients who built the mound had used the cavern as a secret place dedicated to the hunt. Ross's reference to Danny being "in an old hunting camp" finally made sense.

I caught a glimpse of a small body against the edge of the cave. I knew it was Danny. My eyes began to blur with tears. I fought to maintain my composure. I steadied my breathing and studied the pictographs a little longer. I picked up a large spear point, shining my light on it, admiring the skill it took to make it.

"Willie Mitchell," I heard Cheryl call.

I cleared my throat. "Just a minute."

I couldn't put it off any longer. I shined my light on what was left of Danny. I walked slowly toward the fragile remains. The seven-year-old lay in the corner of the cave, naked except for a leather loin cloth. Ceremonial feathers and beads draped his skull and ribs. The Conqueror Worm and his accomplices were long gone, having consumed all of Danny's flesh, leaving only his bones, his mop of hair and a few patches of leathery skin. I had seen enough.

"I'm coming out."

I backed out of the hole and Cheryl guided my feet to the limestone steps. She steadied me on my climb down.

I shined my light on the ledge. No wonder Peewee's men didn't find it. On top of the bank, the small hole disappeared under the outcropping. Even standing in the creek it was difficult to see. If it hadn't been for the albino deer, we would have never found the cave entrance.

I stood in the soft sand of the creek bottom, turned off my light and looked up through the trees at the stars in the black sky.

"He's in there," I said. "It's Danny."

CHAPTER SEVENTY

I sat in my truck at the late Reverend Paul Gray's Ebeneezer Baptist Church at Sophie's Bend watching the giant alligator gars roll in the murky Yaloquena River. It was the afternoon of New Year's Eve, my least favorite holiday. We had driven back from Oxford the day before. Jimmy and Martha were coming for dinner at our house. Susan gave up long ago trying to make me go to New Year's Eve parties.

It had been over six weeks since Robbie Cedars and his crime lab experts processed the cave the day after we found it. I wanted them in there before I called in the archeologists and Native-American experts from Ole Miss to protect the site. Robbie said he would remove Danny's body and check the cave for other recent human remains. Otherwise, he said, he would leave everything the way he found it.

The DNA he took from Danny's remains matched the DNA the crime lab had collected in July in the Thurman home. Just about everyone in town, black and white, turned out for Danny's funeral or the memorial ceremonies at his school, the fire station, and the Little League field. Congresswoman Rose Jackson gave a moving speech about Danny in a special program at the downtown park where he was with Bill and Connie before he was abducted. It was the best Rose Jackson speech I ever sat through.

Nicholas had been in counseling and Walton said the child psychologist thought the boy would be healed in time, that the permanent scars inflicted by Ross would be minimal. I told Walton I was happy to hear that and I hoped they continued the treatment. What I didn't say to Walton was I thought the psychologist was full of it and I believed Nicholas would carry a heavy burden the rest of his life.

Old man Jules picked up the two boxes of legal pads from the Kwik Kopy two days after he killed Ross. They say Jules took a day to read over the legal pads and burned them in the incinerator at the bank. He tried to pay Kwik Kopy but the young clerk said nothing was owed. Discretion being the better part of valor, the clerk didn't volunteer that Ross had paid him generously in advance to scan the pads, add a title page, and download the lengthy scanned document onto a web site Ross provided that dispersed the document immediately into a million servers worldwide.

The Life and Times of Jules Bullard became an e-book sensation. What the posthumous publication of *The Confederacy of Dunces* did for John Kennedy Toole, the e-publication of Ross's version of Jules' life story did for Ross, with a few twists. The stories of Jules' cruelty to Ross as a child and throughout his adult life were lurid, but not nearly as painful to read as the stories of Jules' cruelty to Ross's mother. Ross admitted he relied on information from third parties for those because he was three when she killed herself. One of the online reviewers commented that if only a few of the stories were true, Jules had set a high bar in the field of cruelty to a spouse and child. The reviewer said Jules' cruelty was "Inquisition-worthy."

Ross would have been thrilled to learn that the FDIC and State Auditors descended on First Savings Bank in an unannounced joint audit in the second week of December. The documents Ross removed from the bank were attached as an Appendix to his treatise. Ross's white paper led to the seizure of the Bank's assets and its closure the day before Christmas. Judy left the next day in her BMW for points unknown. Jimmy Gray said the auditors told him Jules would be indicted after the first of the year.

Susan and I accepted Deputy Attorney General Patrick Dunwoody IV's invitation to spend a few days in mid-December with him at Bellingham, his family estate near Charlottesville. He and his long-time partner and executive assistant Donald Monroe were gracious hosts. While Susan and Donald did some shopping one day, Patrick and I had a cup of coffee on downtown Charlottesville's pedestrian mall.

I told Dunwoody I hadn't made a final decision, but I was probably not going to serve my new term as District Attorney. He went into detail describing a special position at the Justice Department he was creating. He said it required a seasoned lawyer with my skills, integrity, and discretion. I was intrigued and promised him I would think about it after discussing it with Susan, Jake and Scott. Governor Jim Bob

Bailey had already told me he would appoint Walton as interim Yaloquena D.A. until a special election could be held if that was what I wanted. I wasn't sure.

After Charlottesville, Susan and I spent the rest of the holidays in her condo on University Avenue in Oxford. Susan told me she wanted us to move there permanently. I'm thinking she may be on to something.

Oxford is a very cool town.

I don't know where any of the bodies are buried in Oxford. If we moved there, I'm sure I would find out after a while.

Scott surprised Donna with an engagement ring for Christmas. They spent the holidays with her family in South Carolina. Jake is still in London and safe for now, but that's all Dunwoody will tell us.

Cheryl Diamond left for Houston the day after our trip to Iron Bridge. I asked her to stay in touch with us. She said she would.

Last night Jimmy Gray and I rode around Sunshine in his big Cadillac drinking bourbon and vodka tonic, respectively, and looking at the Christmas lights. I told him about Dunwoody's offer in general terms and asked him what he thought.

We talked about Oxford, too.

After his second bourbon, Jimmy said he was thinking about accepting the latest offer from the big national bank headquartered in Nashville that had been trying to buy our Sunshine Bank for as long as I could remember. He said if I left town he was going to leave, too. Jimmy said he'd turn out the town's lights as he drove away. He asked me what I thought about selling the bank. I told him it was his call, whatever he wanted to do was fine with me.

When he dropped me off I asked him what he would do to occupy his time if he didn't run the bank. He told me he had gotten a substantial offer from the organization that sponsors National Talk Like A Pirate Day, and was thinking of becoming their national spokesperson.

I told him he was full of crap.

He was still saying "arrrrrrgggghhh" when I closed the car door.

Susan is back to normal, walking, exercising, playing tennis. Nathan said she has a very hard head.

She and I talk about Oxford. We talk about Dunwoody's offer to work for the Justice Department, too. I told Susan I was reluctant to do something that would put her in harm's way again, that it was my fault she had been injured.

She told me to put that out of my mind. Susan said I would be miserable sitting around on my behind, doing things retired people do. She said there were too few people like me and I needed to stay in the game in some capacity. In spite of the trauma we both experienced in the Ross Bullard case, I knew she was right, as usual.

Susan helped me come up with my New Year's resolution, to be more accepting of people. She said that every one of us is just trying to do the best we can. So, I'm going to try to be kinder to everyone I encounter because, according to Susan, each one of us is fighting a tough battle.

Kind of a different tack for the Avenger of Blood, but we'll see how it works out.

I'll keep you posted.

Author Biography

Michael Henry graduated from Tulane University and University of Virginia Law School. He practiced civil and criminal law, including sixteen years as a prosecutor, twelve of those as an elected District Attorney.

Henry currently resides and writes in Oxford, Mississippi.

Made in the USA
Lexington, KY
27 April 2013